Praise for Tl

MW01280223

"The magic is believable, the characters could be people you know, and the twists, turns and mysteries to be solved glue your eyes to the page. You will never forget these characters or their world."
—*Jacqueline Lichtenberg, Hugo-nominated author of the* Sime~Gen *series and* Star Trek Lives!

"Alastair Stone is like Harry Potter meets Harry Dresden with a bit of Indiana Jones!"
—*Randler, Amazon reviewer*

"Somewhat reminiscent of the Dresden Files but with its own distinct style."
—*John W. Ranken, Amazon reviewer*

"I am reminded of Jim Butcher here...Darker than most Urban Fantasy, not quite horror, but with a touch of Lovecraftian."
—*Wulfstan, Amazon Top 500 reviewer*

"If you like Harry Dresden and The Dresden files, or Nate Garrett in the Hellequin series than this series is for you."
—*Amazon reviewer*

"Once you enter the world of Alastair Stone, you won't want to leave."
—*Awesome Indies*

"I've been hooked since book 1."
—*Penny B. McKay, Amazon reviewer*

"It's getting hard to come up with something better than great to describe how good this book was."
—*Ted Camer, Amazon reviewer*

"You cannot go wrong with this series!"
—*Jim, Amazon reviewer*

"Warning—don't start reading this book if you have other things to do."
—*ARobertson, Amazon reviewer*

"Once you start, you need to get comfortable because you will stop reading all of a sudden and discover many hours have gone by."
—*John Scott, Amazon reviewer*

"R. L. King has my purchasing dollars with fun-to-read, suspenseful, character-driven stories…Damn fun reads."
—*Amazon reviewer*

"I have been hooked on this series from the first book."
—*Jim P. Ziller, Amazon reviewer*

"Awesome and exciting. Love this series."
—*Cynthia Morrison, Amazon reviewer*

"Amazing series. The characters are deep and identifiable. The magic is only a small part of what makes these books great. I can't wait for the next one!!"
—*Amazon reviewer*

"Great series, awesome characters and can't wait to see where the story will go from here."
—*Amazon reviewer*

"I have read every book in this series and loved them all."
—*Soozers, Amazon reviewer*

"The writing is extremely good, and the plot and characters engaging. Closest author comparison probably Benedict Jacka and the Alex Verus series."
—*MB, Amazon reviewer*

"The Alastair Stone Chronicles is one of the best series I have read in years…"
—*Judith A. Slover, Amazon reviewer*

"A continued thrill to the urban fantasy reader…"
—*Dominic, Amazon reviewer*

"I consumed the four pack in less than a week. This a great series and one of the best ones I have had the pleasure to read in a long time."
—*Skywalker, Amazon reviewer*

ALSO BY R. L. KING

The Alastair Stone Chronicles

Shadowrun

(published by Catalyst Game Labs)

GATHERING
STORM

ALASTAIR STONE CHRONICLES: BOOK SEVENTEEN

R.L. KING

MAGESPACE
PRESS

Copyright ©2019, R. L. King

The Seventh Stone
First Edition, March 2019
Magespace Press
Edited by John Helfers
Cover Art by Streetlight Graphics

ISBN: 978-0-9994292-8-0

All rights reserved. No part of this book may be reproduced or transmitted in any form or by any means, electronic or mechanical, including photocopying, recording, or by any information storage and retrieval system without the written permission of the author, except where permitted by law.

This book is a work of fiction. Names, characters, places, and incidents either are products of the author's imagination or are used fictitiously. Any resemblance to actual persons, living or dead, events, or locales is entirely coincidental.

| CHAPTER ONE

I F ANYONE HAD TOLD ALASTAIR STONE at the beginning of the year that he'd be sitting at his desk during his University office hour worrying about his son, he'd have laughed at them.

Or called them mad.

Or possibly both.

Parenthood had always been something Stone didn't even think about. It was something that happened to other people—like bowling, or monster truck rallies. The idea of being a father, even to a nineteen-year-old son he'd known nothing about until last month, would have struck him in much the same way as someone suggesting he move into a doublewide in the Amish country and take up woodcarving: in other words, something so foreign to his entire worldview as to be completely out of the question.

Right now, he should already have left for lunch. He had a meeting in less than an hour, which meant going off campus wasn't an option. If he wanted something, he'd have to brave the crowded lunch-hour rush at one of the University's many eateries, and he wasn't sure it was worth it at this point. As almost always happened when his mind was working overtime, his appetite had deserted him.

Someone knocked on his door. Damn—probably some student with a question, which meant the decision about whether to even give lunch a try would be taken out of his hands. "Yes, come in," he called, making no effort to hide his brisk impatience.

"Hey, Doc." Verity Thayer appeared in the doorway, wearing her familiar black leather jacket and jeans. She eyed him critically. "You forgot we were going to lunch today, didn't you?"

"Oh, bugger." He glanced at his calendar: there it was, right there in front of him. *Lunch with V., noon.* "I'm sorry, Verity. It completely slipped my mind."

"You know absent-minded professors mostly happen in the movies, right?"

"You'd be surprised," he said dryly, getting up. "We've still got time, but we'll have to make it a bit quick. I've got a meeting coming up."

"It's okay. Quick's fine." She studied him, her gaze going fuzzy as she shifted to magical sight. "You've got something on your mind, and I don't think it's a meeting. It's Ian, isn't it?"

She always *had* been perceptive—it was one of the things he admired most about her, but there was no denying it could get inconvenient sometimes. "I suppose it is."

"When did he contact you last?" She fell into step next to him as they left the office.

"Last week."

"From where?"

"Prague. He's met up with a collection of young mages over there. Apparently there's quite the magical party circuit around the area."

She chuckled. "Maybe you shouldn't have shown him the portals quite yet."

"Eh, it would have happened eventually. Best he gets it out of his system, I suppose."

"You still haven't taken him to England, have you?"

"Not yet. I told Aubrey and he's desperate to meet Ian, but we haven't managed to get our schedules sorted yet."

She squeezed his hand. "It'll happen, Doc. Don't worry. I know this is all pretty chaotic for you, but maybe a little chaos is a good thing. At least the kind that isn't trying to kill you for a change."

Stone supposed she was right. He hadn't expected Ian would settle down in his old townhouse in downtown Palo Alto, get a job, and begin his magical studies right away. That was what he'd *hoped* would happen, but he'd quickly discovered his son was far too restless for such a settled life. As soon as Stone had taken him to A Passage to India and instructed him in how to use the portals to travel via the Overworld, his aura had lit up.

"You mean I can fly all over the world in minutes, just by going through these things?" he'd asked, looking at the shifting, pastel-colored doorway in the restaurant's storeroom with the wide-eyed wonder of a kid on Christmas morning.

"Well, anywhere the public portals point. You can't access the private ones without permission, but there are a number of public ones all over the globe. As long as you're careful about the mundane authorities discovering you someplace you're not supposed to be, there's no reason you can't go where you like."

"I've always wanted to see the world." Ian gazed at the portal as if tempted to leap through at that moment. "When I was a kid, Mom didn't have enough money. And Bobby—well, he didn't see the point of it. Everybody kissed his ass in Winthrop, so why go anywhere else?"

"What about your magic training? You said you wanted to keep up your studies. I just need some time to find you the proper teacher—"

"That can wait, can't it? I mean, it's waited this long, and I've already got two years done. I'll catch up, right?"

Stone had no doubt he would. His test results, after he'd had finally stopped pretending to have some kind of magical learning disability, had been impressive. And technically, since he started at barely seventeen, he was a year ahead of where he normally would have been. "It's up to you. You're old enough to make your own decisions. Just tell me what you want to do, and I'll help you make it happen."

"That's just it—I don't *know* what I want to do yet. This is the first time in my life where I'm free to explore. Are you cool with me taking some time to do that before I make up my mind?"

"Of course." What could he say? Ian was an adult—and mostly, Stone was glad of that because it freed him from the obligation of being responsible for raising another human. But the downside was that his son had been living on his own ever since he'd fled his abusive stepfather and weak-willed mother to seek his dubious fortune in Los Angeles at sixteen. Stone suspected trying to steer him in any particular direction would likely do nothing but cause friction between the two of them.

So, instead he'd set up a comfortable bank account for Ian and let him go. "I'm not going to support you forever," he told him. "At some point, you'll need to find something to do, whether it's continuing your apprenticeship, going to University, or getting a job. But for now—go have fun, find yourself, do whatever makes you happy. But do come back now and then, and stay in touch. I'll see about finding you a teacher if that's the way you decide to go."

Ian had taken his words to heart, and immediately made plans to set off on a portal-based world tour. True to his word, he'd sent Stone periodic updates, either by phone, text, or even an occasional postcard, but every time Stone had asked him when he planned to return, he'd said he didn't know yet.

Verity walked next to him, content in the silence until they reached one of the small eateries halfway between his office and his classroom. They grabbed sandwiches and sat down at a little table on the patio. It was a brisk spring day, not too cold, but most of the other customers had still opted to sit inside.

"So," she said, "I wanted to talk to you about something."

"Oh?"

"Yeah." She seemed unsettled, and her aura supported it. "You know Scuro's dad does the same thing he does, right? That's where he learned it?"

"Yes." They'd discovered that recently, when the magical tattoo artist had approached his estranged father for information about Trin Blackburn's animated ink. "So?"

"Well…his dad's decided to cut back. He wants to focus on some other things he's been putting off."

"Er…good for him, I suppose." Stone didn't see where she was going with this.

"Yeah. But even though Scuro and his dad don't really get along all that well, Scuro's the only one in the family who inherited the magical-tattooing talent. So that means a lot of his dad's customers will be switching to Scuro."

Stone took a sip of coffee, watching a group of chattering students walk by. "Yes, and—?"

She stared at her sandwich. "Well…with all that extra business, he's going to need more help. He's really come to rely on my healing. It makes the whole process a lot faster and less painful, and his customers have been asking for it." She sighed. "He's offered me a job. Just part-time, but regular. I'd only have to work two nights a week, and he'll give me a big raise. A seriously big raise. Like…enough that I could afford a place in San Francisco."

Ah. So *that* was where she was going with this. Stone glanced at his watch. He'd have to leave soon, but he couldn't bail on Verity now. "So…you want to move to San Francisco."

"Yeah, I'm thinking about it." She still didn't meet his gaze. "It makes sense—I'd be closer to Scuro's shop, and Kyla, and Hezzie. I've been making a lot of headway with the alchemy stuff, and it would be a lot easier to get some regular practice in if I was closer. But…it would mean being further away from Jason. And you."

"Have you talked to Jason about it yet?"

"No. It's only come up in the past week or so. One of the apartments in Hezzie's building is opening up. It's not the best end of town, but the place is nice, and it's bigger than the one down here. I could have my own alchemy setup. She said she'd help me with that." She looked up at him. "So…what do you think?"

"Why are you asking me what *I* think?"

"Because I want to know. It affects you too. We probably wouldn't be able to see as much of each other."

Stone didn't point out that they didn't see that much of each other now—though their unconventional relationship remained as passionate as ever when they spent the night together, their mismatched schedules meant that only happened two or three times a month. He chuckled. "It's not as if you're moving to New York or anything."

"No, but…you know as well as I do that it'll make a difference. There's no portal in San Francisco."

He hated to see her looking so conflicted. "That's true…on both counts. But it's hardly insurmountable. Mundanes commute from San Francisco to Palo Alto every day. If that's what you truly want to do, we'll manage."

She took a bite, swallowed, and sighed. "You took that a lot better than I expected. I wonder if Jason will too."

"Doesn't matter, does it? He's got his own life, and you've got yours. We're hardly all joined at the hip these days."

"You don't know much about overprotective older brothers, do you?" Her eyes glittered, and she shot him a crooked smile.

"Haven't had the pleasure, no."

She finished her sandwich and wadded the wrapper. "Anyway, it's not happening overnight. Hezzie just found out her neighbor's moving out in a month, so I've got a little time to make up my mind. And it's not like I couldn't take the job without moving—I could crash at Kyla's when I'm working. But this would make it a lot easier."

Stone leaned forward and touched her arm. "You don't have to convince me of anything, Verity. You're not my apprentice anymore. You've got to do what's best for you."

"Yeah…" She let that trail off and grabbed her bag. "Anyway, let's talk about something else before you have to go, okay? I saw something I thought you might like." She pulled a folded newspaper out and pushed it across the table toward him, eyes twinkling with mischief.

Stone scanned it. She often showed him strange articles either she or Jason had found, usually amusing crackpot pieces about bat boys, mysterious bigfoot monsters, or other fanciful supernatural beasts. Most were from publications he was familiar with that got their "stories" from the reporters' fertile imaginations and relied on the gullible for their subscriber base.

This one was different. It was on a half-page torn from a paper he'd never heard of from some nowhere town in the Midwest, and the story was a small one, barely three column inches instead of the usual sensationalistic splash complete with Photoshopped image.

He read through it quickly. It didn't give a lot of details, but simply mentioned that a group of young people showed no ill effects several days after a series of bizarre events they experienced at a party held in an abandoned paper mill on the outskirts of the town.

"Interesting…" Stone murmured. "They reported feelings of being out of their bodies, sightings of 'ghosts,' and an overwhelming sense of terror." He tossed it back on the table with a shrug. "They probably all went out there and got good and high. Where did you get this?"

"Tiffany from the coffee shop's cousin sent it to her. She's friends with one of the people involved. Tiff showed it to me because she knows I'm into that 'weird shit,' as she calls it." She picked it up and pointed at it. "The really weird thing, according to Tiff's cousin, is that this happened a couple weeks ago, and already everybody involved barely remembers it, even though they were all seriously freaked out at the time."

"Hmm."

She grinned. "You don't sound very interested. I mean, it's not Bat Boy or anything, but I thought I'd at least get more than a 'hmm.'"

Stone snapped back to attention. "I'm sorry, Verity. I'm afraid I'm a bit preoccupied right now, between the meeting and Ian."

"It's fine. You're right—it's probably nothing." She shoved the clipping back across the table toward him. "You can keep it for your collection, anyway." She finished her sandwich and stood. "I'll let you get going now, so you're not late."

"Want to get together later tonight? There's a new Thai place in Menlo Park I've been meaning to try."

She looked rueful. "Can't. Scuro's got a big job tonight so I need to head back up. Maybe later this week?"

"Yes—of course. That's fine."

She bent and brushed a quick kiss across his lips. "See you soon."

Stone slipped the clipping into his coat pocket and watched her go. By the time he got up and hurried off to his meeting, he'd already forgotten about it.

| CHAPTER TWO

S TONE DIDN'T GET HOME until after nine that night. He pushed open the door to find Raider waiting for him, eyeing him in that accusatory, "you realize you haven't fed me in *days,* right?" way, even though he had full dishes on all three levels of the house.

"You're not fooling anyone, you know," he muttered, tossing the bag from the Dragon Garden on the table. He hadn't bothered going to the new Thai place—it hadn't seemed worth the effort to drive all the way to Menlo Park just for takeaway. "And you're not getting any of this—it's spicy, and I don't want to deal with the aftermath of whatever digestive shenanigans it might cause."

Raider almost looked disappointed, causing Stone to wonder once again if Professor Thaddeus Benchley's echo might be hanging around the place on the sly. "Don't look at me like that. It won't work."

When he hung his coat on the rack inside the door, he remembered the clipping Verity had given him. He pulled it from the pocket and glanced at it again. It *was* a bit strange on second look—a bunch of kids getting high on something at an illicit party wasn't anything to be concerned about, but the fact that they all claimed to have forgotten about it several days later was a bit more interesting. Sure, they could all be lying. But Stone had enough experience with young adults from teaching them for over ten years to know getting that many of them to agree on a story for any length of time was next to impossible.

I must be truly bored, he thought as he gathered the Dragon Garden bag and a Guinness and carried them all upstairs to his study. Raider followed him, leaping up to perch on the edge of the desk.

The little podunk town was called Devil's Creek (*how appropriate,* Stone thought wryly) and it was located in Iowa, a couple hundred miles from Des Moines. As he pulled out his United States atlas and located it on a map, he wondered again if he shouldn't take Jason Thayer's advice and get himself a computer. He'd been resisting it for a while now, content to use the one in his office at work when he needed to print something out or look something up. But ever since Jason had opened his agency and gotten a new setup there so he could do internet searches, he'd been trying to convince Stone to get one of his own.

"Come into the twenty-first century, Al," he'd teased. "I promise, it doesn't hurt. And it's not like the thing's going to blow up if you get near it or anything."

Right now, though, his hardcopy map was sufficient for his needs. He examined the area: Devil's Creek was next to a small river (not likewise called Devil's Creek) which made sense given the article's mention of an abandoned paper mill. The dot for the town was tiny, meaning the town probably was, too—likely just another in the interchangeable series of wide spots in road featuring a gas station, a McDonald's, and a whole lot of farms or ranches depending on where exactly it was located. In all his years living in the United States, Stone had never properly sorted out Midwestern geography. He knew where a few of the big cities were—roughly—but most of the states east of Nevada and west of the Eastern Seaboard constituted a giant black box in his mind. He'd taken a road trip a few years back in an attempt to remedy that, but it hadn't helped much.

He was about to close the map and finish his kung pao chicken before getting back to his research when another thought occurred to him. Barely glancing up, he gestured and brought another large, leatherbound tome sailing across the room to settle on the desk. He opened it and paged through until he reached the spot he was looking for, then grabbed the other map and held it next to the new one.

"Interesting..." he murmured, absently nudging Raider away. "Hadn't expected that..."

He examined the clipping with new interest, then pulled his mobile phone from his pocket and punched Verity's number.

"Hi, Doc. What's up?"

Stone heard muffled heavy-metal music in the background—she must be at Scuro's shop. "I'm not keeping you from anything, am I?"

"Nah, not at the moment. Scuro's finishing up the job, so I've got a little while before he needs me. What do you need?"

"Well." He glanced down at the maps again. "Remember that clipping you gave me today? The one I didn't seem interested in?"

"Yeah..."

"Well, I'm a bit more interested now. Can you put me in touch with your friend's cousin?"

The line crackled. "Uh…yeah, probably. Why? What did you find?"

"Probably nothing. But I located the town on a mundane map and compared it against my ley line reference. Devil's Creek, Iowa is right at the confluence of two of them."

"Wow. I didn't even think to check that. So that means the chances it's legit went up, doesn't it?"

"It's still likely nothing, but at least it's worth a look. I want to talk to the cousin. Can you manage that?"

"Yeah. I'll talk to Tiff tomorrow and see if she can have her call you."

"Thank you."

When she spoke again, the grin in her voice was evident. "And there's the curious cat I know and love. Let me know if you decide to go. Maybe I'll come with you."

"I'm not *going*," he protested, even though he knew that wasn't by any means true, depending on what he found out. "I just…want to learn a bit more about it, is all."

She laughed. "Yeah, Doc, you go right on believing that. It'll make one of us."

| CHAPTER THREE

S TONE'S PHONE BUZZED just after his three o'clock class got out the following day, showing an unknown number. He answered on his way back to his office. "Yes, hello?"

"Uh...hi. Is this Dr. Stone?"

"It is. Do I know you?"

"No. My name's Leith McCoy. My cousin's Tiffany Bailey."

"Ah! Right. You're from Devil's Creek." He slowed his headlong pace to a more leisurely stride.

"Well, next town over, but close enough." She sounded wary. "I'm not exactly sure what you want from me. Tiffany said one of her friends told her you wanted to know what happened at the old paper mill."

"That's right. Did she tell you what I do?"

"She said you were some kind of professor at Stanford."

"Yes, exactly. My area of interest is...unusual events."

"Unusual?"

Stone wasn't sure how much he should say—in his experience, using the words "occult" or "supernatural" around mundanes resulted in one of two outcomes: unhealthy fascination or a nervous brush-off. Neither of those was likely to get him the information he wanted. "Er—yes. Unexplained phenomena, that sort of thing. I thought perhaps you might be able to tell me more about what happened."

"You're not a reporter, are you?"

He couldn't miss the suspicion in her voice. "No, of course not. Have you had trouble with reporters?"

"Not many. There were a few local ones sniffing around just after it happened, but that's it. I'm still not really sure I can help you very much, though."

Even at Stone's decreased pace, he still reached his office building quickly. He nodded to Laura the admin and swept by, ducking into his office and locking the door behind him. "I just want to get a bit more information than what I saw in the article. It didn't provide much to go on."

"All I know is what my friend Liz told me. They had a party out at the old paper mill. It's been closed for years, but people sneak in there a lot. The cops keep an eye on it, but they can't always catch 'em."

"I see. The article said something about ghosts, out-of-body experiences, and feelings of terror."

"Yeah. There are rumors that the place is haunted, but I think it's all bullshit, honestly. Pardon my language."

"Yes, I suspected as much too. I'm guessing there were drugs involved. Am I correct?"

There was a pause. "I doubt it, actually. I know some of these guys. They drink, sure, but they're pretty straight-arrow aside from that. I've never heard of any of them getting high. For sure, Liz wouldn't do drugs, 'cuz her job does random checks. Plus, the cops tested some of them just after they broke up the party."

"Hmm." He wondered if she was telling the truth—she didn't know him, after all, which meant she probably wouldn't reveal illegal drug use to him even if she knew about it. "I see. The part that interests me most is the bit about everyone forgetting about what happened."

The pause was longer that time. "Yeah. That *was* weird. I talked to Liz about it the day after the party, and she told me some pretty freaky things. But then I saw her again a few days later and she didn't even remember what she told me. She looked at me like *I* was the crazy one. Like I was making it all up."

"And you don't think she could have been lying to you, or concealing something?"

"Nah. Liz and I have been friends since grade school. I can always tell when she's lying. She was serious."

"And it's not just Liz who's claiming not to remember?"

"Right. It's everybody who was there. The cops are thinking they had some kind of mass hallucination or something. It's freaky."

Stone jotted down a few notes. "Thank you, Ms. McCoy. I appreciate your time, and I won't keep you any longer. I wonder, though—is there any chance Liz would be willing to chat with me directly?"

"I dunno. I think she just wants to forget about the whole thing, to be honest."

"All right, then. Thank you again."

Stone tried to focus on work and put the events in Devil's Creek from his mind for the next couple days, but he kept returning to the strange happenings, turning them over like

R. L. KING

Raider with a new toy. He searched for any other news stories about the situation, and even asked Jason to look it up for him, but found no other pertinent information. It was as if the story had simply passed from collective memory.

Either that or nobody gives a damn about it because it's pointless, he told himself.

But he kept coming back to the ley lines. Confluences of two ley lines weren't that rare—they existed all over the world—but any time more than one of them converged in a single location, it made supernatural events that much more likely.

Finally, on Friday afternoon, he pulled out his map of public portals in the United States and compared it with the location of Devil's Creek. The closest one was in Chicago, nearly a four-hour drive away, but if he caught a short flight from there to Des Moines it would cut his travel time considerably. He didn't have a class until Tuesday—the three-day weekend should be plenty of time to investigate.

He pulled out his phone and called Verity. "Fancy a little trip?"

"Where?"

"Thought I'd pop over to Devil's Creek and take a look at that abandoned paper mill."

She chuckled. "Ah, so your curiosity finally caught fire. Took long enough. Did you find out anything new?"

"No, just been thinking over what I already know. So— want to come along? I was planning to take the portal to Chicago and get a flight from there."

"I can't, Doc." She sounded rueful. "Kyla and I have tickets to a concert tonight, I've got a job with Scuro tomorrow night, and Hezzie was going to show me some stuff this weekend. But if you really want me to come—"

"No, no, it's quite all right." Stone was sure his disappointment hadn't reached his voice. "You do what you need to do. I'll be fine. I'll probably find nothing interesting anyway."

"You sure? If you really need me—"

If you really need me. That was an interesting way to put things. "No—it's fine. Tell everyone I said hello. I'll let you know what I find when I get back. I'll leave plenty of food and water out for Raider, but if you're in the area at all, would you mind stopping by to check on him?"

"Yeah, no problem." A pause. "Be careful, Doc."

"Come on, Verity—it's not as if I'll find a portal to Hell or anything in some nothing little town in Iowa."

"Well, if you do, call me. I've never seen a portal to Hell."

"That's a promise. Enjoy your concert, and don't blow up the alchemy lab."

He broke the connection and put the phone away, wondering at his uncharacteristic melancholy. This wasn't anything new—his schedule and Verity's often didn't coincide these days—but for some reason this time it hit him harder than usual.

| CHAPTER FOUR

S TONE DIDN'T TAKE MUCH with him for the trip. Raider watched him from the pillow as he gathered a few things into an overnight bag in his bedroom. "Don't you worry," he told the cat. "I'll be back soon. You'll probably enjoy having the place to yourself for a couple of days."

He wondered if that were really true, or just wishful thinking on his part. He and the rangy tabby complemented each other's lifestyles surprisingly well, each of them combining a love for solitude with the periodic need for bite-sized portions of company from another living thing. They each had a good sense of when the other wanted to be left alone, though Raider had his species' typical compulsion to be in the middle of anything that might be going on. Stone had evicted him from the overnight bag twice already as he packed.

He zipped the bag, slung the strap over his shoulder, and ruffled Raider's fur. "Right, then. You be good. If I end up staying longer than expected, Auntie Verity or Uncle Jason will be 'round to top off your food and water."

Raider yawned and licked his paw.

❖

A Passage to India was doing a brisk business when he arrived a little after seven. Marta Bellwood, busy filling a complicated takeout order, waved as he strode past but didn't stop him to chat. He'd been frequenting the place fairly often lately, going back and forth between his Surrey house or Caventhorne on weekends, so his appearance now wasn't unusual. He returned the wave and hurried down the hall before she changed her mind, then quickly slipped past the illusion concealing the door that led to the downstairs portal.

Barely glancing at the serene, pastel-colored gateway shifting in front of him, Stone pulled a card from his pocket and consulted it. He knew the coordinates to his typical destinations—the private portals in Surrey, London, and Caventhorne, along with the ones in Lowell, Massachusetts and New York City—by heart, but it had been quite some time since he'd had occasion to visit Chicago.

As he calibrated the portal to take him to his destination, he thought about how much easier this was than it used to be when the Evil was still lurking in the Overworld. Portal travel wasn't exactly what one might call completely safe—you could still get into trouble if you didn't keep your wits about you—but it was a hell of a lot safer nowadays since the Evil were no longer preparing ambushes for anyone who let their emotions get the better of them. In the years since the Evil's gateways had finally been shut down, Stone personally knew of several magical practitioners who were now brave enough to use this handy travel method, when they never had been before. Officially, very few people knew the reasons for why the Overworld was safer now, but people talked and the story had gotten around.

Stone finished his calibrations and hefted his bag. The trip would take only a couple of minutes, and he'd step out on the other side in the unused storeroom of a bar on Milwaukee Avenue. From there, he planned to find a hotel for the night, then catch a flight to Des Moines in the morning. After that, a two-hour drive would get him to Devil's Creek by mid-day.

With one last, brief twinge of regret that Verity couldn't accompany him on the trip, he stepped into the portal.

He paused only a moment, glancing around at the familiar foggy tunnel opening in front of him. As always, swirling gray mist formed a passageway that stretched out as far as he could see, making it impossible to take a wrong turn if you did your calibrations correctly. These days, all the traveler saw was the mist itself; the dark, fishlike shapes of the larval Evil cruising around in the walls, homing in on strong emotion, were long gone. Occasionally, if you paused for several moments and fixed your gaze far out into the grayness, you might see one or two isolated figures patrolling aimlessly back and forth, but the vast majority of them had either given up and gone home to their own dimension or died for lack of sustenance. Stone wasn't sure which one was true, and he didn't care. As long as they were gone, he was fine with it either way.

He began walking, his footsteps silent on the tunnel's floor. His feet disappeared halfway into the fog, and the whole process felt like trudging through a hallway lined with cotton wool. It didn't impede your progress, but the utter silence and deadness of the tunnel contributed to an overall unsettling feeling. Despite the openness of the tunnel, claustrophobic people didn't tend to do well in the Overworld.

Stone maintained a steady, unhurried pace and didn't look back. Based on previous experience and the distance between the Bay Area and Chicago, he expected the trip to take perhaps a minute or two at most, but the Overworld's strange geography had a way of altering perception, stretching seconds into minutes. By the time you got out, you could swear you'd been walking for ten minutes, twenty, even an hour, only to discover barely a couple of minutes had passed in the "real" world. It was weird, but any practitioners who used the portals regularly took it in stride.

Up ahead, he spotted a flash of light. Good—that must be the other end of the tunnel, the one that opened into the Chicago bar. He figured he'd stop in, get a drink or two and catch up with any mages who happened to be hanging about, and then find a place to crash for the night. Maybe he'd even get a little work done in his room.

The flash of light grew brighter, changing to a purple hue. Stone paused, narrowing his eyes. That was odd—normally the Overworld exits either looked like faint glows, or doorway-shaped darkenings in the unrelieved gray of the fog. The place had an eerie way of washing out any color that entered it, deadening voices and dulling even the brightest of shades on its travelers' clothing. One thing Stone had never seen here, and never expected to see, was any kind of bright color.

"Odd..." he murmured. His voice came out in the familiar monotone, the fog catching and damping all its nuance and overtones. He shifted to magical sight, expecting to see what he always saw when he did the same thing: the muted glow of his own aura surrounded by the same gray-white mundane vision revealed.

Instead, the tunnel came alive with flashes of color, in spots so bright and vibrant it looked like the inside of a nightclub. The spots didn't remain in the same places, but seemed to dance around the tunnel—sometimes quick and choppy, sometimes flowing like water. They seemed to chase each other around the fog-shrouded tube, exuberant puppies out for a romp.

Stone stopped, his curiosity overcoming his trepidation. It was never good for unexpected things to happen in the Overworld, but so far whatever this riot of color was, it didn't seem to be dangerous. He saw no sign of the cruising dark forms of the leftover Evil, which he'd think would be drawn to such a display like moths to a flame.

What was going on?

He turned around with magical sight still active, looking back the way he'd come. More color—not as much, though, and when he returned to mundane sight, it disappeared.

Behind him, something rumbled.

Stone spun. *That* was *definitely* not supposed to happen. Sound in here, even if you were foolish enough to scream at the top of your voice, got attenuated, leveled out, until everything from the loudest shout to the softest whisper had the same lifeless plod.

The rumble didn't repeat, but instead a series of sounds approached, filled the tunnel, and then receded. *Birds?* It had sounded for all the world like a flock of squawking birds flying by and disappearing into the distance.

Okay, enough of this. As always, Stone's scientist's mind was tempted to remain here, to shift back to magical sight, to take readings and note down observations. If something weird was going on with the portals, that was a thing the magical community should know about. Especially if it was causing trouble.

But despite the strangeness, these odd phenomena didn't seem to be causing any trouble. Stone felt no sense of dread, no foreboding, no impression that he should get himself the hell out of here before something he couldn't handle showed up.

Still, though, he didn't *know* what was going on here, and he didn't know what might show up if he remained. His best bet was to get out safely, then either ask around in Chicago to see if any of the other mages in the area had noticed anything, or go back in with better preparation.

Already the bright colors were fading around him, even with magical sight active. The tunnel had returned to its former dead silence, his footsteps to their usual soundless trudge.

Up ahead, he now spotted the dimmed, doorway-shaped space that indicated the other end of the portal, just as he'd expected to. As he continued walking, the colors faded further until at last, when he reached his destination and turned for one last glance behind him, he saw nothing but grayness.

He stepped through the doorway, already pulling a notebook from his coat pocket as the gray faded and was replaced by a dimly-lit space, full of wooden crates and smelling strongly of ale. He looked around for a light switch but saw none, so he used the flickering light of the portal itself for illumination as he quickly jotted down everything he could remember about what he'd experienced in the Overworld. He didn't think he'd forget, but you never knew with magic.

Those kids in Iowa probably hadn't thought they'd forget whatever weird experiences they'd had at the abandoned paper mill, either.

He finished his notes and shoved the notebook back in his pocket, pushing past the stacks of crates, through a closed door, and out into a hallway. The only light here was a single, naked overhead bulb. Around him, he heard only silence: no far-off sounds of music, clinking glasses, or muffled shouts of bar patrons who'd had a few too many. In fact, it was almost as silent here as it had been in the Overworld.

"This is getting odder by the minute," Stone muttered aloud, mostly because he wanted to hear his own voice. It sounded normal, not deadened as if he were still in the tunnel. He shifted his bag on his shoulder and pushed open the door at the end of the hallway.

More darkness. This time, he did find a switch; another hanging fixture lit up a narrow staircase leading upward. His heart beating a little faster now, he took the steps two at a time, shoved open the door at the top, and hurried toward the archway ahead.

"Bloody hell…" he murmured. "What's going on?"

The bar was dark and quiet, the chairs stacked in neat rows on top of the tables, the lights turned off, the space empty. Clearly, the place was closed.

Had it gone out of business? Stone didn't always get the most up-to-date information about the magical community outside California, but surely someone would have mentioned a major portal hub closing.

Besides, if it had closed for good, the shelves behind the bar wouldn't still be lined with rows of sparkling liquor bottles.

Stone frowned, looking at his watch. Seven forty-five. He hadn't updated it for the time-zone difference, so it should be two hours later here. That was prime drinking time, especially on a Friday night—the place should be packed.

So why wasn't it?

Confused, he navigated by the glow of the *EXIT* sign to a door at the front, which opened on another stairway leading up. When he got to the top, he found the door there locked. He unlocked it, settled a disregarding spell on himself long enough to ensure no one would spot him leaving, then pushed it open and stepped out, locking it behind him. Public portals worked on the honor system—travelers could use them even when their associated businesses were closed, but were expected to touch nothing and leave the place locked up when they left. There were ways to track anyone who broke the rules if necessary, but it rarely was. If a mage wanted a few free drinks or some food, it was easy enough to get them in other ways, without putting his or her future access to the portals at risk.

Stone exited the bar onto a nearly deserted street.

Now he *knew* something weird was going on.

He paused, looking up and down the sidewalk. Judging by many of the nearby businesses on both sides of the street—more bars, restaurants, and nightclubs—the area should be as packed as he'd expected the bar to be. People should have been ambling along, talking, bar-hopping, looking in shop windows, hurrying to their next destination. The street itself should have been choked with traffic, creeping along and honking displeasure at each other. Instead, the occasional vehicle—a few cars, more trucks—meandered by, their lights fading into the distance as they turned a corner.

"Hey, man, spare some change?"

Stone started. He'd been so focused on the dark, empty street that he hadn't noticed the old man shuffling up behind him. "Er—"

The man watched him with placid patience. He wore a shabby coat and carried a large black garbage bag slung over his shoulder, probably full of recyclable cans and bottles he'd been collecting. "Change?" he repeated, in a tone that suggested he didn't expect to get any.

"Er—" Stone said again. This whole situation had definitely knocked him off his game. He fumbled in his coat pocket and pulled out a small wad of dollar bills he'd stuffed there and forgotten about. He pressed them into the man's gloved hand. "There you go."

"Thank you, sir. God bless."

As the man started to shuffle off again, Stone called, "Excuse me—"

"Yeah?"

Stone noticed him tense, as if he expected his benefactor to laugh and wrest the bills back from him. "Do you know why everything's closed?"

The man did turn back then, regarding Stone with confused suspicion. "Why shouldn't it be?"

"Well—it just seems odd for it to be so deserted when it's not yet ten."

The old vagrant snorted. "You musta had too many, friend."

"Why do you say that?"

"Lost some time, looks like." He gave a philosophical shrug. "Happens. I once got so drunk I lost three days. Couple years back. Man, that was a real bitch."

Stone stared at him. "What are you talking about?"

Again, the man shrugged. "Prob'ly drank too much, lost some time, if you think it's ten."

"Well…then…what time *is* it?"

"I dunno. Don't got a watch. But the bars close at four, so it's gotta be, I dunno, four-thirty, five-like."

Stone's stare became a gape. What the hell was he talking about? Four-thirty or five a.m.? That was impossible! If that were true, it meant he'd spent the last seven hours in the Overworld. He gripped the man's shoulder. "You're having me on. This is some kind of joke, right?"

The bum gave him the side-eye and sidled quickly away, almost as if suddenly considering him a threat. "I-I don't want no trouble, man. Thanks for the money. I'm gonna go on my way now, okay?"

Stone let him go. What else could he do? Either the bum was lying to him or he wasn't, but he didn't feel like hassling the guy further. He shifted to magical sight and studied the man's aura, noting its sickly yellow hue showed the darkening of age and infirmity, but no overt signs of subterfuge.

After the man disappeared around a corner, Stone picked the opposite direction and began walking. He had no idea where he was going and didn't care, except that he wanted to get to a place that had a clock. An old bum who didn't even have a watch couldn't be counted on to have the answers he needed, but surely a gas station or all-night convenience store would.

It took him fifteen minutes at a brisk walk and two changes of direction before he spotted the bright glow of a 7-Eleven ahead. He increased his speed to a jog and shoved inside, glancing around for a clock. Aside from the clerk behind the counter, the place was deserted.

"Help you find something?" the clerk, a burly African-American man with a bald head and a Cubs T-shirt, called.

"Just—looking for the time. My watch stopped."

The clerk glanced at his own watch. "Four forty-five." He eyed Stone as if expecting trouble. "You wanna stay, you gotta buy something, though."

"Er—right." He got a cup of coffee from the machine and dug a twenty from his wallet. "Four forty-five, you say?" He checked the man's aura, but it looked normal, beyond the usual mild tension convenience-store clerks everywhere probably got when lone customers walked into their stores at the ass end of morning.

"Yeah. Somethin' wrong?"

"No—nothing. Thank you." He snatched his coffee and change and headed back outside, heart still pounding. Pausing to take a sip of the hot, black liquid, he discovered it tasted terrible and tossed the rest in a nearby trash can. It was only then that he remembered his mobile phone.

Idiot. You've got a clock in your pocket.

He yanked it out and clicked it on.

Where the screen would normally have displayed the time, a series of garbled characters appeared, all the way across. As he watched, they flickered.

Well. That's lovely.

Before he thought better of it, he hit the button for his contact list—which thankfully displayed properly—and touched Verity's number.

It rang several times before she answered, and when she did she sounded bleary and muddled. "Hmm…Doc? Is that you?"

Of course she sounds that way—you woke her up, you muppet. If it was four forty-five a.m. here, that meant it was quarter to three in California, well past when even his night-owl former apprentice would be asleep. "Verity?"

He heard the muffled tone of another woman's voice in the distance—probably Kyla. "Yeah. What's wrong? It's—"

"It's late. I know. I'm sorry to wake you. Is it really almost three in the morning there?"

"Uh—yeah. Ten till. Why?" There was a pause, and when she spoke again her voice sounded sharper. "What's wrong? You wouldn't call and ask me something like that if you didn't have a reason."

"I…do have a reason. Something odd is happening, and I'm trying to make sense of it. I'm in Chicago. I went through the portal less than half an hour ago."

"That late? That's weird, but—"

"That's the point. It *wasn't* that late. When I went through, it was a bit before eight p.m., California time."

"But—"

"And when I came out, it was four forty-five, Chicago time."

Silence.

"You begin to see my problem," he said dryly.

"Uh…yeah." She sounded fully awake now. "Do you have any idea what happened? Did you get drunk? Pass out?"

"Nothing like that. The Overworld was acting…strange, though." He described the odd lights and sounds he'd experienced on his way over.

"Wow. And you've never heard of anything like that before?"

"Never. I've traveled these portals hundreds of times, and that's the first time I ever experienced anything like that. Clearly I'm going to need to do a bit more investigation. But if I were you, I'd avoid the portals for a while, just to be safe. At least the one to Chicago."

"I'll get right on that." She still sounded nervous, but amused now too. "Canceling that trip to Chicago right away—oh, right, I wasn't planning one."

"Hush, you. Sorry again to bother you. Go back to— whatever you were doing."

"You sure you're all right?"

He almost answered quickly, with a reflexive, "Of course I am," but then he paused. *Was* he? Could it be that whatever he'd seen in the Overworld hadn't been the portal itself, but *him*? He *felt* fine, but that wasn't necessarily an indicator. "I… think so," he said at last. "I think I'll just head to the airport at this point, and on to Devil's Creek. It's probably just an isolated incident."

"A glitch in the Matrix," she said, but didn't sound entirely convinced. "Keep in touch, okay? And be careful."

"I promise, on both counts."

He called a cab, then put the phone away and leaned back against the building to wait for it to arrive. The temptation to go back into the Overworld to see if the same thing happened again nearly overwhelmed him, but for now he resisted it. He'd come here for a reason, so might as well deal with that first.

| CHAPTER FIVE

D EVIL'S CREEK, IOWA turned out to be a bit more than a wide spot in the road, but not by much. After a short, uneventful flight and a longer, equally uneventful drive in an uninspiring rented Ford sedan, Stone pulled into town at shortly after noon. The sign at the edge of town read, *Welcome to Devil's Creek. Stop by and stay a while!* Below it, a smaller sign proclaimed, *Population 2,322.*

He cruised up the main street, scanning both sides of the street. Neat, old-fashioned buildings lined it, interspersed with trees. The cars parked along it were older and mostly American, and the people he saw wore neat but serviceable clothes. Not a pretentious place, but without a doubt a pleasant, homelike one.

He pulled the Ford into the tiny parking lot of a small eatery halfway up the short street, noting it was nearly full. Must be a popular place. He spotted a newsrack outside the front door and paused to buy a paper before heading inside.

As soon as he entered, he realized he probably should have changed clothes, or used an illusion spell to obscure his appearance. The little bell on the door jingled, and then every gaze in the room was on him, with the exception of one baby in a high chair. He supposed he couldn't blame them—his long black coat and Cardinal Sin T-shirt hardly blended in with the jeans and work shirts favored by Devil's Creek's population.

To their credit, the restaurant's customers quickly returned to their business after giving Stone a curious once-over. A middle-aged waitress in a classic uniform bustled over and flashed him a smile. "Welcome. Don't think I've seen you around here before."

"No. Just arrived."

She led him to a booth next to a window looking out over the parking lot and handed him a laminated, single-page menu. "Coffee?"

"Yes, thank you."

Stone settled back in his seat, well aware that a few of the customers were shooting surreptitious glances his way but ignoring them. Instead, he briefly examined the menu, then opened the paper and scanned the front page, wondering if it would include anything about the incident at the paper mill.

He'd found nothing by the time the waitress returned bearing a steaming cup of coffee. "Ready to order, or do you need a little more time?"

"I'll have the special, thank you." He looked over the room again; he could see all the other tables from where he sat, and most of the other customers appeared intent on their meals. "And if you have a moment, I'd like to ask you a question."

She tilted her head. "What kind of question?"

"There's an abandoned paper mill near your town, is that right?"

Suspicion flitted across her plain features. "Why do you ask?"

"Well…I heard something about an unusual incident that occurred there recently."

"Where did you hear that?" Now there was no mistaking the suspicion. "I really can't talk now, sir. I have to get back to my—"

He held up a hand. "No, please. I promise, I'll only take a moment of your time. A friend of mine showed me the story in the local newspaper, and I was intrigued. I was hoping to find out a bit more about it."

"Why would you want to do that? It wasn't anything."

Stone shifted quickly to magical sight, and noticed that not only did the waitress's aura seem uneasy, but the couple at the next booth had both become a lot more attentive while pretending not to be. He flashed his best charming smile, the one that almost always worked on middle-aged straight women. "I'm a bit interested in that sort of thing. I was in the area, so I thought I'd pop by and see if I could find out anything that didn't end up in the papers."

She sighed. "Listen, sir. I'm sorry—I hope you didn't come too far. That story blew the whole thing out of proportion. Lots of young people sneak into that old mill. They've been doing it for years. This time, they just had a party and things got a little out of hand. That's all it was."

Stone nodded. "I heard they all claim not to remember what happened."

"That's probably because they were doing something they shouldn't have been and now they're afraid they'll get in trouble with the police." She rolled her eyes. "Honestly, I don't see why people are so worked up about it. It was nothing."

"I see." Stone handed her the menu. "Right, then. I won't take any more of your time. But could you perhaps tell me where I might find this old mill?"

"Why?" The suspicion edged up again. "You shouldn't be going out there, sir. There's a fence around it, and if they police catch you, you could get yourself in trouble. My advice is to leave it alone."

Stone considered her words. "Fair enough. Thank you for your time. The coffee's excellent, by the way."

Mollified, she nodded. "Your order will be up soon. Please excuse me."

While he waited for his lunch, Stone sipped his coffee and unobtrusively studied the rest of the customers. Most of them had once again returned to their own conversations, but a couple were still casting occasional curious glances his way. One of these was a young man in a workman's jacket, who was sitting at a table on the other side of the room with two other similarly-dressed men. All of them looked between late teens and early twenties. Stone met his gaze for a moment and held it; the young man looked away and returned to his food.

Stone's order arrived soon after, delivered by the diner's only other waitress, who dropped it off with a quick smile and hurried off before she could be drawn into conversation. He finished it quickly; the food was simple but tasty, and he scanned the newspaper's few remaining pages as he ate. As he suspected, the incident at the paper mill wasn't mentioned on any of them. When he finished, he paid his check, left a generous tip, and headed outside. As he left, he noticed the young workman was no longer seated with his two friends.

The parking lot had cleared out some since he'd arrived. As he headed to his car, he half expected to find the man waiting for him, but he saw no sign of him.

Instead of getting back in the car, he left the lot and strode at an easygoing pace down the street, looking in shop windows. Devil's Creek was clearly not a tourist town, but it did have a small business district with quaint shops, old-fashioned buildings, and a diminutive but handsome brick church next to a tree-lined park. Stone thought about Winthrop, the stifling little town where Ian had grown up under the thumb of his tyrannical, homophobic stepfather, and wondered if the people here were any different. He had little experience with small-town America outside the Bay Area, and wondered, not for the first time, if he should consider taking a sabbatical from the University to drive around and explore some of its local legends. He might even get a paper or two out of it.

Except Hubbard would flay you alive if you leave before they hire another professor, he thought with amusement. Especially now, since his colleague had been furiously writing away on his next horror novel following the news that his previous one had finally been accepted for publication.

His thoughts of Ian reminded him of what had happened in the Overworld last night. He wondered if it was an isolated incident, a "glitch in the Matrix," as Verity had called it, or a symptom of something more widespread. If Ian was using the portals a lot in his travels, he should probably at least warn his son to be careful. As he walked, he pulled out his phone and dashed off a quick text: *Had problem with portal to Chicago last night. Take care when traveling.* He sent it and waited a moment to see if Ian replied, then kept walking when he didn't. He'd go a couple more blocks and see if he could find a library or other place where he might find the location of the abandoned paper mill, then head back to the car and find a place to stay. Regardless of whether he found the mill's location right away, he planned to wait until after dark to head out there. Safer that way, and less likely the wrong people would notice him.

He located the library, a neat little building a block away from the church. Before he went inside he thought about using magic to change his appearance, but decided against it. If this small town was like every other one he'd ever encountered, the story of his arrival at the diner would be all over town before the day was over. No point in adding yet another stranger to pique their curiosity.

The librarian didn't ask questions when he stopped by her desk and inquired about any reference materials she might have regarding the old mill. Although Stone could tell from her aura that she was curious about why he wanted to know, she led him silently to a room full of large, dusty books containing reference issues of the town's newspaper, along with a couple of microfiche readers. She pointed him at the drawers where the microfiche reels were stored, told him to come back if he had any other questions, and turned to leave.

"Oh—I do have one question," he called. "Can you tell me when the mill was built, and when it was taken out of service?"

"It was built in the late eighteen-hundreds, and shut down in…1938, I think. There was a fire, the owners went bankrupt, and then the war started. By the time it was over, nobody wanted to put up the money needed to get it back in business."

Stone thanked her and settled down to his research. For the next two hours, no one bothered him as he pored through the books and swapped out reels on the ancient machine, trying to get a sense of the place's history. It wasn't easy since nothing was indexed, but eventually he located what he was looking for. The librarian had been wrong about the date of the fire, but not by much—he found the account on the front page of a paper from June of 1939.

"Hmm…" he murmured. "I can certainly see why they might have thought the place haunted."

The account of the fire that gutted the inside of the Ainsbury and Son Paper Mill was sanitized, as such stories often were in those days, but Stone had no difficulty reading between the lines to reveal the truth: Marvin Ainsbury and his son Milton were unscrupulous businessmen, driving their workforce of mostly desperate young men and women to put in long hours in unsafe conditions. When a fire broke out one night, rumored but never proven to be caused by the improper storage of oily rags, many of the workers had been unable to escape and had succumbed to either the flames or the smoke.

Afterward, the relatives of several of the workers had sued the Ainsburys, and though they were never found guilty of any wrongdoing (*probably because they bribed the right people,* Stone thought), the negative publicity and cost of the trial drove them to bankruptcy. They fled the area to somewhere in Europe and were never heard from again, leaving the mill in a legal snarl nobody ever bothered to unravel.

After that, Stone found few other references to the mill, beyond brief accounts of a couple of abortive attempts to refurbish it and a few comments about the local children believing it to be haunted. It was declared condemned and the local government had arranged to have a fence built to keep curious explorers out.

"That's not working out too well for you, is it?" Stone murmured, taking the last reel off the machine and returning it to its spot in the drawer.

He thanked the librarian and left, his mind still on the workers who'd perished in the mill because of the Ainsburys' greed and neglect. He wondered if there *were* echoes lurking around the place, and the rumors of hauntings came from people occasionally spotting them. With that many dead in such a tragic way, it wasn't at all surprising that some of their echoes had unfinished business. He'd have expected to find many more stories of sightings.

Ah, well. If echoes were all that was causing the problems, he could verify it and be home by tomorrow. They were interesting, certainly, but no more than any others he'd encountered. Perhaps he could even do something to help them, but he doubted it. Echoes were tricky and persistent, and he didn't see any immediate way to deal with them. That wasn't why he was here anyway.

He headed back to his car and located a small, brick-fronted bed-and-breakfast called the Lamplight Inn near the edge of town, the only one of its kind he'd discovered. Devil's Creek definitely wasn't much of a tourist destination.

By the time he settled into a small, country-kitschy room and took a hot shower, it was already late afternoon. He decided to stay in for an early dinner, calling one of the two pizza-delivery places on the flyer he found on the nightstand. He'd already piqued enough local curiosity at the diner today; best if people thought he'd moved on so he could make his trip out to the mill after dark in peace.

The pizza was good, at least. By the time he finished half of it and put the other half in the room's mini-fridge for the morning, the sun had gone down. He pulled on his overcoat and slipped out the back door, walking casually. The fewer people who suspected what he was up to, the better.

He'd parked his car behind the building. The tiny lot was dark now, illuminated by only a single streetlight. By the small number of other cars, Stone suspected he might be one of only a few other guests, if that. That was all right—it made it even less likely someone would notice him leaving. He reached the sedan and fumbled in his pocket for the key.

A vehicle pulled into the lot, its headlights dazzling Stone's eyes as it slowed down, coming to a stop directly behind his car.

| CHAPTER SIX

TARTLED, STONE STOPPED, taking a step back to put more distance between himself and the new vehicle. "Can you move, please?" he called. "I was just about to leave."

The truck's lights switched off.

Stone blinked as his vision adjusted. He could see it a little better now in the faint streetlight: it was an old Chevy, dusty and dented. The window rolled down and a figure leaned over. "You were asking about the thing at the paper mill."

Stone tensed. It was a man, but he still couldn't make out any detail. "Yes, and?"

"I have some questions for you. I heard you were stayin' here."

"Step out of there—let me have a look at you."

The door opened, and the figure jumped down and moved into the light. "Remember me? From earlier?"

Stone relaxed. With a better look, he recognized the young man who'd been sitting at the diner with two friends— the one who'd left. "I remember you. What do you want?"

"Would you get in? We can talk in the truck."

Without hesitation, Stone hurried over and climbed into the cab. It wasn't as if he had anything to worry about from some farm boy in Armpit, Iowa. Immediately, the young man pulled out of the parking lot and began driving at a leisurely speed down the main street.

"Who are you?" he asked Stone. "You're not from around here. Not anywhere *near* around here. That's pretty obvious."

"No, I'm not. My name is Alastair Stone, and I've come from the San Francisco area."

"Why?" The young man didn't look at him as he drove. He appeared to be heading out of town. "I'm Mitchell Kirkson, by the way."

"Pleasure to meet you, Mr. Kirkson." Stone studied him. He looked to be about twenty, tall and solidly muscular—the type of build Verity called "cornfed." In addition to his workman's jacket, he wore a plaid shirt, well-worn jeans, and scuffed leather work boots. His dark-blond hair was cut in a short, no-nonsense style, and his deep tan and calloused hands suggested he spent a lot of time outside.

"Why did you come looking for me? I got the impression from my reception at the diner that my questions weren't exactly welcome."

"People don't like to talk about what happened. I think they're all tryin' to forget it. Even the ones who weren't there."

"And why is that?"

Mitchell Kirkson turned onto another road just outside town. "I'm just gonna drive around for a while, if that's okay with you."

"Of course. Don't want to be seen with me, I take it?"

"Makes it easier."

"Fair enough. So what's going on? How much do you know about what happened? Were you at this party, or gathering, or whatever it was?"

For the first time, Mitchell looked troubled. "Yeah."

"What was it, exactly?"

"It wasn't anything, really. Not a party, not exactly. Just a few friends getting together to drink a little booze and blow off some steam. We've done it before. Nellie's right—the mill's been kind of a hangout for years, long as anybody can remember. Everybody in town knows who's too young to drink, so we can't go to the bars."

"So this sort of thing happens often?"

"Hanging out at the mill? Yeah, fairly often. The police come by and run people out of they catch 'em, but mostly they don't bother as long as nobody drives drunk."

"Mr. Kirkson—do you know a young woman named Leith McCoy?"

"Name sounds sorta familiar, maybe. Why?"

"She's the one who put me on to this in the first place. Her cousin lives in my area, and she's a friend of good friend of mine. I spoke with her on the phone recently."

Mitchell narrowed his eyes. "You're not makin' much sense, Mr. Stone. You want to tell me why somebody like you gives a damn about some weird stuff goin' on in podunk Iowa?"

"I'll tell you that, but first I'd like you to tell *me* something."

"What's that?"

"Why did you seek me out? Why are you willing to talk to me when the others seem reluctant?"

For several seconds, the only sound was the rumble of the truck's powerful engine, and the faint strains of a country music song coming from its old speakers. Mitchell gripped the steering wheel tighter, and as Stone watched with magical sight, his aura roiled with sudden unease. Stone got the impression he looked tired, and not the kind of tired you got from doing hard physical work. *Psychic* tired.

"Mr. Kirkson?"

"Yeah." He swallowed. "See, here's the thing—the other folks who went to the mill don't remember what happened. But I do. And it's scarin' the devil outta me."

| CHAPTER SEVEN

STONE TWISTED IN HIS SEAT. "You remember what happened that night at the mill?"

"Yeah."

"And nobody else does?"

"I don't think so. They could be lyin' like I was, I guess, but I don't think so."

"I...see. And why are you telling me this, if you haven't told anybody else? You don't even know me."

Again, Mitchell didn't answer right away. The country song faded, replaced by another one about a man whose wife had left him to run off with a traveling salesman. "Maybe that's why," he said at last.

"What do you mean?" Stone settled back, projecting unruffled calm even though he wanted to grab the young man and wrest the story from him. That would be a mistake, he could tell—Mitchell Kirkson was like a skittish deer, wanting to trust him but ready to bolt if he pushed things too fast.

"I mean, you're a stranger. Sometimes it's easier to tell stuff to a stranger."

"I could be a reporter, you know."

"You ain't a reporter." Mitchell's tone held certainty.

"How do you know that?"

"Reporters don't look like you. There's some-thing...strange about you. And I don't just mean the way you dress." He glanced sideways. "You look like the kind of guy who might believe what I have to say without either laughin' or callin' the guys in the white coats."

"I promise, I won't do either. Mr. Kirkson—"

"Call me Mitch, okay?"

"Mitch, then." He hesitated, wondering if he was going too fast, too soon. They were heading up an arrow-straight road now, stretching out before them as far as he could see. On both sides, white fences marked pasture fields dotted with cattle and sheep. "Would you be willing to show me this mill, after you tell me your story?"

Mitch's aura flared. "I don't know. I don't really feel like goin' back there anymore. Especially not after dark."

"All right. That's fine. Just—tell me what happened. I promise I won't laugh. Do you mind if I take some notes?"

Another sideways glance. "You can't tell anybody where you heard this. You have to promise, or I won't tell you anything."

"I give you my word, I won't reveal your identity to anyone. I just want to know what happened."

Mitch considered his words, then tightened his grip on the wheel again and fixed his gaze straight ahead. "Like I said, bunch of us go out there sometimes on weekends to blow off steam. Mostly the ones who are out of high school, workin' but not old enough to go to the bars yet. We take some cases of beer, play some music, just hang out. The mill's pretty big and mostly empty, except for some of the big broken ma-chinery too big for the scavengers to haul out. People have been doin' it for years."

"You mentioned beer," Stone said. "What about drugs?"

Mitch shuddered. "No, sir. No drugs. Well, maybe a few folks bring a little weed now and then, but never anything harder than that. Lot of us have jobs at a couple factories around here that do random drug testing. They can't afford to get fired, so nobody takes chances."

"Was it all beer that night? No weed?"

"Yeah. I'm sure of it. Even if somebody went off to smoke on their own, we'd've noticed the smell."

Stone nodded. "Go on."

"Okay. So, it was about midnight. We'd been up there for a couple hours. Somebody'd brought an old portable CD player and we were just sittin' around drinkin' beer and listenin' to tunes like always."

"How many of you were there?"

Mitch shrugged. "Maybe fifteen. Twenty at most."

"And no one new? Nobody brought a friend you'd never met before?"

"No, sir. Everybody knew everybody else, same as usual."

"All right, go on." Stone settled back and watched the truck's headlights pick out the scenery, which still hadn't changed from flat pastures broken up by the occasional mailbox or trundling farm truck.

"Yeah. So...like I said, we were just listenin' to music. Some folks were dancin'. I was sittin' in a folding chair, lookin' at the machines and thinkin' about what it must have been like there when the mill was runnin'. And that was when I saw 'em." He shifted in his seat, clearly uncomfortable.

"Saw who?"

"People."

"What people? New ones? Did some other people show up?"

"You don't get it, Mr. Stone. They were people, but...they were dressed strangely. Old-fashioned. And...I could see through 'em."

Stone tensed. "You're saying you saw...ghosts?"

"I don't know *what* I saw. I mean, I've heard the rumors that the place is supposed to be haunted—everybody has. But far's I know, nobody's ever seen any ghosts. But I wasn't the only one who did. Everybody there saw 'em. As soon as they showed up, people in our group started pointin' and freakin' out."

"What were they doing? Did they appear to notice you?"

"Nope. They were hangin' around the machines. Looked like maybe they were workin'. It was pretty dim so I couldn't get a good look, but I thought I saw men, women, even a few kids." He shuddered. "And that was when things got *really* weird."

"How so?" Stone made a few notes and forced himself not to urge Mitchell to go faster.

He let out a long blast of air. "You are seriously not gonna believe this, Mr. Stone."

"Try me. I've heard some fairly incredible stories."

"Okay. Okay." He was shaking now. He pulled the truck off the road next to a fence and switched off the ignition. "So... I was watchin' these weird figures...ghosts are what they looked like, okay?" His tone took on a challenge that was almost confrontational, and he glared at Stone as if expecting him to comment. After a moment, he sighed again. "I was watchin' 'em, and then suddenly there was this bright flash of light over by one of the machines. It was—I can't even

R. L. KING

describe it, not really. It looked like the air split open and this glow came out. It was like somethin' out of a science fiction movie. I almost felt like I could see…somethin' on the other side, but not clear enough to make out."

"Bloody hell. Did the others see it too?"

"I don't know. I can't say what happened to them, because suddenly the glow was gone and I was…somewhere else."

"What do you mean, somewhere else?"

"I don't *know!*" Mitch's voice shook with strain. "That's what I'm tryin' to tell you. None of this makes a damn bit of sense. It was like I was suddenly lookin' back at my friends from…somewhere else. Like I was seein' 'em from the other side of the room, over by where the new people were. And then suddenly I was scared out of my mind. Like I knew I was gonna die and there wasn't anything I could do about it. All around me, the other new people started screamin' too, runnin' around, flailin' their arms. One of the women picked up one of the kids and headed for the door, but they both screamed and disappeared. All I knew was that I had to run, I had to get out, or I'd be dead too."

"What did you do?"

"Nothin'. Because right after that, I felt this strong jerk, like somebody had a rope around me and was yankin' me across the room, and then I was back in my own body, lookin' at the world just like I expected to. Except I still felt this kind of overwhelming fear, like I still had to get out of there before something terrible happened."

"Did you run? What were the other people in your group doing?"

"I sure as hell *did* run. I took off like the Devil himself was chasin' me. All around me, everybody else was freakin' out, runnin' around, lookin' like they were seein' the same thing I was. We all took off, leavin' the beer and stuff behind. The way people were screamin', you'da thought the whole place was on fire or somethin'."

"That sounds terrifying," Stone said. "Did you see the ghostly figures anymore after that?"

"I looked back over my shoulder when I ran, to check if anybody was chasin' me. Nobody was. I saw the ghosts, back there by the machines where they were before. They were runnin' around too. They looked as scared as we did, but they weren't chasin' us. I didn't look too closely, y'know? It seemed like they faded in and out—you know, like if you're watchin' an old movie and the projector's screwed up? Then there was another bright flash and everything disappeared."

"Everything?"

"The ghosts, the scared feeling, everything. It was like it just…switched off."

Stone twisted in his seat, aware he was gripping the arm-rest so tightly his fingers dug into it. "So you all…just stopped, outside the mill building?"

"Yeah. One minute everybody was runnin' around, and the next they…weren't. Everybody just stood out there after that, lookin' at each other like they couldn't believe what had just happened."

"But they remembered it?"

"Oh, yeah, they did then. Everybody was talkin' about it when the cops showed up. A couple of us tried tellin' the cops what had happened, but even by then the story started gettin' all muddled up. People were tellin' different versions, gettin' confused…it was like they were all drunk off their asses. But they weren't. The cops did sobriety tests. Everybody was a little buzzed, but definitely not enough to forget somethin' like that."

"What did the police do? Did they arrest anyone?"

"Nah, they let most of us off with a warning. A couple folks were more freaked out than the rest, though, and they took 'em in. I found out later they were actin' like they were comin' down off a bad trip or something, and ended up havin' to talk to a shrink. My younger sister even got sent off to Morris Park—that's a mental-health place in Des Moines—'cause she couldn't calm down. But by the next day, every single person there didn't remember what happened. Even the one who got sent off. The folks I talked to all said it felt like they passed out, and woke up later with no memory of anything except the usual drinkin' and talkin' out there."

Stone considered. "That's… a fascinating story, Mitch."

Mitch shot him a glare. "You don't believe me, do you?"

"I do. I absolutely believe you."

The young man's expression relaxed, but only slightly. "You aren't messin' with me, are you?"

"No. I promise, I'm not."

"Do you…have any idea what the hell might be going on? Did we all have some kind of mass hallucination or something? The cops checked the place out after we kept tellin 'em about seein' the…ghosts or whatever, inside, but they didn't find anything. They even tested the beer to make sure somebody didn't put some kinda drugs in it. Nothing."

"In answer to your question—no, I've no idea what might have happened."

"Do you think we really did see ghosts?"

"I can't say. I was doing some research on the history of the mill earlier today—I found accounts of a catastrophic fire that occurred in the Thirties. Things like that do tend to spawn ghost stories, and sometimes people can be...suggestible. See what they expect to see. I've heard it happen many times before."

"Yeah...that makes sense. But believe me, Mr. Stone— this wasn't any suggestion. I saw those people plain as I'm seein' you right now. At least I *think* I did." Mitch's brow furrowed and his expression grew uncertain. "There's something else I wonder about, though."

"What's that?"

"Why do *I* remember what happened, and nobody else did? I think I'd be happier if I *didn't* remember anything. I've been havin' nightmares ever since that night. That same feeling, like I have to get away from something before it catches me and kills me."

"That's a damned good question." Stone had his suspicions—if something supernatural was going on out at the mill, it was possible Mitchell Kirkson possessed some minimal level of latent magical potential. Not enough to get him in trouble, but enough that his increased sensitivity would make him more susceptible to arcane anomalies. Stone suspected it would wear off after a time. "I'd definitely like to get a look at that mill. Would you take me there?"

Mitch shook his head with emphasis. "No way. I already told you before: there is no way I'm going back there. Like I said—I'm done with that place." He was a big man and didn't look like the sort to back down from any mundane threats, but the naked fear in his tone was impossible to miss.

That didn't surprise Stone. He thought it might be the case, and at any rate it was probably safer not to take a sensitive mundane out there. He had no idea if the events had occurred on their own, or if something about one or more of the group of friends had triggered them. "All right. It's fine," he assured him. "Will you at least tell me where it is? If you'll take me back to my car, then, and I'll go on my own."

"I don't think that's a good idea, Mr. Stone. Goin' out there on your own, I mean."

"Believe me, Mitch, I've got experience with this sort of thing. You've trusted me with your secret—can I trust you with one of my own?"

"Uh…sure. I guess."

Stone pulled one of his business cards from his coat pocket and handed it over. "This kind of thing is what I do."

Mitch studied it, then glanced up at Stone. "Occult Studies? You're a professor at Stanford?"

"Yes. And phenomena like this are what I study. I'm hoping to add yours to a paper I'm working on." It wasn't even necessarily a lie—not entirely, at least.

Surprisingly, that seemed to calm the young man down, but he still looked nervous. "Why don't you want me to tell anybody else?"

"Because it can make things…inconvenient if it gets around. As soon as people find out what I do, I end up having to listen to a whole load of tiresome stories about people's haunted golf clubs and whatnot. I'd rather focus on the mill."

"Uh…yeah. I guess that makes sense." He sighed. "I feel bad about not takin' you out there myself, but like I said, there's no way I'm gettin' near that place again. Not ever. Once was enough to last a lifetime. I'll tell you how to get there, but you need to be careful. The cops have sealed off the hole in the fence folks used to get through, and if they catch you out there, you'll probably get arrested."

"I'll take that chance. Thank you, Mitch."

Mitch pulled a battered notepad and pencil from the truck's glove compartment and drew a crude map. "Mill's at the end of Old Grady Road, a few miles from here. It's out by the river. Not much else out there these days."

Stone took the map and studied it in the dim light as Mitch turned the truck around and headed back toward town.

The young man said nothing else on the trip back, until he pulled into the Lamplighter's parking lot next to Stone's sedan. But as Stone opened the door, he said tentatively, "Mr.—uh, Dr. Stone?"

"Yes?"

"Will you let me know if you find anything out there? Or even better, if you don't? Just...for my own peace of mind?" He took back the map and wrote his phone number on it.

"Of course." Stone swung out of the truck. "Thank you, Mitch. I appreciate what you've told me."

As soon as he closed the door, the truck rumbled out of the parking lot. Clearly, Mitch Kirkson was having second thoughts about talking to Stone. He watched it go, then got into his own car. Before he left, he paused to call Verity.

"How's it going, Doc? Find any ghosts and goblins?" She sounded amused.

"Possibly. I had a very interesting conversation with one of the locals." He told her what Mitch Kirkson had described.

"Wow." Now her tone was more impressed. "I kinda wish I'd come with you now. Sounds like there really is something going on out there."

"It does. I'm planning to go out to the mill now and do a bit of poking around. It might have been an isolated incident, but from the sound of things, nobody's been out there since it happened."

"Well, I'd tell you to be careful, but this sounds like pretty garden-variety stuff for you. Just don't get arrested or anything."

"I'll do my best. I should go now, though—I want to get out there before Mr. Kirkson changes his mind and tells his friends about me. The last thing I want to deal with is a bunch of drunken farm boys playing ghost."

| CHAPTER EIGHT

ONE GOOD THING about the Devil's Creek area being so flat: it was hard to get lost. Stone followed Mitch Kirkson's scrawled map out to the mill. By the time he made it a couple miles out of town and had left the highway, he saw no sign of other vehicles. Either people went to bed early around here, or there was nothing out here to see. Either way was fine with Stone, since the last thing he wanted to do was explain to some cop or other curious lookie-loo what he was doing out here.

He spotted the dark bulk of the mill looming ahead well before he reached it. As Mitch had said, the whole area was surrounded by an imposing chain-link fence, with signs every twenty feet or so proclaiming things like *NO TRESPASSING* and *DANGER – UNLAWFUL ENTRY PROHIBITED*. A couple of the signs had graffiti sprayed on them, and the rusty, uneven pockmarks on another suggested more than one person had used it for target practice over the years.

Stone pulled the car off the road and parked it near the fence, pausing to weave a disregarding spell on it. It wouldn't fool anyone determined to spot it, but it was the best he could do without more effort than he was willing to expend.

It was pitch dark out here once he shut off the headlights, the only illumination coming from the slivered moon. The air was chilly, with a hint of a damp bite. Stone paused a moment to shift to magical sight, glancing around to spot any obvious oddness in the area's astral footprint. He wasn't sure what he expected to see, but even the derelict mill itself showed him nothing out of the ordinary. "Guess I'm heading in, then," he muttered.

A quick levitation spell got him over the fence, and another disregarding spell hid him from any prying eyes, even though he was sure there weren't any. Less than a minute later, he stood next to the mill building.

It rose three stories above him, looking far more imposing up close than it had from a distance. He didn't want to risk a light spell until he was inside, but even in the moonlight he could see it was very old and had at one time been substantial, but the years had not been kind to it. The glass was long gone from the massive windows far above; some of them were covered with heavy plywood, while others yawned open to let in the elements.

Once again, Stone paused for a quick glance with magical sight, and once again he was disappointed to see nothing. He could hardly expect a whole contingent of echoes to be waiting outside to welcome him, but even the ley line—one of the pair that converged somewhere near the area—looked undisturbed and serene.

As he levitated upward again to enter through one of the broken windows, he considered once more what might have gone on here. That was the thing about magic—its manifestations were sometimes inexplicable even to those who made it their life's work to study it. It was one of the rules his own master had drilled into his head from the time he was an apprentice: *never take magic for granted.* It was a useful tool, and if you could harness its power you could use it for many things. In some ways it was like any other force: like gravity, electricity, or solar power, it had rules it followed and could be expected to behave in certain quantifiable ways—most of the time. But unlike those other forces, it also included a chaotic element, or at least one modern magical science had not yet gotten a full handle on. Because at its core it was a force connected with and shaped by living things, its manifestations likewise took as many forms as there were practitioners to manipulate them. What that meant, when it came down to it, was that magic was controllable—until it wasn't. And that meant good mages needed to stay on their toes if they wanted to live long enough to become *old* good mages.

Stone crouched on the edge of the window for a moment, peering down into the interior. It was even dimmer down here since most of the moonlight didn't make it inside, but he had no trouble picking out the towering forms of ruined machinery. He dropped down and summoned a light spell, looking around.

The smell of dust and dampness hung heavily in the air, combined with the faintest hints of old beer and motor oil. Clearly Mitch Kirkson hadn't been wrong that the place had been a clandestine hangout for the local young people for many years. Aside from the rusting, derelict machinery, most of the grimy floor was clear; Stone spotted piles of trash, boxes, a broken lawn chair, and other indications that people had been here, but no smaller machines or other leftover items from when the mill had been in operations. That didn't surprise him—as old as the place was, he was sure the scavengers had picked it clean of anything that could be sold. Even most of the interior walls were gone or crumbling, and anything that might have existed on the second or third floors had long ago been destroyed.

Keeping his light spell up, Stone paced the floor, taking care not to trip over any of the debris strewn around. It would be fairly embarrassing if he weathered any magical threats unscathed, only to brain himself on the corner of some piece of hundred-year-old machinery because he tripped over his own feet.

His mundane explorations proved fruitless. He paid particular attention to the area near the machinery, where Mitch Kirkson had claimed to see the group of echoes clad in old-fashioned clothes, but whatever had shown itself to the group of drunken partiers two weeks ago didn't seem inclined to make an appearance tonight. Stone began to wonder if Mitch and his friends *hadn't* had some kind of shared hallucination, reinforcing each other's memories of what had occurred.

But most of them claim to have *no memories. And that's odd.*

Unless they're all lying, of course. It was possible. From what he'd seen, the Devil's Creek population seemed fairly buttoned-down and conventional. Perhaps what had started out as a joke got out of hand, and the townspeople's disapproval had led the participants to a consensual response of "just kidding" to keep them from real-world consequences.

Stone didn't believe it, though. He'd been watching Mitch Kirkson's aura while he told his story, and the man couldn't hide his fear.

"All right," he murmured, unslinging the bag from his shoulder. "If it takes magic to make you show yourselves, then let's give you some."

Working quickly, he drew a small circle on the floor with chalk, then arranged a few candles around it and lit them. He'd only brought a subset of his magical gear, supplementing it with a few common items he'd purchased in town earlier today, but they should be enough. All he was trying to do here was a sort of magical "jump start"—if he'd been right that Mitch or one of his friends had latent magical potential, his working theory was that it had interacted with the magic in the area to cause the manifestations. If he could re-create that with an even stronger magical kick, he hoped he could duplicate it.

As soon as he took his position in the center of the circle and began to feed power into it, he knew he was right. He wove a protective shield around himself and tilted his head back, studying the contours of the machinery while reaching out with pure magical energy. "Come out and play..." he whispered. "Let's have a look at you, shall we?"

It started slow—there was no jarring jerk, no yanking sensation like the one Mitch had described. Stone felt power growing around him, a low, subsonic hum combined with the sensation of something pressing against his shield. All around him, magical energy arced and danced around the rusting mill machinery, lighting the place up.

"There we go..." Satisfied, Stone took a moment to augment the shield surrounding the circle. He got no sense of danger or foreboding from the growing energy, but best not to take chances.

Near the floor in a shadowy area on the far side of the machinery, something flickered. Stone focused on that area, and after a moment, spotted a series of figures fading in and out of sight. He couldn't get a clear image of them through all the arcing magical light and the glow of the candles, but his brief impressions suggested the same thing Mitch had spoken of: men, women, and children dressed in rough, old-style clothes, clambering around the structure as if performing work.

Stone wanted to rise from the circle and get a closer look, but he didn't. Something big was clearly going on here, and leaving the protective confines of the space he'd prepared wasn't a good idea, especially since he was alone. Instead, he continued watching.

Off to his left, something caught his notice: a brighter, more solid glow. Tearing his gaze from the echoes, he studied it, tensing.

"Well..." he murmured. "*This* is interesting."

Interesting, and not good.

The glow was irregularly shaped and shifting. Roughly six feet in diameter but not even close to circular, it appeared to be some kind of...hole in the air. Around it, he could still see the uneven, rusting forms of the old machines, but where it existed, it showed...something else. Moving, dark-colored shapes surrounded by a yellow glow. In spots, shafts of yellow poked out through the irregular contours, illuminating bits of the mill with light Stone was sure wasn't physical. He was certain if he shifted to mundane sight now, everything here would fade from view as if it had never been here.

The feeling of something pressing on the shield increased, and with it, a growing sense of fear. Stone recognized it for what it was—some manifestation of the energy surrounding the strange shape—and once again bolstered his defenses to compensate.

What was going on?

He'd never seen anything like this before—not exactly. But as he continued to study the shifting yellow shape hanging there in the air, he realized it did share certain characteristics with something he *had* seen before.

If he didn't know better, he'd say it resembled a portal.

That was absurd, though. Portals didn't just pop up in remote locations without provocation. They didn't just *happen.* Even the temporary ones had to be constructed. He remembered what Mitch had said, about seeing a similar structure appearing here before.

Keeping his concentration focused on the shield around the circle, Stone pulled a notebook from his pocket and began dashing off readings, impressions, and questions. Had his presence here caused this manifestation? If he shut down the circle now, could he duplicate it later? Was this something that could be studied?

And what the hell was that shifting yellow hole in the world?

He reached out to his connection to Calanar, pulling in more energy. If he was going to make any sense of this, he'd need all the power he could get.

Suddenly, with no warning, the yellow energy flashed a bright glow, like a thousand flashbulbs going off at once. Stone flinched back, clamping his eyes shut and throwing his arm up to shield them further, dropping magical sight. As he did, he felt the intensity of the light battering the shield, combined with an equally sudden increase in the force pressing against it. He rocked back on his heels, nearly falling over backward as something shrieked in his head.

His head lit up—not with pain, but with a sensation of *clashing,* as if two powerful forces had slammed together and repelled each other.

His mind whirled with images he couldn't begin to follow.

Then silence, and nothing.

| CHAPTER NINE

STONE AWOKE IN DARKNESS.

For a moment he had no idea where he was, but then the cues came back: the smell of dust and burned-out candles and motor oil; the shadowy shapes of the mill machinery, the faint shafts of moonlight through the broken skylight high above.

He lay on his back, splayed out on the grimy floor. Slowly he sat up, putting a hand to his head, testing for damage. Aside from a bit of leftover wooziness and stiff muscles from his awkward position, he felt nothing. No splitting headache, no pain, only the fading vestiges of uneasiness.

He risked a quick light spell to glance at his watch, and let his breath out in relief: only a few minutes had passed.

But what had taken him out in the first place?

Was he still alone?

He dragged himself up and looked around. "Anyone here?"

His voice echoed faintly, but he heard no response—no answering voices, no breathing, no shifting around from someone hiding in the shadows. "Hello?"

Still no reply. He brushed the dust off his coat and switched to magical sight with some reluctance. He still had no idea what had happened—what if it happened again? What if his magic use had *caused* it to happen?

Apparently that wasn't to be the case, though. The place remained as dim and unremarkable to magical sight as it had to mundane vision. The yellow glow was gone. The echoes had disappeared. Nothing remained in the space except trash and debris and the normal, everyday smells of an abandoned building.

What the hell had just happened?

Stone quickly gathered the remains of the circle, tossing the spent candles into his bag and using a little magic to obscure the chalk lines until they blended with the darker dust. He walked over to where he'd seen the yellow glow and examined the area more closely, but even when he stood on top of the spot he found nothing. Whatever he'd coaxed out with his little ritual had apparently tired of him and departed as if it had never been there.

Or else something he'd done had driven it off.

He paced, mind whirling, trying to remember exactly what had happened there at the end. He'd been using magical sight to examine the echoes, the yellow glow, and the feeling of pressure against his shield. He remembered the notebook—he'd been writing notes when the surging energy had hit. Quickly, he hurried back to the spot where he'd come to and cast his light spell around until he found the little book lying open on the ground a couple feet away.

The notes didn't help much. His fast scrawls showed only what he already remembered. Until the last page, when one of the words—he couldn't make it out—tailed off into an unintelligible scribble and disappeared off the bottom of the page. That must have been when he passed out. But what had he been doing then?

The memory returned as he levitated back to the overhead window. He gripped the frame, tensing.

Just before the flare, he'd opened a larger conduit to the Calanarian energy he used to power his magic.

He'd been using it all along, of course—ever since he'd gone black, he couldn't use normal magic without taking power from other people, and he hadn't done that in months. He hadn't needed to—Trevor Harrison's magic-rich dimension provided all the punch he'd ever want, and then some. But in his curiosity to make sense of the strange portal-like glow, he'd opened that conduit wider, pulling in a larger quantity of the energy to help him sharpen his reading.

That was when the glow had lit up like the sun, and that was when the strange *clashing* sensation had hit him and knocked him out.

It had been almost as if two opposing forces had come into contact with each other—like what happened when you touched a pair of magnets with two opposite poles together.

Curiouser and curiouser.

The scientist in Stone wanted to remain behind, to study the phenomena in more detail, make more notes, but he'd used up the ritual materials he'd brought with him. That, and he wasn't entirely sure there would *be* anything left behind to study. His examination after he'd awakened had revealed nothing—not even any vestiges of leftover magical energy. It was entirely possible that the bright flash of light that had knocked him out had obliterated whatever had been there. That was bad for his scientific curiosity, but good for the population of Devil's Creek. Eventually, any remaining reluctance to visit the place would fade, and a bunch of mundanes wandering regularly into an unpredictable magically-active zone was unlikely to produce positive results.

He dropped back to the ground, quickly crossed the open yard, and levitated over the fence to his car. He didn't have to be back in the Bay Area until Monday; if he wanted to, he could gather some more ritual materials and come back here tomorrow for another look. Perhaps he could verify his theory that whatever magic had suffused the place was gone. For now, though, best to get back to town before somebody spotted him out here.

As he got in the car, he remembered his promise to tell Mitch Kirkson what he'd found. He hesitated, wondering if he should "forget" about the promise, but figured it couldn't hurt to give the young man a little peace of mind.

"Yeah, hello?" Mitch answered quickly, and sounded breathless.

Damn. It's after nine—bit late to call. "Er—Mitch? This is Alastair Stone. We spoke today, remember? I'm sorry to disturb you so late. I'd forgotten everyone doesn't consider this too late to ring."

"Oh—no problem, Dr. Stone. My dad's asleep in front of the TV, so I wanted to grab it before it woke him up." There was a pause, and when he spoke again his voice dropped to a near-whisper. "Did you...go out to the mill?"

"I did."

A longer pause. "And...did you find anything weird?"

"I...don't think you were hallucinating, if that's what you mean."

"Did you see it?" The voice struggled to remain soft, but the urgency came through. "Did you see those weird people?"

"No," Stone lied. He hated to do it, but there was no helping it. "I…did get some odd feelings inside, but I didn't see anything. Honestly, if it were me I'd avoid the place for a while, but I don't think there's any danger."

The silence stretched out to nearly a full thirty seconds.

"Mitch? Are you still there?"

"Yeah."

"Is something wrong?"

"I—"

Stone could almost see the struggle on the other side of the line. "Mitch, what's going on? Are you all right?"

"Dr. Stone…I…I want to show you something."

"Show me what? Something at the mill?"

"No. Are you…gonna be in town tomorrow?"

"Yes, I'd planned to return home on Monday. Why?"

"Can you come by my place tomorrow morning? I can pick you up from where you're staying and bring you here if you want."

It was impossible to miss the tension in Mitch's voice now. "What is it? What do you want me to see?"

"I…" A muffled sound, followed by mumbled words in a deep voice. "I can't talk now. Please—will you come? Tomorrow morning?"

"Er—yes. Of course I will."

"Thank you." Relief tinged the uneasiness. "I'll come get you at nine. Thanks, Dr. Stone. Gotta go."

Before Stone could say anything else, Mitch hastily hung up.

| CHAPTER TEN

WHEN MITCH'S BATTERED PICKUP pulled up in front of the Lamplight Inn promptly at nine a.m. the following morning Stone was waiting for him, sipping a cup of strong, black coffee in the inn's tiny sitting room.

He hadn't slept much the previous night, spending most of it either writing more notes of what he'd encountered at the mill while his memory was fresh or tossing and turning in bed, plagued by strange dreams of shapeless things pouring through bright yellow portals. Part of him wondered if he too would experience the strange memory fade that had claimed everyone except Mitch, but when he finally tired of bad sleep and got up to take a shower, the events at the mill last night remained in his mind as clear as ever.

His first impression when he saw Mitch was that the young man had slept even less than he had. Despite being neatly dressed and clean-shaven, he had a haunted, peaked look that was impossible to miss. His blue aura, shot through with the red flashes of deep unease, added to Stone's suspicions.

"Morning, Dr. Stone. Thanks for doing this."

"Not a problem." Stone swung into the pickup and closed the door. "But I'll admit I'm a bit confused about what you've got to show me at your house, and why it had to be now."

"It's...hard to explain. Better to just show you. And the reason it's got to be now is because Dad's at church."

"So...you don't want him to see whatever this is." Stone's curiosity increased. Was Mitch hiding something at his home? Something he'd picked up at the mill, perhaps?

"No...not exactly. It'll just be...easier that way." He glanced sideways. "Please—can I just show you? It'll make more sense when you see it."

"Whatever you like. Let's go."

Stone kept a close eye on both Mitch's aura and their route during the drive. He didn't *think* the stressed-out young man was driving him out of town to murder him or anything, but it was always good to keep a healthy suspicion when you were dealing with the unknown, either supernatural or mundane.

But no, Mitch drove the truck a couple miles up another of the Devil's Creek's arrow-straight, fence-lined roads, and turned into a long dirt drive leading up to a neat, two-story white house with a wraparound porch, a massive oak tree with a swing in the front yard, and a large barn off to the side. A small flock of sheep grazed in a fenced field on one side of the road, and a few goats occupied the other.

"Are your family farmers?" Stone asked.

Mitch chuckled, his unease breaking for the first time since he'd picked Stone up. "Nah. Grandpa was, but he's been gone for years. Dad works as a machinist, and I'm a mechanic. These guys are just kind of a hobby thing these days, for a little extra money."

He pulled the truck in front of the house and stopped, but didn't get out. "So…" he said. "I have to tell you, this isn't easy. Trusting you, I mean. I'm not even sure I should be doing it, to be honest. I hardly know you."

"What are you so bothered about?" Stone scanned the house with magical sight, but spotted nothing out of the ordinary. "Are you going to show me something you took from the mill?"

"No. Not the way you think. Come on." He shoved open the truck's door, got out, and slammed it shut. Everything about him, from his tone to his posture to his aura, suggested his resolve to do this was fading.

Curious, Stone followed him into the house. Despite no mention of a motherly presence, the place was neat and tidy, and smelled of home cooking and wood polish. Stone got the impression of an old, well-loved space, which usually indicated a happy, relatively conflict-free family. He wondered if Mitch and his father did the housework, or if the sister—the one who'd ended up at the mental-health facility—had handled it.

"It's upstairs," Mitch said.

When they arrived at the top of the stairs, he walked to the end of the hall and stopped in front of a door, then turned back to Stone and swallowed hard. "Remember yesterday when we were talkin', I told you my sister had to go to Morris Park 'cause she freaked out at what happened?"

Stone glanced at him, startled. Odd that Mitch would mention the sister just as he was thinking about her. "Yes, of course."

"Well…" He didn't meet Stone's gaze. "That was a lie. That's what most folks think. But the truth is, she's right here."

"Here? In this room?"

"Yeah."

"But—why? Is there something wrong with her? Is she ill?"

"She won't come out. She's been in here since we left the mill two weeks ago. Nobody knows it but us and Reverend Oakley. Dad doesn't know what to do—he doesn't want to take her to some facility for real, but…"

Stone glanced at the door. It had a poster of a band he'd never heard of taped to it, as well as a little plaque that read "Cathy's Room." The plaque looked so old it might well have been there since the room's occupant was a much younger child. "Something happened to her at the mill."

Mitch nodded miserably. "Not then—just after. On the way home." He regarded the door, then turned back to Stone. "You don't have to do this if you don't want to. Like I said, I shouldn't have brought you here at all. This is our family's problem, and it's…pretty unsettling. But…"

"It's all right. I don't know if I can help, but I promise, I won't reveal your secret to anyone."

He considered. "Okay," he said at last, and knocked tentatively on the door. "Cath? It's me. I brought somebody to see if he can help. Can we come in?"

"Go away," came a muffled voice from inside. "Nobody can help. I don't want anybody to see me like this."

"Cathy…come on. You can't stay in there forever. You know Dad's gonna have to do something eventually."

"Go away," she called again. "You shouldn't even be here. You should be at church with Dad."

Stone narrowed his eyes. Magical sight didn't help him with the door closed, but he thought he'd heard an odd, strained overtone in the young woman's voice. "Can you get in there?" he murmured.

Apparently Mitch had picked up the same overtones, because he looked suddenly concerned. He rattled the doorknob and appeared surprised to find it locked. "Cathy—open the door! Please!"

"No. Go away, Mitch. It's better this way!"

"Cathy!" Mitch took a step back and gathered himself, obviously intending to kick the door down.

"Wait!" Stone whispered. "Let me."

"How are you gonna—"

He moved forward, shielding the knob with his body, and used magic to pop the lock. "Try it now."

Mitch didn't ask questions, but instead grabbed it and flung open the door. He surged inside. "Cathy!"

Stone pushed in behind him. What he saw shocked him into forgetting to use magical sight. "Bloody hell..."

Mitch's sister, a young woman who appeared a year or two younger than he was, sat cross-legged in the middle of her bed, wearing a floppy T-shirt and pajama bottoms. Her straggly blonde hair hung down in a jumbled curtain over her face. In one hand she held something that glinted in the dim light filtering in through the room's closed drapes, raising it over her opposite wrist. "Stop!" she yelled. "If you come closer, I'll do it! I swear to God, I'll do it!" She fixed her crazed gaze first on Mitch, then on Stone.

Her eyes were the same solid, golden yellow of the strange portal from the mill.

| CHAPTER ELEVEN

"CATHY! DON'T!" Mitch made as if to lunge forward, to grab her, but stopped himself. Panting, he reached out toward her. "Please—put that down!"

Behind him, Stone shifted to magical sight. Cathy's aura lit up, blazing the same bright yellow as the glow he'd seen back at the mill last night. Her eyes glowed in the same color but brighter now, shining out of a face streaming with tears.

With barely a thought, he summoned a precise telekinetic spell and pulled the razor blade free of Cathy's hand, gently but inexorably tugging it from her grip.

"*No!*" she screamed. She tried to hold on to it, but Stone's spell was too strong. The blade flew from her hand and sailed across the room, landing on the floor in the midst of a pile of laundry.

Cathy screamed again, then flung her hands up and collapsed onto the bed, sobbing. "No…no…you should have let me do it…It's better…it's better…"

Mitch swallowed hard, turning back and forth between Cathy and Stone, his face awash in confusion. "What just happened?"

"No idea. What's going on here? What's happened to her?"

"Make it stop…" Cathy sobbed from the depths of her balled-up comforter. "Oh, please, God, somebody make it stop…"

"This has been going on since we got back from the party," Mitch said softly. "She's worse now…not sure why. Before, she just refused to come out and see anybody, because of—" He gestured at her, obviously referring to her eyes.

"Just the eyes?" Stone asked. He took a tentative step closer to the bed, still with magical sight up. Her aura looked strange and disjointed; on closer examination, he could see flashes of blue among the brighter gold, along with jagged streaks of red indicating her mental turmoil.

"No…not just the eyes. But that's the part folks can see. That's what Reverend Oakley said…" He turned away from Cathy and lowered his voice to a whisper. "…said maybe meant she's got the Devil inside her. He's been prayin' over her ever since, but it hasn't helped."

Stone sighed. Mundanes—it never failed. Every time anything supernatural occurred around them, assuming you could get them to acknowledge it at all, they invariably blamed it on the Devil. Stone didn't believe in the Devil, but if he did, he was certain the old bastard would have more important things to do with his time than spend it turning teenage girls' eyes solid yellow and trying to drive them mad.

"Do you mind if I try to talk to her?" he asked gently.

"Why? There isn't anything you can do to help, is there? I just wanted to show you—" Once again, Mitch looked as if he regretted bringing Stone up here.

"There might be. I don't know. But it's worth a try, isn't it? You said yourself Reverend Oakley's approach isn't working."

The stricken young man shrugged. "Fine. Go ahead, I guess." He glanced at his watch. "Dad'll be home in about an hour, so we need to clear out before that. He won't be crazy about me bringing strangers home."

Stone, with magical sight still active, pulled the white wooden desk chair next to the bed and sat down. "Cathy...can you hear me?" He used a soft, persuasive tone.

Cathy hitched a sob and remained face-down in her blankets. "Who are you? Go away! I'm disgusting..."

"You are not disgusting. Please...will you talk with me for a few moments? I want to try to understand what's happened. I might be able to help."

"Nobody can help."

The depth of despair in her voice gripped at Stone. How horrible it must have been for this miserable young woman to spend the last two weeks shut up in a dim room, refusing to allow anyone but her family and the local clergyman to even look at her. The room smelled sour, a combination of sweat, unwashed clothes, and a faint hint of something floral. He hadn't noticed it before, but a radio played softly from somewhere unseen.

"Cathy...please. Mitch has brought me here because he thinks I can help. My name is Dr. Alastair Stone." He used his title in the hope that if he was lucky, the girl wouldn't ask questions about what kind of doctor he was. "Come on. Look at me. I promise, I'll do everything I can to help. What have you got to lose, if you were already thinking about suicide?"

Behind him, Mitch gasped a little at the starkness of his words, but they seemed to get through to Cathy. Slowly, still shaking, she rose from her slump and cast a tentative glance at Stone, her glowing, solid yellow eyes unsettling and expressionless with no irises or pupils. "How…how can you help?" she muttered. "Nobody can help."

"Well, I don't know if I can," Stone admitted gently. "Not unless you tell me what's happened to you. Can you do that?"

"I don't *know* what happened!" She scrabbled at the blankets, clutching them in thin, clawed hands.

"Do you remember the party? At the mill? Do you remember being there with your brother?"

Her gaze fixed on him, and she tilted her head. "You're…different."

"What do you mean?"

She shook her head violently and clamped her eyes shut. "I just want it to stop."

"You want what to stop?" Stone struggled to keep his voice even, comforting. "What's happening to you, Cathy? Are you in pain? Is something hurting you?"

"No…it doesn't hurt…but it won't stop!"

"What won't stop?"

"The *colors!*" she wailed, snatching a pillow and clutching it tightly to her chest. "The *colors!* They're everywhere! I want them to stop! I'm going crazy!"

Stone looked up at Mitch, who hovered at the foot of the bed, his posture tight with tension. "What's she talking about, 'the colors'? Has she mentioned this before?"

Mitch gave a miserable nod. "None of us know what she's talking about, though. She says she sees these weird glowing colors all over the place—especially when people are around."

Stone went still. *Bloody hell, could it be—?*

With care, he turned back to face Cathy. "Cathy…I want you to answer a question for me. Can you do that?"

She muttered something unintelligible into the top of the pillow.

"When you say the colors are 'everywhere,' do you mean literally everywhere? All around you? Or just around people?"

"What are you—" Mitch began.

Stone held up a hand to stop him. "Tell me, Cathy, please. Where do you see the colors?"

She swallowed, her head still buried. "Mostly…around people. But…other places too. People are brighter. And they won't stop! I can't shut them off!" More red flashes erupted around her aura.

"All right…" he murmured. It was getting harder to keep his voice even as it began to dawn on him what must be going on here. "All right. We're going to sort you out, Cathy, I promise. Can you look at me, please?"

"Don't want to…too bright…hurts my eyes."

"What's she *talkin'* about?" Mitch demanded. "It sounds like you know what's going on here! How can that be?"

"Just—give me a moment. Please. Cathy—what do you mean 'too bright'?"

"You!" she wailed. "Who are you? What do you want? You hurt my eyes! All that weird purple and gold light—it's too bright!"

Stone regarded her in wonder as her words confirmed his suspicions.

Somehow, the strange phenomenon at the mill had done something to this young woman, allowing her to see auras. Not only see them, but be unable to *not* see them, as if she were in a constant state of magical sight. It would be terrifying enough for and unprepared mundane to get a glimpse of the astral realm, but if she couldn't shut it off it was no wonder it had nearly driven her to suicide.

Mitch's strong grip on his arm jolted him out of his thoughts. "What is going *on* here?" he yelled. "If you know anything, you tell me *right now* or get out of here!"

Stone took a deep breath. This would be tricky. He stood and walked over to the window, where he looked out into the front yard. "I'm—not entirely sure I know what's going on. But I have some ideas."

"Well, *tell* me." Mitch joined him at the window, glancing down at his watch. "If we're not out of here before Dad gets back—" He swallowed. "Look—I just want my sister back to normal. Whatever this is, I want to help her. If you know what's wrong—"

"All right," Stone said. "If you really mean that, I might be able to help. You say you go to church—so you're used to taking things on faith, right? That's what I'm going to ask you to do here. I can help, but I can't explain everything. Fair enough?"

"I...have no idea what you're talking about. But if you can help her—"

"I think I can. I've never seen a case like this before, but I've dealt with things that are...similar. I think whatever it was that happened at the mill affected your sister differently than it did anyone else. You too, to an extent—that's why you remember what happened and no one else does."

Mitch's face was wreathed in confusion as he looked back and forth between Cathy, the view out the window, and Stone. "I don't get it, Dr. Stone. I'm sorry, but you're not makin' sense."

"I don't have to make sense. That's where the faith part comes in." Stone began to pace. "But I think what's happened is that the phenomenon, whatever it was, opened your sister up to seeing…something called auras."

"Auras? What are those?"

"Well…some say they're the energy that surrounds every living thing. Some people claim to be able to see them."

"Wait…" Mitch's suspicion increased. "Are you talkin' about some kind of psychic stuff? You know, like palm reading? That stuff's all fake. Everybody knows that."

"Do they?"

"Well—yeah. Don't they?"

"Apparently Cathy doesn't think so. You said you'd have faith—are you willing to do that?"

Mitch looked like he wasn't sure whether to scream, punch Stone in the face, or run from the room. Finally his shoulders slumped. "Yeah. Okay. Guess I don't have much choice, do I? So these…aura things are real?"

"They are, yes."

"Can you see them?"

"I can."

He looked back and forth between Cathy and Stone again. "But—if you can see them, how come you're not—"

"Like her? Because I've got a lot more experience, and this didn't get thrust on me without any warning. I suspect that something in the energy you were all exposed to at the mill opened up a sort of…window for Cathy."

"So…what does that mean? If it's a window, can we…close it?"

"That's what I'm going to try to do."

"How?" Mitch glared at him. "What *are* you, Dr. Stone? You know, come to think of it, it seems pretty damn weird that you just showed up in town from outta nowhere just after this happened."

"Not really. As I told you when we first met, I'm interested in this sort of thing. It's part of my job to be interested, so I keep my eyes open for odd occurrences like this one."

"So you're sayin' this isn't the first one?"

"Well, it's the first one like *this* I've encountered," he admitted. "But certainly not the first strange phenomenon I've investigated. I'd offer to send you a couple of my academic papers, but frankly you'd probably find them quite dull. *I* find them a bit dull sometimes, and I wrote them."

Stone's words seemed to settle at least a small bit of Mitch's suspicion. "So…what are you gonna do? How can you help her? What's makin' her eyes like that?"

"I'm not certain. But if I had to make an educated guess, I'd say it's connected to the energy she encountered at the mill. It's as if it's attached itself to her and she's…channeling it somehow." He chose his words carefully, aware of how easy it would be to lose his audience. If Mitch decided he was a crackpot and kicked him out of the house, he didn't have much hope that Cathy would come to a good end. "Tell me— did anything odd happen with her last night, somewhere before nine o'clock? Before I called you?"

Mitch glared at him. "How did you know that?"

"What happened?"

He gripped the windowsill. "I don't know if it was nine exactly, but right around there she screamed. Really loud, like she was in pain or somethin'. Dad and I ran upstairs to check on her, but by the time she got there, she was asleep like nothin' had happened. If we hadn't both heard it, I'd figure I was havin' some kind of bad dream. But we did. He went back downstairs and fell asleep in his chair after that, and not too long after you called. That's…that's why I decided I had to show you what happened with her."

Stone nodded. "I thought something might be wrong last night. I could hear it in your voice when we spoke."

"So what's it mean? Why did you expect it?"

"Because I did see something out there. I thought I'd dealt with it, but apparently your sister might be its last connection."

"Connection?" Mitch thrust his hands into his pockets. "What the hell are you talking about, connection? What do you mean, you *dealt with it?*" His voice took on an edge of anger that was a clear substitute for panic.

Stone sighed. He'd been afraid of this: Mitch's strong desire to help his sister had driven him to step farther outside his comfort zone than he ever would have done under normal circumstances. Stone admired that—he always admired mundanes who were willing to widen their worldviews—but in this case, he didn't think it would be enough. Mitch Kirkson wasn't Stan Lopez or Edwina Mortenson. Trying to open his eyes to the wider world of magic would be pointless, take time they didn't have, and would likely cause more problems than it solved.

All of that would make things more difficult, but sometimes it was best to know when to cut and run.

"Listen." Stone strode across the room and gripped Mitch's shoulders. "Here's the bottom line, Mitch: I think I can help your sister. I'm fairly sure I can. But I'm not going to explain to you *how* I'm doing it. I can't. You don't have the frame of reference for it, and I haven't got time to give you a crash course. So my question for you is this: are you willing to trust me, for the chance to get your sister back to normal?"

"But—"

"No," he said firmly. He didn't like doing it, but they had less than half an hour before Mitch's father was due back from church, and already he wasn't sure that would be enough time. "Yes or no, Mitch? Do you want my help or not?"

Even without magical sight, he could see the young man's struggle. Mitch's expression shifted between anger, suspicion, and despair, and his entire body thrummed with tension.

"Mitch…?"

Cathy spoke from the bed, her voice shaky and barely audible.

Stone turned. He'd nearly forgotten about the actual, living girl in the bed in his focus on what had afflicted her.

Mitch approached the bed, moving with hesitation. "Hey, Cath. You okay?"

With effort, she pulled her face out of the pillow and opened her eyes, fixing her brother and Stone with her eerie, flat yellow gaze. "I…want it."

"What?"

"I-I want him to help me, if he can. I can't take this anymore, Mitch."

"But—Cath, weren't you listening to him? All this stuff about auras? It's...*wrong*. Reverend Oakley says—"

"Reverend Oakley says I've got the Devil in me." Her voice still shook, but it was stronger now. "I don't believe that. I don't feel...evil. I don't want to hurt anybody. I just want the colors to stop. I want to be *normal* again!" To Stone, she begged, "Please...if you can help me...please do it."

Stone gripped her shoulder. "I think I can." He glanced at Mitch. "It's up to you. I can't do it if I have to worry about you braining me with a lamp or something while I'm working. It will take concentration. Can I trust you to stay out of the way?"

"What are you gonna do?" Mitch's eyes narrowed. "I'm not leavin' you alone with her."

"You don't have to. Just sit down over there and stay out of the way. We don't have much time."

"*Please,* Mitch." Even with her flat yellow eyes, Cathy's expression was pleading. "Do what he says. Dad'll be home soon. If he can't help me...you might as well send me to Morris Park before I try to kill myself again."

For several seconds, the tense silence hung thick in the air, interrupted only by the faint strains of the rock tune coming from the unseen radio. Finally, Mitch growled and slammed his fist down on the end of Cathy's bed. "Fine. Do it, if you can. God help us."

Wasting no time now, Stone pulled the chair next to the bed and sat down alongside Cathy. "I'm going to have to touch you," he said. "But only your forehead. Just lie back and try to relax."

"Pretty..." she murmured.

"What?"

"Your…glow. The one around you. It's so pretty. Purple and gold. Mitch's is pretty too, but it's just blue."

"I think yours is blue too," Stone said. "Hard to tell now, but I think it is."

"I wish…it would be nice to be able to see them when I want. But…not all the time. I feel like something's pressing on the inside of my head."

"Just lie back and relax. We'll get you sorted."

He shifted to magical sight and focused fully on Cathy, blocking out everything else in the room. He'd be vulnerable if Mitch lost his nerve and tried to do something to him now, but it was the chance he'd have to take.

Narrowing his field of view, he picked through the blazing yellow nimbus shining around Cathy's body, separating it from the blue of her base aura and the red of her agitation, damping them all so he could try to find the connection he was looking for.

When he investigated the mill last night, after he woke from whatever had knocked him out, he'd found no remaining vestiges of the strange energy. He thought he'd somehow managed to destroy it, block it off, or otherwise stop it, but he had no idea exactly *what* he'd done to do that. The only thing he remembered was opening in the conduit to Calanar a little wider for more power. Perhaps if he did that again…

There. He hadn't spotted it before because it was so hard to see, but the extra power did the trick: a tiny thread of yellow extended from Cathy's body, meandering upward and then disappearing. But *where* was it disappearing to? What was its source? If he could study this for a little longer, trace it back, he might be able to—

"It's Dad! He's home early!"

Mitch's voice came from far away, but the urgency got through Stone's concentration. *Damn!*

All right—no time for study now. He'd have to do this fast. Regret gripped him as he pulled back, reaching out with his power to grab hold of the little yellow tendril and ease it free of Cathy's aura. Even now he couldn't do it too fast, or he'd risk doing irreparable injury to her psyche.

There. Just a little more...

Something grabbed his shoulder. "He's pullin' into the yard! Hurry up!"

Without thought, Stone swept a hand behind him, magically shoving Mitch backward. He barely heard the young man crash into the wall as he focused his concentration for one last time. He pinched the tendril and tugged it loose.

Instantly, the little thing collapsed and disappeared. He felt Cathy slump beneath his hand on her forehead, and then a second later strong arms grabbed him from behind and yanked him backward. Mitch shoved past him and dropped to his knees next to his sister's unmoving form on the bed.

"What did you *do* to her?" he demanded, voice bright with fear. He took her hand and stared into her face. "What did you *do?*"

Stone didn't answer, but likewise gazed down at the still form, his heart pounding. Had he done it too quickly? He'd had very little idea what he was doing—without further study, he didn't know anything about the strange energy or where it came from. If it had somehow attached itself to Cathy's life force, then removing it could have—

She stirred, then opened her eyes, blinking in confusion. "Mitch...?"

Her eyes, bloodshot and shadowed with fatigue, were pale, cornflower blue.

Stone and Mitch let out simultaneous sighs of relief.

"Cathy—do you see the glows anymore?" Stone asked.

She blinked again, and looked at him as if she'd never seen him before. "Who...are you? What are you doing in my room? What glows? Mitch, what's going on?"

Downstairs, a door shut, and a booming male voice called, "Mitch? You here? I brought Reverend Oakley by for a cup of coffee."

Mitch, who'd been looking at Stone with a combination of horror, confusion, and distress, went stiff and took a step back. "Uh, yeah, Dad! I'll be down in a minute."

He glared at Stone, eyes narrowing. "I don't know what you just did. I don't think I want to."

"You probably don't," Stone agreed. He inclined his head, already knowing the score. He neither expected nor desired thanks or accolades for what he'd done, which was good because he wouldn't be getting any this time. "But in any case, I think that's done the trick. She'll be fine, given a bit of time to rest. I...should go, before your father and Reverend Oakley find me here."

"Yeah." He put his hand on his sister's forehead. "You...sure she's gonna be okay?" He didn't look convinced. "You...you're sure you did it?"

"I'm quite sure." He took another look at Cathy's aura; all traces of the yellow glow were gone now, replaced by an unremarkable, medium blue similar to her brother's. Even most of the red flashes had departed—those that remained didn't surprise Stone, even if she apparently didn't remember anything of what had occurred.

The way Mitch looked at her, though, nervous and un-certain, told Stone the trouble the exposure to the unknown astral energy had caused this family probably wasn't over yet—but what remained was purely mundane and beyond his ability to fix. They'd have to work through it on their own, and decide how far they were willing to stretch their minds to encompass what they'd experienced. The conduit that had attached itself to Cathy Kirkson, for whatever unknown rea-son, was gone, but as was almost always the case when magic came into contact with mundanes, the aftereffects would likely linger for quite some time.

Another door closed downstairs.

"Dad's in the bathroom," Mitch said. "You should go."

"Right. You needn't take me back to town. It's only a couple of miles, and frankly I could use the walk. I've got a lot of thinking to do."

| CHAPTER TWELVE

STONE HEADED HOME EARLY, catching a flight from Des Moines to Chicago Sunday afternoon. But first he drove back out to the abandoned mill to verify what he'd suspected: whatever anomaly had infested the place was now gone, with no traces remaining even when he tentatively opened a wider connection to the Calanarian energy to check for anything he might have missed. He thought about checking in with Leith McCoy again, but decided against it. It was probably best for this little town at this point if nobody stirred up uncomfortable memories. The whole thing would likely pass into history with surprising speed if he didn't poke the embers again.

With everybody but Mitchell Kirkson, anyway. Stone doubted Cathy's brother would be forgetting anything anytime soon.

The Chicago pub that housed the portal was busy when he arrived, packed full of people enjoying an early dinner or getting a jump start on their evening's drinking. Stone didn't recognize any of the customers as mages, but he asked around until eventually someone pointed him at the proprietor, a florid Irishman named Dermot McClellan.

"What can I do for you, friend?" McClellan looked busy, but amiable.

"I was wondering if anyone had reported any sort of…travel anomalies recently."

The man's expression changed from amiable to concerned. "Don't think so. Whatcha talkin' about?" He motioned for Stone to follow him to a more secluded area. "Don't think I've seen you 'round here before."

"I don't come this way often. But I left the Bay Area on Friday night around seven-thirty, and when I arrived here, it was almost five a.m. I thought the place had gone out of business."

McClellan gaped at him. "You're pullin' my leg."

"Believe me, that's not the sort of thing I'd joke about. It was…unsettling." He described the strange colors and sounds he'd heard while traversing the Overworld. "I assume you get quite a lot of traffic through here."

"Oh, yeah. Dozens every day, from all over. We're the central hub for this whole part of the country."

"And no one's said anything?"

"Not a word." He studied Stone. "You sure you weren't— you know—impaired when you were goin' through?"

"I'm certain." He sighed. "Ah, well. It was probably just a one-time glitch if you haven't heard anything else. I'm heading home now—I'll give you a ring if it happens again this time."

"Yeah…" McLellan pondered. "Never a good thing, the portals actin' up. Thought things were settled, once those nasty beasties hangin' about went away a few years back. Hopefully you're right and it won't happen again."

It didn't happen again. Stone stepped through with a bit more trepidation than usual, scanning the fog carefully for any signs of anomalies, but the shifting gray-white tunnel remained as still and muffled and unremarkable as it always did. He walked a little faster and kept his attention focused a little more than he'd do on a standard trip, but by the time he exited the portal in the downstairs storeroom of A Passage to India, the only unusual effect was that his muscles were tense and he was beginning to develop a stress headache. He quickly pulled out his phone and glanced at the time: only three minutes had passed since he'd left Chicago.

That was more like it.

Before he left, he took Marta Bellwood aside and told her about the portal glitch, asking her to contact the other portal-keepers she knew and spread the news.

"It's probably nothing," he said when her expression turned worried. "Probably an isolated incident and won't happen again. But best if people know the potential problems before they travel."

Raider was happy to see him when he arrived home. He dropped his bag on the floor and paused to scratch the tabby's head before heading upstairs. Idly, he wondered how the cat—or any animal—would react to being taken through a portal. As far as he knew, nobody had ever done it. He'd never risk it with Raider, though, even if the portals weren't acting up.

Upstairs in his office, he settled in to make a few calls. Even though the situation in Devil's Creek was probably as much of an anomaly as the portal issue, both had disturbed him enough that he wanted more information. He phoned a few of his associates, starting with Eddie Monkton, and described his experiences.

"That's...the oddest thing I've 'eard in a while," Eddie admitted. "Do you think the portal glitch and what 'appened in the town are related?"

"No idea. I want to doubt it—one was in Chicago and the other was several hours' drive away—but it does seem strange that they both happened so close to each other. I'd almost wonder if it had something to do with me, since I was the commonality between the two, except the business in Devil's Creek had already occurred two weeks before I ever heard of the place."

"Magic's like that," Eddie said. "Doesn't matter how much you study it, there's always gonna be things we don't understand. It's perverse that way—sometimes I think it changes itself around every now and then just to keep us poor sods on our toes tryin' to make sense of it."

Stone chuckled. "Wouldn't be surprised. But if you can look into it for me, I'd appreciate it. Let me know if you can find any references to similar occurrences, either modern or historical."

"Oh you can count on it. You've already got me intrigued. I'm gettin' together with Arthur at the pub in an hour or so after we finish up at Caventhorne. Maybe we can find somethin' there tomorrow. You should stop by, anyway—we've mostly got the collection sorted, so now it's just a matter of meetin' with Kerrick to figure out how we want to get the place ready for visitors."

"I'll see—a bit busy with things now, but I'm overdue for a visit. And I want you to meet Ian, if he ever gets tired of traveling around and settles anywhere long enough to bring him over."

Eddie chuckled. "Yeah, lookin' forward to it. Still can't quite get my mind around you 'avin' a long-lost kid with old Jessamy."

"Join the club. But I think you'll like him. Anyway, I've got more calls to make, so I'd best go."

Stone called a few more associates around the United States, other mages who were either frequent portal users or scholars like himself, and gave them an abbreviated description of both the portal glitch and the events in Devil's Creek, though he didn't share the specific location of the latter. The last thing that mundane little farm town needed was a bunch of curious mages descending on the place to poke around looking for vestigial energy traces. In each case, he asked the other mages to contact him if they heard of any other similar situations. He had enough of a reputation as a maverick that most of them treated his request with amusement—usually, magical scholars preferred for the interesting problems to come to *them,* and didn't seek out potentially dangerous adventures on their own without a lot of planning—but promised to pass along anything they might hear.

"There," Stone said, pausing to pet Raider, who'd planted himself on the desk in front of him. "They can't say I didn't warn them, anyway."

Next, he called Verity. "Are you home?" he asked when she answered.

"Yeah. Got back this morning. Are you?"

"Just got in a bit ago."

"Everything okay? No more weird portal behavior?"

"No, the trip home was quite uneventful—just the way I like it. Listen—do you want to come by for dinner tonight? You and Jason, actually."

"Uh—sure. Want me to check with him?"

"Please do. I want to tell you about what happened. You're welcome to stay after, if you like, of course." He made sure his sly smile came through in his voice.

"Yeah, I'd like that." Her tone matched his. "I'll tell Jason he'll need to bring his own ride."

Verity and Jason showed up around the same time that evening. "So, what's this story V's telling me about magical weirdness?" Jason asked.

Stone led them out to the dining room, where he'd used a barrier spell to keep a confused Raider away from the collection of cartons from Thai Lotus he'd spread out there. He levitated plates to everyone and described the weekend's events to them as they ate.

"Wow," Verity, who hadn't heard the end yet, said. "So you still have no idea what's going on?"

"Not a bit. I wish I could have had more time to do some in-depth analysis while I worked on the girl, but between her brother and the threat of both their father *and* the local clergyman turning up, I thought it best to get the job done with minimal extra effort."

"But it sounds like you don't even know what you did," Jason said. "You—what—cut off a connection between her and some other place? But where?"

"No idea. The only thing I'm certain of is that whatever happened to her was related to what happened at the abandoned mill two weeks ago."

"But it didn't happen to anyone else? That's the weird part. They all just…forgot about it?"

Stone spread his hands. "Your guess is as good as mine at this point. I plan to go over my notes, and I've got Eddie looking into more information for me, but I might have to end up writing this off as not reproducible."

"That might be a good thing, though," Verity pointed out. "I'm sure nobody wants stuff like that popping up all over the place, right?"

"Especially not with the portals." Jason glanced at Verity with concern. "V, you're not planning to go anywhere anytime soon, are you?"

"You're so cute when you worry. But no, other than the City, I don't have any trips planned."

Stone chuckled. "I see where I rate here."

"Yeah, like you'd listen if I asked *you* not to go anywhere…"

"True." He refilled his plate, picked out a couple pieces of beef, and offered them to Raider on another plate. "But I *did* want to ask for your help, Jason. You're getting to be quite good at mundane research with that computer of yours. When you've got a bit of spare time, can you keep an eye out for any other strange news stories? Anything where something's happened and people can't explain why?"

"You think there'll be more of them?" Verity asked.

"No idea. I hope not. But if there are, perhaps I can look into them a bit more discreetly and see if I can get any useful information."

"Sure, yeah, no problem. I'll put Gina on it—she's a wiz at the computer stuff. I'll just tell her I'm helping you out with some stuff for your classes. I'm goin' out of town tomorrow on a case, but I'll get her started before I go."

"Where are you going?" Verity asked. "You didn't say anything about it to me."

"It just came up on Friday. I'm tracking a cheating husband, and it looks like he might be in Reno."

"Anything exciting?"

Jason rolled his eyes. "It's seriously the polar opposite of exciting. Some old dude's wife thinks he's got a young chick on the side, so she wants some photos so she can divorce him and take him for everything she can get." He shrugged. "Me, after meeting her I think the poor guy's just tryin' to get some peace and quiet for a few days, but hey, she's payin' my fee, so it's off to Reno I go."

"Yeah, was gonna ask if I could go along, but maybe I'll pass on that one. Not really into spending a couple days stalking the buffet line at Harrah's."

Jason left early; he claimed he had to prepare for the trip tomorrow, but Stone thought he might be clearing out to give him and Verity some time alone together. After he left, Stone used magic to gather the cartons and plates.

"This is probably nothing, you know," Verity said, trailing him out to the kitchen.

"You're likely right. Magical anomalies pop up now and then—it's just the nature of magic."

She chuckled. "Sometimes I think you're not happy unless you've got some mystery to track down. Sherlock Stone." She came up behind him and put her arms around him as he stuffed the cartons in the trash bin. "You sure are a lot different from when Jase and I first met you."

"How so? I was tracking down magical mysteries back then too. What do you think the Evil were?"

"Yeah, but before you had this 'I don't really want to do it, but I have to because nobody else will' kind of attitude. Nowadays, you almost seem to *enjoy* it."

He thought about that, turning around to face her. "I suppose you might be right. I mean, I'd prefer they didn't happen—losing several hours on a trip that should have taken less than five minutes can get inconvenient—but as long as they're occurring, I won't deny it's intriguing to track down what's behind them."

"Maybe you should team up with Ian and run around the world looking for magical weirdness."

He led her into the sitting room, poured them both glasses of wine, and settled on the sofa. "Not sure he'd be interested. From the look of things, he's inherited my sense of adventure, but not as much of my curiosity."

"Give him time. This is all new to him, and he's got a lot to explore."

"Yes, but…"

"But what?"

"Well, from what I've been hearing from him, he seems more interested in exploring the local party scene than anything to do with magic."

She snuggled into his shoulder. "Mind some unsolicited advice from somebody a lot closer to his age?"

"Do enlighten me. I miss these things sometimes, being in my dotage."

She punched his arm. "Shut up, silly. I'm just trying to say—he's young, he's had a lot of stuff change on him fast, and for the first time in his life he's got the freedom to be himself. I think it's good for him—and I also think it's good that you're *letting* him do it."

"I can't very well stop him," Stone pointed out. "He's over eighteen—and besides, I doubt I could control him if I wanted to."

"Yeah, I know. But you gave him some money and told him to go have fun. That will mean a lot to him. From the sound of it, all his life he's had people not only telling him what to do, but forcing him to pretend to be what he isn't. That's hard, trust me. Let him get it out of his system he'll come back to you."

Stone nodded, but didn't reply.

"You're worried he won't be as focused on magic as you think he should be, aren't you?"

As usual, she'd zeroed in on his concern. "Not...worried, *per se*. But I am concerned about his being a black mage without a teacher. It can be dangerous for black mages if they're given incorrect or incomplete training during their apprenticeships. He's got such potential, and I don't want him to lose the opportunity to take advantage of it."

She took his hand. "Have you tried to find him a teacher?"

"I've sent out a few feelers. The difficult part is that I don't know that many black mages. I even contacted Matthew Caldwell, but he wouldn't even take my call. He's never forgiven me for…" He dropped his gaze.

"For what happened with Deirdre," she finished softly. "I know. I'm sorry." She snuggled in closer and sipped her wine.

"Hey, what about that guy you always go to for magical information? The one who always makes you pay for lunch?"

"Stefan?" Stone blinked, startled. "No—I don't think that would be a good idea."

"Why not? You said he's really powerful. And he's local, so Ian might stick around more."

He pondered. He *hadn't* ever considered Stefan Kolinsky as a potential master for Ian. He hadn't even revealed his son's existence to his friend, and he wasn't entirely sure why. It likely had to do with the nature of their relationship: he thought they might have grown a bit more amicable over the years they'd known each other, but essentially they still maintained a trader's give-and-take regarding any information, favors, or magical items they exchanged. If Stefan were even willing to take Ian on as an apprentice, what would he ask in return?

That wasn't the only problem, either, if he had to admit it. "He's…I don't think he'd be right for Ian. You've never met him—if you had, you'd see what I mean. He's…quite old-fashioned. Rigid. Set in his ways. I suspect if he'd even consider such an arrangement, he and Ian wouldn't be terribly compatible in their styles."

"Are you hinting around the fact that he'd have a problem with Ian being gay?"

"I…honestly don't know. It's not the sort of thing we've ever discussed. But even if he didn't, based on my nearly ten-year acquaintance with Stefan, I have a feeling his teaching methods would make William Desmond look like an easygoing slacker by comparison."

She took another sip of wine. "Maybe. But people can surprise you sometimes. Would it hurt to ask him? You

108 | *R. L. KING*

should at least tell him about Ian. From what you've said about him, he'd probably be pretty offended if he found out from somebody other than you, right?"

"Well…yes, I suppose he would. And it's not as if I've got anything to hide." He finished his wine and levitated the glass to the table, holding it in place long enough for Raider to lose interest in knocking it to the floor. "In any case, I should probably ask him about the anomalies—he's likely to be my best option for finding out what's going on."

Her wineglass joined his on the table and she snuggled closer. "Great. So, now that I've solved all your current problems for you, how about you solve one of mine?" Her eyes glittered in the dimness, and the way she looked at him left no doubt as to the nature of her "problem."

He rose, pulling her up with him. "Brilliant idea. Always happy to be of assistance."

| CHAPTER THIRTEEN

STONE DIDN'T HAVE A CLASS the next day, so on a whim he drove over to Stefan Kolinsky's shop in East Palo Alto. He had no idea if Kolinsky was even around—the man seemed to be away more often than he was home these days—but he figured he could at least tell Verity he'd tried.

To his surprise, he found the black mage in his usual place in the back room, crouched next to a solid black, humanoid construct the size of a small child.

"Never thought you were the type to play with dolls, Stefan," he called, chuckling.

Kolinsky rose gracefully to his feet, removing a pair of wire-rimmed glasses with several lenses attached to them. "Good afternoon, Alastair. It has been a while."

"Been busy, as usual." He studied the object, shifting to magical sight. As he suspected, faint arcane energy hung around it, but he couldn't identify its exact nature. "So, what is that thing, if you don't mind telling me?"

"It is a piece I acquired recently from an...unusual source. The lore around it claims it is a receptacle for a human spirit...a soul, as it were."

"Indeed?" Interested now, Stone moved closer. "Anybody we know?"

"I do not believe it is functional any longer. It is at least a thousand years old, and if it did in fact contain a human soul, it has long since departed." He removed the glasses and waved his hand, moving the black construct to the other side of the room, where he covered it with a cloth. "But surely you have not come to examine my acquisitions. What can I do for you, Alastair?"

"I thought I might take you to lunch and discuss a couple of things with you."

Kolinsky's eyebrow crept up. "I will never turn down lunch and intriguing conversation. I have heard good things about the new Eritrean restaurant in Los Altos."

"Eritrean it is, then. We'll go when you're ready."

Stone didn't say much on the way to the restaurant, and Kolinsky seemed content to look out the window and leave them both to their thoughts. Stone still wasn't sure whether he'd bring up Ian—he supposed the magical anomalies would be a sufficient topic to keep them engaged for an hour or so, but he decided to play the rest of it by ear.

The restaurant was small, set back on a side street, but the crowd was large enough Stone was glad he'd thought to make a reservation. When they were seated at a secluded booth near a party of khaki-clad tech workers and sipping wine, Stone studied the menu, then regarded Kolinsky across the table. "So," he said. "Something odd happened to me this weekend, and I wanted to get your thoughts about it."

"To hear you call something 'odd' must mean it is unusual indeed," Kolinsky said calmly.

"Well, I've certainly never heard of anything like it." The server came by and they both took her recommendation for their order; Stone watched her go until she disappeared around a corner, then recounted the story of the portal glitch and the events in Devil's Creek.

Kolinsky listened attentively, leaning forward a bit, his obsidian-chip eyes never leaving Stone. When the story ended, he remained silent.

"So? Any thoughts? Have you ever heard of anything like that before?"

"I...am not certain." Kolinsky paused for another sip from his drink. "I have heard of peculiarities in the portals—most recently the events from a few years ago, with the extra-dimensional entities."

"Yes, but this has nothing to do with the Evil. I'm certain of it. The Evil drove people mad, or occasionally tore them to pieces. They never caused time glitches."

"And you are certain it *was* an issue with time inside the portal?"

Stone narrowed his eyes. "What else would it be? It doesn't take several hours to go from Sunnyvale to Chicago."

"No...but when considering situations such as this, there are two likely causes: either something is amiss with the portal, or you yourself experienced an event."

"You're saying something happened with *me*? I thought about that, but it doesn't fit. I didn't pass out in the portal, Stefan. I'm certain of it. I walked through just as I always do. I saw the colors and heard the sounds."

"*Are* you certain?" Kolinsky still sounded calm and untroubled.

Stone thought about it. *Was* he sure? Illusions were insidious things—they were one of the few types of magic that could affect people regardless of power level, because they relied on the mind more than magical ability. He hadn't been expecting an illusion in the Overworld. Why would he? It would be like expecting to see an illusion on the Tube in London. It *could* happen, of course—hell, it *had* happened to him. But the likelihood was so low it wouldn't be the first—or even the tenth—explanation he'd settle on for something strange going on.

"Well…" he said slowly, "I suppose I can't say I am, now that you mention it. Are you suggesting I was fooled by an illusion and something or someone—what—knocked me out for several hours? It doesn't make any sense. Why would they do that? And in any case, wouldn't I have noticed when I woke up?"

"It is an intriguing question," Kolinsky admitted. "You may well be correct: it was simply a one-time anomaly. For something that is used as frequently as the Overworld portals, the level of understanding as to their nature and their specific operation is surprisingly low. You know this as well as I do."

Stone did know it, and it often troubled him. Most of the public portals had been built many years ago, and each new generation of mages showed less inclination to study the difficult, calculation-intensive branch of magic required to design and construct new ones and keep the old ones functioning if they experienced problems. Stone himself was one of the few mages he knew of with any kind of deep understanding of portal science, and even he wasn't confident in his ability to diagnose this kind of issue, let alone fix it.

"All right, well, let's put that aside for the moment. I'm willing to accept the 'one-time anomaly' hypothesis if I don't hear of anyone else experiencing similar issues. But the business in Devil's Creek has me a lot more nervous."

Their meals arrived, and Stone paused to sample the unfamiliar cuisine, a tangy meat stew called *tsebhi* served over a flatbread called *injera*. "Good call, Stefan. This is excellent."

"It is indeed. And I think you are wise to be concerned about the events in Devil's Creek. Usually I hear of such things, but this one, regrettably, slipped through my information network."

"Not surprised—even you can't hear about everything. I only heard of it myself because a friend of a friend lives in the area. But what do you think it could be?"

"I should ask you the same question, since you observed the phenomenon firsthand."

Stone sighed. "I've been going over my notes since I got back, and I'm not coming up with much. Based on what I saw, I'd almost say it looked like some sort of rift opening to—somewhere else. But I've no idea where, or why. There were quite a lot of echoes in the old mill, but I've never heard of echoes opening dimensional rifts. Have you?"

"I have not."

"I suspect the man I spoke with and his sister might both be latent talents, which could explain why the energy affected them differently—or even that they were the catalysts for bringing it into being in the first place. But once I managed to block the energy, the sister doesn't remember anything about what happened to her. And the brother is so hopelessly mundane that I doubt I'd get anything out of him. His father and the clergyman have probably already convinced him he dreamed the whole thing up, or the devil was giving him visions. He probably wouldn't talk to me even if I went back there."

"And you got no useful readings from the energy?"

"Not really. Whatever the rift was, the energy wasn't strong. I suppose I should be glad for that—if it was, those kids would probably be dead. And I couldn't get any decent data from the girl because her brother practically chucked me out the window before the others arrived."

Kolinsky considered. "Fascinating."

"Do you have any idea what it might be? What might have caused it? And most importantly, whether it's likely to occur again?"

"Let me do a bit of research—on both the portal and the other events. I will contact you if I discover anything."

"Thank you. And what do you want in payment?"

"This intrigues me—I would have heard of it eventually through my sources, and investigated even if you had not approached me with it. So I will say in this case, the information itself can serve as payment."

"All right, then," Stone said, surprised. "Thank you. And if you hear of any similar situations, please let me know. I'm probably winding myself up over nothing—these events were likely isolated incidents—but if not, I'd like the chance to go in with a bit more preparation and get some better data."

"Of course."

Stone settled back, forcing himself to concentrate on the excellent meal instead of his continuing mental turmoil about whether to reveal Ian's existence to Kolinsky. It was one of those situations he experienced now and then—the ones where he pictured himself standing on the edge of a cliff or poised in a doorway, and his next steps had the potential to be irrevocable. As much as he valued his association with Kolinsky, the man and his motivations remained nearly as much of an enigma now as he had been when they'd met almost ten years ago.

"Alastair?"

Stone jerked his head up. "Yes? Oh—sorry. Checked out there for a moment."

"You look as if you have something else on your mind. Were there any other anomalies you wished to discuss?"

Stone chuckled at the thought. *Is Ian an anomaly? I suppose in a way he is.* He could never do anything the normal way, that was certain. "There is something else, but it's a...different subject."

Kolinsky waited.

Here goes... "I'm looking for someone willing to take on an apprentice."

"An apprentice." Kolinsky tilted his head. "I would have thought you had other resources better suited to—"

"A black mage, Stefan."

"Indeed." He set his fork down. "That is...unusual. Black magic at the apprentice level is uncommon, as I am sure you know."

"Yes, believe me, I'm aware. And this one is more unusual than most. He's nineteen years old, only recently discovered his magical abilities, and was trained for two years by a black mage who had few strictures against pursuing the darkest corners of the Art."

"I see. And where is this teacher now?"

"Dead."

"At whose hand, if I may inquire?"

"It's...complicated. I suppose ultimately it was mine, but I didn't kill her directly. I don't want to go into the details— they're not relevant at present." Stone had Kolinsky's full attention now, but that didn't mean he intended to spill everything. "The relevant bit is that I'm looking for a teacher for this young man, and circumstances have limited my options. He's got the potential to be a brilliant mage, but as I'm sure you understand he needs to be handled carefully. Complicating matters is the fact that he's had a difficult life, and now that he's got his freedom, he's understandably reluctant to focus on a rigorous program of study."

Kolinsky sipped his wine. "I will begin by asking the obvious question: why do you not teach him yourself? It seems the most logical choice."

The precipice loomed. Stone studied the black mage for a moment, meeting his calm, settled gaze. "I can't do that, Stefan."

"Oh? Why not?"

"Because he's my son."

Both of Kolinsky's eyebrows elevated, but all he said was, "Indeed."

"Long story. I'd rather not go into it right now. But I've done the necessary checks, and he *is* my son. I'm certain of it. I tried training him for a bit on my own before I knew he was a black mage, and it…didn't go well. There were extenuating circumstances." He sighed. "I'm at a bit of a loss, to be honest. As I said, he's got immense potential—I can see that already. He's irrevocably black, since he ashed someone while studying under his former master, but he's not interested in pursuing that path any longer. He's also quite…stubborn."

"That does not surprise me, if he is truly your son," Kolinsky said with a faint, arch smile.

"Yes, well, I can hardly argue with that. I'm actually a bit surprised you hadn't already heard. I thought that information network of yours would have picked it up, and I was afraid you might be offended that I didn't tell you earlier."

"Your business is your own, Alastair, and no, I had not heard. Where is the boy now?"

"Who knows? I think he's still in Prague. He's met a group of mages over there who seem more interested in the local nightlife than rigorous study."

"And you approve of this?"

"It's not my place to approve or disapprove."

"He is your son."

Stone waved that off. "Let's not get into that, Stefan. I suspect you and I have very different approaches to dealing with offspring, and debating their relative merits won't get us anywhere. The point is, Ian's an adult now. He can do what he likes, and frankly, after the life he's had, I don't begrudge him some time to have a bit of fun and discover what he truly wants. But he's told me he wants to study magic, and I've promised to try to find him a teacher he can deal with—and more importantly, who can handle his power level and his unique situation."

Kolinsky took another sip of wine. "Are you asking me to train the boy?"

"I don't know. I've never heard you mention an apprentice, aside from the work you did with Zack Beeler—but he hardly counts in this regard. And to be honest, I'm not sure you and Ian would get on. No offense, but you might be a bit...old-school for him, especially after what he's already experienced."

"None taken. I suspect you might be correct—although I will admit to being intrigued. I am aware of your power level, and if you are impressed by the boy's potential…"

"*Potential,*" Stone reiterated. "But as my friend Jason pointed out to me, just as some students with amazing academic potential don't ultimately live up to it, it's entirely possible that Ian's situation has affected him to the point where he won't have any desire to put in the work required to truly excel."

"This disappoints you." It wasn't a question. Kolinsky was watching him now with shrewd intensity.

He sighed again, tossing his napkin on his empty plate. "I don't know, Stefan. I suppose it does to an extent—a couple of months ago, I had no idea I even *had* a son, and then he turns up with all this power…of course I want to see him achieve what he's capable of. But I can't force him to do it. I wouldn't want to. And even if I did try it, I'd be more likely to drive him completely away from magic, or send him off to seek training on his own, which is dangerous for a number of reasons. So at present, I've got to be content to let him explore and hope he'll at least let me offer him advice." He flicked his gaze up. "Do you have children, Stefan?" It occurred to him that he still had no idea exactly how old Kolinsky was.

"I do."

The frank answer was unexpected. "Did you go through this with them?"

Kolinsky chuckled. "No. It was…many years ago, and circumstances were quite different. I am afraid I am not the best source of advice on such matters. But if you like, I will make a few discreet inquiries. Perhaps I can locate some candidates your son might find palatable."

"I'd appreciate it. I'll owe you for that."

"Yes, you will. But let's not speak of that until we determine if I am successful."

"Fair enough. To be honest, right now I'm more interested in any repeats of the Devil's Creek situation. I don't expect to see Ian for quite some time, and there's no point trying to steer him toward study before he's ready."

The check arrived, and he picked it up without pause. "Thank you, Stefan. I appreciate our conversation, as always."

"As do I."

As they left, Stone couldn't help wondering whether he should have told Kolinsky about Ian. It didn't matter now, though—the proverbial cat was out of the bag, and there was no putting it back in. He'd just have to deal with the consequences, if there were any.

| CHAPTER FOURTEEN

J ASON COULD HAVE TAKEN A PLANE to Reno—his fledgling agency had enough business now to allow for a coach-class ticket, even if he didn't touch the rest of the money Stone had fronted him as part of his investment—but he liked to drive. Getting out on the open road and away from the Bay Area crowds helped him clear his head, something he could definitely stand to do now and then. He wished it had been in his red Mustang instead of the unassuming gray sedan he'd bought for company business, but even this thing could manage respectable speed when you opened it up on the freeway.

He'd gotten good start, leaving late the morning after having dinner at Stone's place. As promised, he'd left a message with Gina, asking her to hunt any other odd occurrences she could find around the country, with instructions to call Stone if she found anything interesting. He wondered what she'd think of the request, and whether she'd be able to find anything. Personally, Jason was convinced Stone was chasing ghosts—not even literally this time—and the weird situation he'd encountered in Iowa wouldn't be repeated. Either that, or crazy things like that went on all the time in hidden corners of the country and this was the first time Stone had heard of one. In any case, he was glad Verity had assured him she didn't plan to use the portals for travel any time soon. He'd never tell her, of course, but the thought of her routinely walking through that silent tunnel of fog, even without the Evil lurking around looking for snacks, terrified him. He supposed it was only because he didn't understand it—that, and the only time he'd gone through himself, he and Stone had nearly been devoured—but either way, he had no intentions of letting either Stone or Verity take him through there again. He'd travel the old-fashioned way. Slower, but safer.

As he continued up highway 80, his thoughts turned to the last time he'd driven this road, when he, Stone, Verity, and Verity's girlfriend at the time had set out in a luxury RV on the way to Burning Man. He chuckled when he thought about what they'd actually *arrived* in—a Jeep SUV towing an ancient, rickety wooden horse trailer after the RV had broken down—but his amusement quickly evaporated when he remembered the level of death and destruction the Evil had caused with their attempt to summon a massive gateway to let them into this world after their own portals were destroyed. Dozens of people had been killed and hundreds more injured by fire, vehicles, magic, and even gunshots from the Evil's soldiers.

For a while, it hadn't even been a certainty that Burning Man would ever happen again—aside from the massive liability issues, many of its attendees felt the tragedy had tainted the peaceful energy of the location. It had been cancelled the year following the event, but the year after that the organizers managed to regroup and get things rolling again. After everything went off as planned with no further unexpected happenings, the horrific events began, as all such things do, to pass into memory. Jason had heard from some friends who'd attended one of the later Burns that the organizers erected a memorial each year, burning it along with the Man to commemorate those who'd lost their lives.

Occasionally he thought about trying to go again, but it never got past the "what if?" stage. He didn't think Verity would be interested, and he was sure Stone would probably laugh at him if he suggested the mage come along. Maybe if he ever got himself a serious girlfriend, it might be fun.

He watched the forest flash by and tried not to think about that. Lately, his love life was getting to be as spotty as Stone's used to be before he and Verity got together. He thought he'd found someone down in Ventura when he'd met Kristen—he and the tall, blonde EMT had hit it off on their first meeting and seen each other for long enough Jason had begun to think about getting serious with her, but then had come the business with Verity healing the injured motorcyclist. Kristen couldn't handle the idea of magic, and that had been the end of that. Jason knew Verity still didn't believe him when he'd told her she was more important to him than any woman who couldn't deal with the stranger aspects of his life, but it was true. When both your sister and your best friend spent the biggest part of their lives up to their necks in a world most people would never even see, it simply wasn't practical to allow anyone that deeply into his life who couldn't handle it. If that meant it took him a while to find someone, so be it. He was so busy with the agency he didn't have time for a serious relationship anyway, and even though he'd been casually dating a paralegal from the law firm next door to his office, it hadn't reached the point where they were seeing each other exclusively. He didn't think it would, honestly—she was fun, but the two of them were too different for things to go beyond the casual.

He'd moved on to thinking about his case when he pulled into Truckee. He hadn't intended to stop—Truckee was only half an hour or so away from Reno—but the car was getting low on gas and he needed a pit stop anyway, so he figured he might as well break for lunch. That way, when he reached Reno he could find a place to stay, dump his stuff in the room, and get started tracking down the cheating husband. With any luck, he could find the guy, get the pictures of him pursuing his secret tryst, and be back at the office late tomorrow.

Or maybe, a sudden thought popped into his head, *you could take a little detour afterward and go down to Tahoe. That's where Tony said he was…*

Damn it, no. He slammed the door closed and stalked into a sandwich shop, trying to push the thought out of his head before it took root. That way lay madness, or at least danger, and he knew it.

It didn't work, though. The thoughts persisted as he hit the restroom and then came back out to order a footlong sub and a big bottle of water, and when he found a table near the front window, he finally gave up and let them have their way with him. It wasn't as if he was going to *do* anything about them.

But he *did* have enough information to find Tony, if he made a little effort. He was sure of it. The man wasn't exactly trying to hide, after all—he, Verity, and Stone had saved his life, breaking him out of Marciella Garra's horrific laboratory where he was being drained of his blood to fuel her mad alchemical workings. Would it be such a bad thing to ask him if he'd be willing to—

No. Get that right out of your mind. It wouldn't matter anyway: even if he could manage to convince the bear shifter to share some of his blood with him—either out of sheer gratitude or for a price—Verity had already told him she wasn't going to make the elixir again. She didn't know how to do it herself yet, and her prickly friend Hezzie didn't seem inclined to help. Jason didn't know the reason for Hezzie's dislike and distrust of men, but whatever it was, she'd made it clear to Verity that brewing potions to make them stronger, faster, and nearly impossible to damage wasn't something she was in any hurry to do.

So stop thinking about it, damn you. He ripped bites from his sandwich with a ferocity that startled the woman and two young children at the next table, and forced himself to calm down and flash them a reassuring grin. He didn't have time for this—he had a job to do, and he needed to focus on that. Even though the agency had been doing well so far, he couldn't count on that continuing if he slacked off. He was determined not to touch any of the remaining money from Stone; it was safely stashed away in the bank, and there it would remain, so he'd have to hustle if he wanted to keep things running with his own work.

He finished the sandwich at a slightly more sedate pace, wadded the wrapper, and took the half-full water bottle with him. It was around two p.m.—if he left now, he could be in Reno before three, which would give him plenty of time to hunt down Mr. Cheater. He pulled out onto the road to make a left, edging around a parked car he couldn't see past.

The screech of brakes joined the squeal of tires as a silver SUV smashed into the left front side of the sedan, rocking it sideways. The airbag deployed, slammed Jason hard into his seat and then deflated, revealing steam wafting from beneath the crushed hood.

"Fuck!" he snapped, glaring at the SUV. Why couldn't people just pay attention when they drove? The damn idiot was probably on his phone, or messing with his radio, or—

The door opened and a woman erupted from the SUV, hurrying over to the sedan's driver side. "Oh, my God," she said. "Damn it, I didn't see you! Are you okay?"

He took quick inventory before unhooking his seatbelt and scrambling free of the car. He'd probably have bruises and general aches from the airbag, but aside from that he didn't think anything was broken or damaged. "What the hell?" he demanded, glaring at her. "Didn't you see me coming?"

"Yeah, I'm sorry, it's my fault. I was going too fast." She looked flustered, but not out of control. "Are you sure you're okay?"

"Yeah." Jason smacked the sedan's side and stalked around the front to view the damage. The left front tire was flat, the wheel cocked at a sideways angle, and the quarter panel and left side of the hood were both crumpled. He had no idea what was going on under the hood, but the steam didn't promise a quick fix. He wasn't getting to Reno any time soon, at least not in this car. Even more frustrating, the SUV didn't show nearly the same amount of damage: a heavy winch on the front had protected it from most of the impact, leaving it with some crumpled sheet metal and a broken headlight, but everything else looked fine.

By now, other cars were creeping past them, the usual rubberneckers slowing to examine the scene before moving on. Off in the distance, Jason spotted the whirling lights of a police car approaching. "Fuck…" he murmured. At this rate, between trading information with the woman, making a police report, and figuring out what the hell to do with the car, he wouldn't be out of here before dinner time at the earliest—and that assumed he could find another way to Reno.

"I'm really sorry," the woman said again. "This is totally my fault. My mind was on something else and I was going too fast."

He glanced up to study her. She looked to be in her middle to late twenties, with shoulder-length brown hair, a healthy tan, and a solid, athletic figure. She wore jeans, a leather bomber jacket with the sleeves pushed up, a blue T-shirt with the logo of a local bar on it, and a Dodgers cap. Aside from a fresh, dark bruise flowering on her forearm, she appeared uninjured from the crash.

In spite of his anger at this frustrating setback to his plans, he appreciated her straightforward candor. No trying to weasel out of the fact this mess was her doing. That was one point in her favor. "Yeah, no kidding," he muttered.

She pulled a brown leather wallet from her jacket pocket. "Don't worry—I'm insured. We should probably get out of the street and exchange info."

"Yeah." Jason retrieved his overnight duffel and camera bag from the trunk, then moved off to the side as the police finally made it to the scene.

The cops did their jobs quickly and efficiently, taking Jason and the woman aside separately to get their information and statements, snapping photos of the accident from several angles, and verifying that neither of them needed medical attention. The policewoman who spoke with Jason encouraged him to stop by the local urgent-care facility to get checked out, but he assured her he was fine. The car's frame and airbag had done their job, and it hadn't been a serious crash—though he couldn't tell that from looking at the mangled front end of his trusty gray sedan. He wondered if it could be fixed, or if he'd have to total it and get a new one. The latter would almost certainly involve dipping into the money from Stone.

The cops soon left, just as a tow truck arrived. Jason wondered who'd called it. As it approached, the woman came over to him.

"Listen," she said, still looking apologetic, "I don't know how to make this up to you. The least I can do is buy you a cup of coffee while we wait to find out what's going on. Why don't you figure out where they're taking your car. I'll run you over there so you can give them your information."

Jason almost turned her down—it felt like consorting with the enemy—but then dismissed that thought as stupid. He didn't have Stone's or Verity's ability to read auras, but even so he was fairly sure she *hadn't* meant to hit him, and genuinely did feel bad about it. Being a dick to her for an honest mistake was hardly a good look for him. "Yeah, okay," he said, a little reluctantly. "Looks like I'm not going anywhere anytime soon in my own car."

He spoke to the tow-truck driver; the nearest Ford dealership was in Reno, so he asked the guy to tow it there, then tossed his gear in the back seat of the woman's SUV and swung into the passenger seat.

"Looks like you made out better than I did," he said as she started it up. The engine rumbled smoothly, showing no signs of difficulty.

She patted the dash. "Yeah, this thing is built like a tank. That's probably why it did so much damage to your car." She sighed ruefully. "I can't say 'sorry' enough. I'm not going to lie—my mind wasn't on driving, and I didn't see you poke your nose out."

"Eh, it's okay. As long as you've got good insurance. I just hope they can fix it and don't have to total it."

"Yeah, that would suck. My name's Amber, by the way, in case you didn't notice it on my driver's license. Amber Harte."

Jason *had* noticed it—he'd be a pretty poor private investigator if he hadn't—but didn't say so. "Jason Thayer."

She flashed him a quick smile. Her eyes were a rich brown, serious but with a twinkle of mischief. "Nice to meet you, Jason Thayer. I'd have picked different circumstances, but hey, whatever works." She made a vague wave in the direction of the accident site. "I saw your license plate frame—you're not from around here, area you? Bay Area?"

"Yeah. I was driving over here for some business." Once again, he winced—if he didn't get to Reno by this evening, he'd probably miss the cheating husband, and then he'd either have to track him down again or extend his time in Reno.

"What kind of business? Are you one of those tech guys?"

"Nah. Private investigator."

"Really?" Her eyebrows rose, and she looked intrigued. "That's not one I would have expected."

"Well, that's kind of the point, isn't it? If I wore a fedora and a trenchcoat, it would make it harder to blend in." In spite of himself, Jason liked Amber. She reminded him a bit of Verity: down to earth but with enough whimsy to keep her from being boring.

She laughed. "Good point. So, why don't we get that cup of coffee and then I'll give you a ride to Reno? Least I can do."

"I'll take you up on the coffee, but I can't let you drive me. I'll get a rental or catch a bus or something."

She shook her head. "Nope, you have to let me give you a ride. Like I said, it's the least I can do after messing up your car and your plans. After that—where are you headed? Is your business here in town?"

"Actually, Reno *is* where I was headed."

"Well, then, that makes things easy." She pulled into a parking lot and stopped in front of a local coffee shop with a log façade. "C'mon—this place is good. A lot better than the chains."

Jason followed her into the shop, which continued the rustic, rough-hewn theme on the inside. Some indie-folk band he'd never heard wafted out from hidden speakers. They got steaming cups of coffee and took seats at a table near the window, where he could keep an eye on the SUV.

"So, what are you investigating in Reno, if you're allowed to say?" Amber settled back and sipped her coffee. She looked mostly relaxed, but Jason could see she was still hiding some stress.

"Cheating husband. His wife hired me to get some photos of him with the woman she thinks he's seeing."

She wrinkled her nose. "Ugh, cheaters are the worst."

"Yeah, but they pay the bills. I haven't been in business too long, so I can't be choosy about the cases I take. What about you—what do you do?"

"Oh, this and that. A little bartending, a little freelance stuff...I don't like to be pinned down to anything for too long."

She was being evasive, but that was fine—Jason didn't need her life story. "Hope everything's okay—I'd hate to think you took out my car because you were thinking about your grocery list or something." He smiled to take the edge off his words.

"No grocery lists, I promise." She toyed with her cup, not meeting his gaze. "Just...some stuff going on in my personal life. Nothing to worry about."

Jason didn't push it. Once again, it was none of his concern, and he didn't expect to see Amber Harte again after she dropped him off in Reno. Part of him regretted that—she wasn't wearing a wedding ring, and if he'd met her in San Jose under better circumstances, he might have asked her out. But he was already late, and he didn't have time for that sort of thing right now. "Coffee's good," he said.

She looked grateful for the change of subject. "Yeah, it is. This is one of my favorite places, actually. I come here sometimes to just clear my head, which is definitely something I could use right about now." She finished her coffee and set the cup down. "We should go, though. It sounds like you need to be—"

She stopped, looking at something past Jason's shoulder. "Oh, damn."

"What?" Jason twisted in his chair to follow her gaze.

The door had opened to admit a man. Tall, broad-shouldered and bearded, he wore jeans, a green flannel shirt, and a belt with bull's skull on the oversized buckle. When he spotted Amber and Jason at their table, his brow furrowed and his face twisted in anger.

Before Jason could react, Amber was out of her chair, moving quickly forward to put herself between him and the man. "Hey, Hank. How's it going?"

Hank stopped, glaring between Amber and Jason, and made an obvious effort to get himself under control. "Hey, Amber. Thought I might find you here. What happened to your rig?"

"Got in a little fender-bender. It's fine. What do you want? Shouldn't you be at work?"

His expression clouded, and once again he clearly made an effort to control his anger. "Yeah, I took a break. Was hoping to find you so we could talk." He glowered at Jason. "Who's this guy?"

Jason stepped forward, but once again Amber moved between them. "His name's Jason. I ran into his car, so I'm buying him a cup of coffee and giving him a ride to Reno."

"Like hell you are. Let him take the bus or somethin'." He jerked his head toward the door. "Come on—I don't have too long before I gotta get back, and we need to talk."

She didn't budge. "No, Hank. I told you—I'm taking Jason to Reno. We can talk when I get back."

"Uh—" Jason inserted. The last thing he wanted to do was get in the middle of some ongoing argument between these two. "Listen, it's fine. I can rent a car, or—"

"No," she said, in a firm *don't argue* tone. "This is bullshit, and he knows it. He can bluster all he wants, but it won't change anything."

"Amber—" Hank began.

"I mean it, Hank. We'll talk later. Go on back to work. I'll call you when I get home."

Hank remained where he was, fists clenched, his body trembling with anger. Jason recognized the signs and prepared himself for what might happen. Would Hank go after him, or worse yet, Amber? He stepped forward, next to her, and glared back at the big man. Hank might be at least three inches taller and outweigh him by a good fifty pounds, but he'd fought guys his size before.

Surprisingly, Hank did neither. Instead, he subsided, relaxing his fists but still glowering. "Damn straight we'll talk about this later. Call me as soon as you get back." Then he turned and stalked out of the shop, slamming the door so hard the pleasant little bell on it clanked and jangled like an angry cowbell.

"Well. *That* was something you didn't need to see," Amber said. She sounded neither fearful nor angry, but did glare at the shop's few other customers until they returned to their own business.

"Uh...yeah. Listen—I don't want to cause any trouble. Maybe you should—"

"Maybe I should give you a ride to Reno, just like I said I would. Don't worry—Hank won't mess with you."

"I'm more worried about what might happen when you get back." He glanced toward the door. "Are you two...together?"

She waved it off, heading for the exit. "Sort of. He thinks it's a lot more serious than I do, though. He can get...protective."

"Sounds like more than protective to me." Jason looked around the parking lot, but didn't see any sign of Hank lingering around outside. "You sure this is okay? I don't want to be the cause of anything."

"Eh, he gets like that any time he sees me with another guy. Hell, last week he got pissed because he thought I talked to the checkout guy at the market too long, but he'd never lay a hand on me. He knows better."

Privately, Jason wondered about that. Amber was solidly built, with the kind of athletic frame that suggested she did actual physical work, but he didn't like her odds if it came to a fight between her and the much larger Hank. Besides, people who used their size and strength to bully others pissed him off. "Well...even so, I don't want to cause trouble. Let's get to Reno so you can get back. And let me give you my number in case you need a little backup."

She chuckled. "Thanks, it's appreciated, but not necessary. Trust me, I've dealt with guys like Hank all my life, and I know how to handle them."

They drove off. Jason watched the scenery go by, unsatisfied with the way things were going but reluctant to push it any farther. If he did, he'd end up being every bit as annoying as Hank had been. He had enough issues in his life without getting in the middle of other people's, especially when they were doing everything but holding up neon signs telling him to back off. Still, he was happy he already had Amber's phone number, and she his, from when they'd exchanged information at the accident.

It took about half an hour to reach Reno. Amber drove fast but safely, and her SUV seemed to have suffered no lingering ill effects from the accident. Jason contented himself to listen to the rock music on the radio until Amber pulled into the parking lot of the Ford dealership.

"Here we are," she said briskly. "Let me say it one more time—I'm *really* sorry about hitting your car. I know it's messing up your plans, and I hope you won't hold it against me."

"Nah, it's fine. It's a pain, yeah, but this kind of stuff happens." He got out and retrieved his gear from the back seat. "You take care, Amber. And I'm serious—you have my number. Give me a call if you need anything."

"I will—but don't count on it. Good luck with your car!" She reached across to shake his hand.

"Yeah, thanks. I—" He took her hand, and stopped.

The dark, spreading bruise he'd spotted on her arm less than an hour ago had vanished.

"Everything okay?" she asked, frowning.

"Uh…yeah. Fine. Have a good one."

Jason remained where he was, watching the SUV until it had turned a corner and receded from his line of sight. As he turned to walk back to the dealership's service area, his thoughts had moved far away from the accident.

| CHAPTER FIFTEEN

T O HIS CONTINUED ANNOYANCE, Jason soon discovered the service department wouldn't even have time to look at his car until the following day. "Sorry," the advisor told him. "I wish I could move you up, but we're crazy busy these days. We'll give you a call tomorrow after we get a chance to look it over." He glanced at his computer. "But from the look of the initial assessment, expect it's gonna be in the shop for several days at minimum. That's assuming they don't find any hidden damage."

"Great," Jason muttered. Well, there was nothing to be done about it—he couldn't force them to work faster, and he'd worked on enough cars in his life to know they were telling the truth. He might get lucky and not end up having to total the car, but he wouldn't be getting it back any time soon.

The dealership set him up with a rental. They tried to offer him an upgrade to something sporty, but he chose a boring beige sedan similar to his own. That much might work in his favor, at least: there weren't too many things less likely to be noticed than a beige rental car. He found a cheap motel, checked in, took a shower, and verified the accident hadn't damaged his camera gear. Now all that was left was to wait till dark and get the photos.

This part of his adventure, at least, went off without any problems. He found his client's husband, a sixtyish man dressed in the style of someone twenty years younger, right where she'd told him he'd be: at one of the bars at the Silver Legacy, laughing as he shared dinner and a bottle of champagne with a woman about Jason's age in a tight, sparkly cocktail dress. He got a secluded table where he could keep an eye on them and observed them for several minutes, verifying without any doubt that he'd found the right guy.

Carefully glancing around to make sure nobody was watching, he pulled out his tiny digital camera and snapped a few shots. He'd gotten good enough at deploying the little thing that nobody appeared to spot him—certainly not the couple, who'd clearly had more than one glass of champagne before Jason had arrived. He'd brought a larger camera with a big telephoto lens along too, in case he'd have to shoot outdoor photos, but this one would work just fine for what he needed.

Just to be safe, he stowed the digital and pulled out another small camera, this one using real film, and snapped a few more. He did it quickly and still nobody appeared to notice him. He finished his drink and left the casino, and was back in his room at the motel in less than fifteen minutes. After checking the digital photos to make sure he'd gotten what he needed, he emailed copies to Gina back at the office, then stowed the memory card and the roll of film in a secure portion of his bag and settled back on the bed.

Now what? He'd hoped to get the photos and drive back to the Bay Area first thing tomorrow morning, but he couldn't do that until he found out what was going on with his car. He didn't feel like going out drinking or gambling on his own, and although the hot shower had taken the edge off the mild aches and pains from the accident, some of them still lingered. Maybe it would be best just to hit the bed early so he could be at the dealership when they opened.

You could hunt up Tony, you know. You've got time.

He slammed his fist down on the bed. Damn it, he needed to stop thinking about Tony! Even if he could manage to find the man, what was he going to do? Show up wherever he was and say, "Hey, man, my friends and I saved your life, so how about forking over some of your blood so my sister can make a magic potion to give me superpowers?"

Yeah, that would go over great.

Besides, he didn't have any idea where Tony was, aside from "the Lake Tahoe area." That was a big area—bigger still because, as a bear shifter, he probably didn't have a nice two-bedroom apartment in town. Hell, where *did* bear shifters live? Did he have a cave in the woods or something? Was he the only one, or was there a whole colony of them? Pissing off a clan of people who could change into grizzly bears was not high on his list of intelligent life choices.

He settled back on the bed with a loud sigh. *Just give it up. Get a movie on the TV, have a beer, and forget about it. It's a bad idea to poke bears, remember?*

But Foley knows where Tony is...and you do *have his number.*

Damn. That was true, as much as he'd tried to put it out of his mind.

Officer Foley had fled Marciella Garra's compound with Tony and the baby jaguar shifter Diego, and Foley had been the one who'd told him Tony was in Tahoe after they'd met to return Diego to Viajera. If anybody still knew where the bear shifter was, it was the cop.

Jason swung up to sit on the edge of the bed and snatched his wallet from the nightstand where he'd tossed it. He stared at it long and hard, trying to talk himself out of this. It was a bad idea. At best, even if he could find Tony, the shifter would probably gape at him in astonishment for having the nerve to make such an insulting request. At worst, he might anger the man and any friends or relatives he had knocking around, and gain a powerful enemy he had no hope of dealing with. Not without his magically-powered associates, anyway, and the last thing he wanted to do was drag Stone and Verity into this mess.

Just be happy with yourself the way you are. You've done fine so far.

Growling, he flipped open his wallet and withdrew the slip of paper with Foley's number on it. Before he could talk himself out of it, he grabbed his phone and punched in the number.

"Yeah, Foley. Who's this?"

Jason didn't hear any of the background noise to suggest Foley was at the tiny police station where he worked. "Hey, Foley. It's Jason Thayer. Remember me, from the animal compound?"

"Oh—uh, yeah, of course I do. Little hard to forget, though to be honest I've been trying to."

"Yeah, sorry about that. Sorry to call so late, too."

"It's okay. What's up?"

Jason gripped the phone tighter. "Listen—I was wondering if you were still in contact with Tony. You mentioned before you two had talked after...what happened."

There was a pause. "Uh...I wouldn't say I was exactly in *contact* with him. We never went out for beers or anything. Like I said, I'd really rather just put this whole thing behind me. It was all way too weird for me, you know?"

Jason could certainly sympathize with that. Sometimes he thought his whole *life* was getting too weird for him, and he'd had several years to get used to it all. "I get it. But I was thinking about giving Tony a call—got something I want to talk to him about. So do you know where he is?"

"Yeah. In Tahoe. Or at least he was. Actually, I think he's away, now that I remember it—took a trip up to Canada to visit some relatives, last I heard. Said he didn't know when he'd be back. In fact, he mentioned he might just decide to stay up there." He paused again. "I kinda think what happened spooked him pretty bad too, so he wanted to get away from this area, at least for a while."

Damn. Jason sighed. "Okay, man. I guess I can't blame him for that." Getting captured, held in a cage, and having your blood drained to power some old witch's alchemy business had to be hard on the psyche, even for somebody who was more bear than human.

"What did you want to talk to him about?"

"Ah, nothing important. It can wait. Mind giving me a call if he turns up? Or passing my number along to him if he contacts you, and asking him to call me?"

"Yeah, sure, no problem. Everything okay with you guys?"

Jason snorted. "Oh, yeah. My friends eat this kinda stuff for breakfast. And I'm learning to."

"I don't envy you, man. My life's gone back to the way it used to be before I started using that stuff, and I couldn't be happier about it. Never thought I'd be this satisfied with the wife, the kid, and TV after dinner, but I am. Not just satisfied—*happy*. I feel like I've been given a second chance, and I don't want to screw it up this time."

"That's great, Foley. I'll back off so I don't accidentally drag you in to anything else. You take care."

"I appreciate that." Foley sounded relieved. "You too."

Jason tossed the phone on the bed, shoulders slumping. Well—that was that. There went his last realistic chance of getting hold of some shifter blood for Verity to experiment with. He had no idea how to reach the pair of wolf shifters who'd also been held prisoner at Garra's compound, and there was no way he'd talk to Stone about contacting Viajera. If he knew or had met any other shifters, he had no idea who they were; it didn't matter anyway, because only the fact that he'd helped save their lives gave him the courage to approach them about a possible deal. The rest of them would either laugh or use him for a light snack.

Just forget about it.

Yeah. Just forget about it. Frustrated, he stripped off his shirt and jeans and climbed into bed. Maybe he'd get up early tomorrow and go for a long run or find a gym to help him blow off some steam and focus on the important stuff—doing his job and growing his agency into something he could be proud of. He didn't need alchemy-based powers for that.

As he snapped off the light and pulled the covers up, an image flashed into his mind again: Amber Harte's warm brown eyes and impish, straightforward smile. He wished he could give her a call, but she'd already told him she was seeing someone. The thought of the brutish, possessive Hank made him tense with anger, but she'd claimed she could handle him and the whole thing was none of his business. But what if—

In his mind's eye, Amber's face swirled away, replaced by the large, spreading bruise on her arm. He hadn't been seeing things—the bruise had been there. He pictured the sleeve of her brown bomber jacket shoved up to reveal it, and then her arm when they'd shaken hands before she left him at the dealership. The bruise had been there, and then it was gone. Not just faded, either—vanished as if it had never been there.

Damn...

He sat up, shoving the covers down. He was sure he'd seen it—that wasn't the kind of thing he missed. And bruises didn't just vanish that fast.

Not on mundane humans, anyway.

He scrambled out of bed, retrieved his bag, and dug through it to find the sheaf of paperwork from today's accident. There it was, just as he'd remembered: Amber's phone number, along with the rest of her contact information.

He glanced at the clock on the nightstand: a little after ten p.m. That was late to call, especially someone he barely knew. What if she was already asleep? What if she was with Hank? And even if he was right about her being something other than vanilla human, was it any of his business?

He tapped in her number and waited as it rang, heart pounding hard.

"Hello?"

It was Amber's voice. She sounded puzzled. He swallowed.

"Hello?" More suspicious now. "Who is this?"

"Amber?"

"Who *is* this?" The suspicion grew firmer, with an edge of anger.

"It's Jason Thayer. From today. The accident?"

"Oh, right." Calmer now, but still not friendly. "Hello, Jason. It's a little late to call—is something wrong?"

He listened for a moment, trying to pick up any rumbling bass tones in the background to indicate Hank might be nearby, but heard none. "Uh—sorry to bother you so late. But I've been thinking about something, and it's been bugging me."

She sighed. "Jason, really. If you're worried about what happened with Hank today, don't be. I promise, he blusters a lot but he wouldn't dare lay a hand on me. I'm fine. We talked and everything's good."

That was a relief, anyway—assuming she was telling the truth. "Okay. That's—good. But it's not what I was calling about."

"Well…what is it, then?" Now she sounded impatient, like she wanted to get him off the phone.

He paused a moment, trying to decide if he wanted to take the plunge. If he was wrong, she'd no doubt think he was crazy. But people had thought worse things about him and he'd survived. "So, today, right after the accident, I noticed you had a big bruise on your forearm."

"Yes, and?"

He could almost see her frown and her furrowed brow. "Well—later, when you dropped me off in Reno and we shook hands, it was gone. Like, completely gone. Like it had never been there in the first place."

Long pause. "Jason, come on. That's crazy. I didn't have any bruise."

"You did. I saw it, clear as day on your arm."

"Come on—don't you think I'd know if I had a bruise on my own arm? You probably just saw a shadow or something. Maybe you saw my other arm later, or I had it turned at a different angle. I don't know. But bruises don't just disappear."

Jason didn't reply.

"Jason?"

"Yeah. I'm still here." He didn't mention that he'd picked up the odd undertone in her voice that he associated with nervousness, if not outright lying. He couldn't see auras like Stone and Verity could, but part of the training Fran Bartek had given him had been in how to spot subterfuge in people's expressions, postures, and tones of voice.

"Are we good? I promise, everything's fine. There really wasn't any bruise. I'm fine. I was more worried about you, in that little cracker-box of a car."

He wondered what she'd say if he asked if they could get together so he could see for himself, but he didn't do that. "Okay. Yeah, you're right. I must have been seeing things. Sorry to bother you."

"It's no problem. You getting your car back any time soon?"

"Don't know yet. I'll find out tomorrow."

"Hope the news isn't too bad. I know I've said this too many times already, but I'm *really* sorry. You take care, Jason, okay?"

"Yeah." He tightened his grip on the phone, and the words came out in a flood before he could stop them. "Amber—listen. I think I might know what you are, and if I'm right, I've met others like you. I've got friends who deal with this kind of thing all the time. So—if you ever need help…" He trailed off, heart pounding harder than ever, part of him aghast at what he'd just said. But he leaned forward, holding his breath, and waited for her reply.

When she did finally answer, after several seconds' worth of silence, her voice had an odd edge: calm, but with a definite overtone of controlled anger. "Jason—I don't know what the hell you're talking about, whether this is some kind of roundabout way of hitting on me, but—knock it off. I told you, I'm not interested, and I mean it. So don't call me again, okay? Just…leave me alone."

The line went dead.

Jason sat there, staring at the phone. His hand shook.

He didn't miss the fact that she hadn't denied anything he'd said.

| CHAPTER SIXTEEN

STONE HAD BEGUN TO BELIEVE the events in Devil's Creek and the portal *were* nothing more than random magical glitches. When two weeks passed and no new odd happenings turned up for any of his sources, he began to think his hypothesis about the whole thing being one of those unexplained incidents that happened with magic sometimes was a valid one. Idiopathic, they called it in medicine, which meant *yeah, it happened, but damned if any of us can figure out why it happened.* This looked to be just that: idiopathic magic.

Neither Eddie, Arthur, Verity, Jason, nor Kolinsky discovered anything definitive about other, similar events. His friends from England and Kolinsky didn't contact him at all, and the only things Verity and Jason (who'd returned from Reno two days late after getting into a fender-bender on his way there) had found was more of the "Bat Boy" style, obviously fake stories. Even Gina Rodriguez, Jason's computer-wiz assistant at the agency, came up empty.

"Sorry," Verity told him one night when he stopped by her place for dinner to help her with her flurry of packing as she prepared to move to San Francisco later in the month. "I wish I could spend more time on this, but I've been so busy between Scuro and getting ready for the move, and…"

And living your life, he thought. He understood completely, though the whole thing was a bit of an adjustment. He'd thought when his two friends moved back to the Bay Area, they'd see each other more often, but between his own busy schedule, Jason hustling to drum up cases for his agency, and Verity splitting time between Scuro, Kyla, Hezzie, and the other Harpies in San Francisco, he was lucky if he saw either of them once a week anymore.

Ah, well. He had his own things to do. It wasn't as if he sat around his big old house pining away of loneliness with only Raider for company. He had his work, his research, and The Cardinal Sin to keep him busy, as well as his weekends spent in England helping Eddie, Arthur, and Kerrick put the final touches on Caventhorne in anticipation of its grand opening. Quite a buzz had begun to grow in the magical community now that the date was getting closer. Stone was sure much of it was simply the curious who wanted to get their eyes on some of William Desmond's rumored magical storehouse of treasures, but scholarly interest was high as well. He was sure Stefan Kolinsky would be one of the first to stop by, probably arranging some kind of private visit so he didn't have to deal with anyone else. He'd already decided to offer Kolinsky a private tour of some of the areas not generally available in exchange for unspecified future assistance.

Even with the complete lack of further evidence of magical oddness, though, Stone found himself unable to simply give up and let the matter drop. Events like Devil's Creek and the glitch in the Chicago portal didn't just *happen.* There was a reason for them, even if he didn't know what it was. Even if they *were* one-off events, his curiosity wouldn't let him go without more investigation into what might have caused them.

Finally, one Thursday afternoon after he'd finished the lecture for his entry-level Occult in America class a few minutes early and there hadn't been any questions, he'd leaned against the lectern and regarded the class.

"So," he said briskly, "We've still got some time before the end of the quarter, but how would some of you like the chance for a bit of extra credit?"

A murmur went through the hall. Stone didn't often offer extra-credit opportunities, and when he did, he had a reputation for making them more interesting than the run-of-the-mill research project.

Good. He had them where he wanted them. He pushed off the lectern and began pacing back and forth across the front of the classroom. "Right, then. Here's the assignment: this class is called 'Occult in America.' We've discussed several prominent historical events and individuals, including the Salem Witch Trials, Madame Blavatsky, and the occult influences on early Freemasonry, but all of those were just that: *historical.* Just because we live in a modern, technological society doesn't mean there aren't things out there right now that nobody can explain. Why do you think those ghost-hunting television shows are so popular?

"So here's what I want you to do: find me some. Do some research, look at newspapers and other sources around the country. Talk to your friends and family members who live in other parts of the country. I'm looking for unexplained occult-related events, the more current, the better. Let's keep it confined to America, and I want to see some good research.

That means don't send me anything from the supermarket tabloids, unless you can corroborate it with more credible sources. Obviously you don't have to *prove* anything, but I promise, not only will I not give you any extra credit for Bat Boy sightings, I might actually take points *away*."

Laughter rippled, some of it nervous. Since this was an undergraduate-level course, most of these students had only known him for this quarter, and hadn't learned yet to tell when he was joking and when he was serious. He supposed he'd have better luck if he gave the problem to some of his graduate students, but they were busy on their own projects, and besides, the new kids had the kind of enthusiasm and eagerness to please that might just turn up something unexpected. "Any questions?"

Nobody had any, so he dismissed them early and gathered his papers. It was a long shot—he could hardly expect a bunch of kids to come up with something several mages and a private investigator missed—but it couldn't hurt.

He didn't have another class until Tuesday, and he was surprised to find a young man waiting next to his closed office door when he arrived there after finishing the lecture. He recognized the kid as one of his students from the Occult in America class, a football player who always sat in the back and didn't participate much, so he didn't know his name. "Yes, something I can do for you?"

"Yeah—I just wanted to drop off the extra-credit assignment." He unslung his backpack and unzipped it.

"You found something?" Stone asked, surprised. He'd already glanced through a few papers other students had left with Laura the admin, and so far all of them had been duds—mostly urban legends or haunted-house stories Stone had already heard of. He unlocked the door and motioned the kid inside the office.

"I think so." He withdrew a slim sheaf of clipped-together pages from his pack and offered it to Stone. "I didn't have much luck with the newspapers, but I remembered something a friend of mine said a couple weeks ago. It's just a rumor, so it might not be enough to get the points, but I figured I'd run it by you anyway."

Great. Another urban legend. Stone was beginning to regret giving the assignment, but now that he had, he'd have to deal with the consequences. "Suppose you tell me about it."

The young man perched on the edge of the guest chair and indicated the paper. "I'm from Pennyslvania. Little town outside Pittsburgh. When I was a kid, before I settled down and decided to get serious about football so I could get into a good school, I ran with kind of a wild crowd in the city. Some of my old friends are still into some stuff like that. When you mentioned your assignment, I figured I'd ask one of them, since he hears weird shit sometimes. He said supposedly there's this guy there—he used to live out in the sticks, but the rumor is he suddenly developed some kinda weird healing powers while he was out there." The kid offered a crooked grin. "Yeah, I know it's got to be bullshit, but it did kinda sound like the stuff you were lookin' for."

Stone didn't roll his eyes, but it wasn't easy. "Faith healing" was almost always pure bunk. Not always—he'd met at least one practitioner who had a powerful healing gift, even aside from Verity, but people didn't spontaneously develop the ability. "So—what—has this man discovered the church and started holding tent revivals?"

"No. That's just it. He's disappeared. My friend says the word on the street is that he and a couple of his cousins went to the 'Burgh and tried to make money off it—you know, charging people to fix 'em up. But they weren't too smart, and it wasn't long before one of the local gangs heard about it. Supposedly they grabbed him and now they're usin' him to patch up their own people and makin' money themselves off him. I don't know, though. There's nothing in the papers about it, so all I have is what my friend told me." He indicated the paper Stone held. "Will that be enough to get the extra credit? I could really use it, Doc."

Stone examined the first page of the paper, noting the student's name: Ronald Cobb. "Well, Mr. Cobb, I'll have to read it over and let you know. You've put in all the detail you're aware of?"

"Yeah. There isn't much, though."

"Is the gang named in here?"

"The gang?" Ronald Cobb tilted his head. "You need that?"

Stone shrugged. "Details like that add to the verisimilitude. I'm not implying you made this up, of course, but every detail you can supply, especially those that can be independently verified, makes it look better." He leaned back in his chair. "I'll be straight with you, Mr. Cobb—I've got an ulterior motive for requesting these stories. I'm considering a new paper about modern-day occult or supernatural occurrences, so I thought I'd combine the chance to offer you lot a bit of extra credit with a research opportunity I might not otherwise have access to. I promise, if I end up choosing your contribution as part of the paper you'll get all proper credit, but I'll need to corroborate the story."

Cobb looked relieved. "Ah, okay. I get it. Uh—no, the gang's not named because I don't know what it is. But my friend probably does. I can put you in touch with him if you want to ask him."

"Yes, that would be brilliant." Stone handed back the paper. "Just add the information to the bottom there. I'll let everyone who received extra credit know by late next week."

"Okay. Thanks, Dr. Stone."

As soon as Cobb left, Stone used magic to close the door, then looked down at the paper. The story was almost certainly bullshit—some fanciful tale Cobb's friend had cooked up to help his college buddy. People didn't develop spontaneous magical healing abilities.

They don't suddenly start seeing auras, either.

Still, Cobb's story could explain why no mention of the guy had turned up in the newspapers: if he was some naïve, small-town oaf who mentioned his newfound powers to the wrong people, it would be in those people's best interest to keep the whole thing under wraps, especially if they wanted to exploit the man's gift for their own profit.

He kept a copy of his ley-line map book in his office, so he pulled it down. The presence of a ley line in or near the small town the man had come from would go at least some of the way to making the story potentially believable. It was something to start with, anyway.

It took him only a few seconds to find the right page, and a few more to pinpoint Litton, the tiny town a couple hours' drive from Pittsburgh. "Well..." he murmured. "That's interesting."

Not only did one ley line run through the middle of Litton, but two of them crossed nearby, just as they had in Devil's Creek.

| CHAPTER SEVENTEEN

S TONE WAS APPREHENSIVE about traveling the Over-world again, but the trip, this time to the public portal in New York City, proceeded with no unexpected events. He caught a flight to Pittsburgh, picked up a rental car, and paused behind the wheel to go over what he'd discovered in the last few days.

He was going to have to do some work this time. When he'd called Ronald Cobb's friend, a young man named Jamal Fielder, he didn't have much to add to the story. He said he'd heard it from a friend of a friend, and all he could verify was that the man had supposedly lived far out in some rural area, and had spontaneously developed the strange abilities after a hunting weekend with his two cousins a couple of weeks ago. All three of them had taken off for Pittsburgh to try to mone-tize his new talent, and that was when he and the cousins all vanished. Fielder said he didn't know any more about it ex-cept that he'd heard a rumor that one of the fringe Pittsburgh gangs, called the Sixes Posse, had gotten wind of the man's alleged abilities and promptly grabbed all three of them.

"I think it's all bullshit if you want the truth," Fielder had told Stone. "Only reason I told Ronnie at all was 'cuz he said he needed something for extra cred in that weird-ass class of yours. But anyway, that's all I know and all I wanna know. Even if the story about the guy is bogus, I don't want nothin' to do with the Sixes. Those guys are freaks."

Stone didn't push it—he didn't want a reluctant mundane along if he had to deal with supernatural threats. He *did* regret, though, that Verity had once again begged off on joining him. He didn't blame her—she was right in the middle of packing to move, and had another big job with Scuro scheduled for tonight—but that didn't mean he didn't miss her company.

Ah, well. Couldn't be helped, and he didn't have time to dwell on it.

The area the Sixes Posse controlled was on the east side of the city. He'd consulted Jason for some intel on the area a couple days ago, and his friend had, after checking with some law-enforcement contacts, given him a map showing the boundaries of the gang's influence along with the names of a couple of bars the members frequented.

"You're really gonna go talk to guys in a gang?" he'd asked. "That's probably a bad idea, Al. No offense, but you've got the street smarts of…well, a British dude who grew up in a mansion and went to private school."

"Thanks for the vote of confidence," Stone had replied with a wry grin. "But I'm not worried. I can be very persuasive if I need to be. And it's not as if I haven't spent my share of time hanging about in dodgy pubs."

"Just don't get too cocky. I think you underestimate us mundanes sometimes. We can still catch you by surprise. And besides, the Sixes are rumored to be into stuff like devil worship. That could mean they've got mages, right?"

"It could, but it's not likely. And even if they do, they're almost certainly nothing to write home about, talent-wise. I can handle them."

"Yeah. Just—be careful, okay? You sure you don't want me to come along? I'm working on a case right now, but I should have it wrapped up in a few days, and—"

"No, that's quite all right. I'll be fine, and I haven't got time to wait."

It was dark by the time he reached the hotel and dropped off his gear. A light rain fell, more annoying than inconvenient, and the air had a cold bite that suggested winter here hadn't quite given up its hold yet, even this late in the spring. Downstairs, he calibrated his disguise amulet to make him look like a pale, middle-aged man in a cheap suit and a drab tan overcoat, then hailed a cab outside.

The driver turned around to look at him in surprise when he revealed his destination. "You sure, buddy? That ain't a nice part of town."

"I'm sure. I'm meeting a friend there." Stone used his American accent. He worked on it periodically, enlisting Jason and Verity to give him honest assessments on his success, and they'd assured him that as long as he was trying to sound like a middle-of-the-road guy from California, he was doing fine. When he attempted other accents, he could see from their polite attempts not to laugh that he still had a lot work to do, so he stuck with what he knew.

"Okay..." The driver still sounded apprehensive, but he pulled out into the brisk evening traffic without further comment.

Stone watched the bleak scenery go by, growing bleaker as they got closer. It was no wonder the Sixes and other gangs like them turned to crime, Stone decided, if they had to live in a place that looked like this. He'd seen plenty of bad neighborhoods, both in London during his university days and elsewhere in his travels, but this little corner of Pittsburgh seemed to be in the grip of a debilitating blight. The buildings here were old, with rows of multi-story townhouses giving way to a haphazard business district dominated by grungy brick buildings. Many of both were abandoned or condemned, boarded up and sagging, their facades rotting or crumbling from years of neglect.

"Here y'are." The cabbie pulled into an open spot in front of a check-cashing business with its front picture window replaced by a sheet of plywood. "You sure you want me to let you off here?"

"I'm sure. Thank you."

Morrie's Tavern, next door to the check-cashing place, was in better shape than many of its neighboring structures. It didn't look much different from many other lower-class bars Stone had seen in the States: tiny windows, faded old sign that had probably been there since before he was born, and several flickering neon ads for various pedestrian beers. A couple lounged outside, having a conversation under the slim awning that ran the length of the place. Next to them, several news racks had been broken open, and the only papers remaining were ads for escort services and for-sale circulars. The couple looked briefly up from their conversation as Stone passed them and descended the short flight of stairs to the entrance, but said nothing.

Inside, the place was barely lit. It smelled of beer, some kind of spicy food Stone couldn't identify, cigarette smoke, and cheap perfume. Pounding hip-hop music boomed at a volume level that allowed conversation only if the participants were sitting right next to each other.

The bar was also packed. Stone kept magical sight up as he limped through the crowd, looking for signs of anything unusual even though he had no idea what he was looking for. He saw nothing at the moment, only the typical flares of excitement and occasional lust along with the darker patches indicating poor health in some of the customers. The majority of the patrons were male and most were young, ranging from late teens to early twenties.

Around Ian's age. Stone wondered what his son was up to, whether he was hanging out in places like this, and then chuckled. For a while in his own youth, he'd frequented bars every bit this seedy. It would be worse than hypocritical for him to take issue with Ian's choices.

As he approached the long, scarred bar, he gradually became aware of several young men wearing similar clothing. It wasn't as if they all wore black leather biker jackets with *Sixes Posse* emblazoned across them, but more than a few of them sported Steelers or black Penguins jerseys with either 6 or 66 on the back, others wore black stocking caps even in the oppressive warmth, and all of them had dark circles around their eyes—either naturally or added with makeup. Stone couldn't tell which, but either way it did give them a sinister aspect. A few of them were casting Stone odd, suspicious glances when they didn't think he was looking.

A stool opened up at the bar as a hefty young man slid off and disappeared into the crowd, and Stone quickly moved to occupy it.

The bartender, a dour, solid bottle-blonde woman in a backward-facing Steelers cap, ignored him when he tried to catch her attention to order. At first he thought it was accidental, but when she dropped a plate of chicken wings in front of the man sitting on his left and then, a couple minutes later, brought a fresh bottle of Yuengling to the guy on his right without acknowledging his presence, he knew it was either some kind of test or this place really didn't like strangers.

He studied the area behind the bar, noticing the lifelike human skull behind the ancient cash register, the detailed painting showing some kind of hellish scene of torture and dismemberment hanging at the back, and the upside-down cross suspended from the ceiling. What he didn't notice was any hint of magic, malevolent or otherwise. He almost smiled, until he remembered his disguise: these guys were posers. If there was an ounce of magic in the lot, he'd eat his boots. What that meant for the rumors of a guy with real healing powers he didn't know, but at least it looked like he didn't have to concern himself too much with being jumped by a bunch of wannabe baby mages trying to prove themselves.

As the bartender prepared to walk past him again, he used a bit of subtle magic to stop her forward progress, then shoved a twenty-dollar bill in her direction. "I'll have one of those, please," he said firmly, nodding toward his neighbor's bottle of Yuengling.

She looked startled, but already Stone had dropped the magic. "Yeah," she said with grudging annoyance, sweeping up the bill in a stubby-fingered hand and clunking a bottle down in front of him. "Hang on, getcha change."

"It's fine. Keep the change. I—I've got a question for you." Stone deliberately made his voice sound tentative, darting a quick glance around the area as if he'd suddenly realized he was surrounded by potential hostiles.

"Yeah, whatcha want?" She looked impatient. "I ain't got time to chat."

"Well…" He forced a nervous chuckle. "It's just—I heard a rumor about something, and I sure hope it's true."

"What kinda rumor?"

Now the two guys on either side of Stone were paying attention to his words as well. They hadn't moved, but he could see the telltale flares in their auras indicating sudden interest.

He chuckled again and pulled at his collar. "Well…I know this sounds crazy, but I'm kind of desperate and I'm out of options, so I figured I'd take a chance."

The two guys were definitely listening now, even though they appeared intent on their own thoughts.

"C'mon, spit it out," the woman said, making a 'go on' gesture. "I ain't got all night."

Stone dropped his gaze. "I heard there's a guy around here who can…you know…fix people. Heal 'em. Like they do in those church meetings on TV sometimes. I thought that stuff was all fake, but what I heard is that this guy's the real deal."

The bartender snorted. "You're crazy, man. You musta wandered into the wrong part of town. You sure you're not already shitfaced?" Her aura, however, belied her words, its muddy orange indicating definite interest. She knew something, even if she didn't want to say so.

"Yeah…I know. I figured it had to be crazy." He sighed and fidgeted with his beer bottle, projecting dejection. "Hey, I'm sorry to bother you. Guess I'll just finish this up and head back home. Thanks."

"Yeah, you do that." She moved quickly off to serve another customer, but her aura remained on high alert.

Next to Stone, the guy on his right picked up his beer and melted into the crowd. The guy with the chicken wings continued methodically chewing through them, but like the bartender's, his aura appeared interested as well.

"You know," the guy said as Stone finished his beer and prepared to leave, "I couldn't help overhearin' what you were sayin' to Wanda there." He jerked his head toward the bartender's broad back. "That's pretty fucked up, a guy who can heal like one o' those TV preacher guys. They're all frauds, you know."

"Oh, I know." Stone twisted around, settling back in. He made another exaggerated sigh. "It's stupid. Just wishful thinking, I guess."

"Yeah." The guy sucked the sauce off another wing. "And anyways, even if that kinda guy existed for real, he'd be an idiot to do it for free. Ain't nobody do nothin' for free, y'know? If I could do somethin' like that, I'd charge a shitload of money to do it. Only fair, right?"

"Well, yeah," Stone agreed, forcing his aura to remain calm and desperate on the off chance he was wrong about anyone around here having magic. "Sure, it's only fair. I probably wouldn't even have enough money for a guy like that to look at me."

"You got some kinda problem?" The guy, who had medium-brown skin and stringy black hair under a black Penguins stocking cap, turned his stool toward Stone. He shoved the plate of wings over. "Want one?"

"No, thanks, I'm good." Stone bowed his head. "Yeah, I have a problem."

"What kinda problem?"

He looked around. "I...don't really want to discuss it right here in the middle of the bar, you know?" He sighed. "Ah, what's it matter anyway? Like you said, it's crazy. Stuff like that isn't real—those guys are just frauds, trying to take people's money away."

"Yeah. Maybe so." The guy pulled his wings back and selected another one. "Where'd you say you heard this rumor, anyway?"

"Friend of a friend. You know." Stone deliberately did a bad imitation of a down-on-his-luck schlub trying to sound cagey.

"Yeah, yeah, I know." He considered. "But if a guy like this *did* exist—if he was the real deal—how much would you be willing to pay to get whatever this problem is fixed? Hypothetically, you understand."

Once again, Stone kept his aura under control. "Not enough, I'm sure. I figure maybe I can come up with a thousand. Even that'd be hard. I'm sure a guy like that wouldn't look at me unless I had a lot more than that. I wouldn't, if I was him."

"Yeah, you prob'ly got that right." The guy finished the last wing on the plate, wiped his mouth on his sleeve, and downed the remainder of his beer. "Well, you take care, man.

Hope you find somebody to help out with your problem." He clapped Stone on the shoulder and walked off into the crowd.

Stone watched him go until his dull yellow aura disappeared into the colorful swirl of other ones, then turned back around, unsure of whether he'd accomplished anything. With both guys who'd been listening gone now and the bartender off flirting with someone at the other end of the bar, he wondered if the potential of a thousand dollars hadn't been enough to pique anyone's interest to take a chance on a stranger. He'd played it careful at first, figuring if he threw around talk of too much money, they'd probably just try to roll him in the alley after he left. That wouldn't go well for them, of course, but it would also mean his chances of finding the healer—assuming he existed at all—would likely evaporate. Either that, or he'd be forced to lean on people a lot more than he wanted to.

He finished his beer and was about to try his luck in another part of the bar when another man slid onto the stool to his right, where Chicken Wings had been. This one was a little older, broad-shouldered and thin-faced, with short dark hair and a Penguins jersey over a black hoodie.

"'Sup, man?" he muttered, waving for a beer. Apparently he rated better service than Stone had, because Wanda instantly abandoned her flirting, poured him a pint, and placed it in front of him.

"Hey," Stone said without looking at him.

"I hear you were talkin' to my pal Spud about some kinda crazy-ass thing. Somethin' about a—what—faith healer?"

Stone shrugged. "I didn't mean anything by it. It's just I heard a rumor, so I took a chance. I was just about to go. I don't want any trouble."

"Nah, man, no trouble. You're good. So you got yourself a problem needs fixin'?"

"Yeah. I guess I do."

"Wanna share it?"

Stone glanced up at the man. He was maybe in his late twenties, with a series of tattoos on his neck that disappeared into the top of his hoodie. They included three sixes, one stacked on top of the other two, on the side of his neck. He had the same dark circles under his eyes as the others Stone had spotted, making his narrow face look even more skull-like. "What good would it do? There's no such guy, right? It's just an urban legend."

"Maybe it is, maybe it isn't. Why don't you tell me what you need and maybe I might know somebody who can help."

Stone allowed a little hope to reach his face. His heart pounded, but more with exhilaration than fear. It had been a long time since he'd had to rely on his acting chops, and it felt good. "Really?"

"Let's see."

Stone crossed one leg over the other and pulled up his trouser leg, weaving an illusion as he did. The several layers of gauze wrapped around it were real—he'd put them on in his hotel room before leaving—but the angry wound seeping blood through the bandages was not.

"Holy fuck," the guy said. "What happened to you, man? You should go to the hospital with that shit."

"Yeah, I know." Stone bowed his head again, looking glum. "The problem is, I'm not supposed to be here. My wife thinks I'm in Philadelphia. If I go to the hospital, I'm afraid she'll find out. Especially since I got this...uh..." He offered a sheepish, conspiratorial smile "...from a jealous boyfriend."

The guy's grin matched his. "Oh, I get it. You were steppin' out on your old lady and you don't want her to find out nothin'."

"Yeah. Plus, our insurance isn't that great, so..." He shrugged, then winced. "I tried to take care of it myself, and figured I'd get it looked at there at a clinic or something when I get back to Philly, but it's getting worse. I'm getting scared. So when I heard about this guy..."

"Who'd you hear it from?"

"I don't know the guy's name. Friend of a friend kind of thing." Stone was taking a chance that if these guys were holding the would-be healer and exploiting his talents for profit, they'd have to make it known somehow that those talents were available. If that wasn't true and they were only using him to patch up their own guys, things could go south in a hurry. He tensed, readying magic if he needed it.

"Yeah, right." The guy seemed to take it in stride. "Okay, listen. I might know somebody who can help ya. My man Spud was sayin' you could come up with a grand. That true?"

"Yeah. I got some of my own money put away, that my wife doesn't know about. It'll be hard, but I think I can get that much." He gripped the guy's arm with a hopeful gaze, then quickly pulled back as if realizing that was a bad idea. "Are you saying...you *can* help me? That this guy *does* really exist, and he really can do this stuff?"

"I ain't sayin' nothin'. But here's what I want you to do, if you're serious." He pulled out a scrap of paper and scrawled something on it. "You get the money, cash, then come to this address in a half-hour. It's a few blocks from here. Somebody'll meet you there, check you out to make sure nobody followed you, and we'll go from there. Don't be late. Got it?"

"Uh—yeah. I got it." Stone took the paper, then flashed the guy a worried glance. "How do I know I won't just get rolled for the money? A thousand's a lot to carry around in cash."

The guy patted his arm. "You don't, friend. Ain't no guarantees in this world. But if you don't want your old lady findin' out you been steppin' out on her, maybe you oughtta grow a pair and take a few chances, y'know?" He nodded toward Stone's leg. "Besides, that thing looks like it's gettin' infected. Better not wait too long." He raised his glass and then walked off before Stone could say anything else.

Stone remained where he was for a couple more minutes, staring down at the paper and doing his best to look both troubled and in pain. Then he got up and limped out of the bar. He didn't miss the flares of auras around the room as several of the Sixes watched him leave.

He had to sell it so they didn't get suspicious, so he called another cab, took it to an ATM, and told the driver to wait while he pretended to withdraw money. In truth, he already had the thousand secreted away behind an illusion in the pocket of his real overcoat, though he never intended to let the Sixes keep it—illusions were versatile things, and he'd gotten a lot better at them since Calanar. If he was lucky and smart, he could find the guy and get him out without ever casting an offensive spell.

That was the plan, anyway. Whether it would work out that way was anybody's guess.

He got back in the cab and directed the nervous cabbie to take him to the address the guy at the bar had given him. This time, the driver didn't try to discourage him from going there, but merely pulled back out into traffic without a word.

It only took a few minutes in the sparse traffic to reach the place. It turned out to be an abandoned shop, with any indication of its former purpose stolen, destroyed, or obscured by graffiti. Rusting bars covered the front window, but the door was clear.

Still selling the limp, Stone shuffled to the door and tried it, unsurprised to find it open. Looking around nervously, he limped through and stopped just inside. "Hello?" he called in a shaky voice. "Is anyone here?"

Three figures appeared, stepping from the deep shadows in the room's debris-strewn corners. All three of them wore ski masks and hooded sweatshirts—no Sixes colors now. "You the guy with the problem?" one of them asked.

Stone didn't recognize the voice—it wasn't any of the guys from the bar. "Uh—yeah. The guy at Morrie's Tavern told me to come here."

"You got the money?"

"The guy said you could help me—fix my leg." Stone pulled up his trouser leg to reveal the illusionary wound. "I think it's getting worse. You have to help me. Please."

"You got the money?" the guy repeated, louder.

"Y-yeah. But I want to see this healer guy first. If you can help me, it's all yours." Stone was all too aware that if he were what he appeared to be, attempting to intimidate these men would be about as useful as trying to convince students not to procrastinate on their assignments. If they decided it would be easier to simply beat him up and take his cash, his mundane persona couldn't have done a thing about it.

One of the other guys chuckled. "This little fuck's got some balls. I like that."

"Yeah," said the first guy. "Don't worry, man. We got the goods. But first we gotta see you got the funds, and then check you out. So let's see it."

Stone pulled out his wallet, looking nervous, and opened it enough to show them the thick stack of bills, then quickly tucked it away again as if afraid they might take it from him.

They didn't. "Good, good. Now we gotta check you. You know—make sure you ain't got any weapons, wires, anything like that. Put yer hands on yer head and stand still."

This could get a bit tricky, but nothing Stone couldn't handle. He did as he was told, raising his hands to the top of his head. "I don't have anything, guys. Why would I screw up my last chance at getting this fixed without messing up my life?"

"Shut up."

Two of the guys came over and gave him a thorough frisking, including checking his pockets, then stepped back. "Okay, open your shirt."

"What?"

"Do it, man." The guy sounded impatient. "Gotta make sure you ain't wearin' any kind of wire."

Once again, Stone did as requested, altering the illusion to make his own trim physique look pale and flabby. "Can we go now? My leg's killing me."

"Yeah, yeah. Get yourself back together. And put this over your head."

"This" turned out to be a black pillowcase. "Why?"

The guy snorted. "You're really bad at this, you know? We can't have you knowin' where we're takin' you. Just do it before we call the whole thing off and take your money for wastin' our time."

With reluctance—only some of it feigned—Stone pulled the pillowcase over his head. It was thick enough so he couldn't see anything, and smelled like it hadn't been washed in months. If necessary he could use a clairvoyance spell to see what was going on around him, but even after Calanar that spell worked better with a ritual. He shuffled back and forth as if his leg was hurting badly and waited.

Two of the men took positions next to him, each one gripping an arm. "Okay, come on. We'll go slow so you don't fuck up your leg."

They led him in a different direction, probably out through the back. He heard the slide of a van door opening, and then they settled him into a seat and climbed in next to him. It was hard to smell much past the pungent body-odor aroma of the pillowcase, but Stone detected traces of cigarette smoke, pot, and old pizza. When he shifted to magical sight, he could barely make out three hazy auras glowing around him: the driver and the two men on either side of him.

The trip to wherever they were going took around twenty minutes. Stone didn't bother listening for cues to tell him where he was; he didn't care. All he paid attention to for the duration of the trip was the auras around him, prepared to bring up a shield if any of them showed any agitation. To his relief, all three remained their normal muddy green, yellow and blue hues until the van stopped and the door slid open.

"Okay, out," the guy on his left said, gripping his arm.

Stone followed him out, immediately noticing he stood on gravel now instead of asphalt. He craned his ears for any clues to his location, and thought from the lack of vehicle sounds that they might be outside the city, in the suburbs or even out in the country somewhere. The two men took his arms again and led him up three steps, then opened a door, took him inside, and pulled off the pillowcase.

Stone blinked, rubbing his eyes and looking around. As he'd guessed, they were inside a house now. It looked like it had been quite impressive at some point in its history, though from the look of things whoever owned it currently didn't take very good care of it. The room he stood in, probably a living room, had only a few pieces of mismatched furniture, a big-screen TV on the wall, and a series of DVD boxes scattered in front of it. A haze of pot smoke hung in the air. Two more men in their middle twenties lounged on a sofa watching a pornographic movie with an open, nearly empty pizza box and several empty beer bottles on a coffee table in front of them. They looked up as Stone and his escorts entered.

"We got somebody for Clyde," one of the men with Stone said. "You guys are cool—just keep an eye out in case anybody followed us."

The two on the couch eyed Stone with languid disinterest, then returned to their movie.

"Come on," said the man, taking Stone's arm. "Upstairs."

Stone glanced around with magical sight. So far, he didn't spot any subterfuge or violent intentions in any of the guys.

"So who is this guy Clyde?" he asked. "Where'd you find him? Is he one of your ga…uh, group?" He made a show of struggling up the stairs, and adjusted his illusion again to add some red in his cheeks and sweat on his forehead.

"No questions," the man behind him said. "You ain't here for questions. Unless you want us to take you and that fucked-up leg of yours back right now."

"No, no, I'm sorry. It's fine. I just want this to be over." He stumbled at the top of the steps and would have fallen if they hadn't caught him. They led him into an empty room with a bed, a dresser, and a pair of old easy chairs. The window curtains were drawn tight, allowing no view outside.

"Just wait here," the first guy said, and left the room, leaving the second guy alone with him.

Stone sat down on the bed, wincing, listening to the jangly, *bow-chicka-wow-wow* music from the porno wafting up through the floor. He didn't have to wait long before the door opened again and the first guy came back in, followed by a skinny, stringy-looking man.

"Okay," said the guy. "Clyde, here's your latest client."

Stone eyed Clyde dubiously. "*This* is your healer?" The guy had long, unkempt hair, a stubbly beard, and bad skin. His Lynyrd Skynyrd T-shirt, jeans, and scuffed brown hiking boots looked like he hadn't changed them in a while, and his nervous, twitchy demeanor marked him as obviously scared of something. He looked like a backwoods hick and a tweaker got together and had a baby. A switch to magical sight verified his fear: the guy's blue-green aura flashed with red patches.

It also glowed, very faintly around the edges, with the same odd energy Stone had spotted around the old mill in Devil's Creek, and Cathy Kirkson—a little more orange than yellow, but unmistakably the same general appearance. Unlike Cathy, though, Clyde's eyes looked normal. Bloodshot and fearful, but normal.

"What's the problem, Clyde?" the first man asked. "You look spooked about somethin'. Nothin' to worry about. Just do the same thing you did all those other times."

"Yeah, yeah…I'm gonna need a drink." His voice was as twitchy as the rest of him, high and reedy.

"Get the man a beer, Ski," the first man told the second. Then, to Stone: "You want one?"

"No, thanks. Can we just do this?" He winced, slumping back. "I think I'm starting to get a fever. Oh, God, what if it's getting infected?"

"Chill out," Ski said. "It'll be fine."

"Go ahead, Clyde," the first guy said, indicating Stone. "Fix up this guy's leg and we'll set you up."

Stone pulled up his trouser leg, and Clyde winced.

"What'd you do to yourself, man? That looks bad."

"Can you fix it?" Stone had augmented the illusion again; the "blood" had now leaked completely through the bandage, and he'd added some angry red trails radiating out from beneath it.

Clyde hesitated.

Ski shoved him down next to the bed. "Do it, Clyde." His voice took on a menacing edge.

"Y-yeah." He cast Stone a terrified glance, then began undoing the bandage with skinny, shaking fingers.

Judging from the caked dirt and gods knew what else on Clyde's hands, Stone was grateful the wound wasn't genuine. He watched with interest, keeping magical sight up as Clyde got the bandage off and moved his hand around over the area.

Nothing changed. If anything, the faint yellow-orange glow surrounding Clyde's aura faded a little. Clyde swallowed, sniffed loudly, and waggled his fingers.

Stone "helped" him, adjusting the illusion again so first the red trails, then the bloody edges of the wound itself began to recede. After several seconds, his pale, hairy illusionary leg showed no sign of injury.

Both Stone and Clyde let their breath out, slumping. "Holy…cow…" Stone breathed, feigning a wide-eyed gape of astonishment at Clyde. "How did you…*do* that? That's amazing! It's a miracle!"

The first guy grinned. "Ain't it? No time to hang around and marvel, though. Hand over the cash and let's get you outta here so you can go back home to your old lady. And needless to say, you ain't gonna say nothin' to nobody about this. We seen your info in your wallet. If you say anything, we'll find you. Got it?"

"Oh, God, yes. I won't say anything, I promise!"

"Can I have my beer now?" Clyde's voice shook, if anything, more than it had before. He was still staring at Stone as if he'd sprouted three or four extra eyes.

"Yeah, yeah. Ski, get the man a beer. He's earned it. And you—hand over the cash."

Stone pulled out his wallet and gave the man the sheaf of bills, still feigning astonishment. "This is…this is…"

"I get it. You're amazed." The man turned away to open one of the dresser drawers on the other side of the room.

Clyde took that opportunity to grab Stone's arm. "Help me, man!" he whispered, barely audible over the music. "I don't know what the hell you are, but you gotta help me!"

Stone glanced toward the other side of the room. "What I am? I don't—"

Clyde's grip tightened, and his watery, bloodshot eyes bulged so wide they nearly popped out of his head. "Look," he whispered with more urgency. "Somethin's goin' on here. They're gonna kill me. I can't do it anymore!"

"What do you mean, you can't—"

He pointed at Stone's leg, and when he spoke again his tone was still nearly inaudible, but now strangled with fear. "I didn't do that. I *can't* do it anymore."

Stone glared at Clyde in astonishment. "You can't heal anymore?" he whispered.

Clyde shook his head with vigor. He was about to say something else when the other man slammed the dresser drawer shut and turned back around. "Okay. Time to go. We—"

Ski came running into the room, his aura bathed in red flashes. "We got a problem, PB!"

"What the hell—" The man whirled in his direction, looking past him to the door.

From outside, the unmistakable crack of gunfire went off, followed by the shattering of glass.

CHAPTER EIGHTEEN

"FUCK!" PB YELLED, wrenching a gun from somewhere beneath his sweatshirt. "What's goin' on?"

"It's Hammer's guys!" Ski said, as more gunshots went off and another window shattered. "They musta followed us, or figured out where we were stashin' Clyde!"

Clyde, for his part, looked terrified. "Oh, man, fuck, we're gonna die!"

"We're not gonna die," PB said. "Ski—take Clyde down to the basement. Keep 'im safe—we're prob'ly gonna need 'im." Still more gunfire sounded, this time from inside the house. The Sixes were clearly firing back.

Ski grabbed Clyde's skinny arm and pointed at Stone. "What about this guy?"

"Who gives a fuck about him? He's on his own. Hurry up!" PB swept out of the room.

"Oh God…Oh God…" Clyde moaned as Ski began dragging him toward the door.

"You're not going anywhere," Stone said. He still had the illusion up, but he now spoke in his normal voice, all the trembling nervousness gone.

Ski spun back around, looking for the newcomer in the room, but stopped when he saw only Stone. "Who was—"

"That would be me." Stone swept his hand, and the gun flew from Ski's grip and crashed into the wall. "Let him go and get out of here."

"What the *fuck*? Who the hell are you?" Ski dived after the gun, which had landed on the floor near the dresser.

Stone flung it under the bed, and sent Ski sailing into the opposite wall. "Didn't you hear me? I said *go*."

Ski, eyes huge and jaw dropping in a terrified gape, scrambled to his feet and took off toward the door.

Clyde was already on his way there. He'd almost made it when Stone grabbed him in a telekinetic hold and dragged him backward. "Not you, Clyde. We're getting out of here. I need to talk to you."

"What *are* you?" Clyde demanded, nearly gibbering in his terror.

"I'm like you—only a lot better at it. Come on—we'll go out the window and borrow their van."

He gripped Stone's arms with a madman's strength. "We can't go out there, man! Didn't you hear the *shooting*? We go out there we'll get blown to fuck!"

"No, we won't. I can protect us. But we've got to go. Are your cousins here?"

"How do you know about my—"

Stone grabbed him and shook him as behind them, the bedroom window exploded and several bullets took chunks out of the far wall. "We've got to *go*, you idiot! Where are your cousins?"

"Dead." Clyde's tone turned bitter as his bloodshot, freaked-out gaze shifted to the window. "Buried out back, I think. They killed 'em right after they brought us all out here." He bowed his head. "Fuckin' bastards shot Louie and Pete. *Shot* 'em, man! Just…killed 'em in cold blood."

From downstairs they could now hear loud shouting, along with continued gunfire and the sound of squealing tires outside. "How you gonna get us outta here, man?" Clyde whined.

"Just come with me, and stay close. I promise, I can get us out safely. But you're going to have to answer some questions after we're out."

"What questions?"

The door slammed open. Two shadowy figures appeared, taking cover on either side of the doorway. Yelling in rage, they aimed a spray of gunfire into the room.

Clyde shrieked and dived for the floor, but Stone didn't move. His invisible shield, reinforced with Calanarian power, easily deflected the bullets, sending them ricocheting into the walls, the window, and back out through the open doorway. One hit one of the figures, who screamed and staggered backward, dropping his gun.

"Come *on!*" Stone grabbed Clyde's arm and dragged him back to his feet, which wasn't easy because he had both hands locked over his head. He wrenched harder and used a bit of magic to launch the skinny man to his feet.

"Wha—?" Clyde yelled as he suddenly discovered himself upright through no effort of his own. "I don't wanna—"

The second gunman apparently had no idea what had just happened, which was reasonable given that he couldn't see Stone's shield. He slipped inside the room and leveled his gun at Stone's head. "Hands where I can see 'em, asshole," he ordered.

Stone recognized Ski, who'd found himself another gun. "I don't have time for this." More bullets flew pattered along the house's side, a few finding their way in through the window. This time some of them bounced off the shield. The Hammers' aim was getting better. "Get out of my way."

"I said, hands *up!*" Ski barked, waving the gun. "Do it before I blow your fuckin' head off!"

"Sorry. Didn't hear me, I guess. Let me repeat: I don't have *time* for this." With a gesture, he lifted Ski off the floor and flung him out through the broken window. The Sixer's scream rose and then faded as more gunfire went off.

Stone yanked Clyde up again. "Come *on,* Clyde. I can force you, but it will make things more difficult. Let's move."

Clyde stared at the window Ski had just sailed through, then settled his terrified gaze on Stone. "You're—you're—"

"Yes, I am. And you've got a much better chance with me than you would with this lot. So what's it going to be?"

Clyde swallowed, swiped his arm across his streaming nose, and looked at the door. "Okay. Yeah. Let's go."

"We're not going that way. Come on." He dragged the protesting man over to the window. "Now, this will be a bit tricky, so I need you to stay still and be *quiet.* Do you understand?"

"What are you gonna do? They're *shootin'* in through that window, man!"

Stone slammed him into the wall with telekinetic power. "Last chance, Clyde: do you want to live, or do you want to stay here and let them blow your miserable head off?"

Clyde was nearly blubbering now. "Yeah. Yeah, man. I want to live. I don't wanna die. I'll be good. Just—get us the hell outta here!"

"Good." Stone checked the door to make sure nobody else was coming in, then paused to concentrate. He wasn't lying to Clyde: this *would* be tricky. He'd have to maintain three spells at once: invisibility, levitation, and the shield, and he'd have to do it long enough to get them to one of the vehicles. If Clyde panicked and broke free of his hold, he wasn't sure he could get the man back before the Sixes or the Hammers blew him to bits.

That, and with all this gunfire, the police couldn't be far behind. Whatever he did, he'd have to do it fast. "Right, then—hold on to me, and no matter what happens, *don't let go*. If you let go, I can't protect you. Can you do that?"

"Y-yeah. Yeah." Clyde flung his arms around Stone and clamped his hands together in a death grip, sending up a plume of stench that was nearly visible to the naked eye. "I don't know what you're gonna do, but fuckin' *do* it, man!"

Stone didn't wait for him to have second thoughts. He concentrated a moment longer, then pulled up the spells one at a time: shield first as the highest priority, then levitation, and finally invisibility. He lifted the two of them and zipped out through the window just as more gunfire sounded from inside the house. Either Hammer's guys had made it inside, or more of the Sixes had come back upstairs to secure their prisoner.

"Oh shit oh shit oh shit…" Clyde mumbled, but to his credit he kept it quiet and didn't start screaming in terror as they flew out past the edge of the house, passing over Ski's bloody, bullet-riddled body in the front yard. From here, Stone could see two dark-colored sedans prowling back and forth along the front side of the house. Their lights were off, but the intermittent flashes and staccato *cracks* from their interiors, along with the whooping shrieks of their passengers, gave away their locations every bit as well as the auras of the gunmen hanging out the windows.

Stone dropped them down behind a large tree across the road from the house. "Stay put," he ordered Clyde. "And stay down."

Apparently, Clyde was done arguing. He dropped down to his knees and pressed himself against the side of the tree as if it were his best friend in the world, huffing like an overworked train.

Stone took a moment to catch his breath—the invisibility spell was still tiring even at his upgraded power level—then re-cast it and poked his head out from behind the tree. He waited until the two cars had crossed and reached maximum distance from each other, then focused in on the closer car's tire. A second later, brakes screeched and the gunfire stopped as the car's left front tire exploded with a *bang* every bit as loud. The sedan fishtailed and came to a stop facing the house.

"What the—?" Clyde demanded, gripping the tree.

Stone ignored him and concentrated on the other car, which had spun around and was now coming back toward the first one. "Be ready to move," he told Clyde.

"What're you gonna do?"

More gunfire came from inside the house, dropping one of the Hammers from the stricken car as he exited to assess the damage. The other car pulled between it and the house, laying down covering fire as the remaining two Hammers in the first car scrambled out and climbed in. It had to be a tight fit now, especially if the second car had been full to start with.

As soon as they were in, the second car sped off around the side of the house.

Stone grabbed Clyde's arm and pointed at the Sixes' van, which was parked along the opposite side of the house. "Come on! Head for the van and stay close!"

Clyde didn't ask questions. His skinny legs pumped and his breath wheezed as he ran alongside Stone. They reached the van just as the Hammers' remaining functional car came flying around the corner, tires throwing up plumes of gravel and guns blazing.

Stone wrenched open the door of the van—fortunately, the Sixes hadn't locked it—and used magic to fling Clyde inside. "Stay down!" he ordered, dropping into the driver's seat.

The Hammers' headlights fell on him, illuminating him in a bright glow, and only then did he realize he'd dropped the invisibility spell too soon to conserve his energy. The muzzle-flashes resumed, and this time rounds plinked off the side of the van instead of the house. One shattered the windshield and slammed into the empty passenger seat.

"Oh God oh God oh God…" Clyde moaned from the floor.

"Enough of this," Stone growled. He couldn't see the car's tires well enough to blow them at this distance with the headlights' glow dazzling his eyes, but he had to do something fast. *Let's give this new power a real test, then.*

As the car continued its slow, inexorable approach, Stone gathered the Calanarian energy, shaped it, and took hold of the sedan's front end. He had no idea if he could do this, but now was as good a time as any to try. With a wrench, he lifted the car's front left side and flung it sideways, waiting for his head to light up with pain.

It didn't. The dark sedan tilted and continued tilting until it lay on its side. It hung there for a moment in perfect balance, then did a graceful flop onto its roof, tires still spinning uselessly in the night air.

"Yes!" Stone yelled. He was definitely going to have to do some more tests to discover his new limits. Not now, though. Now, they had to get the hell out of here before the Hammers regrouped or the Sixes discovered their ride was leaving without them.

But they still had a problem he'd forgotten about. "Oh, bloody hell, I don't have the keys!"

"Look under the sunflap," Clyde's shaky voice called from the floor. "Don'tcha ever watch any movies?"

Stone bit back a sarcastic reply and checked the sun visor. To his surprise and delight, a set of keys with a skull keyring dropped into his hand.

"I didn't think anyone was stupid enough to do that in real life," he muttered, jamming the key into the ignition. A moment later, he had the van turned around and was heading as fast as he dared away from the house. In the opposite direction, he spotted faint red and blue lights and heard the far-off sirens of approaching police cars. It was only when they'd made it a mile away that he let himself relax, just a little.

"What...the hell...*are* you?" Clyde poked his head up from the floor and settled himself into one of the van's rear seats. "What is going *on?*"

"That's what I'm planning to ask *you*," Stone said, without taking his eyes off the road. "But first we need to get rid of this van and find a safe place to lie low for a while."

"No way, man. Thanks for the rescue, but I'm outta here. Just let me off somewhere—gas station or whatever—and I'll be outta your hair, pronto."

"It doesn't work that way, Clyde." This time, Stone did turn a little to meet the skinny, twitchy man's gaze. "I've come a long way looking for you, and you're not going anywhere until we have our little chat."

"You can't make me," he said sullenly.

"Oh, but I *can*. Believe me, you do *not* want to try my patience right now. You saw what I did to that car, right? And besides, I saved your miserable hide. You owe me something for that."

"I can't do it anymore." His voice still sounded sullen, and now a whine had crept into it. "I'm tellin' ya, it's gone. I was sure they was gonna kill me when they found out. So if ya got any ideas o' pickin' up where those guys left off, I can't help ya."

"So you're saying you can't heal anymore?"

"No, man. It's gone. I don't know what fixed your leg, but I promise, it wasn't me."

"Don't worry about my leg. It was just a ruse to get me in to see you."

"I'm hungry. Can we stop to get somethin' to eat?"

"Not until we get away from here, and get a different vehicle. So you *could* heal before? That wasn't a lie?"

Clyde sighed. "No lie. It was freaky as fuck, but I could. Just a couple days ago, I fixed up a guy who got stabbed in the gut. It was pretty disgusting. Nearly lost my lunch lookin' at it. Part of his, y'know, intestines were stickin' out."

"Do you have any idea why it doesn't work anymore? Do you feel any different?"

"What the hell is going *on* with you, man?" Clyde gripped the passenger seat and poked his greasy head forward into the gap. "Why all the questions? How did you even know about me? What do you want?"

Stone looked around. They were entering a town now, though he had no idea which one. He spotted a small motel near the outskirts, pulled the van around the back into a poorly-lit parking lot, and motioned Clyde out. "I'm going to get us a room here so we can talk. Say *nothing* until we're inside. Do you understand?"

"Why?"

"Just do it. If you talk, you'll regret it." Stone hated to threaten the man since he was obviously already terrified, but he didn't have a lot of choice. He couldn't leave Clyde in the van until he'd secured a room, since the odds he'd do a runner as soon as he was alone approached certainty.

"Fine. But I want somethin' to eat, man. And a beer."

"Don't worry. Just stay quiet."

Stone was glad he'd decided to wear gloves, since it would be difficult to explain to the cops what his fingerprints were doing in a van outside Pittsburgh when he was supposed to be in Palo Alto. He still had the illusionary amulet going to make him look like a middle-aged businessman, so he quickly wove a second illusion to make Clyde appear as a skinny, pimply teenage boy (not much of a stretch, except for the age). He gripped the other man's arm and strode toward the office.

Fortunately for him, he'd hung on to the thousand dollars he'd pretended to give the Sixes back in Pittsburgh, and even more fortunately, a little cash went a long way to buying the bored clerk's disinterest in their specific circumstances.

Clyde remained silent, unwittingly playing the part of a surly teenage boy, and fifteen minutes later they were safely closed inside a boring, utilitarian motel room with the door locked and the curtains drawn.

Stone switched on the light and motioned for Clyde to sit down. He'd bought a selection of snack foods and soft drinks from the motel's lobby, and he tossed them on the table. "Sorry it's not much yet, but we'll get you more later. Right now, I need you to talk."

Clyde ripped into a pack of Ding-Dongs with the voracity of a starving wolf. He shoved one into his mouth whole, chewed, swallowed, then stuffed in the other one and washed it down with a big swallow of Mountain Dew. "What do you want, man? I mean, I'm glad as fuck you got me out of there, don't get me wrong. Those guys were hardcore. I wish you'd taken 'em all out. They killed Louie and Pete!"

"Yes, I'm sorry about that, I truly am." He took a seat across the table, moving his chair so it was between Clyde and the door in case the man decided to make a break for it. "Clyde—tell me about what happened."

"What do you mean, what happened?"

"You didn't have these healing abilities all your life, did you?"

"I—" Clyde's gaze skated away, and his aura flared. "I dunno, man. I dunno."

"Don't lie to me, Clyde. I'm on your side, but I've got very little patience right now and I'd like very much to deal with this as quickly as possible and go home. So how long have you had these abilities?"

He bowed his head and opened an energy bar with more care. Even if it hadn't been obvious from his posture that the last of the fight had gone out of him, his aura clearly displayed it. "Aw, fuck, man, I dunno what the hell happened. But I do know *when* it happened."

"When?"

"Two-three weeks ago. Me an' Pete an' Louie went out huntin' like we always do this time o' year. We tried a different spot this time—friend o' Louie's had him a cabin out in the woods out near Litton, and let him use it for the weekend. So we headed up there. Took a cooler fulla beer, a buncha sandwiches and some cold fried chicken, and headed out. I took my dog Rocky with me. He's a good dog."

"So what happened?" Stone asked, unwilling to sit and listen to Clyde's hunting stories. "Get to the point."

"Okay, okay." He took another slug of Mountain Dew and scratched his belly. "Sure wish this was beer, though."

"Later."

"Yeah. So we was out there lookin' for some woodchucks, coyotes, that kinda thing. Thought maybe we'd try to get us a deer if we could, even though it ain't deer season. It was early on Saturday morning. Rocky took off, and the next thing I hear, he's yelpin' like somethin' got him.

"So we all run over there and find Rocky tanglin' with a fuckin' *bear!* He musta got too close to its cub or somethin', 'cuz it was tearin' shit outta him. We shot off a couple rounds and scared it off, but I thought ol' Rocky was done for. Figured I'd have to shoot him to put him out of his misery, y'know?"

"But that didn't happen?"

"No, man. That's when things got fuckin' *batshit.* I ran over toward where he was, and suddenly I felt weird."

"Weird?"

R. L. KING

"I can't explain it. Like…*energized,* y'know? I dunno how else to say it. Like I drank about nine o' them Red Bulls in a row. But anyway, I dropped down on my knees next to Rocky, and I don't mind admittin' I was bawlin' like a baby. I love that dog, man. Raised him from a pup. But anyways, I took him in my arms, prayin' to God to help him, and suddenly I just started feelin' this…warmth around me. Almost like somebody turned up the heat, even though it hadda be nearly freezin' out there. And my vision got all…like *yellow.* I thought maybe I might be havin' a stroke or somethin'."

He picked up a Slim Jim, but let it drop back to the table and met Stone's gaze head-on for the first time. "And that's when it happened."

"What happened?"

Clyde swallowed. "One second I was lookin' down into Rocky's eyes, apologizin' to him for what I was gonna have to do, thinkin' about how much I loved him and wished it all hadn't never happened, and then…" He swallowed again, and his voice shook. "And then…He had this big slash on his side. I could see his ribs, it was that bad, and there was so much blood…but I swear to God, as I watched, that slash just…sealed up. Went away. And so did all the other cuts and stuff he had. His eyes got brighter, he licked my hand, and then got up and started jumpin' around like nothin' had even happened."

Stone stared at him in astonishment. Those kinds of magical manifestations under stress or pressure weren't impossible among latent talents, but he'd never heard of one showing up quite that fully formed before. "And…you've never felt anything like that before?"

"Nah, man. Well, like I said, one time I drank a six-pack o' those five-hour energy things on a dare—thought my heart was gonna pop right outta my chest—but I didn't go 'round healin' up no dogs after." He eyed the door. "Hey, man, can we get a pizza or somethin'?"

Clearly they weren't going to get anywhere until Clyde had been fed something more substantial than junk food. "Fine." Still keeping an eye on the skinny man, he used the room's phone to call the pizza delivery joint on the flyer next to it.

"Get meat," Clyde called. "Lotsa meat. An' mushrooms. An' extra cheese."

When the pizza had been ordered, Stone dropped back into his chair. "There. Now tell me what happened next."

Clyde shrugged. "It was Louie who figured it out. After Rocky got fixed up, he said there was some kinda glow around us. He cut his finger and told me to try fixin' it up."

"And did you?"

"Yeah, man. It was trippy as hell. All I had to do was think about how I wanted to fix the problem. I even fixed Pete's cold, so it didn't just work for injuries."

"So that's when you decided to go into Pittsburgh and set up shop as some kind of mystical healer."

"Yeah. Wouldn't you? Louie figured if I had this fuckin' weird new superpower, at least we should make money on it. But I guess we put out the word to the wrong people, because it weren't a day before the Sixes showed up. One of 'em pretended to be hurt, and soon as I fixed 'im up, all the sudden there was guns *everywhere.* They told me I worked for them now. They threw a bag over my head and next thing I knew, I was at that house. They kept me in the basement when I wasn't workin', and kept bringin' guys through with knife wounds, gunshot wounds—even some normal-lookin' people like you. I guess they were advertisin' for clients or somethin', chargin' a big pile o' money for me to do it. I didn't even get none o' the money!" He looked indignant, then bowed his head. "And I know they iced Louie and Pete. They didn't say nothin' about it, but I didn't see 'em no more after I got out here. Them guys told me they let 'em go, but I heard 'em talkin' when they thought I was sleepin', and I heard somebody diggin' out in the backyard a couple days later."

He popped open another Mountain Dew with obvious dejection. "They was good guys, Louie and Pete. We been together since we was kids. They was *family*. I wish none o' this shit had ever happened to me, even if it *did* mean losin' Rocky. I'm glad whatever it is, it's gone now."

"Are you sure it's gone?"

"Yeah, man. When I woke up this morning, I didn't feel that energized feelin' no more. I cut my finger a little and tried to fix it while I was alone, but it didn't work no more. I was scared shitless what they'd do to me if they brought me somebody and I couldn't fix 'em no more. I knew they'd either beat the shit out of me or kill me and bury me out back with Pete an' Louie. Or maybe both."

Stone nodded. "Right, then. So it was a good thing I came by when I did."

"What are you? How did you do all that stuff?"

"Long story, and not one I'm going to tell you. I'm asking the questions, and I'm running this little show right now. Don't worry—I don't mean you any harm. After you help me, I'll give you some money and you can be on your way. But I need something from you first."

Clyde narrowed his eyes. "What do you need?"

"I want you to take me to the place where you first noticed you had these abilities. The place where you healed Rocky."

"Why? There ain't nothin' there."

"I have my reasons. That's my payment for getting you out of there, Clyde. How far is it from here?"

"Man, I don't even know where *here* is!"

It was a fair point—Stone didn't know either. He got up again, located a notepad with the motel's address on it, and dropped it in front of Clyde. "There—does that help?"

Clyde stared at it. "Shit, that's ten miles north o' town, out in the 'burbs."

"How far is it to the spot?"

"I dunno…maybe a couple hour's drive? But it's gonna be dark as the Devil's armpit out there this time o' night. Can't we sleep on it and go in the morning?"

Stone was almost certain if he agreed to this plan, Clyde would try taking off as soon as he thought he had a chance. That, and he didn't relish the idea of spending a night in the same room with this odorous bumpkin. "No. We'll go tonight. Don't worry about the darkness."

"It ain't just the darkness! Didn't I tell you there's *bears* out there?"

"Don't worry about those either."

"Maybe you're not from around here, but you're an idiot if you don't worry about bears. And anyways, I ain't leavin' without my pizza."

Stone sighed, wishing he could just ditch the annoying man and go on his own, but he knew his chances of finding what he was looking for in the back end of rural Pennsylvania were basically nonexistent. "Fine. But remember what I said—if you say anything to the delivery man, it won't go well for you."

Somebody knocked fifteen minutes later, interrupting Stone's impatient pacing. "Yes, who is it?" he called without opening the door.

"Smitty's Pizza."

Stone shot Clyde a warning glare, then opened the door. A kid in a rumpled red and blue shirt and blue cap stood there holding a large pizza box. After a quick aura check, Stone took the pizza, shoved forty dollars in his hand, and said, "Keep the change."

"Hey, thanks, mister! Enjoy your pizza!" The boy scrambled away before Stone could change his mind.

"Oh, shit, that smells good," Clyde called. "Bring it here!"

Stone was about to close the door, magical sight still active, when he spotted something across the street. He paused, hand on the knob, and stared at it.

It was a human figure, too shadowy to identify as male or female, but its shifting orange aura roiled like crackling flame. It was unmistakably watching the motel.

"Oh, bloody hell…" Stone murmured.

"Bring it in, man!" Clyde called, louder. "Whatcha waitin' for?"

Stone glanced his way, then back toward the figure through the partially open door.

It was gone.

| CHAPTER NINETEEN

"**I** STILL DON'T KNOW what you're so worked up about, man."

Clyde sat in the van's passenger seat, the pizza box balanced precariously in his lap and a Mountain Dew can stuck in the cup holder. "Why'd we have to get the hell outta there so fast?"

Stone didn't answer right away, concentrating on both driving and keeping an eye around him for odd auras or police cars.

"Hey! Talk to me." Half the pizza was already gone, and Clyde spoke around a mouthful of another slice, wiping his greasy hands on the side of the seat. "What's goin' on? You looked like you saw a ghost when you came back in."

"I think somebody might be watching us."

"Oh, shit." He dropped a crust back in the box and peered out the window into the darkness. "Oh, shit, the Sixes are after us?"

"I don't think it's the Sixes."

"Those other guys, then? The ones who were shootin' at us?"

"Be quiet, Clyde. I need to think. I don't think it was them either."

"Why not? What'd you see out there?" He twisted around in his seat and looked out through the back window, but the only thing visible back there were the headlights of other cars.

Once again, Stone didn't answer. How could he explain the uneasy feeling he'd gotten when he saw that strange aura? He couldn't even explain it to himself. What he *did* know, however, was that whoever it was, they were almost certainly magically talented. The area across from the motel was a vacant lot, with no trees, cars, or other hiding places. There had been no way the man, or woman, or whatever could have disappeared that fast without magical assistance. Stone had only looked away for a couple of seconds.

Why was someone with magical talent watching him? *Were* they watching him, or were they after Clyde? And if they weren't from the Sixes or the Hammers, where *were* they from?

He hadn't wanted to keep driving the same van. There was too much chance someone would recognize it—either the Sixes or the police—but once he spotted that mysterious figure, he knew remaining even long enough for Clyde to finish his pizza was a bad idea. If the figure was a spotter and had locked in a positive identification of either of them, they might even now be calling for reinforcements, or at least reporting back to whoever sent them.

Clyde had protested loudly when Stone had swept the remaining snack cakes and soda cans into the room's plastic laundry bag and ordered him to gather the pizza, which he'd only just begun to devour.

"What the *hell*, man?" he'd demanded, waving his slice and dripping chunks of sausage onto the stained rug. "I told ya—I ain't goin' nowhere until I finish this—"

"You're going *now*." Using magic, he levitated the box and shoved it into Clyde's hands. "Don't argue with me, Clyde. I won't say it again."

Clyde, suitably reminded that the crazy man who'd snatched him from certain death didn't need a gun to be threatening, gripped the box and trailed Stone out.

Now, in the van, Stone followed Clyde's directions to skirt the Pittsburgh area proper and keep to the less-traveled roads through the outlying towns. "It'll take a little longer," Clyde had said sullenly, "but less chance anybody'll fuck with us. You really are gonna let me go, right? You ain't takin' me out here in the sticks so you can murder me and hide the body?"

"Why would I go through all that trouble to rescue you if I planned to kill you? I could have done that back at the house. Now shut *up*, Clyde, and let me concentrate."

They had to stop once for gas, but other than that Stone kept a steady pace, using his disregarding spell to keep anyone from noticing the van. They had a couple of close calls when he spotted state troopers, but either the Sixes hadn't reported the van stolen or they'd decided they had enough trouble with the Hammers without chasing down their fleeing meal ticket just yet.

Clyde focused on finishing his pizza as they drove. Stone wasn't sure how such a skinny man could put away that much food in that short a time, but as long as it kept him quiet he didn't care. They'd left the Pittsburgh area and driven southwest for nearly an hour before Clyde spoke again.

"So why you wanna find this place, anyway? You think if you go there you'll get superpowers too?"

"No. I already have superpowers, remember?"

"Yeah, I'm tryin' not to think about that, okay? You're fuckin' creepy, if you want the truth. And anyways, Pete and Louie didn't get no superpowers. Just me. Dunno why."

"Maybe you're just special."

Clyde snorted, missing Stone's sarcasm completely. "Ain't nothin' special 'bout me, man. And like I said, I wish it ain't never happened to me. So anyways, why you wanna see it?"

"I want to study it."

"Study it? You some kinda scientist or somethin'?"

"Yes. I am."

"You don't look like no scientist." Clyde tossed the empty pizza box in the back seat, scattering crusts all over the floor. He dug out another Slim Jim, stuck it in his mouth, and looked Stone up and down. "You look like you sell insurance or somethin'. Don't sound like it, though. You from Australia?"

"No. And I don't sell insurance. This isn't what I really look like."

Clyde pondered. "No shit? Pretty good disguise, then. What *do* you look like?"

"That's why they call it a disguise, Clyde. Because I don't *want* you to know what I look like. It's safer that way for both of us."

"What, you think I'm gonna tell anybody about this? If you ain't lyin' and you do let me go, I'm takin' off, man. Gettin' the hell outta this area, startin' up somewhere else. I'm *done* with all this freaky shit around here."

"Wise man."

"Yeah, I think—wait, turn here!" He pointed at a sign half-obscured by low-hanging branches.

Stone wrenched the wheel, flinging dirt and gravel as the van teetered alarmingly for a second before settling back to all four tires. They'd been on a two-lane, rural road before, but this one was barely wide enough for a pair of vehicles to pass each other. The headlights picked out a series of ruts, and scrubby weeds poking up along the middle.

"Are you sure this is right?" He glanced at Clyde's aura, but aside from mild nervousness he saw no sign of deception.

"Yeah. Like I said, Louie's friend's got a hunting shack out here. Ain't nobody usin' it right now, so he let us have it for our weekend. Usually we go up north o' here, but we figured we'd try somethin' new." He sighed in the darkness. "*That* was the worst fuckin' decision we ever made, huh?"

Stone didn't argue with that. He focused on driving, keeping the van in the middle of the narrow road. He didn't expect to see any other vehicles out here, but he maintained a careful watch for any signs of light ahead. Every couple of minutes he switched to magical sight, looking for traces of the yellow energy he'd seen in Devil's Creek, but didn't see any.

The going was slow. Stone fought the temptation to accelerate, but the van wasn't built for speed, especially on bad roads like this. They crept along at barely twenty miles per hour for nearly thirty minutes before Clyde came up from his bag of snack food and pointed out another sign. "There. Turn there. The cabin's just up this road."

The new road made the one they'd been on look like a superhighway. Mostly dirt with scattered patches of gravel, it was so narrow that the branches on either side scraped along the van's flanks. Above them, a slender moon provided the only other illumination, filtering through the trees.

"There it is." Clyde pointed ahead, where a small, dark structure crouched in the middle of a clearing.

"Doesn't look like anyone's here," Stone said, scanning it with magical sight. Aside from the faint green auras of the trees and the occasional brighter one of a small animal or bird, no other glows caught his attention.

"Ain't nobody here. Louie's friend don't let many people use it—he just let us as a favor. What're you gonna do?"

Stone opened the door and got out, pausing to stretch his legs. The air smelled fresh and woody out here, but it had a cold bite, too. "Get out. You're going to show me the place where you healed Rocky."

"In the *dark*? There might be flashlights inside, but it's all locked up and I ain't got the key."

"Let's check." Stone headed to the cabin, motioning for Clyde to stay where he could keep an eye on him, and surreptitiously used magic to open the front door's lock. "I guess you forgot to lock it."

"No way, man, ain't no way we—"

Stone ignored him, heading inside. "Find the lights and let's go."

The wooden cabin was tiny and rough-hewn, with a small living room containing heavy, battered wooden furniture taking up most of its space. It had a minuscule kitchenette with a microwave and mini-fridge, a closet-sized bathroom, and a bedroom barely big enough to fit a set of bunk beds.

Clyde quickly dug two flashlights from a drawer in the kitchenette, switched them on, and handed one to Stone. "Now let's *go*," he whined. "Whatever you wanna do, let's get it over with. I wanna get the hell away from here."

Stone wanted to get the hell away from Clyde, so he didn't object. He locked the cabin door behind him and followed the man out into the forest.

"Aw, man," Clyde said, shining his light around. "I just realized—I ain't gonna be takin' no more hunting trips with Louie and Pete. Not ever." His voice shook.

"I'm sorry, Clyde." Stone couldn't help feeling sympathy for him—sometimes, in his focus on solving magical puzzles, he tended to forget about the human elements involved. This man, annoying as he was, had just lost two close family members in a particularly brutal way.

"Yeah…me too. This whole thing is prob'ly God's way o' punishin' me for tryin' to make money from a miracle or somethin'."

"I doubt that." Stone tramped along beside him, periodically scanning the area with magical sight. Mostly, he was looking for signs of that flickering orange aura or any other human presence, but deep down he had to admit Clyde's tale of roaming bears had spooked him a bit as well. Last time he'd tangled with a bear, it hadn't ended well for him. And this time he couldn't count on his companion to spontaneously develop healing abilities again to take care of the aftermath.

"So what do you think it is, then?" Clyde asked, not sounding convinced.

"I don't know. That's why I want to look at it."

"But *why* do you want to look at it? How did you even find out about it in the first place?"

Stone pondered how much he wanted to say. "It's…sort of a hobby of mine, hunting down things like this."

Clyde stopped, staring at him with big, round eyes. "You're sayin' there's *other* things like this?"

"It's beginning to look like there are, yes."

"Oh, man…" he moaned. "So even if I get my ass outta the area, I might find another one?"

"Doubtful. The only other one I've seen is nowhere near here. I think you'll be fine."

Clyde didn't look convinced, but he swung the light back around and shined it ahead. "We're gettin' close. It was right around here. I recognize that rock there."

Stone though that rock looked like every other rock they'd passed so far, but he had to trust that Clyde's tracking skills were up to the task. He switched back to magical sight and swept his gaze around again.

Wait—was that a flash of color? "Stop."

"What? I told you, it's up ahead."

"Wait. Just…wait a moment." He sharpened his magical gaze, trying to home in on the light, but when he tried, it faded tantalizingly away. Had he really seen it at all, or was it wishful thinking?

If he *had* seen it, it was off to the right, maybe twenty feet away, behind some trees.

"This way."

"But you said—"

"*This* way," he insisted, heading in that direction. There were so many trees here he wasn't sure if they and their auras were obscuring his vision, or whether there was nothing there at all. He definitely couldn't make out any shapes.

Clyde sighed loudly and followed him. "Man, are you sure you're—"

Stone stepped around the last tree and stopped. There it was again, only for a moment, flickering at the edge of his vision, but it disappeared when he tried to look at it head-on. Almost as if it were an—

"Bloody hell…" he murmured.

As he pumped more power into his attempt to view it, the weak illusion faded away to reveal a shimmering rift in the air. This one didn't look like the one at the mill in Devil's Creek, but Stone was certain it was the same sort of phenomenon. It wasn't yellow this time, and it definitely wasn't orange—more of a flickering pale green. Instead of an irregularly-shaped, six-foot hole in the air, it appeared as more of a swirling mist. What the two had in common, though, was the shifting, dark figures moving around in their middles.

But why was this one obscured by an illusion? Who had cast it?

"What's goin' on?" Clyde demanded, breaking into his thoughts. "You see somethin'?"

Stone didn't want to take his eyes off the thing, in case it disappeared again. "You don't, then, I take it."

"I don't see a damn thing but trees. This ain't some kinda joke, is it? Because I'm gettin' pretty freaked out."

"It's not a joke. Do you feel anything? The energized feeling you got before?"

"I don't…Hold on." His voice went from petulant to nervous.

"Do you?" Now Stone did turn his magical gaze on Clyde. He wasn't at all surprised to see the man's muddy blue-green aura traced with bits of the same pale green as the swirling patch ahead.

"Yeah…yeah…Oh, fuck, it's happenin' again!" Clyde scrambled away, holding his hands up, eyes huge. "Oh, fuck! I don't *want* this to happen again! Why'd I ever let you bring me out here? I've had enough of this, man!"

Before Stone could stop him, he turned and took off, running toward a patch of trees. His flashlight beam swung and bobbed, illuminating trunks, branches, and for a second a startled squirrel that immediately darted away.

"Clyde, wait!" Stone spun and flung himself forward, intending to give chase, even as he knew there was no way he'd track the man if he got out of sight. He raised his hand to grab him with a telekinetic grip.

Before he could get the spell off, Clyde stopped moving, jerking upright as if he'd stepped into an electrical current. He screamed, twitching and juddering, and then something sizzled. His scream cut off abruptly as he disappeared. His flashlight dropped to the ground and rolled, its light-beam picking out the mossy bottom of a tree trunk.

And then silence.

"Clyde!" Stone went stiff, instantly bringing up his magical shield. Whatever had gotten Clyde, it hadn't been his telekinetic grab. "Who's out here?" he called, sweeping his gaze around again. "Show yourself! You won't find me such an easy target!"

A figure stepped out from behind the trees. "You aren't a target at all, scion. We must speak."

| CHAPTER TWENTY

S TONE COULD SEE THE FIGURE—it was right there in front of him, perhaps fifteen feet away—but he couldn't make out any of its features. It looked like a slim humanoid shape, probably male, its features and clothing obscured as if it were standing inside a steamy shower cubicle.

What he *did* recognize immediately, though, was the distinctive, flickering orange aura around it—the same one he'd spotted across the street from the motel before they'd left.

"Who are you?" he demanded. "What do you want?" He jerked his head sideways toward where Clyde had disappeared. "And what did you do to him?"

"It was unfortunate," the figure said. "I regret the necessity, but I assure you, it *was* a necessity."

"You've killed him, then?" Stone took a step closer, sharpening his magical gaze to try to see past the swirling fog. "Yes."

"Why? Why him and not me?" He reinforced the shield again, just in case the figure decided to add him to its quota. The thing's words from before came back to him. "And what did you call me? 'Scion'? What do you mean by that? Scion of what?"

The figure waved it off. "We must speak. I cannot remain long."

"I have nothing to say to you. Get the hell out of here and let me get on with dealing with this thing before it causes any more trouble."

"That is an unwise course of action."

"Oh, really? Is that so? Do you plan to stop me, then?"

"I cannot stop you."

"You did a bloody good job of stopping poor Clyde."

"He was a mundane, a child who played with forces he didn't understand. In this form, I don't have the power to affect you, even should I desire to."

"Wait," Stone said. He glanced around quickly, making sure no more weird, orange-auraed figures were converging on the area. "Who the hell *are* you? What do you want?" He gestured toward the swirling green structure. "Are you responsible for this thing?"

"I am not."

"So why do you give a damn about whether I stop it? It's causing trouble. It's been responsible for several deaths already."

"All is proceeding according to plan," the figure said. Its voice was strange, not quite male but not quite female, and a part of it seemed to echo inside Stone's mind. "It would be unwise and dangerous to interfere."

"Interfere with *what*? This thing isn't natural. I don't know what's causing them to pop up, but this is the second one I've dealt with so far. Are you saying there are more of them?"

"I cannot say any more. None of this is your concern."

"Wait." Stone gestured at the swirling red again. "Were you responsible for the illusion? Are you...trying to *hide* these things?"

"Go home, scion. This does not concern you. If you continue to meddle in things you don't understand, you could set into motion events you can't comprehend."

"So *explain* them to me!" Stone snapped. "What are these things, and why are they here? What purpose do they serve?"

The figure flickered, shifting like an unsteady television signal. "I can say no more. It is not permitted. Take this as a warning: do not interfere."

"I can't do that. These things are affecting mundanes. They're killing them. Either explain to me what's going on and who the hell you are, or get out of my way and let me get on with it."

The figure regarded him in silence for several moments, then flickered again. "I must go," it said at last. "I beseech you to heed my words. If you persist in this folly, you could cause untold consequences."

The thing was already fading. Stone launched himself forward toward it. "*Tell* me!" he yelled. "What's a 'scion'? *What* consequences?"

The orange-wreathed figure shimmered one last time and disappeared.

| CHAPTER TWENTY-ONE

S TONE BARELY ACKNOWLEDGED Marta Bellwood's greeting as he trudged out of A Passage to India's dining room the following day. He gave only a perfunctory wave before hurrying out, pausing as the door swung shut behind him.

His shoulders slumped with fatigue. He'd gotten next to no sleep the previous night, between trying to write down everything he could remember about what had happened before he forgot any of the details, and tossing uneasily in bed as he fought with a mind that refused to quiet.

When the figure had disappeared and left him alone in the clearing near Clyde's friend's hunting cabin, he'd immediately tried to find it, to track it back to wherever it had come from. He'd run to where he'd last seen it, kicking his magical sight to maximum intensity, focusing on locking in on any leftover magical energy he could use as a trace.

He'd found nothing. It was as if the figure had never been there at all—or else it was good enough to hide its tracks sufficiently to thwart Stone's efforts. The latter hypothesis unnerved him: he knew his own power level, and these days there wasn't much out there that could hide from him.

When it became clear he wasn't going to follow the figure, he turned his attention back to the rift itself. The illusion concealing it was a weak one, obviously designed to deter mundanes from getting too close to it. Unlike whatever the orange-hued figure had been doing to hide itself, its efforts to hide the rift were easy to undo. Once Stone cleared away the last of the illusion, he spent the next hour examining the rift from all sides, taking readings, and making notes. He even tried tossing a few twigs and rocks through it, but all of them simply flew through and landed on the other side, rather than disappearing as he'd expected them to. So whatever this thing was, it wasn't a portal—at least not for physical objects.

What it was, though, was a power source. Stone wasn't sure whether Clyde had been a latent talent; as with Mitch and Cathy Kirkson, he hadn't had time to perform the level of examination necessary to determine that for sure, and now that Clyde had been vaporized, he'd lost his chance. But whether he was or wasn't, the shifting anomaly *was* putting out some significant power.

Stone remembered what Clyde had said about his cousins Pete and Louie not showing any sign of the "superpowers" he himself had gained. That might have been true, or the rift might have bestowed different abilities on them—ones that hadn't manifested in obvious ways. After all, Clyde might never have discovered his healing abilities if the bear hadn't attacked his beloved dog.

It didn't matter, though: Clyde was almost certainly correct that the Sixes had murdered Louie and Pete, which meant all three of his potential test subjects were firmly out of his reach. All he had left was the rift itself. It was letting in power from *somewhere,* he was sure, but that left two important questions: what had caused it to appear here, and *where* was the power coming from?

The only other things he determined definitively with his testing were that wherever this thing was pointing, it wasn't the same place the one in Devil's Creek had pointed, and it wasn't anywhere he'd ever seen before, like the Overworld or Calanar. Aside from that, he had no idea. He might be able to find out more if he had the materials to do a potent ritual, but he wasn't sure he could find the place again if he left. Hell, he wasn't completely sure he could find the van from where he was now.

And then there was the matter of the mysterious figure. It had told him to leave this alone, that he was meddling with things he didn't understand. It hadn't come out and admitted to casting the illusion to hide the rift, but it hadn't denied it, either—and it *had* denied that it had done something to cause the rift's existence. If both of those were true, that meant the thing had some reason for concealing the rift from others.

It did—or whoever it worked for did. It had spoken of "not being permitted" to say anything else—not permitted by whom?

And what the hell was this 'scion' business about?

Finally, in frustration, Stone had closed his notebook, taken one last hard look at the rift (he couldn't swear to it, but he was fairly sure the level of power it was putting out had decreased slightly even in the hour he'd observed it), and then tried the same trick he had in Devil's Creek: pumping power from Calanar into it in an attempt to overload it and seal it up. He did it with some trepidation, remembering both what had happened last time and the strange figure's warning, but he couldn't go away and leave this thing here if he could do something about it.

This time, the process went more smoothly, perhaps because of the increased time he had for study before making his attempt. He focused his thoughts and his power, feeding energy into the rift until the swirling green fog flared bright, then brighter, then winked out of existence. He quickly spun, looking around as if expecting the figure to have returned, but it didn't. The woods were silent except for the occasional far-off rustle of a small animal or call of a bird.

"There. That's done. Got anything else to say?" he called, keeping the shield up and bracing himself for an attack.

Apparently, whatever it was didn't have anything else to say, because the silence remained. Even the birds and animals shut up.

Before he left, he paused on the spot where the hapless Clyde had been vaporized. "Sorry, mate," he said, and meant it. The skinny, greasy guy might have been annoying as hell, but he hadn't asked for any of this.

As he drove back to Palo Alto after an uneventful trip through the portal, Stone contemplated his next steps. It was too late in the day to pop over to England to discuss this with Eddie and Ward, and he wanted a bit more time to turn things over in his head before he took it to Stefan Kolinsky. Finally, he pulled out his phone and called Verity.

"Hey, Doc!" She sounded happy to hear from him. "Are you back? Did you find anything this time?"

"I…did. Where are you? Up in San Francisco?"

"No, I'm actually at the Mountain View place tonight, finishing my packing. The other guy left already, so the landlord's letting me move stuff in early. You want to come over?"

"No work for Scuro?"

"Not tonight. Not till later this week, actually. I'd love to see you—but this time, don't laugh, but I'll have to feed *you* takeout. All my pots and pans and stuff are in boxes."

He chuckled. "I'll bring something by. I'm on my way home, so I need to stop over and check on Raider."

"He's fine. I was just there a couple hours ago. I refilled his food and water and scooped the litter boxes. He barely acknowledged my presence. I think he likes having the place to himself."

"As long as he doesn't start throwing parties. Brilliant, then—I'll be there shortly."

Stone did stop at home to assure Raider he hadn't abandoned him, but he wasn't sure whether it was out of concern for the cat (who had proven on numerous previous occasions that he had no problem with extended solitude) or whether, deep down, he was reluctant to visit Verity and look at her mostly-empty apartment and collection of stacked boxes.

It seemed only a few days ago when he'd helped her move into that place. She'd been so proud of herself, that she could finally afford an apartment of her own and didn't have to live in Stone's guest room, let him pay half her rent, or share space with Jason. He'd been pleased too—it always made him happy to see his former apprentice take another step toward independence—but now, her next step was taking her far enough away from him that casual dinners or dropping by each other's place on a whim would no longer be practical.

He wondered, as he often did when his mind went to dark places, if moving to San Francisco was her way of gently disengaging from him—perhaps in a way *she* wasn't even consciously aware of. Between her work with Scuro, her relationship with Kyla, and her activities with the Harpies and Hezzie, she was as busy as he was these days. Maybe more so, now that he'd deliberately cut his class load down to three days a week. Even Jason had commented that he barely saw her anymore.

He gave a wistful smile as he bid Raider a good evening and drove toward Mountain View. Perhaps all of this was for the best, all things considered. He cared deeply for Verity, and he knew she did for him as well. That much, he was sure of, because she still hadn't learned how to hide her aura from him. But she also cared deeply for Kyla, and Stone had known from the time he met Verity when she was seventeen, before he'd had even a glimmer of interest in her beyond that of a teacher with a student, that her primary attraction was to women. As strong as her feelings were for him, and as much as they both enjoyed their nights together, he was an anomaly. She'd never mentioned any other relationships with men to him, and Jason had told him once that he was aware of only a couple, both of the one-night-stand variety and neither recently.

He shook his head in annoyance. He was acting like some kind of romantic fool, and he didn't have time for that right now. Verity would do what she would do, and he'd accept it because he loved her and wanted her to be happy.

That was the end of it. Right now, he had more pressing matters to concern himself with.

She pulled him into a tight hug when she opened the door, then kissed him. "It's so good to see you. Come on in."

He held up a bag. "I've brought takeaway from the Dragon Garden."

"Oh, good. I was just gonna call for pizza delivery, but this is better."

He thought about poor Clyde as he followed her in, and was glad he wouldn't have to look at another pizza for a while. He gestured at the stacks of boxes piled around the living room. "All set to go, I see."

"Yeah. Fortunately I don't have that much stuff, so Kyla and I are gonna make a couple of trips this weekend. I'll have to pick up some furniture, though, since the new place isn't furnished. Jason offered to help me carry it in." Her eyes twinkled. "I don't really need him to, of course, but I'll let him so he can feel useful."

"Do you need any help from me?"

"No, it's fine. Thanks for the offer, but I think I've got it under control. I'll invite you over for a housewarming evening when I get settled in."

"Sounds like a plan."

"So," she said, setting a Guinness in front of him as he began pulling cartons from the bag, "how did your trip back East go? Did you find another one of those things?"

"I did, yes. And they're beginning to trouble me."

She took a seat across from him, shoveled some broccoli beef onto her plate, and started on it with her chopsticks. "Why so?"

He told her the whole story, focusing most on what happened after they reached the forest, and ending with the strange figure's appearance and its warning.

Her eyes widened. "Wow. That's pretty unsettling. So there's somebody running around trying to keep people from finding these things? *Killing* people over them?"

"This one, anyway. I didn't see any sign of him, or anyone else, around the last one."

"And you have no idea what he meant when he said you were meddling with things you don't understand?"

"None." He took another swallow of Guinness and contemplated the cartons. "I'm at a bit of a loss about what I should do from here. It's not practical to go running about all over the country trying to track down more of them. The two I found out about were both essentially by chance—one because your friend knew someone in the area, and the other from a student looking for extra credit. I can ask my friends in the magical community to keep a lookout for odd events, but after this last one I'm concerned. I certainly don't want anyone else getting hurt or killed over them."

"Yeah...poor Clyde and his cousins. It always makes me sad when mundanes stumble into magical stuff and end up getting hurt."

Stone nodded soberly, looking down at his plate. "Yes. And if you count the two gangs, this thing has led directly to several other deaths that I know of. True, they were murderers, but that doesn't mean they deserved this."

"What about what that thing he called you—'scion'? Have you had any luck figuring out what that means?"

"No idea. Obviously I know what the word means, but I've no clue how it applies to me. This thing almost seemed as if it knew me somehow, or at least knew who I was."

"Maybe it knows about your family? You *do* come from a long line of mages, right?"

"Yes…that's the only reasonable explanation I've come up with, but I don't see what my family has to do with unexplained rifts opening to other dimensions. I suppose it might be worthwhile to do a bit more research on my family history, as distasteful as that might be. I've been putting it off, but if it's causing trouble…"

Verity finished off the contents of a carton and stacked it inside another one. "Have you considered listening to this guy?"

"What do you mean?"

"Well…it sounds like he thinks you could cause *more* trouble if you keep looking for these things. Have you considered just leaving them alone?" As he drew breath to reply, she continued quickly, "I'm not saying I think it's a good idea, necessarily. But remember, these are only the ones you encountered by accident—you said so yourself. How do you know there haven't been more of them out there for a long time, just…doing what they do without any interference?"

He pondered her words. "You've got a point," he admitted. "I suppose it's possible there are loads of them out there, all over the country—or the world—that I don't know a damn thing about. There *are* stories of supernatural anomalies all around—haunted houses, strange sightings, all the standard stuff. Perhaps they're related to these things." He sighed. "But you know me, Verity—now that I've discovered them, I can't just…not do anything. At the very least, I need to do my best to discover *why* they're here. Things like that don't just pop up for no reason. Besides, I don't have much faith that whatever it was that showed up and killed Clyde has anyone's best interests in mind but its own, and those of whoever or whatever it works for."

"Yeah," Verity said reluctantly. "That's true. If it really thought you were causing problems, why didn't it just tell you why? If it knows who you are, it's got to know you don't just give up because somebody tells you to." She used magic to gather the cartons and carried them to the kitchen. "So what are you going to do?"

"I plan to chat with Eddie and Ward about it this week-end, and probably go by Kolinsky's place sometime this week. He said he hadn't heard anything about the last rift, but maybe he knows something about this 'scion' rubbish. It's worth asking him, anyway, even if I end up having to give him something big from Desmond's collection to get some answers."

"What about Mr. Harrison?"

Stone hadn't thought about Trevor Harrison. He hadn't heard anything from the man since he'd returned from Calanar, and hadn't tried to contact him. "I suppose I could leave a message with Nakamura and see if he'll get back to me, but this doesn't really seem like Harrison's kind of thing."

She drifted back in. "Tell you what, then—if there's nothing else you can do about it tonight, why don't we sit down and…enjoy the evening. It's the one thing I don't like about moving—it'll be harder for us to get together."

He let her lead him to the sofa, where she snuggled in next to him and drew her legs up. "You're worth the drive, love."

She kissed him. "You know I'm not running away from you, right?"

He didn't know that—not completely—but he offered a murmured affirmative. "This will be good for you. Sort of the best of both worlds. Think of it not as getting rid of your safety net, but…dropping it down a couple of levels. Just promise me you'll be careful with the Harpies, all right? You're not fooling me—I expect you'll be involving yourself in their activities quite a lot more once you're closer."

"Probably," she agreed. "And I promise I'll be careful. I'm not fragile, you know."

"Oh, bloody hell, I know that. I've always said you're stronger than all of us, and you've done nothing to change my mind."

Her aura lit up with pride and pleasure. "You're the best thing that ever happened in my life, you know. No matter what happens, don't ever forget that, okay?"

"I won't. But I'll be happy enough to just be part of your life."

She smiled, unfolded herself from the sofa, and stood, offering him her hands. "Come on—let me show you that you have nothing to worry about."

CHAPTER TWENTY-TWO

STONE'S PHONE RANG the following morning, just as he was driving in through his house's front gate. His mind still occupied with both the rifts and his night with Verity, he pulled the car off the road and got out to pick up the mail, idly answering the phone as he did. "Yes, hello?"

"Alastair, hello."

He stopped, astonished at the familiar voice he hadn't heard for months. "Imogen. I—what a surprise. It's good to hear from you. How have you been?"

"I've been very well. I'm so sorry I haven't rung in so long, but I know we've both been so busy…"

"Not a problem—I should have stopped by to visit you during one of my trips to Caventhorne. What can I do for you?"

"Well…" She hesitated. "I've got some news, and I wanted you to find out directly from me."

"What sort of news?" Stone tensed. The last time she'd called him with news, it had been to tell him her father had gone missing. He'd tracked Desmond to a magically warded section of Caventhorne, only to discover him dead in his office.

216 | R. L. KING

She seemed to have caught on to his train of thought, because she chuckled. "Nothing bad this time. Good news." She paused. "I'm…going to be married, Alastair."

Once again Stone went stiff, his hand tightening on the phone. If he'd been stronger, he might have crushed it. "Are you?" he asked with care. "That's—wonderful, Imogen. I'm so happy for you. You and Clifford finally decided to make it official, did you?" He started toward the mailbox again, picturing Clifford Blakeley's pleasant face, graying blond hair, and bankerly suit.

"We did, yes. Neither of us is getting any younger, you know, and he's made me so happy, especially after Dad died." She paused again. "We'll…be sending out the invitations soon, but as I said, I wanted to let you know in person. It's later this summer. A small affair—just a few close friends. You…will come, won't you?"

Stone smiled. "Of course I will, Moggy. You couldn't keep me away. That's brilliant. I really am happy for both of you. Please tell Clifford I said so."

When she spoke again, her voice held relief, as if she'd been holding her breath waiting for his response. "I'm so glad. Your blessing means a lot to me."

"Of course you have it—I told you that before. I want you to be deliriously happy, Moggy. Just send me the details and I'll be there."

"Thank you, Alastair." Something lurking around the edges of her voice told him the thanks was for more than just agreeing to attend the wedding. "I'll let you get back to whatever you were doing, then. I'll talk to you later."

Stone put the phone away almost robotically, slowing his steps as he approached the mailbox. So Moggy—Imogen

Desmond, his old master's daughter and his former almost-fiancée many years ago—was finally getting married. He'd begun to wonder if she ever would. He supposed he couldn't wish for a better match for her: Clifford Blakeley obviously adored her, and if he was a bit...well, conventional...there was nothing wrong with that. After all, lack of conventionality—or at least mundanity—had been what had doomed his own relationship with her. She'd be much happier with Blakeley, a man who was a success in the mundane world while knowing nothing about the magical realm. She could be the center of his universe, in a way she never could have been with Stone. It was what she deserved.

He truly was happy for her, and wished her nothing but the best, but as he reached the mailbox he couldn't help feeling the sensation of another half-open door in his life firmly closing.

He had a lot of half-open doors in his life, he realized. Hell, he hadn't even thought to tell her about Ian yet. He pulled out the phone again and stared at it a moment, deciding whether he should call her back and share the news about his son, but then put it away. He'd introduce her to Ian when the boy came back to England to meet Aubrey. Maybe they could all even get together for dinner in London.

He opened the mailbox and removed a stack of envelopes and advertising circulars, paging through them one by one as he walked slowly back toward the BMW. It was the usual stuff—bills, junk mail, sale flyers—and he barely paid any attention to it. The majority would get pitched into the bin without a moment's glance, as it was every day.

As he climbed into the car and tossed the junk mail on the driver's seat, he noticed one envelope that didn't look like the others. Stark white, it was shaped more like it held a greeting card instead of a bill, and bore neither stamp nor return address. The only writing on the front of it was *Alastair Stone* in dark green ink.

He paused before starting the car and opened it. Perhaps someone in the neighborhood had put it there, inviting him to some weekend get-together. It happened occasionally; so far he'd politely declined the invitations, but the residents of the tiny town of Encantada were a close-knit bunch, and seemed to feel obligated to continue in their attempts to include him in their activities.

Inside was a single, stiff white card. Stone withdrew it from the envelope with growing curiosity. It looked like something Stefan Kolinsky would send, except he recognized Kolinsky's handwriting and this wasn't it. Besides, his black-mage friend would go to Walmart in his underwear before he used green ink.

The card was blank.

Stone tilted his head, turning it over to examine both sides, then pinching open the envelope to see if he'd missed anything else inside. This was odd. Why would someone bother sending him a blank—

Ah. Of course.

He held the card up again and shifted to magical sight.

He hadn't exactly *expected* a series of lines written in firm, old-fashioned script to shimmer into being on the card's surface, but it didn't surprise him, either. He took a quick glance around with the sight still up and saw no sign of anyone lurking nearby observing him, so he turned his attention back to the card.

It included only a few lines:

Dr. Stone:

I hope this finds you well. I regret the need to contact you directly, but I must offer you a warning. It is imperative that you do not continue on your current course of action. If you do, and more specifically if you encourage others to do likewise, your activities could lead to dire consequences. I can say no more, but I hope you will take my words as they were meant. I do not wish you ill; however, if you persist I will be forced to oppose you, and that will not end well for you.

Best wishes to you.
—A Concerned Party

There was no other signature.

"Bloody hell…" Stone murmured.

What the hell had he managed to get himself embroiled in this time, and how much larger was its scope than he'd originally suspected?

He gripped the card tighter, opening the envelope to shove it back inside. He couldn't wait any longer—it was time to bring in the big guns now. If anybody had any chance of figuring out what was going on with this nonsense, it would be Stefan Kolinsky. The black mage was never around on weekends, but tomorrow afternoon he'd drive over there and see if—

As he watched, magical sight still active, the script on the card began to fade. In less than ten seconds, it had dissipated into nothingness, leaving the card once again blank. No trace of magical energy remained around either it or the envelope.

Stone continued to stare at it for several more seconds, but nothing else happened. The card remained text-free, magically inert, and altogether uninteresting.

"Well…" he said. "That's brilliant. This message will self-destruct in five seconds."

| CHAPTER TWENTY-THREE

J ASON WAS TIRED, both physically and mentally, and that hadn't changed much in the last few weeks.

He shoved open the door to his apartment and threw his messenger bag on a nearby chair—or at least tried to. The bag hit too hard, slid off, and fell to the floor. The flap popped open, spilling a stack of papers and file folders all over the floor.

Jason sighed. That was how his life had been going the last few days. Ignoring the bag, he went to the kitchen and got a beer, then flung himself down on the couch without turning on the TV. It was nearly ten-thirty, and if he was smart he'd go to bed and get some sleep so he could get an early start on the morning.

He'd stayed in Reno for two more days following the accident, waiting for the Ford dealership's service department to report the extent of the damage and his insurance company to get back to him about whether it would be totaled. It didn't surprise him when they called back and told him just that—the car had been a few years old on purpose, both to save money and to make it blend in better, and the damage to the front end had been extensive enough to make repairing it more expensive than writing it off. At least Amber Harte's insurance company wasn't dragging its feet about paying the claim, but these things still took time and there was no rushing the wheels of corporate bureaucracy.

He'd thought about calling her again before he left Reno, but didn't. As potentially interesting as she was, mysterious disappearing bruise or no mysterious disappearing bruise, she'd made it clear in no uncertain terms that she didn't want to hear from him. Unlike too many guys his age, Jason knew there was a fine line between romantic and creepy when it came to pursuing a woman he was interested in, and as much as he'd have liked to talk with her again, he'd decided any further contact in the wake of their last phone call would be teetering firmly toward the "creepy" side. Especially since he was even more interested in finding out what was up with the bruise than he was with taking her out to dinner.

Though he wouldn't have turned down the dinner. He wasn't an idiot.

He'd finished his case, retrieved a few more items from the Ford, and driven at a leisurely pace back to the Bay Area. After filling out the paperwork back at the office and updating the case files, he'd told Gina only that he'd had a minor accident in Reno and asked her to look into finding the agency a new boring sedan. He wasn't happy about it, because it meant he'd have to dip into his savings until Amber's insurance paid the claim, but there was no helping it.

What he hadn't done was tell Stone or Verity anything beyond the basic details about the accident. He'd thought about it—considered it fairly deeply, in fact—but ultimately decided to keep the whole situation to himself. Unlike his sister and her former master, Jason hadn't been born with the pathological curiosity of a whole roomful of cats. Sure, he had more than a standard human share—he had to in order to be good at what he did—but he also possessed the ability to let something go when there was nothing good to be gained by pursuing it.

In his estimation, the situation with Amber Harte and her disappearing bruise fell neatly into that category. He was certain if he mentioned it to Verity she'd encourage him to go back to Reno, or at least call Amber again, and if he mentioned it to Stone, the mage would probably hop the next plane over there (assuming there wasn't a magical portal in the area somewhere) and track her down himself. Neither of which would make Jason's life any better.

Besides, it wasn't as if he ever *saw* Verity or Stone these days. Between his own case load, which had piled up a bit following his unexpected stay in Reno, whatever crazy problem Stone was chasing right now involving weird magical events, and Verity's move to San Francisco, he didn't even try pinning either of them down for more than brief meetings. The best he'd done was to get Verity to agree to let him help her move next weekend.

That wasn't exactly the way he wanted to interact with her right now.

He swung his legs around until he was half-sitting, half-lying on the couch and drained the remainder of his beer, debating whether to get up and get another one. Finally, he sighed and stayed where he was, since getting drunk right now wouldn't solve any of his problems and would only make him feel like crap in the morning.

A while ago, he'd thought the discovery that Verity was sleeping with Stone was the most shocking thing she could spring on him. But now she was leaving the South Bay for an apartment in a sketchy San Francisco neighborhood so she could be closer to her girlfriend, her job healing for a magical tattoo artist, and her new mentor, a surly, man-hating young witch who brewed alchemical potions. Not to mention the Harpies, the gang of female vigilantes both the girlfriend and the witch belonged to. Some of them had odd magical abilities of their own, and they all ran around at night taking down street criminals and playing defender of the downtrodden. Not, in his opinion, the best bunch for his sister to get tangled up with.

It wasn't fair for him to get in her way, of course—as much as he wanted to continue seeing Verity as the little sister he could shield from harm and protect from the world, that ship had sailed the moment she'd run away from her halfway house at seventeen and joined up with the Forgotten. Then, when she'd met Stone, the ship had plowed full steam ahead into that part of the map where it said *Here There Be Dragons*. He didn't regret any of this, not exactly, but when he was honest with himself he did wish it would slow down a bit.

That clearly wasn't going to happen.

He grunted, more annoyed at himself than he was with Stone and Verity, and leaped off the couch to gather the untidy pile of papers and folders and stuff them back into his messenger bag. The best thing he could do right now was take a hot shower, go to bed, and try to get a decent night's sleep. He had another case he needed to get started on tomorrow, and dwelling on things he couldn't change wasn't going to help with it.

His phone rang.

Great. Now what?

He grabbed it from the table, expecting it to be either Stone, Verity, or Gina, but he didn't recognize the number. "Yeah, Jason Thayer."

"Jason? It's Amber Harte. Remember me, from Reno?"

Holy shit. He dropped back down on the couch. "Uh—yeah, of course I remember you. How's it going?"

"It's good." There was a pause. "Listen, I hate to bother you this late, but—I need your help."

"My help?" His faint frown deepened. Her voice sounded strained. What could he do to help her, though? Did she want him to go back to Reno, after—

"Yeah. I'm in the Bay Area, and I've run into a little trouble. And then I remembered what you said."

"What I said about what?"

Another pause. "Look—I lied to you before. I'm sorry, but I did. You *did* see a bruise on my arm. Were you serious when you said you thought you knew what I was? And that you've got friends who've dealt with...that kind of stuff before?"

Now it was Jason's turn to pause. "Uh—yeah. I was. What are you doing in the Bay Area? What kind of trouble are you in?"

"Can you come here? I'm at a motel on Monterey Road in San Jose. I need to talk to you, if you're willing."

Despite his annoyance at the way she'd treated him before, it didn't even occur to him to turn her down. But that didn't mean he was going to throw all his caution away. If she was some kind of supernatural being like a shifter, it would be stupid to meet her somewhere on her own terms. "Yeah. Sure, we can meet. But could we do it at a bar or something?"

She paused. "That's…not really a good idea right now. Listen—I'm sorry I called. I shouldn't be dragging you into my problems. Just forget I—"

"No," he said, before he could stop himself. "It's okay. I'll come. What's the name of the motel?"

"You sure? I don't want to cause any trouble for you."

"Yeah. It's fine."

"Okay, then. The place is called the Capri." She gave him the address. "There's a 7-Eleven on one side and a Shell station on the other. Real high-class place. I'm in room 209." Her voice still held tension, but he could hear a smile in it too.

"Okay. That's not too far from me. I'll be there in twenty minutes."

"Great. Just knock twice so I know it's you. And…thanks, Jason."

He stuck the phone back in his pocket and grabbed his leather jacket from the chair. After a moment's hesitation, he grabbed his gun too. He still didn't have a concealed-carry permit, but when dealing with potential supernaturals, prudence trumped legalities. For a second, he thought about calling Verity, or Stone, or both of them. It would have been wiser to have some magical backup, especially since he was fresh out of enhancement elixir.

But he didn't do it. He didn't want to admit it even to himself, but it wasn't entirely because he didn't think a single meeting in a relatively public place would be dangerous.

Part of it was because he wanted to see her again, alone.

| CHAPTER TWENTY-FOUR

THE CAPRI MOTEL was one of those places that dotted certain parts of the San Jose area: it had probably been built in the Fifties, and might even have been nice back when motels were a new thing, Monterey Road was a main drag through San Jose, and more families started taking cross-country road trips.

Right now, though, it looked rundown and old, like the owners were trying to keep up with the decay but didn't bring in enough money to do it. It had two stories, patchy tan stuccoed walls with darker brown doors, and rickety, rusting exterior staircases at each end. A small, kidney-shaped pool, unlit and half-empty, stood in front of the place, surrounded by a high chain-link fence. A sign on the gate read *CLOSED UNTIL FURTHER NOTICE.* Jason had visited several such establishments in the course of his work, tracking down various low-lifes who had reason to hole up in a place that didn't ask questions as long as you paid cash and didn't cause trouble.

He'd brought the Mustang since this wasn't official agency business. He parked it in front of the office and got out, looking around. Aside from a couple guys hanging out smoking near the other end of the ground-floor row of rooms, he didn't see anybody else moving. Something about the guys suggested they might be undercover cops, but they didn't seem interested in him.

Room 209 was at the far end of the second floor, next to an ice machine that looked as if it hadn't worked in this millennium. Jason paused outside the door to consider one last time whether he should have given Stone or Verity a call, then knocked twice, decisively.

For a few seconds, nothing happened. He was about to knock again when he heard the room's chain lock disengage, followed by a deadbolt. The door swung open to reveal Amber in a room lit only by the faint glow of a small, muted TV set.

"Hey," she said.

Something about her seemed off—she wasn't moving with her usual grace, and her tension was unmistakable now that he could see her. "Hey. You okay?"

"I will be. Thanks for coming so late. I appreciate it."

"It's only eleven. Not exactly past my bedtime. What brings you to San Jose?" He wondered briefly if it had anything to do with him, but that was ridiculous.

"Kind of a long story. I'll get to it in a minute. Want a beer?"

"Yeah, sure, thanks."

She walked back inside without turning the light on, crouched next to the room's tiny mini-fridge, and returned with a can of Corona. She already had one of her own open on the nightstand. "Bet you're wondering what I'm doing in such a high-class place."

"The thought had crossed my mind." He narrowed his eyes, trying to pick out what he thought was off about her.

She wore a black, long-sleeved thermal shirt and jeans; a pair of black work boots lay next to the bed and she'd tossed her leather jacket over the room's only chair.

"Place seems fairly well protected, though. Did you notice the two undercover cops lurking downstairs?"

"How'd you know that?" he asked in surprise.

She waved it off. "Eh, cops are cops. There's a look. You learn to notice it."

"Yeah, I guess you do. Didn't expect *you* to, though."

"Do you have experience with cops? I suppose you would, being a P.I."

"Yeah, but that's not all. My dad was one, so I grew up around them. Plus, I got kicked out of the Academy for punching out an instructor. So I took a few years off, then decided it was time to get my shit together and get my license."

She laughed. "Punching out an instructor, huh?"

"It was a long time ago. I've…matured since then. I only punch people out when they really deserve it."

"Well, all right, then." Her grin didn't fade. She settled herself on the bed, moving with slow deliberation, and switched on the bedside lamp. She was definitely stiff, or worse. "Did the instructor deserve it?"

"We had different interpretations." He sipped his beer. "So, anyway, how can I help you? I gotta tell you, I was surprised to hear from you. After the last time I called, I figured you didn't want anything to do with me. Are you okay? I can't help noticing you're moving like you might be hurt."

"How's your car?"

She was clearly being evasive; he wondered why, but decided to go with it for now. Whatever she wanted, she'd get

R. L. KING

to it eventually, and until then he could sit here and have a beer with her. He kept a close eye on the door, though, watching for any shadowy figures moving past the drawn curtains. "Totaled. I'm waiting for the check from your insurance company so I can pay for a new one."

"That sucks. I really am sorry about that, but to be honest it didn't surprise me. Most modern cars might be safer in a crash, but that's because they're designed to crumple up like an old shopping bag when you look at them funny. Give me an old car any day."

"Oh, yeah? You like old cars?" *Careful. Don't get too chummy yet. You still don't know what she wants.*

"Yeah. I grew up with older brothers, and they taught me to work on 'em. I think they thought it was cute at first, but that changed when I got better at it than they were." She flashed him a challenging grin, as if expecting him to tease her about it.

"Nice," he said, and meant it. "I miss it—my personal car is a Mustang, only a few years old, and nowadays they're so complicated under the hood that I'm afraid to touch anything. One of these days I want to pick up an old project car, or maybe a bike."

Her gaze turned appraising, but then she dropped it and sighed. "Sorry. I could sit here all day and talk cars, but that's not why I called. I didn't *want* to call—I don't like to bring other people into my problems—but I'm smart enough to know when I have to."

"Yeah. So…how can I help you?"

She took another swallow of beer and watched him again, clearly trying to decide whether to proceed. When she spoke again her voice was firm but held tension. "When you called me back that night, asking about the bruise on my arm, you said you thought you 'knew what I was.' What did you mean by that?"

"Uh..." Jason considered his words with care, suddenly wondering if this was how Stone and Verity felt when trying to decide whether to spill the supernatural beans with a new acquaintance. "It's...complicated."

"Not really. I want to hear what you think I am. Just spit it out." Her attention was fixed on him now, her gold-flecked brown eyes focused on his.

"Well..." he said. "There's a general answer to that question, and a more specific one that's probably less likely to be right."

"Start with the general one."

He swallowed. If he said something and she looked at him like he was crazy, he could always claim to be joking. *Ha ha, good laugh, right?*

"I...think you're something supernatural."

She didn't laugh. "And what makes you think that?"

"I saw your arm," he said, gesturing toward it. The thermal shirt's sleeve covered it now. "I'm a detective, remember? I'm trained to observe things and draw conclusions. And what I observed was that you had a big, dark bruise on your arm after the accident, and it looked fresh. And then less than an hour later, when you shook hands with me right before I got out of your car, it was gone."

She nodded slowly. "And what conclusions did you draw from that?"

"Either that I didn't see it right—like you said, maybe it was a shadow or something—or..."

"Or?" Her tone was calm, untroubled as she sipped her beer.

"Or else there's something about you that lets you heal injuries faster than you should be able to."

She considered. "That's not the kind of conclusion normal people would come to. You know that, right?"

"Oh, yeah. I know it for sure. A few years ago, I would have convinced myself I was seeing things and never would have called you back."

"But you did call me back. And you said you have friends who...how did you put it? 'Deal with this kind of thing all the time'?"

"Yeah."

"You also said you think you know what I am. You sounded pretty specific about it. So...what *do* you think I am?"

He spent a little more time giving her a frank once-over, figuring she couldn't complain about it under the circumstances. Her shoulder-length brown hair was pulled back into a loose ponytail, framing a tanned, attractive face with a strong jaw, heavy brows, high cheekbones, and a slightly turned-up nose. She wore only minimal makeup, but didn't need it. Her shoulders, wide for a woman, fit the rest of her tall, athletic frame well. She wasn't a slender waif, but she didn't have an ounce of extra fat on her, either.

Okay. Here goes. "I think you might be a shifter of some kind."

"A shifter." Her voice was neutral and gave nothing away.

"Yeah."

"So you know about shifters?"

"Yeah. Some. Like I said, my friends—well, my sister and my friend, actually—had some dealings with some of them a few months back." He leaned back. "So, am I right? And are you going to tell me why you need my help?"

She sighed. "You're sort of right."

"How can I be *sort of* right? You either are or you aren't, right?"

"No, not exactly. I'm *part* shifter."

Jason tilted his head. "You mean like half?"

"I mean like a quarter. My grandmother was one. I got some of the abilities, but I can't…you know…actually get big and furry." She spread her hands and shrugged. "What you see is what you get."

That was odd. Jason was hardly an expert on shifters, but he remembered Viajera was half jaguar shifter, and she could change form just fine. If they interbred with humans too long, did they lose that ability? So it wasn't like mages, apparently, where the talent turned up periodically with no way to predict it. "Uh…okay. So what do you mean you got some of the abilities? Obviously you got the regeneration."

"Yeah…not nearly as good as the real thing, though. I can heal from some pretty bad injuries, but it takes me a lot longer than a true shifter." She took another drink of beer and changed position. "I'm stronger and faster than most normal humans. My sense of smell's better, but again, nowhere near the level of a true shifter."

Jason thought back to the scene at the coffee shop. "So that's why you said you weren't worried about handling Hank. Is he one too?"

"A shifter?" She snorted. "No. He's just a big guy who's used to people kissing his ass because they're afraid he'll beat the crap out of them if they don't. He's okay most of the time, but he gets a little possessive sometimes. As you saw."

"Are there a lot of you over there? What kind are you, by the way? The one I knew most was a jaguar, from Peru, but I also met a bear, a couple of wolves, and a cougar."

Her expression sharpened. "Wait a minute. That was you?"

"What was me?"

"Word got around a few months ago about some crazy old woman who'd kidnapped some shifters and was holding them prisoner, stealing their blood for something. Were you involved in that?" Her eyes narrowed into a predatory glare.

"Yeah. My friends and I were. We were the ones who got 'em out of there." He leaned forward, a ripple running down his back. "Do you know them? The ones who got out?"

"No, not directly. I don't think the wolves and the cougar were from around here. There's a colony of bear shifters out in the wilds between Reno and Tahoe, though. I know a few of 'em, casually."

"Is that what you are? A bear?" It made sense—she did have a bit of a bearish look to her. He wondered if the colony was the same one Tony belonged to.

"My grandmother was a bear, yeah." She focused on him again. "So these friends of yours—your friend and your sister—what are they? Obviously not shifters, or you would have mentioned them before the ones you helped rescue."

Jason looked away. "Yeah. That's the thing—it's not my business to out them. They're both a lot more familiar with the supernatural world than I am—that's all I'll say until I know a hell of a lot more about why you called me and what you want."

"Fair enough." She sounded like he'd successfully passed a test. "So let's get to what I want. I didn't tell you the whole truth when I told you what I did back in Reno."

"No surprise there—I figured you were being evasive, but it was none of my business. So you're not a bartender?"

"Oh, I am, occasionally. But that's not all I do. And it's not why I'm here." She glanced around the room and then leaned in closer, dropping her voice to a lower tone. "I'm...kind of a bounty hunter."

"What do you mean, *kind of* a bounty hunter?"

"I don't have a license, and I don't do the normal kinds of jobs licensed bounty hunters do. I track people down for private clients, and my targets are a little more...special."

Jason stared at her. "You mean you go after supernatural stuff?"

"Yeah, and other things. Not exactly the kind of thing you can take a test for. I'm known in certain communities around the Reno-Tahoe area for being the go-to girl when you need to track somebody down but you don't want to get involved in...legal entanglements."

That made sense, and Jason certainly had no trouble believing she could handle the physical aspects of the job. "So what do you need me for? It sounds like you've got this pretty well under control."

"Yeah...I thought so too. But it turns out there's more to this guy than I thought."

"What do you mean by that?"

In answer, she drew herself to a more upright seated position, and pulled up the bottom of her shirt to reveal a large, white bandage on her side. A small amount of blood soaked through it, and several purple bruises surrounded it.

"Holy shit," Jason said, leaning in for a closer look. "Who did that to you? Do you need a doctor?"

"No, I'm okay. It's already mostly healed up. Like I told you, I got the regeneration ability, but it takes longer for something like this."

"So…who's responsible for it?"

"I don't know his name. He showed up in Tahoe a week ago and caused some trouble—broke into a jewelry shop and stole a bunch of high-value stuff. Obviously he got in, but he didn't set off any alarms or show up on any of the security tapes except as a blur. The people who owned the shop called the cops, but one of them knows about…the other world and thinks the guy's connected to that. That's why they called me."

Jason nodded. "Okay. So you tracked the guy out here to San Jose?"

"Yeah, but then I lost him. It's like the guy doesn't leave traces. I was trying to figure out my next step when I got jumped."

"*You* got jumped?" If she was even part shifter, Jason was surprised anyone could manage to sneak up on her.

"Right?" She looked as indignant as he did. "That's not supposed to happen. That's my whole shtick—people can't hide from me. I track them down and deal with them. I've never met a man I can't take in a fight, except for true shifters."

"This guy isn't a shifter, is he? Because I'm flattered that you'd think of me, but I'm just a guy. I work out and I'm good in a fight, but—"

She eyed him critically. "Are you familiar with magic?"

He stared at her. "Magic?"

"Yeah. I know you know about shifters, but what *else* do you know?"

"I've…got some knowledge in that area," he said, narrowing his eyes. Once again he glanced toward the curtained window, but still saw nothing moving outside.

"Good. That'll make things easier," she said. "I'll be honest with you—unless you've got abilities you're doing a good job hiding, it's not you specifically I need help from. I was hoping you might talk to one of these friends of yours. I've got some intel that the guy I'm after met up with a couple friends here—including the one who winged me. I think he's trying to sell his haul and leave this area by tomorrow, so I need to find him fast. If he gets out of the area, I'll have a hell of a time finding him."

Jason finished his beer, frowning. As much as he wanted to help Amber, he wasn't sure he wanted to drag Stone or Verity into the situation. "You think this guy has magical talent?"

"It's the only reason I can come up with for why he can do what he does." She pointed at the bandage on her abdomen. "This isn't supposed to happen. I'm not just bragging, but *nobody* sneaks up on me. This guy isn't just sneaky—he's got some way of evading tracking, and I'm damned if I know what it is." She winced and lay back down again. "Damn, this sucks. I know it'll be fine in an hour or so, but if he's turned the tables and he and his buddies are after *me* now—"

"Yeah." Jason had already thought of that. From the sound of things, the rickety chain and inadequate deadbolt on the door wouldn't hold these guys back. Hell, they wouldn't hold *him* back, if he were determined to break into this room. "What about the shifters? Do you know any of them? Could they help?"

"They don't get involved. They're very reclusive, and they rarely leave their home territory. But one of them heard some of the townspeople talking about the break-in, and he convinced them to hire me to grab him." She sighed. "At first, I thought the guy *was* a shifter. Not a bear, but some kind of sneaky one."

"But now you're sure he isn't?"

"Yeah. As soon as he got wind I was on his tail, he took off. I tracked him to this area, but there's something more to him, and I can't put my finger on what it is. It's almost like he's taunting me—letting me get a whiff of him and then disappearing again. And then when I didn't even expect it, he attacked me. I'd be an idiot to go after him and his guys alone, especially before this heals up, but I can't let him get away."

"What makes you think he hasn't already left the area?"

"A hunch. Guys like that enjoy playing the game. I'm sure he likes evading me because it feeds his ego. And it hurts *my* ego to admit he got the better of me—I've never failed to bring in a target before, but this time I've got nothing. So when I remembered what you said, I figured it was worth giving you a call and seeing if you were serious about these friends of yours."

"Well…I'm definitely serious about them. They're both pretty busy, though. My sister's in the middle of a move up to San Francisco, and my friend…Yeah, I'd rather not get him involved unless it's necessary. He's damn good, but he also has a tendency to…complicate things. I'd rather keep this simple, if it's all the same to you."

"I like simple." She finished her beer and swung her legs off the bed. "So, will you call your sister and ask her, at least? I can offer her a cut of my fee if she can help me find this guy and get the stuff back. Plus she'll be helping out a lot of nice folks who don't deserve this kind of crap. If the shop owner can't get his stuff back, he's in trouble. His insurance won't cover all of it. He might have to close the place, and he's got a wife and four kids."

Jason studied her again. He barely knew this woman, and had no idea how much of what she was telling him was true. His gut told him she wasn't lying to him—but he had to make sure it really was his gut he was listening to, and not something further south.

"Yeah," he finally said. "I'll call her. But I think you should get out of here. This place isn't safe. What if you come to my place and we call her from there?"

She gave him an appraising look, as if trying to determine his motives.

"Look," he said. "You don't know the area like I do. If he decides to come after you again, this isn't the place you want to be, undercover cops or no undercover cops. I promise, I'm not trying to hit on you. I just want to go someplace safer while we figure this out. Okay?"

She studied him for a few more moments, then sighed, stuffed her feet into her boots, and stood. Already, she moved with a little more limber grace than before. "Yeah. I don't like it, but I guess you make sense." She grabbed her jacket off the chair. "Thanks, Jason. You didn't have to do this. I mean, so far I've totaled your car and told you to get lost, and you're still willing to help me out. You're okay."

"Yeah, that's what they tell me. And just to be clear: I *am* gonna help you out. I want to be in on this. I'm not just gonna put you in touch with my sister and step out. We're a package deal."

"Fair enough."

"Also..." Jason added, wondering if he shouldn't just leave well enough alone.

"Yes—?"

He leaned forward. "I know I said I wasn't trying to hit on you, and I'm not. But if we get this guy...will you at least let me buy you dinner sometime? Assuming you meant it about you and Hank not being serious."

Her expression remained impassive for several seconds, long enough to make him think he'd blown it, but then she smiled. "Yeah, sure, why not? And yeah, I did mean it. Hank's a good guy, but I can't deal with that possessive shit. And anyway, what's one dinner? You've got yourself a deal." Her eyes twinkled. "But I'm warning you now—I know you Bay Area types love your vegetarian restaurants, but this girl's pure carnivore."

| CHAPTER TWENTY-FIVE

EVEN THOUGH IT WAS AFTER ELEVEN by the time Jason called Verity, she answered promptly. "Jason?" Her voice sounded concerned. "Everything okay? You don't usually call this late."

"I'm fine. But I've got a little...situation you might be able to help me with. Are you in San Francisco?"

"Nah, sleeping over here tonight—was doing a bunch of cleaning today. What's up?"

He glanced at Amber, who was sitting on his couch drinking a beer. "I've got a...friend here who could use a little help. *Your* kind of help. You up for hearing her out?"

"Yeah, sure." He didn't miss how much her voice perked up, and then it took on a sly edge. "*Her*?"

He sighed. Little sisters could be a pain sometimes, even when they could blow things up with their minds. "Yeah. Her. You coming or not? We're at my place."

"Be there in twenty minutes."

R. L. KING

She showed up in fifteen, dressed in leather jacket, jeans, and combat boots. "Okay. What's this problem—and who's your *friend?*"

He gave her a dirty look he knew wouldn't do any good, then waved her inside.

Amber leaped from the couch—she seemed to be completely healed now—and the two women eyed each other appraisingly.

Jason stepped in. "Amber, this is my sister Verity. V, this is Amber Harte. I met her a few weeks ago—she's the one who totaled my car."

Verity grinned. "Well, hey, that's not the way I'd pick to meet somebody, but I guess you take what you can get. Hi."

Amber's tense posture relaxed a little. "Hey. Good to meet you."

Jason noticed Verity looking Amber over with the fuzzed-out glance indicating magical sight. "So, uh…"

"You said something about *my* kind of help," Verity said. "I think I know what that means, but suppose we get it out in the open so there aren't any misunderstandings."

Amber nodded approval. "Good. Straightforward. I can work with that."

"Amber's part shifter," Jason said.

"*Part* shifter?" Verity tilted her head. "So—what—you grow a tail and pointy ears or something?"

"You didn't tell me your sister was a comedian, Jason." Amber sat back down on the couch, looking amused.

"Yeah, there's a reason for that."

She laughed. "No. It means I got some of the perks—strength, speed, tracking, healing—but nowhere near as fast as a real shifter. And that's all I got."

"So you can't change into a—what?"

"Bear." Amber appeared to be relaxing more as Verity continued to take her words in stride. "And Jason tells me you might know something about magic."

Verity shot Jason a questioning glance.

He shook his head. "Didn't tell her much. Just said you might know some stuff that could help her."

"Help you with what?" She turned her attention back to Amber. "What's the problem?"

With a little help from Jason, Amber explained the situation.

Verity listened in silence, perched on the edge of a chair across from her. "So..." she said at last, "You think this guy who broke in to the shop is some kind of mage?"

"That's my theory, yeah. I don't have a lot of experience with mages, but I do know shifters. And they can't break into buildings without a trace." She finished her beer. "Can mages do that?"

"Oh, yeah. I can think of several ways they could do it." She got up and began pacing. "You said you think this guy is working with at least one other person?"

"I think he stole the stuff from the jewelry store and transported it here—maybe he has a buddy here he can fence it to. I'm not sure. But he's definitely in the area, or was a couple hours ago, and there's definitely more than one of them. At least two, maybe three."

Jason watched Verity pace, amused at how much some of her unconscious habits were growing to resemble Stone's. "What do you think, V? Could you find the guy?"

"Maybe. Depends." She addressed Amber again. "In order to find him, I'd need something of his to use as a tether object. Did he leave anything behind at the scene?"

"Like what?"

"Anything that belonged to him—the more important it was to him, the better. It'll be harder to find him if he really is a mage—if he's got any kind of power, he can protect himself against tracking."

"But that takes effort, doesn't it?" Jason asked. "Would he even bother, if he doesn't know a mage is looking for him?"

"Let's hope not. Doesn't matter, though, if I don't have a tether object."

"Damn," Amber said. "I didn't stay long at the scene back home—just long enough to get the story and pick up the guy's scent." She bowed her head with a dejected sigh. "Well, it was a good try, anyway. Thanks for coming over here."

"Let's not give up yet," Verity said. "You said you fought these guys, right? Did you get any good hits in?"

"Why?"

"If you did, maybe you got some blood on your clothes or something. Blood's one of the best tether objects around."

Amber jerked her head up and grinned. "Hang on a second." She hurried over to a duffel bag she'd tossed next to the sofa, rummaged in it, and came up with a brown leather glove. She tossed it to Verity. "This work? I got one good shot in on the guy before his friend took me down and they got away."

Verity examined the glove, fuzzing out again. "Yeah, this is great. If this really is his blood and he hasn't put up shielding, I can use this." She glanced at Jason. "And if I can't…I know somebody who can."

"Yeah…" Jason shook his head. "I really don't want to get him involved, though. You're good, V—you got this. Let's keep this one to ourselves, okay? He's got enough on his plate."

She grinned. "You're not fooling anybody, big bro."

"What?"

Amber was shifting her gaze between the two of them as if watching a tennis match, but said nothing.

Verity's grin widened. "You want to keep the weirdness magnet as far away from this one as possible."

"Well…yeah. I mean, I know it's rubbed off on you too, but you haven't had as long for it to sink in. This one should be pretty straightforward, right? You find the guy, we go there, take 'em out, get the stuff back, call the cops, and call it a day."

He narrowed his eyes and turned to Amber. "You're not planning on killing anybody, are you? Because I'm not down for that."

"No killing. I hope I can take the guy back, but the people who hired me really only want their stuff back." Her expression took on a predatory aspect. "I *do* want to show him it's not a good idea to try this again, though."

"That I can get behind. C'mon—the sooner Verity does the ritual, the sooner we can get this taken care of."

They went back to Verity's apartment to perform the ritual. That was where her materials were, and now that she was all packed up, she had floor space.

Jason prowled the room, casting occasional glances out the window as his sister worked. He couldn't help her with this, and neither could Amber, so they stayed out of the way as best they could.

"This magic stuff always freaks me out," Amber said under her breath, watching Verity as she carefully placed candles around the outer edge of the boundary she'd drawn with chalk on the floor.

"Have you seen a lot of it?" Jason, as he often did when hanging out with either Stone or Verity, wondered how many people were in the know about the magical world and didn't say anything about it for fear of being thought crazy.

"Not really. Mostly heard about it. A couple guys at the colony know people who can do it, and I'm pretty sure one of the guys who runs the shop where this stuff was stolen from is peddling a little magical gear out of the back room. That may be why this guy I'm chasing went after it."

"How well do you know the colony in Tahoe?"

She shrugged. "Casually at best. Like I told you, my grandma was a shifter. My dad kept contact with them until he married Mom, and then they moved away. Dad made sure we knew about our heritage, though. When I got old enough I went back and re-introduced myself, but…"

"But what? Oh, wait—is it like the other part-shifter we know? She never really felt like she was part of her clan since her parents took her away when she was a little girl."

"Nah. Like I said, I know them. We hang out occasionally. One of my brothers still lives closer to them, but mostly the true shifters live in their animal forms. One of them's got money and owns a huge section of land out in the middle of nowhere in the forest, and they're based there. Not a lot to do for those of us who are stuck on two legs."

He narrowed his eyes. "Stuck? You mean you'd rather be a bear?"

"Sometimes. Life's a lot less complicated for them, you know? But not always. Some of them are pretty strange…really a lot more bear than human."

"Yeah…" Jason fell silent, looking out the window again.

"You look like you have something on your mind."

He jerked, startled. Oh, right—even part-shifters could apparently pick up faint changes in scent that indicated un-ease or agitation. "Yeah…I guess I do have a lot on my mind right now."

"Jason…" She took his arm and gently turned him around, though he could feel the strength in her grip. "Come on. What is it?"

Her eyes were beautiful, medium brown with golden flecks. "Remember before I told you one of the shifters we helped rescue from that compound was a bear?"

"Yeah."

"His name was Tony. I kind of lost track of him after we split up. Do you know him?"

"I don't think so. They keep to themselves a lot, and I never met all the younger ones. Why?"

"No reason, really. I just wanted to maybe see him again—see how he's doing, you know?" He wondered if he sounded as lame to her as he did to himself.

She gave him an odd look, but before she could answer, Verity spoke up.

"Okay, we're ready to go here. Give me a few more minutes and hopefully we should have something."

Jason and Amber returned to the circle, taking seats on the couch nearby to watch as Verity lit the candles and sat down in the center with the bloody glove. Jason pulled out the map of the San Jose area he'd brought with him and unfolded it, ready to hand it over.

The ritual didn't take long; barely ten minutes had passed before the candle flames shot up and died, and Verity's shoulders slumped.

Jason leaped up. "Did you find them?"

"Yeah. Give me the map."

She spread it out in front of her, studied it a few moments, and then stabbed her finger down on a location. "There."

Jason and Amber knelt next to her. Amber pulled out a flashlight. "Do you know where that is?" she asked Jason.

"Yeah. It's kind of a sketchy area—lots of warehouses and industrial parks."

"Makes sense—they might be holed up there waiting for whoever they're fencing the stuff to. If they're still there, that might mean they still have it." She jumped to her feet in a single strong, graceful motion. "I gotta go."

"Wait—I'm coming with you," Jason insisted. He couldn't quite duplicate her leap, but came close.

"*We're* coming with you," Verity added.

"Hang on." Amber held up her hands. "I really appreciate your help, but I can't ask you to—"

"You're not asking," Verity said. "We're volunteering. At least I am. If this guy's a mage, you might need magical back-up anyway."

"Yeah," Jason said, pulling on his leather jacket. "Come on, Amber—I know you're tough, but this guy took you out before. Let us help you."

She flicked her gaze between the two of them, then sighed. "Fine. Can't say I mind having some backup, magical or otherwise. Let's do this."

They piled into Verity's SUV ("In case they recognize your Jeep," Jason told Amber). With Verity driving and Jason navigating with the map, they arrived in the general area of San Jose in twenty minutes.

"Why would they go here?" Verity asked, looking around at the run-down industrial parks, many of which had *For Lease* signs on them, and old warehouses.

"Guy probably has a local buddy who knows the area," Amber said. "They grabbed quite a bit of stuff, so they need a place to hide a truck and take care of the handoff to the fence without any cops or lookie-loos around."

"There it is," Jason said, pointing forward. "Pull off here, V. Can you do that disregarding thing?"

She grinned. "Yeah, don't worry. I got this."

He didn't say it, but once again he found himself apprehensive of just how much his sister seemed to be enjoying adventures like this. He supposed it wasn't anything more unusual than what she did with the Harpies in San Francisco, or some of the stuff she got up to with Stone, but he tried not to think too hard about either of those two things.

"Okay," Amber said. "Let's do a little recon. I want to be sure they're really in there before we do anything. I'll go around the back. Jason, you take the side. Verity—"

"I'm going up," Verity said, pointing. "I see some windows up high, and they won't be expecting anybody to be peeking in on them from twenty feet up."

"Nice. Meet back here in ten minutes?"

"Got it," Jason said.

"Be careful," Amber said. "These guys took me down hard, and that's not easy to do."

As he crept around the side of the warehouse, Jason found his thoughts focused more on Amber than on the thieves inside. He moved silently, using the moonlight to navigate, wondering how many guys they'd end up having to deal with. He wasn't worried—between him, Amber, and Verity, he doubted they'd be much of a match, even if they did have a mage. With a cold little smile, he pictured what Amber must look like in action—strong, fast, and fearless, her brown ponytail whipping around behind her. He wondered if she knew any martial arts, and if she did, whether she'd be interested in sparring with him. And maybe a few other activities after they finished…

Cut it out, he told himself, but he didn't feel guilty. Amber was an attractive woman. Even if nothing came of it, you couldn't blame a guy for fantasizing.

Up ahead, he heard voices. Tensing, he stopped moving and slipped sideways behind a dumpster, then rose high enough to peer over the top.

Ten feet ahead, a door had just opened. Two figures exited but stopped inside the doorway, and one bent to prop it open. A few seconds later, tiny lights flared as they lit cigarettes.

Jason remained where he was, feeling in his pocket to thumb off the ringer on his phone in case somebody picked that moment to try calling him. From his hiding place, he could barely hear the two talking if he strained his ears.

"When are those guys gettin' here?" one asked. "I'm sick of waitin' around with this weirdo."

"They're payin' us enough," the other growled. "Just shut up and wait. Cops ain't comin' out here. We'll be outta here in less than an hour."

Jason rose a little more, trying to get a better look. There was no light above the door, and the cigarettes' glowing tips didn't provide much illumination, but he made out the bulky silhouettes of light body armor on both of them, and the one with his back turned had what looked like an SMG slung over his shoulder. What did they have in that truck that was worth that kind of protection? What were they expecting to go after them? Maybe Amber was more dangerous than he thought.

For one brief moment he considered trying to take them down himself. He had the element of surprise, and if he moved fast he might be able to get the drop on them. That would definitely impress Amber…

Then he shook his head in disgust. *Come on, idiot—there are two of them, and at least one has a gun.* Stupidity wouldn't impress her—and if he got himself killed, it wouldn't matter. No, they'd need to be smart about this one, and work together.

As he prepared to duck down and sneak back to the rendezvous point to share what he found with the others, one of the men spoke again, freezing him in place.

"Hank's gonna have to give us a bonus if that chick shows up again."

"Don't he know her or somethin'?"

"I dunno, maybe. But he didn't say nothin' about no psycho chick attackin' us."

"Don't worry. We took her down good. She's off lickin' her wounds somewhere now, if she knows what's good for her."

"C'mon. Let's go in before Freak Boy gets jumpy."

The two figures stubbed out their cigarettes and disappeared back inside, closing the door behind them with a *clang*.

Verity and Amber were already waiting when Jason returned, huddled next to the corrugated side of the building away from the light.

"Where have you *been?*" Verity demanded. "We were about to come looking for you."

He joined them in the shadows. "What did you find?"

She pointed up. "I looked in through a broken window up there. They've got a small truck parked inside—like one of those rental jobs, but plain. I barely saw a couple guys heading outside, but I didn't see the mage anywhere. Either he's hiding or he's not there. I was worried those guys had spotted you."

"I saw the truck too, through the side window," Amber said. "I didn't see the mage either, but I can smell him. He's in there somewhere."

"Yeah," Jason said with a sigh. "He's in there. Those two guys you saw went outside for a smoke, and I heard 'em talking. They called him 'Freak Boy.' Can't figure that could be anybody else." When Amber started to say something, he held up his hand and met her gaze. "There's something else, Amber, and you're not gonna like it."

"I don't like any of this. What is it?"

He spoke carefully, keeping his voice even. "They mentioned something about somebody named Hank having to give them a bonus if 'that chick' showed up again. They thought maybe he knew you."

Amber stared at him in silence for several seconds. "You're…sure?"

"Yeah. I'm sorry, Amber."

"Who's Hank?" Verity asked.

"A guy I know back home. A guy I *thought* I knew, anyway," she added bitterly. She studied Jason a moment. "It makes sense, though. He never liked Darryl—the guy who owns the shop. They had a falling out a year or so ago, and Hank never forgave him." She let out a sigh in the dim light. "Damn it, I never thought he'd—"

Verity touched her arm. "Hey," she said softly. "I'm sorry too—it sounds like this guy's a friend of yours. But we need to do this if we're going to. If the other guys show up it'll be harder."

"Yeah…" She stood and straightened her jacket. "Three of them, three of us. Sounds pretty straightforward."

"They have guns," Jason said. "SMGs, from the look of it. And body armor. We can't just punch our way in. They'll take us down before we get near them."

"We'll have to be sneaky, then," Verity said.

"Can you get us in there without anybody seeing?"

"It'll be tricky—disregarding won't work, and maintaining an illusion spell on three people at once would be hard. I might drop it at the wrong time."

"You can unlock doors, right?" he asked.

"Yeah, that's easy."

"This place has two doors. What if you unlocked them, and we came in from two sides. You could keep yourself invisible long enough to hide somewhere inside, right?"

"Yeah, but…" She looked at him in concern. "You said they had guns. And not just handguns, either. You don't have any armor, and you don't regenerate." Her expression turned to a sly grin. "Hang on—I have an idea."

The others leaned in as she whispered her plan, and by the time she was done, both of them were smiling too.

"I think I could get to like your sister, Jason," Amber said with approval. "Come on—let's do this before anybody else shows up."

| CHAPTER TWENTY-SIX

J ASON CROUCHED next to the warehouse's side door, alternating between checking his watch and looking back and forth to make sure nobody was sneaking up on him. He didn't often think about just how long five minutes was when you were waiting for your friends to get into position, but every second seemed to take an eternity. Were Verity and Amber okay? Had the guys inside, or somebody else they hadn't even seen, caught them? He hadn't heard any yells or gunshots, but his mind spun terrifying scenarios of someone taking Verity out with a long-range sniper shot from one of the nearby roofs, or dropping Amber with a spell, or poison, or—

There! That was time. Forcing himself to move with care, he pulled open the door Verity had unlocked earlier, just in time to hear something heavy slamming to the floor inside, and a loud voice booming, *"This is the police! Put your hands up and drop your weapons!"*

That was the diversion Verity had promised. He'd forgotten illusions could be auditory too, but her deep-voiced cop sounded plenty real to him. As startled yelps sounded from near the truck inside, Jason slipped in and hurried to the side, gaining cover behind a stack of boxes before peering out to see what was going on.

The two guys in body armor, the ones he'd seen having a smoke outside, had leaped up from two sides of a large box they'd been using as a card table, their SMGs in hand. They took off in two different directions, both generally away from where the slam had come from.

Jason crept sideways, looking around the other side of his cover for a better view. He'd have to cross a large expanse of empty floor to get to the two gunmen, but they both had their backs to him. If he moved fast, he could—

He sensed the presence behind him an instant before it struck, which might have saved his life. Even so, he barely managed to throw himself sideways before the strangest feeling he'd ever experienced send his body into jerking spasms. As he dropped, still twitching, his mind locked on the closest thing he could compare it to—the time he'd been hit with a Taser back at the academy. His body crashed to the ground, his arms and legs flailing around, and spotted the skinny, grinning figure of a man moving past him, around the corner of the boxes.

"There's no cops!" the man yelled. "They've got a mage! Get 'em!"

Beyond them, Jason heard a gunshot, deafening as it echoed off the warehouse's metal walls and roof. *Amber? Verity?* Had one of the men hit one of them? *Damn it, get up!*

"Jason!" Verity came pounding around the other side of the boxes and skidded to a stop, dropping to her knees at his side. "Are you hurt? What happened?"

He struggled to speak, his voice shaking as he got his limbs under control and pushed himself unsteadily up. "I—think that guy—the mage—did something to me."

"Yeah. I think he's a wild talent. It looked like he—I don't know—phased? Teleported?" She gripped his arm and helped him up as another gunshot sounded from the other side, followed by several crashes as more boxes hit the floor. "His arm went right through you. He—"

Jason spotted the shadowy figure as it poked its head and its gun out from behind yet another stack of boxes. "Look out!" He dived forward, taking Verity and himself down just as a fusillade of shots zinged past them and buried themselves the wall.

Verity acted fast, twisting around and firing off a blast of magical energy with a loud roar. The man ducked back behind cover, but not fast enough: the blast hit his arm and he shrieked in pain.

"Come on!" Verity whispered, leaping back to her feet. "We need to get some height on this."

Another gunshot went off on the other side. "Where's Amber? We gotta find her."

"We need to get to that mage. Going up?" She pointed toward the top of the large stack of boxes.

"Yeah. Do it."

She didn't hesitate. He felt the wrench of her power on him, and then both of them shot upward to drop neatly on top of the crates. They were about fifteen feet up, crouched on a solid platform.

Jason was already looking around even before they landed. He spotted Amber on the other side, perched on a metal shelving unit bolted to the wall not far from the truck. The other gunman was down below, trying to get a bead on her.

She didn't give him a chance. Leaping with grace and precision, looking more like a jungle cat than a bear, she dropped down on top of him. He got off a couple of shots, but obviously hadn't expected the "crazy chick" to go for the direct attack. The rounds *spanged* off the shadowy ceiling high above as the guy went down with her on top of him. His gun flew from his grasp and clattered on the floor.

"I gotta find the mage!" Verity panted. "We can't let him get away." Without waiting for Jason to reply, she took off toward the other end of the stack. Jason caught a glimpse of her fuzzed-out, magical-sight expression before she once again levitated away.

Much as he wanted to follow her, he knew he couldn't. She was a damn good mage, and she could handle herself. Amber and the second gunman continued to wrestle on the floor on the other side of the warehouse, both of them trying to get to the gun, but he didn't know where the first one—the one Verity had winged with her spell—had ended up.

He hurried to the edge of the stack and crouched low, peering over at the fight in progress. Amber seemed be holding her own, and neither of them were getting any closer to the SMG, which somebody had kicked several feet away. If he could leap down and grab it before they did, he could—

He caught a movement directly below him. The first gunman slipped around the crates, training his SMG on the writhing pair as he tried to get a bead on Amber.

Jason didn't think, but only acted. Using the sounds of the fight as cover, he gathered himself and jumped down, landing on top of the first gunman just as the second one scrambled away from Amber toward the fallen SMG.

The guy never saw Jason coming. The two of them went down with Jason on top, but the guy kept hold of his gun this time. Jason caught a quick look at Amber, moving faster than any normal human, diving toward her own opponent the instant before he reached the gun, but then he had to focus on his own fight.

The gunman was strong, fast, and agile—probably not a supernatural, but definitely combat-trained. Jason didn't care. All his frustration at perceiving himself the weak link in the team bubbled up, along with his fear that if he didn't take this guy out, he'd go after Amber and Verity, drove him to fight with a madman's strength—but it was a strength fueled not by madness but by a controlled sense of rage. He slammed his fist into the guy's unprotected face—one of the few parts of him that wasn't armored—and satisfaction surged when the man's nose broke with an audible *crunch*.

The guy brought the gun around, trying to get a shot, but Jason stayed inside his reach, grabbing the man's gun arm with both of his and slamming it against the concrete floor. The guy struggled under him, aiming blows at his unprotected side and head with his other arm, but couldn't manage to fling Jason free enough to get a good shot with either his fist or his weapon.

"Jason!" Amber called, followed by another crash and yet more gunshots.

He didn't know if she was in trouble, but her words gave him a jolt of fresh energy. Keeping hold of his opponent's gun arm with one of his, he got a handful of the guy's hair with the other and slammed his head down, probably harder than he should have. Bone impacted concrete with a *thunk;* the guy's eyes rolled up into his head and his body went limp.

Jason didn't stay to see the results. "Amber!" he yelled, leaping upward, afraid of what he was going to see.

He needn't have worried. He spun toward them in time to see Amber unleash a fast, punishing kick into her opponent's jaw. The guy's head jerked around and he dropped the SMG, which he must have regained at some point, as his body did a graceful three-quarter pirouette. He smacked into a pile of boxes and then slumped down to a half-sitting, half-lying position, his chin resting on his chest.

Jason hurried over to her, panting but satisfied. "You okay?" She didn't seem to be bleeding except for a couple small cuts on her face; like him, she was breathing hard but her eyes blazed with energy and adrenaline.

"Yeah. You?" Already she was crouching next to her fallen opponent, kicking the SMG away and pulling a handful of long zip-ties from her pocket. She slipped one around the man's wrists and tightened it, then put another around his ankles and tossed two more to Jason. "Get the other one before he wakes up."

He caught them but threw a glance back over his shoulder. "Where's Verity?"

"I don't know. She took off, but I lost sight of her."

"Fuck—she went after the mage!" He threw the zip-ties back to her. "I gotta find her!"

"Wait!"

He didn't want to stop, but he did. "What?"

"Get this other guy trussed up and I'll go with you. I can follow their scent."

Once again, Jason chafed against even a few seconds' wait, but he couldn't hear his sister and had no idea which way she'd gone. "Hurry up, then. And check him—I slammed his head pretty hard."

Amber quickly examined the other guy. "He's breathing. We'll call the cops and they'll get him an ambulance." She zipped him up, made sure the pair of SMGs were well out of reach for either of them, and then hurried after him, pausing to sniff the air. "This way," she said, pointing toward one of the side doors.

Jason only then noticed the door was open. Had the mage fled outside? Verity had said he was a wild talent—if the phasing ability was his only power, he'd never stand up against all three of them, and he probably knew it. Better to cut and run while he still could. He hurried through the door and paused to listen. "V! Where are you?"

From somewhere in front of him, an inhuman shriek of terror sounded, and abruptly cut off.

Amber tore past, taking off across the street toward a building under construction. "Come on!"

Jason put on a jet of speed to catch up with her. The shriek had sounded like a man, not a woman. Had Verity caught the mage? Had she killed him? "Where'd they—"

"There!" Amber gripped his arm and pointed.

He stopped, a chill running through him. He recognized his sister's familiar figure up ahead, but she wasn't moving. Instead she stood still, appearing to be looking at something in front of her that Jason couldn't see.

"Something's wrong," Amber said. "I smell blood, and fear."

Jason ran up next to Verity and grabbed her shoulders. She was shaking. "V! What's going on? Where's the mage?"

In answer, she pointed in front of her. Her breath came hard and fast, but she said nothing.

Jason looked where she was pointing, but couldn't see anything but the concrete wall of an incomplete building. There was no sign of the mage. "Did you find him? Did you—"

Amber arrived, stopping on the other side of Verity. "Oh, fuck…" she breathed.

"What?" Jason demanded. "What happened?"

She too pointed, but not at the middle of the wall as Verity had, but rather at the bottom. Jason wrenched a flashlight from his pocket and shined it at the area.

A narrow puddle of blood seeped from beneath it.

He still didn't get it. "What's going on?" If the guy had run into the wall, there should be blood up higher, but aside from what he saw on the ground, the concrete was pristine. "Where is he?"

Amber took hold of Verity's shoulder. "He tried to go through, didn't he?" she said softly.

She nodded, making no effort to shake off either Jason's or Amber's hands. "I was catching up with him, so he tried to go through the wall." Her voice was a monotone, steady but clearly disturbed. "I don't think he realized it was as thick as it was."

Only then did Jason get it. "Oh, fuck…" he whispered. He rounded the corner and hurried through an open doorway several feet down, expecting to see the mage's body hanging half-in, half-out in some kind of grotesque state, but he didn't. He narrowed his eyes as Amber came around to join him, leading Verity by the hand. "This doesn't make sense, though—this wall isn't thick enough for him to be stuck inside."

"I don't think he is," Verity said. She still sounded shaky, but stronger now. "I think he tried to phase through, but either lost his nerve halfway in or he was just too tired to make it. It probably took a lot of energy to do that. I think his body must have just...dissipated."

Jason gripped her arm. "It wasn't your fault, V."

"I know that." She pulled herself up and let out a long breath. "I know. He did it before I could stop him. But still..."

"Yeah." Amber regarded the wall for a moment. "That's a shitty way to die, any way you look at it. And all over a truck full of stuff." She glanced back toward the warehouse across the street. "Come on. We need to call the cops on those other guys. Maybe if they're lucky they'll get the fence too."

"Don't think so," Jason said. He indicated a large panel truck coming down the side street on the warehouse's other side. It slowed for a moment, then took off at a high rate of speed in the opposite direction.

"Ah, well." Amber didn't seem bothered. "I did my job. I got the stuff back, and that guy won't be messing with anybody again. Sucks that it had to go down that way, but..." She trailed off and shrugged. "Anyway, thanks again—both of you. I couldn't have done that without your help."

"Yeah...no problem," Verity said.

"You gonna be okay?"

"Yeah. I'll be fine." She gave a faint smile. "You call the cops. I'll go bring the car around so I can drop you off and you two can be alone."

"V…" Jason glared at her.

"Hey, none of my business. But I do want to get out of here. I still have cleaning to finish up tomorrow." Without giving either of them a chance to reply, she jogged off toward where she'd parked the SUV.

Jason exchanged glances with Amber, feeling suddenly awkward. "Uh…Yeah. So, we should go call this in. Probably not from our cells, either. I saw a pay phone just up the street. We can call anonymously."

"Better that way," she agreed. "And I need to call Darryl and let him know his stuff's safe. And then head back home and deal with Hank."

"You…want me to come with you? I still owe you that dinner."

She leaned in and brushed a quick kiss across his cheek. "I haven't forgotten—but it'll have to be another time. I need to leave for home right away so I can grab Hank before he hears anything and takes off." She flashed a lopsided smile. "Rain check? You ever get back my way?"

"I'll make a point of it." A pause, and then, "Sorry about Hank."

She waved him off. "It happens. Not too happy that I missed that part of him, but maybe I wasn't looking for it, you know?"

"Yeah. I get that." He wanted to say something else, but suddenly his tongue felt like it weighed ten pounds and his brain wasn't helping. Finally, he settled for, "Anyway, that's a definite on the rain check. I'll give you a call, okay?"

"I'll be waiting." The smile she gave him this time wasn't lopsided, but it *was* still amused. "Don't take too long, though."

| CHAPTER TWENTY-SEVEN

B Y THE TIME Stone stopped by Stefan Kolinsky's shop the following day, he'd come no closer to unraveling the mystery of the vanishing note.

He'd pulled out his notebook immediately after the text had disappeared, trying to reproduce as much of it as he could remember before the details faded from his memory. He thought he'd done a fairly good job of re-creating the message, though he had less success at capturing any of the nuances of the handwriting. By the time he thought to examine the envelope a few seconds later, the text there had faded as well.

Somebody was definitely trying to send him a message, but they didn't want to give him any chance of figuring out who it was.

He spent the remainder of Sunday going over all his notes again, beginning with the newspaper clipping about the Devil's Creek incident and ending with the now-blank note-card. To help him visualize the timeline, he taped them to the whiteboard in his downstairs library, scrawling notes beneath each section. He hadn't been completely convinced the two events were related before, but now he had more certainty about it. Even though the pair of rifts didn't have many

R. L. KING

similarities in appearance, they did share two important traits: both of them were shedding power into this dimension from somewhere else, and both existed on or near ley line confluences.

To his frustration, though, the facts he *didn't* know far outnumbered those he did. Had these things appeared naturally, or had someone created or summoned them? Why was the strange figure in Pennsylvania trying to conceal one with an illusion? Who was the figure working for, and why didn't he want Stone investigating further? What "dire consequences" might occur if he did? What, in this context, was a 'scion' and why did the figure call him one? And why had the figure killed Clyde?

A cold thought gripped him: if the thing was killing any mundanes who knew about the rifts, did that mean Mitch and Cathy Kirkson were in danger, or already dead? He made a note on his board to check that out—he didn't want to contact them directly again, but perhaps he could ask Jason to have Gina search recent obituaries in area papers.

As usual when Kolinsky hadn't left a note behind his wards indicating he was away on one of his acquisition trips, the black mage was in his shop. He sat at his usual spot at his roll-top desk, a large, thick tome open in front of him. "Good afternoon, Alastair," he said without turning.

It struck Stone again, as if often did, to wonder why Kolinsky spent so much time in his shop. In the ten years he'd known the man, he had literally never seen a customer in it; in fact, the only other living soul he'd ever observed there had been Zack Beeler, the night the thief had tried breaking in. Other than that, the place had remained almost unchanged in all that time, with the exception of the ever-revolving collection of new artifacts he often found Kolinsky examining at his desk or his worktable.

"Don't you ever get bored hanging about in here by yourself, Stefan?" Stone closed the door behind him and glanced around, but didn't see anything new other than the book. The humanoid figure the black mage had been examining last time Stone had visited was gone now.

"Boredom is the burden of the weak-minded," Kolinsky said. He swung his chair around and regarded Stone with his usual calm expression.

From anyone else, it would have been an insult—especially anyone who knew how much Stone himself loathed forced mental idleness. From Kolinsky it was...just Kolinsky. "I could argue with you about that, I suppose, but I won't waste both our time."

"A wise choice. How can I be of assistance?"

"I've discovered some new developments regarding that strange case I was telling you about last time I spoke, and I was hoping you might have some new insights. You *haven't* got anything new about what I've already told you, do you?"

"I am afraid not."

Stone didn't take the offered chair, but instead paced around the shop. "Well, I've got some new data for you. It's happened again, and this time I'm even more concerned about it."

Still pacing, he told Kolinsky the whole story of the events in Pennsylvania. He left nothing out, but paused before he got to the part about the strange figure in the forest. "Does that sound like anything you might be familiar with?"

Kolinsky thought about it. "It does seem related to the previous event you described. Are you certain the two...rifts, for lack of a better word…were not emitting the same sort of energy?"

"Positive." Stone pulled out his notebook and rattled off a few figures. "Similar, yes, in that they were definitely both putting out energy of *some* kind. If I had to guess, I'd say it was coming from two different dimensional spaces. But at least with the second one, when I tried to toss something through it, it passed directly through while remaining in our space. So it wasn't a gateway. More like a…wound, bleeding energy into our world."

He sighed, studying the spines on a bookshelf without processing them. "But I haven't told you the rest yet. Remember the strange figure I mentioned, the one I saw outside the door when the pizza deliveryman arrived?"

"Of course."

"Well…he—or it, or whatever—showed up again. It gave me a warning."

"What sort of warning?" Something about Kolinsky's posture subtly changed as he leaned ever so slightly forward in his chair.

"It told me to leave the matter alone. That I could cause untold harm if I continued on my current path." He consulted his notebook again, reading the being's words exactly as he'd written them down.

Kolinsky's calm gaze went still. "You say it referred to you as 'scion'?"

"Yes. Do you know what the hell it was talking about? I'm guessing it's got something to do with my family, but how would this thing know about that?"

The black mage returned to his relaxed, attentive posture. "That is possible," he said. "Lineage is, of course, quite important in the magical world."

Stone let out a louder sigh and resumed his pacing. "None of this is making a bloody bit of sense, Stefan. This thing was *hiding* the rift with an illusion. Not a powerful one, but it didn't need to be. If I hadn't known it was there, I'd never have found it. And it killed Clyde. Why would it do that? Was it because he knew the location of the rift? And if so, why not kill me too? Why did it say it couldn't stop me?"

"Alastair. Please—sit down."

"I can't. I've got too much energy to sit down. I need to get to the bottom of this, and I haven't got any idea how, short of traveling around to every ley line confluence in the country and hunting for more of these things. That's hardly practical, even if I took a year-long sabbatical." Again, he sighed. "There's one more part I haven't told you yet. Maybe the most important part of all."

"Oh?"

He pulled the blank card in its envelope from his inner coat pocket and tossed them on Kolinsky's desk. "Yesterday, I got this. It was in my mailbox."

Brow furrowing slightly, Kolinsky picked up the envelope. He examined it for a moment, then glanced up at Stone. "May I?"

"Of course."

With care, he plucked the card from the envelope and examined it with the same level of care. "I am not certain I understand, Alastair. Both the card and the envelope are blank."

Stone wasn't sure whether he was glad Kolinsky hadn't found any traces he'd missed, or disappointed. "They weren't yesterday. Well, they looked blank until I switched to magical sight, but I'm sure you've already done that."

"I have. And still they appear blank."

"The envelope had my name on it. The message, which revealed itself only to magical sight, remained for only a few seconds—long enough for me to read it—and then faded. I wrote it down as quickly as I could. I'm reasonably confident I got the phrasing right, but I couldn't reproduce the handwriting. It was in green ink, by the way, if that's relevant." He opened his notebook to the page where he'd written the message and passed it to Kolinsky.

This time, the black mage stared at the message for more than five minutes in silence. Stone was tempted several times to say something, to ask him if it meant anything to him, but he didn't. Instead, he remained still, watching closely with magical sight.

Kolinsky's aura didn't budge. The only indication of his focus was a slight tightening of his hand on the notebook, and an even slighter tensing of his posture. Finally, he closed the notebook and handed it back.

"Well?" Stone demanded. "You looked at it long enough. Have you got anything for me? I'm not kidding, Stefan—I'm stumped this time. This person claims to be 'a concerned party,' but what are they concerned about? It sounds like they're afraid I'll cause some sort of calamity if I continue my investigation, but I don't believe that for a second. I think they're trying to protect their own hide, and whatever vile little experiments they're up to."

Still, Kolinsky didn't reply. He was gazing into the middle distance now, almost as if he were seeing something that wasn't there. Either that, or he was deep in thought.

"Stefan?"

Kolinsky let out a long, slow breath. "Alastair…this matter is not something with which I can assist you."

Stone narrowed his eyes. "What are you talking about? Do you know something?"

He didn't answer.

"You *do* know something, don't you?" He rubbed his forehead, shoving his hair up into spikes. "Right. Sorry. Got a bit caught up in things and forgot about the protocols. What do you want in exchange for the information? You've got me where you want me, Stefan, and I don't mind letting you know it. So name your price."

Kolinsky's expression was oddly expressionless. "There is no price, Alastair. I cannot help you with this matter."

"What do you mean, you can't help me? Are you saying you don't know the answer, or you do know it and won't give it to me?" He whirled and his pacing turned to stalking around like a cat in a cage. "I don't think you get it: I don't make offers like this very often. I want the answer to this, and I'm willing to meet your price to get it. I know you were interested in that old multi-volume set Desmond had on ancient black magic techniques. You tell me what's going on with these things and it's yours. Not just access—I'll pop over there and bring it back to you tomorrow."

Kolinsky bowed his head.

"Come *on,* Stefan! What's wrong with you? I've never seen you turn down an offer like that before. But—all right, then, if you don't like that one, name your own." Somewhere deep inside Stone's mind, a part of him realized the danger of what he was saying. He was acting like a rube who'd set his sights on some shiny bauble, and was ready to give up far more than it was worth to get it. That was not a tactic you ever wanted to take with Stefan Kolinsky—the man ate desperation for lunch. But as he stood there, his gaze fixed on his friend, something likewise told him Kolinsky had the answers he sought—if only he could find the key to unlock them.

"I am sorry, Alastair."

To his credit, Kolinsky almost—*almost*—looked like he *was* sorry. A muscle in his jaw twitched, and his long, elegant fingers tightened around the fine fountain pen he held. But other than that, he didn't move.

"Bloody hell." Stone felt sudden anger rising, and fought to contain it. "How long have we been associates? How many things have we helped each other with over the years? This isn't the time to start hoarding information like some kind of gods-damned dragon on a pile of gold. This thing is *killing* people, and these rifts are leaking magical energy into our world. Altering mundanes. Even possibly mucking with the way the portals work. None of that can be good. Somebody's got to get to the bottom of it and stop it. If you've got information that can help with that and you're keeping it to yourself—why would you do that?"

Still, Kolinsky said nothing.

Stone glared at him. This was it, then. This was real. Kolinsky wasn't going to help him. For any price, it appeared. Why, after all these years of being a dispassionate information broker, would he suddenly refuse to part with a bit of data?

A chilling thought gripped him, bringing with it sudden dread.

He stopped his pacing, slowly turning to face Kolinsky as the black mage remained seated at his desk. "Stefan...are you *involved* with this situation somehow? Is that why you won't tell me anything?"

Silence.

The chill running down his back intensified. "Dear gods, you *are*. You're...are you *causing* these odd rifts somehow? Or someone you're connected with?"

He didn't expect an answer, so he was surprised when Kolinsky said softly, "No."

"What?"

"I am not responsible, nor is anyone I am associated with."

"Well, *what* then?" The question came out as an explosive demand. Stone's voice shook with anger, but did nothing to stop it. "What the *hell* is going on with you, Stefan?"

Slowly, very slowly, Kolinsky turned his chair around. His face was as impassive as ever, but his obsidian-chip eyes held uncharacteristic tension. "Alastair...as you have pointed out, we have been associates for many years. I value our relationship, and my word is of paramount importance to me. All I can say is to repeat: I cannot help you with this matter. What I *can* do, however, is offer you a bit of advice."

"Advice?" Stone's anger simmered, threatening to bubble up again. "What kind of advice?"

He met Stone's gaze, and his face could have been carved from granite for all the expression it showed. "I know you are a curious man—in fact, I am well aware that curiosity is both your defining trait and potentially your undoing. But in this case—you would do well to walk away."

Stone could not believe what he was hearing. "Walk *away*? You're honestly suggesting I—what—just forget about the whole thing? Stop investigating why someone is hiding dangerous dimensional rifts? Why they're killing people or mucking with their minds to prevent them from revealing their locations? You want me to put it out of my mind like yesterday's news and go back to teaching mundanes about the Salem Witch Trials?" His voice rose at the end until he was nearly shouting.

"You have told me about your son, and his need for training. Perhaps you might focus your energy on him."

"Don't you *dare* tell me how to handle my son, Stefan," Stone snarled. Once again in the back of his mind, warning klaxons were going off: *Danger! Danger! Hazardous area ahead! Turn back!* But he ignored them as definitively as if he'd plowed through a physical barrier with a fleet of tanks. "This isn't about Ian. This is about *you*."

Kolinsky did not reply.

Stone spun away, turning so the black mage couldn't see his face, even though he was sure his aura was in turmoil. His heart pounded, adrenaline coursing through him and fueling his growing anger and confusion. But when he spoke again, his tone was even and composed.

"Stefan…I'm going to say it one more time: if you know something about this situation—if you want me to walk away from it and forget what I know—then you've got to tell me *why*. You should know me that well by now. You should know how absurd it is to expect I'll back off because of some vague warning with nothing to back it up. I've already been threatened by one other person—assuming it wasn't you all along—and that's going to do exactly bugger-all to dissuade me from looking into this. So unless you want me to toss your advice in the bin where it belongs along with that card there, give me a *reason*."

For a second—only a second—something smoldered in Kolinsky's black eyes. His jaw tightened, his posture tensed, and for a brief moment Stone wondered if he'd finally pushed too far and goaded the black mage to attack him. If that happened, he could be in trouble: even after Calanar, Kolinsky was one of the few mages left whom Stone doubted he could take in a magical battle.

Kolinsky didn't attack, though. He drew a deep breath, another, and then the tightness in his shoulders relaxed and whatever had appeared in his eyes receded. He leaned back in his chair and steepled his fingers, continuing to regard Stone with his usual hawk-like, probing gaze. "You must do as you will, Alastair. My advice is offered to you as a valued associate...and if I may dare say it, a friend. If you choose not to heed it, I will be unable to involve myself in what might follow."

"In what might follow." Stone spoke in a monotone, all the anger drained from his voice. "But you won't tell me what that is."

Kolinsky said nothing.

Stone let his breath out. "Fine. You do what you have to do, Stefan. I'd have thought by now we could be straight with each other, but apparently your little secrets are more important to you. That's all right." He regarded the black mage for another moment, then turned and walked away. "I hope this is worth it to you. Because I'm not stopping. In fact, now that I'm certain something *is* going on and somebody of your power level has his fingers in the middle of it, I'm planning to step up my efforts to get to the bottom of it."

He stopped at the door without turning back. "Want to stop me now? Wipe my memory? Kill me?" He spread his hands and remained facing away from Kolinsky. "Now's your chance. Have a go, if that's what you want."

He waited, tense and ready, but no attack came. Once again, Kolinsky said nothing.

"Right, then. Goodbye, Stefan."

As he closed the door softly behind him, left the shop, and trudged back to his car, Stone didn't look back. He did, however, wonder if he'd just made a big mistake—or a dangerous enemy.

| CHAPTER TWENTY-EIGHT

STONE ALMOST WISHED he had a class to teach on Monday afternoon; it might have done something to distract him from his growing unsettled thoughts.

When he'd gone to Kolinsky's shop, as he'd done dozens of times before over the years, he'd expected at best to get some insight into the situation with the rifts, and at worst for the black mage to tell him he hadn't come up with anything but would keep looking. He'd never in his worst nightmares expected that Kolinsky might be *part* of the problem.

No, that wasn't fair. Assuming his friend (is *he still my friend?*) had not lied to him, it sounded as if he knew what was going on but wasn't actively involved with it. Stone wasn't even sure how that could work: how could he know about interdimensional rifts popping up at random ley line confluences and not want to do something about them, or at the very least study them? Kolinsky was the only person Stone knew whose curiosity exceeded his own. If some mystery existed, especially one that pertained to magic, the black mage wouldn't stop until he'd ferreted out every corner of its secrets. Whether he did that on his own or by trading information, items, and data with other people, his ultimate aim had always been to accumulate as much magical lore as he could manage. And, given his wealth and power level, that was undoubtedly a lot of lore.

Stone stopped at University Perk, his old favorite coffee shop when he'd lived at the Palo Alto house, and pondered his next move over a cup of industrial-grade brew. Now two different people had warned him off his investigations. But why? What could Kolinsky and this unknown being stand to gain from allowing these rifts to exist? Hell, what did Kolinsky and this being even have in common? He didn't have enough data to even make a guess at this, since he'd seen the thing in Pennsylvania as barely more than a human-shaped glow of energy. He hadn't spotted it in Iowa—true, he hadn't been looking, but it hadn't hidden itself from him when it had killed Clyde. He couldn't even be sure the creature that had killed Clyde was the same one that had left the note in his mailbox.

He sighed in frustration. Kolinsky had been his best hope of gaining more information, a potential ally in the kind of search both of them relished. Without the black mage's help, he didn't know where else to turn. Eddie and Ward were already searching through the archives in England trying to find out more. His students' extra-credit efforts hadn't turned up any other credible leads, nor had Jason's computer whiz. Verity was busy with her move, Scuro, and her friends in San Francisco, and even if she wasn't, it was unlikely she could locate anything that he couldn't find faster. She didn't have those kinds of resources. Same with Ian, who was probably drunk off his arse at a party somewhere.

On a whim, he pulled out his phone and punched the private number for Nakamura, Trevor Harrison's assistant at the Obsidian in Las Vegas. It was unlikely to get him anywhere, but he had to try.

"Hello, Dr. Stone." Nakamura's brisk voice came on the line after the first ring. "How are you?"

"I'm...confused," Stone told him. "I don't suppose there's any chance Mr. Harrison is around? Or...reachable?"

"I'm sorry, Dr. Stone. He hadn't been back here in quite some time. And as you know, I have no way to contact him directly."

That was what Stone had expected, but he still felt a twinge of frustrated despair at Nakamura's words. "Damn. I suppose I shouldn't be surprised, though. But in any case—if he does pop in any time soon, could you give him a message for me?"

"Of course."

Stone considered his words, and how much he wanted to reveal to Nakamura. Finally he decided there was no point in keeping secrets. Harrison trusted the man, and Harrison didn't trust many people. "Tell him...something very odd's going on with random rifts opening to other dimensional spaces, and I think there's some kind of high-level conspiracy to keep anyone from finding out about them. I've been warned off pursuing an investigation, but no one will tell me *why* I should give it up."

Nakamura chuckled. "So, naturally, you're proceeding with it, full speed ahead."

"Well, yes." Stone chuckled too. "You know me too well, Mr. Nakamura—or else Mr. Harrison's told you about me. But in any case, he'll want to know about this, I think. Please ask him to contact me when he gets the message."

"I will do that, Dr. Stone. But once again, I can't in any way predict when he might return."

"Not a problem. Better than nothing, I guess. Ta."

He put the phone away and sighed. Well, that was that. Harrison was either on Calanar, or off traveling somewhere else, but either way he was out of communication. Stone supposed if he were truly desperate for answers he could do the ritual that would take him back to Calanar personally, but even as tantalizing as his current puzzle was, he wasn't ready to take that step yet. Too many variables, and besides, he had no guarantee he'd even find Harrison if he did it—or that the man could get any further with the problem than he could. It was worth asking if he happened to be around, but not worth a chancy interdimensional jaunt yet, especially with the portals acting up.

So here he was, back at square one, out of reasonable options. For all his bold words to Kolinsky about continuing his investigations regardless of dire warnings, he found himself with nowhere else to go.

He drained his coffee cup, smacked it down on the table in frustration, and tossed a five-dollar bill next to it for a tip, then stalked out of the shop. Perhaps he'd study his ley-line map again and see if he could predict any other possible locations for rifts to appear. It wasn't very scientific, but it was all he had.

He'd parked the BMW in front of the Dragon Garden, his go-to Chinese takeaway spot when he didn't want to think about eating. He hadn't had lunch yet, and briefly contemplated picking something up to take home, but as usual when he was focusing on a problem, his appetite for anything but coffee and alcohol had deserted him. As he passed the restaurant, however, another thought came to him suddenly.

He'd almost forgotten about her because she'd been away from the area for so long, but he did have one other associate with vast knowledge about the magical world. He hadn't even checked in to see if Madame Huan had returned from her latest trip abroad—perhaps she had, and if so, she might have some ideas. If nothing else, she was always an excellent sounding board for him, listening patiently and offering insightful comments as he rambled on about whatever magical puzzle currently troubled him.

Huan's Antiquities, Madame Huan's combination junk shop and antique store, looked much the same as it always did—a neat little place on a tiny downtown Palo Alto street, sandwiched between a noodle shop and a clothing store catering to the kind of elderly woman who wanted to relive the styles of her youth. It was the sort of place you wouldn't even notice if you weren't looking for it, but even though it was often closed, it never looked abandoned or shabby. In a way, it was similar to Kolinsky's own East Palo Alto establishment, except that while Stefan's place looked like a good place for an unwary person to blunder into and disappear, Huan's Antiquities had a welcoming air.

Stone parked down the street and hesitated. This was foolish. Of course she wouldn't be at the shop—she was never there these days. He still suspected she maintained a private portal in the back; he'd never seen it and she'd never mentioned it, but it could explain how she managed to move so easily between her three shops (that he knew of) here, in London, and somewhere in China.

To his surprise, the *By Appointment Only* sign wasn't present, and the door opened for him with a pleasant tinkle of an unseen bell. Even more surprisingly, the first thing he saw was a customer: a teenage boy rummaging through one of the shelves that brimmed with the familiar eclectic assortment of mismatched items. The boy glanced up at Stone as he entered, then returned to his efforts.

"Good afternoon! May I help you?"

Stone snapped his gaze up at the unfamiliar voice, and he tensed in surprise. Standing behind the cluttered counter was a pleasant-faced Asian woman—but it wasn't Madame Huan. He'd never seen this woman before.

"Er—I was looking for Madame Huan. Is she here?" Unspoken in his tone was, *who are you?*

She seemed to pick up on this, though she didn't answer it. Instead, she smiled ruefully. "I'm terribly sorry, sir, but she's not here. She was here earlier today, but she's been called away on urgent business. Is there something I can help you find, perhaps?"

"I didn't know she had any other help here." Stone glanced around; the place looked no different than he remembered it, with its rows of dusty, overstuffed shelves and collection of wares that appeared to have been sorted by someone with a deep aversion to organization. It was one of the hallmarks of the shop, and Stone was convinced it amused Madame Huan to keep it so. For those in the know, the good stuff was stored—in a much more structured fashion—in the back, but nobody got back there without Madame Huan's permission.

The woman chuckled, but didn't reply directly. "So, how may I help you today? Are you looking for something in particular?"

You have no idea, he thought. "Well—yes. Madame Huan. Do you know when she'll be back?"

"I'm sorry, sir, but I don't. I got the impression she might be away for some time, actually."

Well. That was bloody inconvenient. Stone sighed, annoyed with himself. If he hadn't stopped for coffee, and thought of coming here straight away after he left Kolinsky's shop, he might not have missed her. "Damn," he murmured. "All right. Thanks. Have you got a way to contact her?"

"I can pass a message along when she checks in. I'm afraid I can't give you her contact information directly, though."

"Fine." It was one of the problem with old, powerful mages—they were difficult to contact using standard, modern means. Unlike Kolinsky, Madame Huan didn't eschew the telephone, but she didn't have a mobile, either—or at least if she did, she'd never told him about it. "Please tell her Alastair Stone would like to talk with her, and it's rather urgent. She has my number."

The woman wrote down the message, then flashed him another kindly smile. "Done, sir. I'll pass the information along as soon as I can."

"Thank you." Stone paused a moment, appearing to look at something on the shelves behind her, but actually switching to magical sight. The woman's aura was a clear, calm green, and he saw no duplicity or uneasiness in it. He sighed and headed back down one of the narrow aisles toward the door. Another avenue of investigation blocked.

As he passed the boy, who had crouched and was now examining an ancient bowling bag full of broken toys, the kid looked up at him. "You looking for the other lady who was here?"

Stone stopped. He glanced back over his shoulder, but the shop assistant had moved off down another row of shelves. "I am, yes."

"She was literally just here. Like fifteen minutes before you got here. Bad luck, you missing her like that."

"Indeed?" Stone crouched next to him, studying an old, elaborate world globe nestled next to a shaggy brown teddy bear.

"Yeah. Some guy came in and talked to her, and then both of them left through the back. The guy seemed…" He struggled for the word. "Not upset or anything, but like he had something really important on his mind."

"Is that right?" Stone checked again, but the assistant was still nowhere to be seen. "What did this man look like?"

The boy shrugged. "Not like the usual kind of guy you'd see in a place like this. Tall, dark hair, old-fashioned black suit. I didn't get a good look at him, sorry." He indicated the shelves with a wave. "I'm looking for cool stuff to use in a video I'm making. That's why I've been poking around in here so long. This place is awesome."

Stone went still. "Old-fashioned black suit? Did you hear him speak?"

"Yeah, just for a couple seconds. He had some kinda accent. Like Russian, maybe."

Bloody hell.

Stone rose to stand. "Thank you. I'm sure I'll find her—we're old friends. I hope you find what you're looking for."

"Thanks, dude. Hope you find your friend!" The boy was already focused back on his search, putting the bowling bag aside and picking up a wig form.

Stone got out of there without speaking to the shop assistant, and he didn't stop until he was back in his car.

What in the *hell* was going on? Stefan Kolinsky had been here—had apparently come here with some haste after their conversation—and now Madame Huan had disappeared less than fifteen minutes ago following his visit?

Stone gripped the steering wheel, taking a couple of deep breaths.

If he didn't know better—and he *didn't* know better— he'd swear that not only had Kolinsky come to warn Madame Huan that he might be looking for her, but she'd fled her shop to avoid talking to him.

"Why would he do that…?" Stone murmured.

And worse yet, did that imply what he was fairly sure now it did: that not only did Kolinsky have some knowledge of what was going on with the rifts, but Madame Huan did as well, and neither of them wanted Stone to find out what they knew?

He slammed his fist on the wheel with a growl. Why were his two most trusted sources of magical information avoiding him, and why did it seem they wanted these strange rifts to go uninvestigated—at least by him?

As hard as he tried to fit this new information into a framework, it didn't make sense. Sure, Kolinsky had always hoarded information and been immensely secretive about what he revealed, but in the ten years of their association he'd never outright refused to share something. There had always been a price, and sometimes that price was higher than Stone was willing to pay, but the whole thing had always been a business transaction.

But Madame Huan—her absence troubled him even more. She hadn't been around as much as Kolinsky over the last couple of years, usually away on some artifact-hunting expedition on the other side of the world, but when she *was* around, she'd never been reluctant to talk to him. He'd known the kindly mage since his apprentice days, and visiting her had always been a pleasant, peaceful experience—also usually fruitful, when he was looking for information about something.

In fact, he'd always had the impression that while Kolinsky and Madame Huan respected each other, they were hardly the best of friends. That wasn't surprising: Kolinsky never apologized for his black magic, and Stone had never met a more benevolent white mage than Madame Huan. Even though she had been the one to introduce Stone to Kolinsky shortly after he moved to the Bay Area, he remembered she'd done it with some reluctance, cautioning him to remain on his guard around the man at all times.

Hardly the mark of a pair who'd casually pop in and out of each other's shops—which meant there had to be some urgency around Kolinsky's heads-up to Madame Huan.

A sudden, chilling thought gripped Stone. He fired up the BMW and drove as quickly as he could get away with back to East Palo Alto, mentally cursing every other car on the road to get out of his way. He parked directly in front of Kolinsky's shop and ran to the door, but he already knew what he'd find when he got there.

The door was locked, and the familiar sign behind the wards indicated that Kolinsky was away, and would be for the foreseeable future.

"Bugger!" Stone yelled, slamming his fist on the wall so hard it hurt. "Gods *damn* you, Stefan, what are you up to?"

Two young men walking by on the street glanced at him nervously and picked up their pace to get past him.

Stone rubbed his face, shoving his hair up, and considered his options. He knew from past experience that if Kolinsky didn't want to be found, he had no option there. Even though he knew where the black mage's home (or one of them, anyway) was, he likewise knew that if Kolinsky was avoiding him, he wouldn't respond there either.

He stalked back to the car, slammed the door shut behind him, and let his breath out.

What *now*?

You could just give it up, you know, said a little voice inside his head.

Don't be ridiculous. Something's going on, and I'm going to find out what it is.

Yes, but two powerful people you trust are giving you a fairly good hint that you should stay away from it. Maybe they know something you don't?

So why don't they just tell *me then? If they've got a good reason I should stay away from this, all they'd have to do is share it with me.*

Would that stop you?

He didn't answer right away. Would it?

If rifts were opening in random locations, causing trouble with the local mundane population, why would anyone think it was a good thing to simply leave them to it?

Another chill went through him.

Kolinsky and Madame Huan were both powerful mages—certainly more powerful than he'd been pre-Calanar, and probably still more so now. He was sure they were both considerably older than he was, and had a lot more experience with magical phenomena. He didn't doubt for an instant that both of them had access to resources he wasn't even aware of. Both of them had always seemed almost to operate on another plane of power than even the most potent mages Stone had met—people like William Desmond and possibly even Trevor Harrison.

What if they simply didn't *care* how the rifts affected mundanes?

Stone sighed. He could believe that about Kolinsky, but not about Madame Huan. If the two of them were conspiring to keep this information from him, there had to be another reason.

If he was going to find out what it was without their help, he'd need to change his approach.

He pulled out his phone and punched Verity's number. "Are you busy?" he asked when she picked up.

"Uh—no, not really. Just doing some last-minute packing and cleanup before this weekend. What's going on?"

"Will you come by the house this evening? I have a dilemma, and I need a sounding board. Perhaps the fact that half the time I can't follow your thought processes will help in this situation."

"Doc, you give the nicest invitations." He could hear the wry smile in her voice. "Yeah, sure. See you then."

| CHAPTER TWENTY-NINE

VERITY'S EYES NARROWED in concern when he opened the door to her later that evening. "You don't look so good. Are you okay?"

"I...don't know." He trudged back inside, leading her to the living room. Raider perched on the sofa, watching both of them warily. "Have you eaten? I could have something delivered if you like, or I've got—"

"No, it's okay, I'm good. Doc, what's wrong?" She steered him to the sofa. "You look like something's really bothering you. What's this dilemma you mentioned on the phone?"

Stone sighed. He'd been trying ever since he got home to quiet his mind enough to work through the problem on his own, to try to see some aspect of it he'd missed before, but all he'd succeeded in doing was stressing himself out even more. Sometimes, when faced with a problem he couldn't solve, his mind seized up and refused to function properly, leaving him with no other choice than to put the matter aside for a while and hope the diversion was sufficient to break the barrier. He'd gone for a run around Encantada earlier, but it hadn't helped.

"Is it still the business with the rifts?"

"Yes. There's been a new development, just today, and I've no idea what to think about it." He raised his hand and levitated a bottle of scotch and two glasses to the table from the liquor cabinet, poured, and took a healthy swallow. "I went to see Stefan, hoping he might have some insight."

"And did he?"

"Yes…and no."

"What's that mean?"

Wearily, he told her about his conversation with Kolinsky. By the time he was done, his glass was empty. Raider sniffed at it, and he contemplated pouring another.

She stared at him. "So you think he knows what's going on, but he won't tell you?"

"Yes. And I can't work out why. I essentially offered him anything I could provide, and he still refused. That's not at all like him. And it gets worse." He did pour another glass then, and told her about his trip to Madame Huan's place.

"Wait." She still hadn't touched her glass. "So you're saying you think Stefan went to Madame Huan's and—what—*warned* her you were coming, so she could get out of there before you could ask her about this?"

"That's exactly what I think, as absurd as it sounds."

"But why would he do that? It sounds like both of them know what's going on, and for whatever reason they don't want to tell you."

"And now you see my dilemma. Not only am I at an impasse trying to locate any more of these rifts so I can—I don't know *what* the hell I should do about them, to be honest— now two of my most reliable sources of information about the magical world seem to be conspiring to keep me in the dark." He narrowed his eyes, and felt himself tense. "And I don't like it. Not one bit."

"So what will you do about it? It sounds like you can't hunt down either one of them, right?"

"Right. If they don't want to be found, they could be anywhere. Hell, Madame Huan could have gone back to China to get away from me, if she's trying."

"What about Mr. Harrison?"

"He's not available either. I called Nakamura today and asked, but he hasn't seen him for a long time."

"Do you think *he's* avoiding you too?"

Stone hadn't thought about that. "Hmm...possibly, but he's always difficult to get hold of. This isn't anything new for him. I'm inclined to think not unless some new development pops up."

She stroked Raider, who was sitting on her as she leaned back. "So it sounds like your two angles here are either to find someone who knows what's going on and will tell you, or else tracking down more of these rifts so you can study them, right?"

"Yes, those do seem to be the most logical next steps."

"And you don't know any other mages who might know, right?"

"No. I've already got Eddie and Ward hunting through the archives at Caventhorne and the London library looking for any references to odd magical anomalies, but so far they've come up with nothing."

She got up, gently evicting Raider from her lap, and paced the room, staring out the window into the darkened front yard. For a long time she said nothing, but then she turned back to him with a contemplative look.

He sat up straighter. "Have you got something?"

"Probably not. But I'm trying to think about why Stefan and Madame Huan would even *know* about stuff like this. You said they're both really old, right?"

"To be honest, I've no idea. I get the distinct impression they've been around for some time—Madame Huan doesn't look a day older than she did when I was an apprentice, for example, and I don't think Stefan's aged in the ten years I've known him—but I've got no proof of that."

She nodded, as if distracted. "Let's go with that for a minute. If they *are* really old and they know about magic, could it mean they know about these rift things because they've seen them before?"

Stone considered. It was a line of reasoning he hadn't examined. "I suppose it's possible. You're suggesting these rifts might have opened up previously?"

"Who knows? I'm just free-associating, hoping something will lead you somewhere you haven't been before." She turned back to the window. "But let's keep going with that. If these things have been around before, and those two know about them—then maybe others did too. Maybe somebody noticed them if this has happened before."

"Possible," Stone said again. "But I don't see where you're going with this."

"Me neither, not entirely. But I'm thinking if you haven't got any chance of finding Stefan or Madame Huan to talk to and you don't know any other mages as old as they are, maybe hunting through old archives *is* the way to go."

He sighed. "But I told you—we're already doing that. I spent several hours going through the library at my place, and Eddie and Ward haven't turned up anything in any of their or Desmond's reference books yet."

She plopped back down on the sofa next to him with an even louder sigh. "Yeah…that's what you said. I know. And I know how good Eddie is at finding stuff like that. If it was in one of those books, then—" She stopped, going stiff. "Wait!"

"What?"

"Well…what if he can't find it in books because it *isn't* in a book?"

"I don't follow."

"You said these rifts were popping up in random places, right? Near ley line convergences?"

"Yes…"

"What if the information's not in a book, but on a map somewhere?"

"I've already checked all my ley line maps, but I haven't found anything unusual."

"No, that's not what I mean." She gripped his arm. "Have you got any really old maps at your place or Caventhorne? Maybe if this has happened before—especially if it happens in specific spots—somebody might have marked the locations on one of them."

Stone stared at her in amazement, then spun and took her by the shoulders. "Verity! You're brilliant! That's a brilliant idea. I hadn't even thought to check other maps, after I didn't turn up anything on my usual ley line ones." He kissed her. "Oh, bloody hell, I need to get back home. I've got loads of old maps at the house, and I know there are more at Caventhorne and in the library."

She grinned. "See, that's why you keep me around, Doc."

"Indeed it is. The only reason, in fact."

"Yeah, I always thought so. You're not leaving now, are you? It's like three in the morning in England."

He wanted to. Now that he had new information to investigate, his body thrummed with nervous energy. But she was right—there was nothing to be gained by heading over now. Whatever this was, it had been going on for some time, and it could go on until tomorrow. "That depends. Can you stay?"

A slow, sly smile spread across her face. "Not to look through dusty old maps."

"Oh, believe me, that's suddenly the last thing I've got on my mind at the moment." He took her in his arms and hugged her tight. "But seriously, Verity—thank you. No doubt I would have arrived at that brainwave soon enough, but you might have saved some lives by getting me there faster."

"Just be careful. If Stefan and Madame Huan are trying to keep you from finding out about this, it might be because they want to keep you safe."

"That's the charitable thought. Or it might be that they've got something to gain from letting it continue. That's why I want to get to the bottom of it. I hope it doesn't lose me two powerful friends, but I don't like being kept in the dark." He raised an eyebrow. "Most of the time, anyway. Right now, the dark sounds quite nice."

| CHAPTER THIRTY

STONE CALLED LAURA at the University in the morning and told her he needed to take a personal day. He felt a bit guilty about it, but weighing the potential harm the rifts could do against his students' having to put up with a TA for a day or two took care of that.

"You sure you don't want me to come with you?" Verity asked as they sat at the kitchen table sipping coffee. It was early for Stone to be awake, but he'd found it difficult to sleep as his brain continued chewing over possible locations for maps.

"No, you'd be bored senseless. This is the sort of thing Eddie and Ward love to do, so they won't mind helping. You keep going with your packing. The move's this weekend, right?"

"Yep. I've got Kyla and Hezzie lined up to help me with the last of it, so you're off the hook."

He shot her a mock-indignant glare. "What, you don't think I can carry boxes?"

"Oh, sure I do, especially since you've been hitting the gym. You've been doing a great job keeping it up, by the way. Jason and I had a little bet that you'd slack off."

Stone didn't ask which one of them had bet against him. "Off you go, then," he grumbled. "I've got things to do, and so do you."

She kissed him with a grin. "Let me know how it goes."

After she left, he gathered what he'd need before leaving. As he reached the front door, he paused, thinking about the morning commute traffic he'd invariably be stuck in on the way down to Sunnyvale. Things would certainly be a lot more convenient if he had his own personal portal at the house.

It occurred to him that the two major reasons why he'd never seriously considered building his own portal no longer applied. First, when he'd lived in the townhouse in Palo Alto, he'd been renting. Portals—permanent ones, anyway—weren't movable, and he could hardly build a persistent magical structure in the basement of a place he didn't even own. That had put the whole matter out of the question all on its own.

The second reason had been cost. The materials needed for a private portal were beyond the financial means of all but the wealthiest mages. When portals were built at all anymore—and they almost never were these days—they were almost always the result of a group of local mages getting together to pool funds, either to add one to a geographical area that wasn't served by the current network, or to build one for the use of some private association.

Stone didn't have that problem anymore. He'd never exactly been poor, but before William Desmond had died and bequeathed him a sizable fortune, the materials would have strained his means to the point where it wasn't practical.

Now, though, all that had changed. He owned his own home—one that included numerous locations where he could conceal a portal room behind wards and illusions—and he had enough spare funds to turn a "someday maybe" proposition into a reality. He already had the knowledge to build the thing himself, after all. He'd have to brush up a bit since he was out of practice, but he was confident that wouldn't be a problem.

Also, it would make popping back and forth to England a *lot* more convenient. He could still go to A Passage to India now and then to visit Marta, but he wouldn't have to fight traffic and drive for a minimum of half an hour every time he needed to head over there for some minor reason.

"Right, then," he said to Raider as he opened the door. "I'll give that some thought. After I've sorted out this whole rift thing, anyway. You be good."

He took the portal straight through to Caventhorne, emerging in the familiar basement room. He'd already phoned Eddie and Ward to let them know to expect him, so he headed immediately to the main library where he knew he'd find them.

The two of them, along with Kerrick, had done an exemplary job in preparing the place for its eventual use as a resource center for the world's magical community. When Stone had first heard that part of Desmond's will, he'd been doubtful about whether it would be possible. Caventhorne was a massive, rambling place, full of hidden areas, warded caches of magical books and artifacts, and a fortune's worth of antiques, artifacts, and old-world décor. In his later years,

Desmond had spent more time in the London house—the one Stone now owned—and commuted through a pair of private portals to Hertfordshire when necessary; in the meantime, the place had been maintained by a skeleton staff whose only jobs had been to keep the place cleaned, dusted, and presentable when its master was absent.

For the past several months, Eddie and Ward had been spending nearly all their time going through the books and artifacts, deciding with Stone's help which would be made available to researchers and which would be kept private, either at Caventhorne itself or at Stone's Surrey house. Because Desmond had left his entire magical collection directly to Stone, he had to make choices about each individual item, some of which were too potent or dangerous (or both) to make public. The result was that the whole process had taken considerably longer than any of them had expected. Finally, they were beginning to see the proverbial light at the end of the tunnel.

Eddie and Ward were, as he expected, seated at one of the carved antique tables in the library. They were poring over a pair of massive, illuminated tomes that predated the printing press, but looked up as Stone entered.

"Afternoon, mate," Eddie called, grinning. "What brings 'Is Lordship all the way over 'ere on a school day, anyway? You've got us dyin' o' curiosity."

Stone didn't bother to grumble. Ever since Eddie's research had turned up a few random nobles in his family tree, his friend had been teasing him mercilessly about it. He was used to it by now.

"Still working on this thing with the rifts." He quickly caught them up with the latest information, including the part about Kolinsky's and Madame Huan's unexpected reactions. "I was feeling fairly stumped last night, but something Verity said gave me an insight."

"Always thought that girl's brighter'n you are." Eddie's grin widened. "So what's the big revelation?"

"Maps. I've been looking at my ley line maps, but if Stefan and Madame Huan know what's going on and won't tell me, that could mean it's happened before. So I plan to dig into some older maps and see if I can turn anything up. Want to join me?"

"Try to stop us," Ward said, getting up.

Eddie closed his book. "Now't you mention it, I've got a few things back at the London library that might be 'elpful. You two stay 'ere and 'ave a butcher's, and I'll pop down and see if I can find anything. I'll ring if do."

Several hours later, to Stone's disappointment, none of them had turned up anything useful.

He sighed, using magic to switch on a lamp in the library and rolling up the latest in a series of oversized vellum maps he'd been examining. "Nothing," he said with a sigh.

Ward looked equally discouraged. "Doesn't appear so," he agreed. "It was a good idea, but so far all I've found is variations on the standard ley line maps."

Stone had found the same. Some of them had been quite old and beautifully rendered, and a few had been magically active or interesting in other ways, but neither he nor Ward had discovered anything out of the ordinary regarding the locations of magical rifts. A call to Eddie in London had verified that he hadn't either.

"Sorry, mate," he said when Stone phoned him that evening. He sounded tired. "I've dug clear down to the second basement—there's stuff in there I 'aven't looked at in *years*—but there's nothin' like what you're lookin' for. All you've done is given me a big pile of interestin' stuff I'm gonna need to find time to go through now, so thanks for that."

"Well, I appreciate your looking, anyway. I suppose I should head back to Surrey and see if I can find anything in my own library. I doubt it, though. If it's not here or in the London archive, I can't imagine I've got it squirreled away someplace."

"Come on down here first. After spendin' a whole day diggin' through a bunch of dusty old maps, I have *got* to have me a pint or two at the Dragon. Or three. And you and Ward are comin', so no arguin' about it."

Stone thought about begging off, but what was the point? A few pints and a couple hours' worth of relaxation sounded like just the thing—he was too tired to do any more serious study tonight anyway, and his head ached from hours of peering at the tiny, crabbed print on centuries-old maps.

"Fine." He glanced at Ward and mouthed, *Pub?* When his friend nodded with enthusiasm, he said, "We'll be down in half an hour. I suppose you two might as well get back to the usual tomorrow. No point in wasting too much more time on this."

"Somethin' will turn up, mate," Eddie said with surprising sympathy. "Maybe you just need to lubricate your brain or summat."

❖

To his surprise, Stone managed to put the whole situation with the rifts and the maps out of his mind for a couple hours once he and Ward met Eddie at the Dancing Dragon Pub in London. Seated at their favorite table in the back room, the three of them, by unspoken agreement, talked about everything *but* the day's failed task.

Stone didn't do a lot of talking himself, but a couple of pints did relax him enough that Eddie's endless football stories didn't bore him as they usually did. By the time they rose to leave at nearly eleven p.m., he was feeling a pleasant combination of tipsy and tired that told him he'd probably manage to get a good night's sleep tonight.

"Thanks," he told his friends as they left the pub and stepped out into the cold, sleety night. "That wasn't what I would have chosen to do tonight, but I think I needed it."

Eddie clapped him on the back. "You should listen to us more often, Stone. I think we know what you need more than you do. Ain't that right, Arthur?"

Ward smiled. "If you don't know by now that Stone never listens to anybody, I can't help you."

"Stubborn, 'e is." He grinned. "Anyway, got an early mornin' tomorrow—back to the old grind. I'll let you know if I turn anything up, mate."

Stone thought about heading back to Surrey so he could get an earlier start in the morning, but by the time the black cab dropped him at the London house, his eyelids were drooping so hard he could barely trudge up the stairs to the front door. Easier to just sleep here tonight and take the portal to Surrey in the morning. That also meant he'd be less likely to disturb Aubrey by showing up so late. He made a mental note to call the University in the morning about taking one more day, then headed upstairs to the bedroom he used on the rare occasions he stayed at the house.

Even though he was dead tired, he had a hard time falling asleep. It might have been the unfamiliar surroundings, the house's chill (he hadn't bothered with the heat since he'd only be here for the night) or all the pints catching up with him, but for whatever reason he found himself tossing and turning. Every time he managed to drop off to sleep, bizarre, half-remembered dreams woke him up, leaving his head pounding in confusion. The only thing he could recall about the dreams was that they seemed to center around maps, which made sense given how he'd spent his day. They swirled through his mind in a jumble: huge ones unfurled on tables, smaller ones in books, old and yellowed ones on globes, spinning so fast he couldn't even make out the details—

He snapped awake.

That time, the dream had been different. The previous ones had featured only the rolled maps and the ones in books, but this time his subconscious had added in a globe.

Ah—then he remembered. It must have come from the globe on the shelf at Madame Huan's shop, next to the bowling bag the boy was looking at. Something in his tired brain must have put together "maps" and "globes" and added yet another layer of confusion to his dream.

He settled back to the pillow and had almost dropped off to sleep again when another image swirled into his mind— not a dream this time, but an actual image.

A familiar image, of the sitting room in this very house.
Bloody hell.

Stone leaped out of bed, snatched his T-shirt and jeans from the floor, and yanked them on as quickly as he could, heart pounding hard.

It was probably an absurd thought—he was misremembering, or his vision was based on things he'd seen years ago.

But what if it wasn't?

He pounded downstairs in his stocking feet, sliding to a stop in the doorway of the formal sitting room on the third floor. He fumbled for the switch to turn on the overhead light, then cast his gaze around, hardly daring to hope.

William Desmond's sitting room had not changed appreciably since the first time Stone had seen it, at age fifteen when he'd first met Desmond while being evaluated for his potential apprenticeship. Back then, he'd thought it looked like something out of a museum, full of antique furniture, priceless oriental rugs, heavy drapes, and walls paneled in exotic wood. Every wall sported a painting that would have been at home in an art gallery, and several of its surfaces included classical statuary or finely-wrought lamps. Everything in the room was in a style of old-world class; Stone remembered being nervous about sitting on one of the fine sofas because he'd come in out of the rain and feared his damp clothes would damage the fabric.

Desmond, however, had not been fussy or touchy about his homes and possessions; the man had been so comfortable with his vast wealth and so gracious in his manners that Stone soon realized he probably could have walked in covered head to toe in mud and Desmond wouldn't have done more than offer a patrician look of disapproval. True, he probably had a cleaning spell to deal with the problem, but that was beside the point.

If the item Stone sought was still here, it would be on the far side of the room, near the fireplace and behind one of the massive sofas. He hurried across the room, heart still pounding. Even if it was there it almost certainly wouldn't help, but he had to check every possibility.

There it was, right where he remembered it. The large globe, nearly three feet in diameter, sat on the floor in a carved wooden stand that allowed it to rotate freely. It was of an old-fashioned style, done all in rich, antique browns with the oceans shown in lighter tan. Stone had no idea how old it was; the labels on the land masses, tiny and difficult to read, revealed it was definitely older than the founding of the United States, but yet the outlines of the continents appeared far more accurate than other maps from the same time period might have indicated. What had undoubtedly made it more interesting to Desmond, though, was the interconnecting network of lines that crisscrossed its entire surface: a three-dimensional rendering of the same ley lines Stone had been studying in his books and maps. It also included a few locations of magical interest, most of them in Europe, but nothing that corresponded to the sites Stone had visited.

He let his breath out in a disappointed sigh. Well, it had been a thought, but in truth he wasn't surprised it hadn't panned out. Perhaps Verity's theory that Kolinsky and Madame Huan somehow knew about the rifts from previous appearances wasn't correct after all. Perhaps they merely had information from some other source he didn't have access to.

He was about to turn and leave the room when another idea occurred to him and he spun back around. He tried to remember if he'd ever looked at the globe with magical sight before—it seemed almost impossible that he hadn't, but then again, even back when he was an apprentice he hadn't sat around examining every place he ever entered. He'd probably taken a quick look around, noticed that a large number of items in the room glowed with magical energy, and then moved on. Large numbers of items in *every* room of both this place and Caventhorne glowed with magical energy. He probably would have been more surprised if they *hadn't*.

He crouched next to the globe and shifted his sight.

Instantly, it lit up with arcane illumination.

"Yes…" he murmured, resisting the urge to pump his fist. Instead, he leaned in closer, turning the globe until North America was in front of him.

Immediately, he spotted two things: the ley lines shone with faint glows, and a number of other glowing areas were scattered around—not just on the North American continent, but the others as well. He didn't see a lot of them; the first thing he looked for was whether they all existed at ley line confluences, and he quickly discovered that they did. He couldn't find one example of the larger glows ("larger" being a relative term, since they were barely bigger than pinpricks and only slightly brighter than the ley lines themselves) that didn't occur at a convergence of at least two ley lines.

They didn't occur at *all* the ley line confluences, however. In fact, even more oddly, there didn't seem to be any logic to where they *did* occur. He found several at places where only a pair of lines crossed, but none in far more potent locations. The first places he checked—the site of Caventhorne with five converging ley lines, his own house in Surrey with three, and the northern-Nevada area where Burning Man had been held, which featured a gargantuan nexus of ten—did not include the glowing pinpricks.

Stone frowned, leaning in closer and sharpening his sight. That was odd. Almost invariably, ley line convergences corresponded with power: the more ley lines crossed in a given area, the more magical potential that area possessed. So if these odd rifts were popping up at locations of power, it seemed logical they'd appear where the power was greatest.

That could mean one of two things: most likely, that the glows *didn't* represent the locations of potential rifts, but rather something else Stone had no idea about. That made them interesting and ripe for later study, but not useful to his current problem. The second was that the glows *did* indicate rift spots, but their placement had nothing to do with relative power level.

Carefully, he spun the globe again and leaned in even closer. He wished he had his jeweler's loupe, but didn't want to take the time to retrieve Desmond's from his office. Instead, he waved his hand and shut off the light, bathing the room in darkness except for the unearthly arcane glow from the globe and the other nearby magically-active items.

In the darkness, the pinpricks stood out a bit more against the faint ley lines. Stone turned the globe again, focusing in on the eastern and Midwestern parts of the United States. Obviously there weren't any labels indicating state borders since the globe predated states, and Stone's American geography outside the West Coast was spotty, but he immediately noticed a pair of the glows in the approximate places he expected the Pittsburgh and Iowa areas to be. He'd have to check them against a conventional map, but he was fairly sure they were close enough not to be coincidences.

The other thing he noticed with his closer examination was that the pinprick dots were slightly different colors.

Confining his search to the United States, Canada, and western European areas, he discovered that the dots varied from pale yellow-green to a more solid blue, and that similar colors seemed to congregate in clusters. For example, the three dots in the UK area were all blue, the five in western Europe were more of a teal hue, and the ones in the United States—about twenty, though he couldn't be sure he hadn't missed any— varied between yellow in the north and orange in the south.

Stone sat back on his heels, barely aware that his legs were protesting his uncomfortable crouch. Why would the lights appear clustered? Were those in proximity to each other somehow related?

He leaped up, ignoring the pain in his knees, and hurried over to the bookshelf. He retrieved a handsome, leather-bound world atlas and a book of modern ley-line maps, then used magic to drag the globe's wheeled stand over next to a low table and pulled a chair in front of it. Seated comfortably now facing the globe, he opened the atlas and the ley-line book to two-page spreads of the United States, then began comparing those maps against the one on the globe.

No doubt about it: the pinpricks on the globe corresponded to ley line convergences in Iowa and the Pittsburgh area. Stone's heart began beating faster again: it appeared he was on to something after all. The only problem was, the globe, though large for its type, still didn't show enough detail to allow him to home in on precise locations. He found three other yellow dots spread along the northern part of the United States, but couldn't place them specifically enough to make them useful. If only he could zoom in on an area, like you could with a map on a computer.

"Hang on…" he murmured. "Who says I can't?"

The globe was obviously a highly magical object, and it didn't make sense for those pinprick locations to be there at all if they didn't give the user enough information to find them. There had to be a way to do this.

He scanned the bookshelves near the globe's initial position again, until he found a familiar, large magnifying glass. He'd seen Desmond use it many times while poring over tiny print in books during his apprenticeship, and had occasionally felt a brief, smug pride that his own young eyes didn't need the same kind of augmentation. But what if Desmond hadn't been using it in lieu of reading glasses after all?

He summoned it to him, noting that when it came into proximity with the globe, it too began to glow with magical energy. Barely breathing, he moved it into position over the globe's map.

Instantly, the tiny features snapped into focus, revealing details Stone hadn't noticed before. In fact, it almost seemed as if the map's topographical features took on a pseudo-three-dimensional appearance. As he moved the glass around in wonder, minuscule mountains, rivers, and other points of interest rose into view.

That was fascinating, but it still didn't completely solve Stone's problem. Because the map predated the United States, it included only intermittent labels, and most of the ones that did appear were no longer accurate. If he was going to do this, he'd have to do it by geographical features rather than place-name labels.

It was hard, painstaking work. By the time Stone had managed to locate the three yellow dots' locations on his modern map, two hours had passed. He set the map aside, fighting against his drooping eyelids, the pain in his back from hunching over the map, and the growing dull headache from peering through the magnifying glass to examine tiny geographical features on the globe. He'd planned to do the same thing for the dots in the UK, but reluctantly had to admit he didn't have the energy. He'd have to get some sleep. At least now he had three more potential locations to check: one in northern Oregon, one in central Wyoming, and one in southern Michigan. If he'd had it to do again he probably would have concentrated on the UK locations first, since he was here now and they'd be easier to check, but he did need to get back to the US. *Might as well check those out first,* he decided.

For now, though, sleep. It had been a productive evening after all, and he was sure, now that he had a next step, his spinning mind wouldn't trouble him further tonight.

Tomorrow, he could get started tracking this problem. And if Kolinsky and Madame Huan had a problem with it, they could bloody well show up in person and tell him why.

| CHAPTER THIRTY-ONE

THE FIRST THING STONE DID when he got back home was call Verity.

"Did you find anything?" she asked, sounding sleepy.

"I think so, yes." He explained what he'd discovered on the globe. He'd taken an hour after he'd gotten up that morning to study it again, verifying that he hadn't made mistakes locating any of the areas due to fatigue, but no, they were right where he expected them to be. He made a mental note to come back and check the ones in the UK if his theory with the US locations panned out.

"Wow. So you think these places—Oregon, Wyoming, and Michigan—will have more of these weird rifts?"

"That's the theory. I've got a meeting on Friday, but I plan to head out to check on them on Saturday. I figure I can get at least one of them done over three days. If they're there, I can close them, and if they aren't...well, then I suppose it's back to the drawing board, isn't it?"

"You want me to come with you? I could put off the last of the move for a few days."

"No, I know you've been looking forward to getting settled in. I'll be fine."

"Oh! Even better. If this stuff is urgent, I don't have anything going on this week. No jobs for Scuro until the middle of next week. I could check one of the places out for you, and tell you if I find anything, and that way I could be back by Sunday for the move."

Stone hesitated. "I'm not sure that's a good idea."

"Why not? I can hunt down magical weirdnesses as well as you can. I won't get near it or try to do anything about it if I find one, but it'll make things easier for you. I can do a little advance recon."

He thought about it. Verity wasn't his apprentice anymore—she was a competent mage in her own right, and even possessed a few skills at a higher level of expertise than he did. If the rifts were messing with people's minds, her own was strong enough to block it out, and she might be able to detect things that would take him longer.

"I suppose," he said, still with reluctance. "It *would* make things easier. I just don't like the idea of you going alone. We still don't know the extent of these things' influence."

"Don't *you* start getting overprotective, Doc. I get enough of that from Jason already. He's my brother so I can't really do anything about him, but you don't get away with it."

"I'm not being overprotective. I'm being prudent. If you run into difficulty, I'd feel better if you had someone else along to help out. Is Jason available?"

"No. He's away on another case for a few days, and I'm not gonna drag him off it to babysit me." She paused. "Hey, wait, I know. I could take Kyla with me. We could make a little mini-vacation of it. If we find anything I'll call you, but if we don't...I could stand to get out of California for a few days."

Stone didn't say it, but her words relieved him. He didn't know Kyla all that well—they didn't have much in common beyond their mutual connection to Verity—but she was good in a fight and he suspected she had some kind of physical-based magical ability that made her stronger and more agile than the average person. "Yes, that sounds like a good idea. Which one do you want to check out?"

"Let me call her later today and ask if she's up for it and if she has a preference. I'll be seeing her tonight anyway. Can I let you know?"

"Yes, of course. Whichever one you choose, I'll check at least one of the other two this weekend. Thank you, Verity."

"No problem, Doc. Happy to help."

He didn't hear back from her until late that afternoon. He'd gone to the University and delivered his lectures by rote, and during a break he went to the library to find more detailed maps of the three states. By comparing them to the ley-line map he'd brought with him, he determined that both the Oregon and Wyoming locations were near tiny towns, and the one in Michigan appeared to be out in the middle of no-where with the closest settlement more than twenty miles away. That was good for two reasons: first, it was unlikely to affect any mundanes—at least not on any kind of scale—and second, he could probably save it until last.

On a whim, he made a quick call to Madame Huan's shop, but no one answered. He didn't bother driving by Kolinsky's place—it would have been pointless.

Verity's call came as he was walking to his car.

"Okay," she said. "I talked to Kyla. She's a little skeptical about the whole rift thing, but she likes the idea of getting away for a couple of days. So we're in."

"Excellent. Do you have a preference? It looks like the Michigan one can wait until last, since it's in a remote location. So, Oregon or Wyoming?"

"Wyoming," she said instantly. "Kyla said she took a trip to that area with her parents when she was a little kid, and she'd like to see it again."

"Brilliant. Put all the expenses on your credit card, and I'll reimburse you."

"I've got money now, Doc."

"I know you do. But you're doing this for me, so you shouldn't have to pay for it. Neither of you should. I do appreciate your help, by the way. Tell Kyla for me." He gave her the name of the small town near the ley line confluence. "Just—you know what to do. Talk to people, have a look around with magical sight, that sort of thing. And call me immediately if you find anything. I mean it, Verity—I know you're quite capable of handling yourself, and I don't doubt it for a moment. But if this is a situation Kolinsky and Madame Huan are trying to steer me away from, you're not ready to take it on yourself. And if you see that figure I told you about, get the hell away."

"Yeah." Now she sounded serious, rather than indignant. "I get it. I promise, I won't mess with anything on my own. If we find any weird stuff, you'll be the first to know. I'll even call if we *don't* find anything, because I expect if that happens, Kyla and I will be out of communication for a couple days."

"Fair enough. Good luck."

"You too." She paused. "And you be careful too. I know you think you can handle everything on your own, but like you said—this is big stuff. Don't let that famous curiosity get you in over your head."

"I don't plan to."

"You *never* plan to," she said wryly. "That's kind of the point."

"*Touché.*"

Stone had trouble containing his impatience for the next couple days. He knew he could have taken more time off and gotten an earlier start on his own investigations, but he deliberately chose not to do that. As the years had gone on, his magical dealings took more of his time than they used to, resulting in a lot of days away from the University. He felt guilty about it: this was his profession, after all, and he owed it to his students and his colleagues to be as present and engaged with them as he was with hunting down magical anomalies.

Not for the first time, as he sat in his office on Friday morning preparing for his meeting, he wondered about his future with the University. Following Adelaide Bonham's bequest and the endowment, he'd had much more freedom to set his own hours and determine his own coarse load— that was why he only taught three days out of the week now. He fit his research into his free time, and even used some of his magical investigations as seeds for his papers, but if he wanted to continue teaching students—the thing he loved to do—he'd have to prioritize his work here at least as much as he did his "other life."

That, and until they found another professor to replace Edwina Mortenson, he couldn't leave Mackenzie Hubbard with an increased workload. If he stepped back from teaching and they couldn't find anyone else to take up the slack, it was entirely possible the higher-ups in the Cultural Anthropology department might axe the Occult Studies program. They were doing well now and had moved long past any financial concerns they'd had when Stone had first arrived, but the program couldn't go on without instructors, and Hubbard couldn't carry the load himself with nothing but TAs for assistance.

Stone sighed, gathering the papers on his desk and sorting them into neat piles. This situation would bear a lot more thought before he made a final decision. At least he had his green card now, so they couldn't kick him out of the country if he decided to leave the University. He'd thought about applying for dual citizenship, and even begun the process a few years back, but ended up not pursuing it. Even though he considered California as much his home now as he did Surrey, he didn't feel any compelling reason to make things official. Not yet, anyway.

He finished stacking the papers and glanced at the clock. His meeting was in half an hour; if he left now he could grab something quick to eat before he had to show up. He hadn't heard anything from Verity since she and Kyla had landed in Casper at midday yesterday, when she'd called him with a quick "We're here, everything's fine." Their plan had been to head to Mason, the tiny town near the ley-line confluence, and begin their investigation, but it was a couple hours' drive and she'd told him they weren't in a hurry.

After grabbing an energy bar and a to-go cup of coffee, he headed immediately to the administration building. Even though this was generally a day off for him, he found himself wishing if he had to be here, it could be to teach a class instead of to attend some tedious bureaucratic exercise. Despite his constant, low-level focus on the rifts lately, he still found himself caught up in the material when teaching, energized as he always was by the students' interest. He wasn't vain about it, but he knew his engaging, theatrical lecturing style was one of the major reasons the Occult Studies department had gained so much popularity over the years since he'd joined. True, his world-class expertise in the subject drew in the relatively smaller group of serious students, but quite a number of others from different departments took his courses as electives as well. He usually had to turn some away at the beginning of each quarter.

The meeting droned on as it always did, and Stone struggled to project an interest he wasn't feeling. As soon as the last agenda item was ticked off the list, he hurried outside and pulled out his phone to check for voicemail. He had three: one from Laura the admin and two from unfamiliar numbers. He listened to them as he walked.

Laura didn't want anything important, and the first unknown number was some resort trying to convince him he'd won a contest he'd never entered. He deleted it and hit the *next* button.

The number wasn't familiar, but the voice was. "Dr. Stone? It's Kyla." Even though the staticky connection, Stone couldn't miss the stress in her voice. "Please call me back as soon as you get this. Something's wrong. Verity's disappeared, and I can't find her!"

| CHAPTER THIRTY-TWO

S TONE WISHED there were some way to make a commercial plane fly faster. He sat back in his seat, forcing himself not to fidget or to spin out wild scenarios of what might have gone wrong in Wyoming.

Something *had* definitely gone wrong, though.

He'd called Kyla back immediately, and she'd answered on the first ring. "What's going on?" he demanded without greeting. "Where's Verity?"

"I don't *know*," she said. "We went off this morning to investigate something, and the next thing I know I'm back here and she's gone and she's not answering her phone."

"Hold on, hold on," Stone urged. He'd only met Kyla a couple of times, but she'd always struck him as an unflappable, straightforward kind of person. Now, she sounded like her world was falling apart. "Tell me the whole story. What were you investigating?"

"That's what I'm trying to tell you. I don't remember. We drove out somewhere, but I don't remember getting back here. When I checked my watch, half an hour had passed that I can't account for. What the hell is going on, Dr. Stone? What did you send her out here to check on?"

Stone was still walking, lengthening his stride as he headed back toward his office building on the far side of campus. "Kyla—listen to me. If I'm going to help you, I need the whole story. Tell me everything you can remember, and don't leave anything out."

"Okay. Okay. Uh—we landed in Casper, rented a car, and drove to Mason, the town we were supposed to be investigating. That's where I am now. Seriously, this place is tiny, and it's out in the middle of nowhere. Took us a couple hours to get there. They only have one motel. We checked in and V wanted to go out and look around right away, so we did."

"Did you find anything?" Stone swept through the door to the office building and slowed his pace as he headed down the hall.

"No. Not a damn thing. V looked around with magical sight, but she didn't find anything out of the ordinary. We walked around town a little—it's not much of a tourist place, but people were friendly enough, I guess. Talked to a few of them, asked if they'd noticed anything odd around the area."

"But they hadn't?"

"Nope. Nothing out of the ordinary at all."

"What did you do then?"

"That was yesterday. This morning, V got the idea to go driving around the area outside town—she said maybe your map wasn't completely accurate, and whatever it is might be out in the boonies somewhere nearby."

"Good thought," Stone agreed.

"So we got up, had breakfast, and drove out of town, following where she said one of the ley lines was. According to the map, there weren't any other towns within like a half-hour's drive, so we just tooled around on some of the smaller roads. Every once in a while, we'd stop and she'd get out and check for—I don't know—magical traces or whatever she does."

"Did she find any?"

"Yeah. We were out this little road—it was paved, but barely two lanes wide. We were stopping like every five minutes, so this had to be like thirty minutes or so out of town, and she suddenly got all stiff like she'd spotted something."

"This was near the road?"

"Yeah." She sounded miserable. "Fuck, this is all my fault."

"Why do you say that?"

"We were stopping so often, and she wasn't ever finding anything. So that one time, I stayed in the Jeep to check my voicemail. She'd only be gone for less than five minutes, so I figured if I kept her in sight, she'd be fine."

Stone tensed. "But she wasn't?"

"That's the part I don't remember." She growled, obviously frustrated with herself. "The last thing I remember clearly was sitting in that fucking Jeep, watching her wander around like she always did. But then, next thing I know, I'm waking up in our motel room and she's not with me. I can't find her anywhere, and she's not answering her phone."

"Bloody hell…"Stone muttered. Then, louder, "All right. I'm coming there, but it will take some time. Do you think you can retrace the route you took?"

"Yeah…I think so. Maybe not exactly, but I know what road we were heading out, so if you can do the magic thing, you should be able to find it. Should I—"

"Kyla, I know you won't like what I'm about to say, but what I want you to do is stay where you are. Do *not* go out there and try to find her or rescue her. I don't know exactly what's going on, but whatever it is, she's better equipped to deal with it than you are."

"I can't just sit here on my ass and—"

"You can, and you must. If she's found another rift, all sorts of things could have happened. And unfortunately, blundering about without any idea of what you're doing is more likely to get both of you killed than to help anything. So stay put, and I'll catch a flight and get there as soon as I can."

"Yeah. Fuck. Hurry, or I don't know how long I can do that."

She'd hung up then, and Stone, heart pounding, had immediately informed Laura an emergency had come up and he'd have to leave. He hadn't given her time to ask any questions.

Cursing the fact that there weren't any portals close enough to Wyoming to make it worthwhile to take one instead of flying directly from San Francisco, he'd quickly packed a bag, called Brandon Greene to look after Raider, and headed for the airport. He thought about calling Jason, but Verity had said he was off on a case somewhere. Stone wasn't willing to wait for him; if something truly was wrong, he'd call from Wyoming.

The only spot left on a nonstop flight to Casper leaving soon was a middle seat in coach, all the way in the back of the plane. Stone sat wedged between a doughy man in a Denver Broncos jersey and a chatty old lady, barely noticing either, and tried not to speculate too much about what might have become of Verity. He'd tried to call her himself before the plane took off, but not only didn't she answer, he didn't even get voicemail. It rang four times and cut off.

By the time they landed in Casper, it was late afternoon. As soon as he stepped off the plane, Stone was already calling Kyla. "I'm in Casper. Did she turn up yet?"

"No. I've been trying to call her, but nothing. I did find out one weird thing, though."

"What's that?" Stone was nearly running now, dodging slow-moving knots of tourists on his way to the rental-car counter.

"I asked some people about what's out that way—if they'd ever heard of anything strange. A couple of them mentioned there's a town out there. I found it on the map—it's even smaller than the one I'm in now—but I'm sure we didn't see it."

"Are you sure you were on the same road?"

She sighed. "I don't know. I can't be certain. Like I said, I lost like thirty minutes, and I don't know how that happened. Listen, I'm not sitting here much longer. If you don't get your ass out here soon, I'm going without you to try finding that town."

"I'm moving as fast as I can. Getting a rental now. Please, Kyla, don't do that. You'll be more help if you wait for me and we'll go out there together."

"I'm sure as hell not waiting till tomorrow morning. Who knows what's happening to her out there?"

"No—we won't wait until morning. Just stay put. If you want to do something useful, ask around about the other town. See if anyone can tell you anything about it. The more information you can gather before I get there, the better off we'll be."

"Yeah…okay." She sounded reluctant. "But hurry."

"Fast as I can. Call me if anything comes up in the meantime."

There weren't many customers at the rental counter, so in less than half an hour he was on his way out of Casper in a Jeep SUV with four-wheel drive. He remembered what Kyla had said about their having one, so he didn't want to take chances that he might need it. He barely had any idea what it was like in Wyoming, but had a mental image—which he was fairly sure wasn't entirely accurate—of lots of trees, snow, and large herds of buffalo or something.

He was wrong about the snow, anyway—the weather was overcast and chilly, but as he pushed the Jeep as fast as he dared under a disregarding spell, he saw no sign of rain or snowfall this late in the spring. By the time he pulled into Mason two hours later, the sun had already set. He pulled out his phone and called Kyla as he drove down what appeared to be the main street.

"I'm here. Where are you? Oh—wait. I think I see the motel."

He'd almost passed it, since it barely looked like a motel at all. The sign next to the road wasn't even lit up, and he'd be surprised if the place had more than ten rooms. He pulled into the tiny lot and parked next to another Jeep with a rental plate.

"I'm coming out now," she said. A couple seconds later, one of the doors opened and a figure hurried out into the lot.

Stone took a quick glance at Kyla's aura as she approached, and wasn't at all surprised to see its normal deep blue alight with agitation. She wore a black leather motorcycle jacket, jeans, Suicide Girls T-shirt, and combat boots, and her shoulder-length dark hair looked like she hadn't combed it recently. Smudged circles stood out on her brown skin, making her eyes look like they were set into hollows.

"About time you showed up," she snapped before he'd even gotten out of the car.

Stone didn't hold it against her—he knew he'd have felt the same way if someone had forced him to sit on his hands and wait for help to arrive when he knew someone he cared about was in danger and he couldn't do anything about it. He *had* felt that way, both on the plane journey and the drive out here.

"What did you find out? Anything? I assume she hasn't turned up."

She glared at him. "Like I wouldn't have called you if she had. Come on inside. I need to grab a couple things, and then we're leaving."

Stone followed her, grateful for the chance to stretch his stiff legs after two hours of driving.

The motel room was clean, serviceable, and hadn't had a décor upgrade to its Old-West theme in at least twenty years. An old-fashioned tube TV droned in the background, playing some action movie from the Eighties.

Kyla dug a flashlight and a couple of energy bars from an overnight bag on the unmade bed, then snatched a legal pad from the small table under the window. "Okay, come on. You drive, and I'll tell you what I found out on the way." She held up a bar. "Want one?"

He realized he hadn't eaten since she'd called him. "Thanks. Did you find out anything else while you waited?"

"Yeah. There *is* a town out there, or at least there's supposed to be. It's called Cinder, and it's only got less than a hundred people."

"But you didn't see it?" As soon as Kyla was in the passenger seat and had the door closed, he pulled out of the parking lot.

"Not that I remember. All I remember seeing out there was a whole lot of nothing."

"But Verity said that was the direction the ley line was running?"

"Yeah. I had to take her word for it, of course. Turn here."

Stone had already consulted his maps and had a general idea which direction the ley lines ran and where they were located, but it had been difficult to get a definite answer without being at the actual site. He pulled the Jeep off the road before turning and twisted around to wrestle a pair of books from his bag in the back seat.

"What are you doing?" Kyla demanded. "Keep going."

Stone ignored her. He opened each book to a page he'd marked and passed them over to her, then drove off again. "Compare those two maps with each other. One shows the location of the ley lines, and the other is a basic road map. See if you can find Cinder."

He kept his eyes on the road as Kyla switched on her flashlight and studied the two books. The road out here was nearly deserted, with only a couple of cars passing them going the other way, back toward Mason.

"I don't see Cinder on here," she said after a couple of minutes. "But the ley line map V had wasn't this precise. I can't be sure because I don't remember exactly where it was, but it looks like the spot where the two ley lines cross is near where we stopped."

"That's not surprising." Stone would have been surprised if it *hadn't* been so. "But it's odd that the town isn't on the map at all."

"Maybe it's so small they don't bother. Or else it's newer than your map."

"Doesn't matter too much. If you can show me where you last remember stopping, I can see how things compare with the actual ley lines." He glanced over at her. Despite her calm façade, her aura practically thrummed with tension. "We'll find her, Kyla. I'm sure she's fine. She's well trained to deal with this sort of thing."

"How can you say that? You don't even know what 'this sort of thing' *is*. She was telling me about the other stuff you discovered, and how you're still not sure what's going on with it."

"You're right: I'm not entirely sure yet. That's why I'm checking out these locations—so I can get more data to help me work this out."

She switched off the flashlight and sighed into the darkness. "This sucks, you know? I don't get how she could just *disappear*."

"Are you sure she did?"

"What the hell's *that* supposed to mean?"

"Well—you said the last thing you remember is watching her looking around for something, and then the next thing you knew you were in your motel room. It's possible from her perspective that *you* disappeared."

She drew breath to protest, but then let it out. "I guess that's true. But why wouldn't she answer her phone? Why wouldn't she call me?" She snorted. "This whole magic thing is kind of a pain in the ass, you know? At least the way you guys do it."

"What do you mean?"

"I know a couple other people who have some magic—I mean, you know Hezzie does, and one of the other Harpies does too—but they don't do *this* kind of stuff." She spread her hands out, encompassing the area. "They don't fly off who the fuck knows where tracking down magical freak zones. They just...*use* it. You know, to make their lives better. To help people."

Stone kept his gaze fixed straight ahead, watching the road. "You don't approve of me, do you, Kyla?"

"What?"

"You're not exactly hiding it, even if I couldn't see your aura."

She shrugged, but didn't answer.

"May I ask why? Is it because Verity and I are—"

She remained silent for so long he thought she still wouldn't answer, but then she finally said grudgingly, "That's part of it, I guess. But not the main part."

"Oh?"

By this time, they'd left Mason behind; even its faint glow no longer showed in the rearview mirror. Out here the land was mostly flat and rocky, and the combination of no traffic and the overcast sky obscuring the moonlight made the road ahead look as desolate as the surface of the moon. "I don't think you're good for her," she said at last.

He glanced her way, then returned his attention ahead. "Why do you say that?"

"Look, I just want to find her, okay? I didn't sign on for some long discussion."

"I get that. I want to find her too, as much as you do. But if we're going to work together effectively, I think it's best to get these simmering resentments out in the open, don't you?"

She wadded her energy-bar wrapper and jammed it in her pocket. "It's not *resentment*. I don't resent you. She cares a lot about you. Anybody can see that. It's good that you help make her happy. But…"

"But what?"

She didn't answer.

"Kyla…"

"You want the truth?" She didn't raise her voice, but he couldn't miss the tension in it. "Okay, I'll tell you the truth— I'm afraid you're going to get her killed."

"*What*?" He cast another quick look her way.

She spread her hands, indicating the view outside the Jeep's windshield. "Look what we're doing now. You sent her out here to check out some fucking magical thing, and now she's gone. She might be dead for all we know. And if she is, it's your fault."

Something inside him clenched at her words. He tightened his grip on the wheel and sighed. "Kyla…I'm not going to say you're wrong. But you also don't have the whole story. Verity *wanted* to come out here and investigate this. I didn't want her to go, but she insisted."

"You let her."

He barked a laugh. "Seriously? Do we both know the same Verity? Since when does anybody *let* her do anything? Or prevent her from doing it if she's got her stubborn mind set on it?"

"Yeah…I guess you have a point there." She rubbed her neck. "She's tough, and I know she knows what she's doing. But—"

"I could say the same to you, you know. You and that vigilante association of yours are the ones who encourage her to do things that could get her arrested—or worse."

She snorted. "Come on. That's not even the same level of dangerous. We hunt down street scum, and occasionally somebody with minor magical ability. With V's level of magic, she can handle anything we go against with one hand tied behind her back. Blindfolded."

"Mages aren't immune to bullets," Stone pointed out. "Trust me on this one. If someone caught her with her shield down, she's as vulnerable as any mundane."

"That's why nobody goes out alone. We look out for each other." She shifted in her seat, almost as if she were physically uncomfortable. "You—we talk a lot. She's told me about you. About how you have to solve all the puzzles, even if they put you in danger. This one's like that, isn't it? She wouldn't tell me everything, but she did say there were some people trying to scare you off looking into this."

"There are. But I made her give me her word that if she spotted anything unusual, she'd call me and wait before checking it out further. *Especially* if she saw anyone lurking around. She's not a fool, Kyla. And I trust her to keep her word."

"But she's gone. So what's that mean?"

"Either that she *didn't* keep her word, or more likely that she ran into something she couldn't get away from."

"So you think she *could* be dead."

Once again, Stone tensed. It was possible, of course. Magic was dangerous. And if she *was* dead, Kyla was right: it was his fault, at least indirectly. "I don't think so," he said at last. "As I said, she's well trained in magic, smart as hell, and fast on her feet. I think we should refrain from wild speculation until we get there and see what's going on."

"Yeah…" she muttered, obviously not happy about it. She settled back in her seat and stared out the window at the wide-open darkness, occasionally flicking on the flashlight to check the maps.

Another twenty minutes passed before she spoke again. "We should be getting close. I recognize that sign. It wasn't much past this where we stopped and she got out on her own."

Stone slowed the Jeep, switching to magical sight. He could already feel the ley line energy out here—the combination of the confluence and the fact that there wasn't much out here to get in the way made it particularly easy to notice.

They drove for another couple of minutes, then Kyla pointed. "There. I remember there was a speed-limit sign right near where we pulled off."

Carefully, Stone guided the Jeep off the road and parked near the sign. So far, nothing unusual had turned up to his magical sight—aside from his and Kyla's auras, the faint, pale green ones of nearby scrubby vegetation, and a single ley line that stretched out roughly in an east-west direction, nothing stood out. He opened the door. "You say she went off away from the road?"

"Yeah." She pointed again. "That way. She'd walked for maybe five minutes before she disappeared."

"All right. I'll check it out." When Kyla opened her own door more slowly, he added, "You don't have to come along if you don't want to."

"Like hell I don't." She got out and slammed the door shut. "First, I want to find V. Second, there's no way I'm gonna sit on my ass in the car again while *you* disappear too."

"All right. Stay close. I mean it. We don't know what's going on out here, and if you wander off, I won't be able to protect you."

"I don't need *protection*," she snapped.

"Normally I'd agree with you. But unless you've got any magical powers you're keeping under your hat, you're better off swallowing your pride and listening to me this time. All right?"

"Let's go." She stalked off.

Stone sighed and hurried to catch up with her. The air was chilly out here, and a brisk wind blew his coattails behind him like a cloak.

She still had the flashlight, and was shining it around ahead of her as she walked. When Stone caught up, she slowed her pace. "I don't see anything on the ground, but I guess it doesn't make sense she'd drop anything. You aren't any good at tracking, are you?"

"Seriously? Do I *look* like I spend much time in the wilderness?"

She snorted. "Yeah, me neither. Do you see anything magical?"

Stone had magical sight up, and was already scanning the area. "I see the ley line. The other one's nearby, but not right here. I'm looking for any traces of Verity's aura."

"But you don't see any?" Her voice sounded tight.

"That's a good thing. Normally, people don't just leave bits of their auric energy hanging about in the air after they leave an area. If they do, it means something happened—either she used magic, or she was injured or agitated."

"But how could she just *disappear* if nothing happened?"

Stone stopped, still scanning. "Let's be clear on this: you didn't actually see her disappear, right? It wasn't a situation where one second she was there and the next she was gone?"

"No." She kicked the ground. "Like I said before, the last thing I remember clearly was watching her walking around, somewhere near where we are now. I didn't see her wink out or anything."

"Okay. Let me think a moment."

He stared straight ahead, still trying to spot any sign of a rift, an anomaly, the orange-hued figure he'd seen in Pittsburgh, or anything else unusual. Had Verity spotted something? Had someone shown up and taken her away, wiping Kyla's memory in the process so she couldn't follow?

Wait...

The last rift, the one he'd found with Clyde, had been hidden under an illusion—and not a very good one—but the one in Devil's Creek hadn't. On the other hand, the Devil's Creek rift caused memory lapses in almost all the people who'd been near it. Judging by the note Stone had received, there was *someone*—perhaps more than one someone—out there who didn't want him messing with the rifts, and these someones obviously possessed some significant power. Hell, Stefan or Madama Huan, or both of them, could be involved with this.

"Also," he murmured, talking more to himself than Kyla, "obviously at least one person knew where these things were located at some point in the past, since they created the globe."

"What?" Kyla demanded. She still stood next to him, but looked as if she might erupt into motion at any second if he didn't get on with it. "What globe?"

Stone ignored her. "So if one person knew, it makes sense others could as well. Which means if they knew I was looking, they might have put up better illusions to protect the remaining rifts."

"What are you talking about?" Kyla sounded annoyed. "Who's 'they'?"

"Just—give me a moment." Stone's thoughts were moving so fast now that he barely registered her words. "Let me talk this out."

Hardly realizing he was doing it, he began to pace, still muttering to himself. "Obviously the minimal illusion didn't stop me—it wasn't meant to, because at that point they had no idea I was coming. It was put there to keep mundanes from blundering into it."

"Doc, if you don't start making some sense right fucking *now,* I'm gonna keep going."

He blinked, snapping back to reality. "Sorry. Trying to work something out. Just bear with me for a moment or two—I want to check something. Stand back, please."

"What are you going to do?"

"I think there's got to be something here. I can almost feel it, but not quite. So I'm going to add some more power to my effort."

"Effort to do what?"

Stone didn't answer. Instead, he took a couple steps back, drew a few centering breaths, and opened a wider conduit to bring in more Calanarian energy. He didn't normally use it for this kind of thing, but he saw no reason why it shouldn't work. If he could punch up his detection magic sufficiently, perhaps he could see through any illusions that might be concealing a nearby rift.

At first, nothing happened. He walked around, scanning in front of him, feeling the Calanarian energy singing through his body. It was an odd feeling, channeling this much otherworldly magic for this long—not exactly unpleasant, but he got the definite impression that he shouldn't do it at this level for too much longer without a rest. If there was an illusion here, it would be harder to punch through it because he had no idea what he was looking for. Would he see the rift itself? Verity? Someone else? One or more structures? He didn't know.

"Doc? You okay? You look pale." Kyla's nervous voice seemed to come from miles away.

"Hush. I've almost got it…"

There! He'd nearly skimmed over the faint shimmer in the air, but it was definitely there. He took a step forward and focused in closer, trying to pick it apart, pumping more energy into the effort until his nerve endings tingled and he felt as if some vast well of power was building within his body.

He couldn't keep this up much longer. But if it was an illusion, all he'd have to do was get past it, and it should crumble like dust—at least for him. He had no idea how he'd help Kyla see through it, but that problem was for later. First he'd have to—

What?

He stopped, stiffening.

R. L. KING

"What?" Kyla demanded, grabbing his arm. "Did you see something?"

He didn't answer.

"*Tell* me, damn it! What did you see?"

"It's not possible…" he whispered. "The sheer power alone would be…"

She spun him around. "Tell me. *Now.* What are you seeing? What's impossible?"

He didn't even bother to shake free of her. Now that he'd seen it, he didn't need to. He knew what he was looking for now, and he could find it again instantly. "It's not an illusion." He spoke in a tone of wonder.

"What is it, then? Do you see the—rift thing? The thing V was looking for?"

"Sort of." With effort, he forced himself to turn his attention fully to her. "It's—I still think the rift is around here somewhere, hidden behind a small illusion. But I think I know now why we haven't found Cinder."

"Why?" She cut a quick glance sideways, toward the area where he'd been looking.

"Come on—we've got to go back to the car. I need to check something."

Her grip on his arm tightened, holding him in place, and her eyes blazed. "Dr. Stone—neither one of us is going anywhere until you tell me what the hell is going on."

He held her gaze until she left go. "I don't believe it myself, but it's the only thing that makes sense. I think the rift has somehow…shifted the entire town of Cinder—somewhere else."

| CHAPTER THIRTY-THREE

K YLA, WHO WASN'T SHORT, had to jog to keep up with Stone's long, swift strides as he headed back toward the Jeep.

"What are you *talking* about? Shifted somewhere else? What does that even mean? Where are you going?"

Stone didn't answer until they were both back in the car and he'd driven off. He wasn't doing it to be unkind or evasive, but rather because his mind was moving so fast he could barely keep up with his own thoughts. "I hardly believe it myself," he said. "I've never seen anything like this in my entire magical career—"

He stopped in midsentence, gripping the steering wheel so tightly his knuckles whitened. "Bloody hell, yes I *have.*"

"How the fuck does V put *up* with you?" Kyla yelled. "Listen—you tell me *right fucking now* what's going through your head, and why we're leaving instead of trying to find V!"

Stone took several long, deep breaths, forcing his heart rate down and trying to wrangle his madly careening thoughts. Finally, he pulled off the road again and let the Jeep idle. "Okay," he said, a bit breathlessly. "I'm sorry. I'm not doing it on purpose. Let me try to explain this to you and then we need to get going."

He twisted in his seat, grounding himself by looking at her angry, worried expression. Kyla cared about Verity as much as he did, and Verity was their primary objective. "Okay," he said again. "I don't know how much Verity told you about the previous rifts, so if I tell you something you already know, just—keep listening. I've seen two of them before—one that caused a number of people to suffer a memory lapse, and one that was hidden by an illusion. I expected this one to be similar, but perhaps with a better illusion since powerful people are trying to dissuade me from hunting them down."

"Yeah, I got that part. But what did you mean, 'shifted'? How do you shift a whole *town*?"

"Damned good question. But I've seen this sort of thing once before—an entire *skyscraper* shifted between dimensions."

She gaped at him. "You're…fucking…*kidding*."

"I'm not. I didn't think I'd ever see something like it again—the factors involved don't seem to exist here, so I didn't think there was enough magic to do it. If I'm right, that means this rift is far more powerful than the last two."

"Fuck…" she said, letting her breath out in a long blast. "So you're saying the town's here, but it's…*not* here?"

"That's exactly what I'm saying. I think the rift either shifted Cinder to whatever dimension its power originates from, or else the town is stuck between that dimension and ours." He took a few more breaths and, convinced he could manage both his thoughts and his driving, pulled back out onto the deserted road.

"So…what are we looking for? And where's V?" She paused. "Are you saying…she might have gotten too close to…whatever this thing was, and now she's shifted too?"

"Yes. I'm just speculating, obviously—can't do any more without more data—but my theory is that she wandered too close to something, investigated it, and ended up getting shifted over. Then you noticed her missing, went to investigate yourself, and for whatever reason got hit with some kind of memory-altering magic."

"But why? Why would I get my memory altered but V didn't?"

"Probably because she's a mage and you're not. She's got strong mental protections against that sort of thing. But she's never dealt with anything like this, so once she got shifted, she probably didn't know how to get back."

Kyla gripped his arm. "So you think…she's in there somewhere? Inside Cinder on…another dimension?" She snorted a bitter laugh. "Listen to me. This is fucking unreal."

"Good word for it. And yes, that's precisely what I think. She may not even realize anything is wrong. Time can run differently between dimensions, so she might think she's only been gone for a few minutes."

"Time runs differently between dimensions. *Listen* to yourself."

He shrugged. "It's true. I've experienced it."

"So what the hell are you looking for now? Why are we leaving the area?"

"We're not leaving the area. We're just moving forward a bit, while I look for—that," he finished in triumph, pointing up ahead at a small sign. He pulled off next to it and stopped.

It read: *Cinder*, ¼, and included an arrow pointing to the right. Just beyond it was a narrow road, barely two lanes wide.

Kyla looked at the sign, then down the road. "Quarter mile. That's not far—we should see lights or something, right?"

"We should, yes. But if I'm correct and the town is shifted, we'll get to where it's supposed to be and find nothing but bare land."

"Shit…" she gripped the dashboard. "Well, let's go, then. If that's where V is, we have to find her. We have to get her out of there."

"Yes. And figure out how to get Cinder back where it belongs as well." He turned onto the narrow road, then stopped again. "But first, I need to make sure you're not going to get hit with the same memory-lapse magic as before."

"How are you gonna do that?" she asked, eyes narrowing.

"By putting some protection around your mind, with your permission."

She glared. "Protection?"

"Sort of a block. It won't be perfect, but it should keep the influence out long enough for us to figure out what's going on here. The alternative is that you wait here and let me investigate—but I doubt you'll go for that, will you?"

"Hell, no." But she still looked nervous. "How are you gonna do this protection thing? Can you mess with my mind? V's never talked about anything like that."

"She's probably never had to, but I assure you, she's capable of it. Don't think of it as 'messing' with your mind, though. Think of it more as putting up a shield." He chuckled. "A magical tinfoil hat, as it were."

"This isn't funny."

"No, it's not. But that's how I deal with situations like this—I try to keep my sense of humor. Are you willing to let me put up a block? If you're not, it's probably best if you stay here. If the memory lapse hits you again, you won't be any help to me *or* Verity."

She regarded him with suspicion. "You can't read my mind, can you?"

"No. Mages can't read minds. I promise, all it will require is a momentary contact. You won't feel anything."

He could tell she didn't want to do it. Despite their mutual connection with Verity, it couldn't be any clearer that she didn't entirely trust him. She looked at him, then at the road ahead where the faint lights of Cinder should have been shining, and finally let out a loud sigh.

"Okay. Do it. But make it quick."

"Yes. Just hold still a moment."

He reached out, moving slowly so he didn't startle her, and put three fingers on her forehead. Between the physical contact and magical sight, he sensed her disturbed aura more than ever. She was doing a very good job of hiding the fact that this whole situation was freaking her out.

The process took only a few seconds, and then he pulled back. "There."

"That's it?"

"I did say you wouldn't feel anything. I could do a better one if I had more time, but that should at least protect you from wandering off and forgetting why you came here in the first place."

He put the Jeep back in gear and drove slowly up the road toward where Cinder should be, watching the odometer carefully and stopping short of the quarter-mile mark. He pulled off the road and got out, and Kyla followed.

"What are you going to do?" she asked. "I don't see a damned thing. No lights, no buildings, no nothing."

Out here, the darkness was nearly overwhelming. When Stone switched off the headlights, the enter area was bathed in an inky black that seemed almost palpable.

"I need to look around. This is where the town should be, but obviously it's not here. That supports my theory. Will you stay here while I check something?"

"Check *what*? I'll come with you."

"I'm just going to levitate up and see if I can see anything from above. I doubt I will, but I want to know before I start bringing out the big guns. It will only take less than a minute."

"Fine. But hurry *up*."

He couldn't see her face in the darkness, but he could hear the growing tension in her voice. "I'll hurry."

He lifted off the ground and, keeping magical sight up, rose to a height of about fifty feet, then drifted over into the area where Cinder should be. As he suspected, he still saw nothing below him, beyond the pale green auras of vegetation. There was no sign of any human or animal auras in the vicinity. He floated back down and landed next to Kyla, who'd opened the Jeep's door to provide some light.

She nearly pounced on him. "Anything?"

"No. If there was a town here, it's gone now."

"Are you saying it's literally gone? You said something about it being shifted. What's the difference?"

Stone pulled his bag from the back seat and removed a smaller bag from it. He hadn't brought much in the way of ritual materials with him this time. "The difference is the magnitude of the magic we're dealing with. Either way, it's got to be immense—you can't simply shift an entire town—even a tiny one like Cinder—to another dimension without putting out some massive amounts of energy. But the question is, is it simply shifted out of phase, which would take less power and be easier to reverse, or did something literally move it—buildings, people, livestock, and all—to another plane of existence? If that happened, I'm not sure I know a way to reverse it."

She grabbed his arm. "You mean you can't get V back?"

"Hold on. As I said, I'm not sure yet what's happened. And even if the town *has* shifted over bodily, that doesn't mean I can't get her, and the other residents, back. It will be harder, but it's possible. I'm saying I doubt I can get the *town* back. Buildings can't walk through portals."

"I thought you said you were looking for a rift. Something you can close." She released his arm and paced around, fists clenched.

"I was. I *am* looking for a rift, but until I know more about what's going on, I can't just close it. That could seal all those people on the other side, and if I close it without a clear idea of what location it's pointing at, then the odds of finding them again get a lot lower."

"So what *are* you going to do?"

He turned to face her. "Kyla, listen to me. I know you're worried about Verity. I am too. But if I'm going to do this, you've *got* to let me think. You can't help me with this part, but you can hinder it. I don't mean to be rude, but you'll do the most good at this point by going back to the car and letting me work this out. The longer we wait, the more likely something might happen—like the rift closing spontaneously on its own, or someone turning up to investigate."

She made a noise that was halfway between a snort and a snarl. "*Damn,* but you're an arrogant bastard, Stone."

"I know," he said softly. "But that doesn't change the facts. If you don't let me get on with it before something happens, Verity could be lost forever. And I don't fancy letting that happen. Do you?"

She held his gaze for several seconds with a smoldering one of her own. Finally, she let her breath out and unclenched her fists. "Fine. On one condition, though."

"What's that?"

"If you find anything, you'll tell me. You won't just—cross over or whatever without me. We go together."

"I promise."

"Okay. Do it, then. Find her." She stalked back to the Jeep, threw herself into the passenger seat, and sat there with the door open, still glaring at him.

Stone didn't waste time. He hadn't been kidding about his fear that the rift, wherever it was, would close spontaneously. He didn't have enough data about the rifts yet that he could reliably predict their behavior. Muttering to himself, he began pulling items from his small bag. He felt as if he was blundering around in the dark, and that wasn't good—before, the whole thing had been little more than an interesting magical problem, but now, with Verity likely in the same place Cinder was, the stakes had become a lot higher. If he couldn't figure something out soon, he might never get her back.

Finally, he settled on a wooden rod with a red crystal attached to the end of it. He smiled a little as he remembered using it once before, way back when he'd first met Jason and Verity, to help focus his thoughts during a magical procedure. They'd teased him about his "magic wand," and he supposed to a layman that was exactly what it looked like.

But focus was what he needed now, more than anything. If he had any chance of figuring out what had happened to Cinder—whether it was shifted or literally transported—he'd need to figure out exactly *where* the other dimension in question was. Was it the same as one of the others, in Devil's Creek or Pennsylvania, or a third and completely different one? Had Verity been present in the town when it had happened, or had she inadvertently walked through some sort of gateway?

Hell, was she even here at *all*? He realized he had no way to know her disappearance was even connected with Cinder.

Stop it. Where else *would she be?* He had to continue with that assumption for now, because if he didn't, he had no other reasonable hypothesis to pursue.

He glanced back over his shoulder toward Kyla. She sat in the passenger seat, one leg dangling out, her gaze fixed on him. Her posture and her aura jangled with impatience, fear, and anger. He sympathized—he would be the same way if their positions were reversed—but he couldn't concern himself with her right now. She couldn't help him.

Turning back, he raised the rod, feeding magic into it until the red crystal glowed. Then, still holding it up, he began pacing around the area, looking for either a way around whatever illusion that was concealing the rift, or any sign of Cinder. As he paced, he increased the power, opening the connection to Calanar wider until his body thrummed with energy. Whoever had done this was good—damn good. It wouldn't be easy to—

Wait.

He stopped as something shimmered in front of him.

Had he truly seen it, or were his eyes playing tricks on him? He held the rod higher and added more power. Now, not only was his body thrumming, but the rod was too. The little crystal seemed to resonate with it. *Something* was out there. If he could get the two of them in sync, then he could—

There.

This time there was no mistaking it: faint images appeared a short distance away. They were so indistinct he couldn't make out any details, but he didn't need to. He recognized a building when he saw one, even though it was nearly transparent.

The little crystal began to hum, and the rod shook in his hand. The wooden part remained cool, but he could feel the heat coming off the crystal.

"Hold on…" he muttered, still concentrating. If Cinder *had* been shifted rather than transported, its energy was foreign to whatever dimension it was trapped in. It was one of the fundamental principles of portal science: any entity's energy—living or not—had an affinity for the dimension where it originated. It *wanted* to exist on its own dimension, and sending it somewhere else, or holding it halfway between two somewheres, required delicate balance and a lot of power. To do it to a whole town would take even more, so if he could somehow disrupt that balance…

Just a little more, and I'll have it—

The red crystal exploded with a *pop*, sending shards flying in all directions. Stone flinched, barely bringing his arm up before he got a faceful of tiny missiles. He took a step back, but before he could lower his arm a strange feeling—half heat, half swelling power—hit him and blew him over backward.

Off in the distance, he thought he heard Kyla yell something, but the wind carried the sound away before he could be sure.

| CHAPTER THIRTY-FOUR

S TONE SCRAMBLED BACK to his feet, and stopped. His breath caught in his throat.

His view had changed from only seconds ago. Now, instead of nothing but desolate, scrubby plain, the dark hulks of buildings rose in front of him. He stood on a narrow paved road; on his left he spotted a gas station, a tiny general store, and a few unlit structures beyond them, and on his right was a fenced corral with a few head of sleepy sheep milling around. Farther up the road he made out the faint glows of streetlights and a few more buildings.

"Cinder, I presume," he muttered.

He turned and looked behind him. As he suspected, there was no sign of the Jeep or Kyla. When he walked back in that direction, he made it about ten steps before something in his brain shifted and suddenly he was walking back toward the town again. He wondered if the only reason he even noticed was because of his mental protections—would the residents of Cinder even realize they were trapped here?

He looked around, trying to locate any sign of other living beings—even a stray dog running around in the street—but saw nothing. What did that mean? Were they dead? Had the town shifted but not the people?

He set off at a slow jog, stashing the rod in his pocket. Kyla had said Cinder had fewer than a hundred people, which meant its core probably didn't take up much geographical space. Maybe everyone had simply gone to bed early; it didn't seem like there was much to do out here after dark even under normal circumstances.

His first stop was the gas station. It was small and dusty, with only two pumps and a building that housed a tiny mini-mart and a closed garage space big enough for one car. The main lights were off, but a couple of beer signs flickered in the front window, giving the place an ominous, horror-movie aspect.

"Anybody around?" Stone called as he approached. A single car was parked at one of the pumps, but no one was behind the wheel. He edged around it and ducked through the door to the mini-mart.

The first thing he spotted inside was the figure sitting behind the counter. The bored-looking, gangly teenager in a green John Deere cap and Guns 'n' Roses T-shirt was slumped on a stool, an issue of *Penthouse* in front of him and opened to the centerfold. He neither moved nor acknowledged Stone's presence, but merely sat with his gaze fixed downward as if the smiling, naked woman in the magazine were the most interesting thing in the world.

"Hello?" Stone said.

No answer.

He shifted to magical sight, but no aura registered. When he added more power to his examination, he caught faint flickers around the boy. Every few seconds he could barely make out intermittent flashes of the row of cigarette cartons on the rear wall as the kid's form went insubstantial.

"Hmm." Stone waved his hand in front of the boy's face and got no response. Shifted, then, and not transported. That was good—at least it would probably be easier to reverse. Was everyone in town like the boy, held in some kind of suspended animation between the dimensions? Would they remember anything if Stone managed to restore them to their proper place?

And where was Verity?

He hurried back outside. "Verity!" he called, as loud as he could. "Where are you?"

No answer.

"Bugger…where did you go?" He took off at a faster jog and quickly checked the general store, which was closed. In a couple of small residences just off the main street, he found more of the suspended, unmoving figures—a man seated in front of a dead TV set in one, and a family gathered around a board game in the other. He left them alone and exited back out to the street.

But where was Verity? Was she in the same suspended state as everyone else? His mental protections were stronger than hers—or perhaps she hadn't expected this, so she hadn't bothered reinforcing them until it was too late. But then, why wouldn't she have stopped moving as soon as she crossed the perimeter into the shifted area?

Of course. Maybe she did.

Clearly he needed to get more sleep, because his brain wasn't functioning at full capacity. Pausing a moment to orient himself, he summoned a light spell around his hand and ran out of town to the south, toward the spot where he and Kyla had first pulled off the road—the location she last remembered seeing Verity.

It didn't take him long to reach it; his long strides covered the ground fast, and the light spell prevented him from tripping over rocks or uneven terrain. He slowed as he drew closer to where he suspected the edge of the phenomenon was, not wanting to be caught again in the strange, direction-altering field he experienced before. As he moved, he reinforced his mental shields. If he got trapped in the suspension effect, he doubted anyone else would ever find any of them again.

He spotted a figure up ahead when he was still fifty yards or so away. He couldn't make out detail yet, but whoever it was stood unmoving like the rest, as if they had simply wandered out of town for a walk. Heart pounding, he tensed and approached even more slowly? "Verity?"

No answer.

Closer, with magical sight up at full strength, he had no doubt the figure was indeed Verity. She wore a black hoodie, leather jacket, jeans, and black boots, and her still, unmoving gaze was fixed somewhere toward Cinder. As Stone came up next to her, he couldn't miss the same kind of flicker he'd seen around the boy in the gas station and the people in the houses. In her, though, it was stronger; bits of her emerald-green aura shone through along with red flashes arcing around her body.

She's fighting it. He watched her for a moment longer, but aside from the flickers and flashes, he saw no movement—not even in her eyes. Clearly, if she *was* fighting the effect, she wasn't strong enough to break free.

That meant wherever this rift was, it had to be a potent one. He'd have to be careful.

"Verity—can you hear me?"

Still no sign of movement—but did the flashes around her aura change, just for a moment? He couldn't be sure.

He paced around her, magical sight still up. "Verity! If you can hear me at all, give me some kind of sign. I'm going to get you sorted."

Nothing happened for several seconds. But then, as he continued to watch, her aura seemed to blaze brighter for a moment, and the some of the red flashes diminished.

"Good! That's it! So you're still in there after all. Just give me a moment…"

He focused his concentration. This would be a tricky bit of magic, because he'd need to reach her not only on this dimension, but on their home one as well. Like everything else around here except him, she was stuck between the two, and thus unable to act in either. To bring her back, he'd need to get her fully into phase with either this dimension or the other one—and it made more sense to bring her back here, then go in search of the rift and exit through it. It had to exist on both dimensions, or Cinder wouldn't still be shifted. Once the two of them got back to their home plane, he could close the rift from there. It wouldn't be easy and he couldn't be sure it would work, but since dimensional energy tended to want to return to its home location, disrupting the energy from the rift should cause it to snap back.

At least he hoped that was how it would work. It wasn't as if he dealt with this kind of interdimensional magic every day.

But first he had to get Verity back.

From his shoulder bag containing his ritual components, he pulled out a small sack of sand and used it to trace a crude circle to enclose her. Fortunately, this shouldn't take an elaborate working—it would have been much worse if she'd been fully transported here. Using magic, he placed four small candles around the circle at north, south, east, and west (assuming those values even had any meaning here) and then stepped back and lit them. Theoretically, all he'd have to do to get Verity back was to grab hold of the energies from the two separate dimensions and bring them into sync with each other long enough for Verity to return. After that, he could reinforce her mental shields, or she could do it herself now that she knew what she was up against.

"Hang on just a moment longer…" he murmured, moving next to the circle without crossing it. He took a couple of deep breaths to center himself, then reached out with his power, opening the conduit to Calanar. As he did, it occurred to him with some shock that it was even more fortunate than he'd thought that the rift had only shifted Cinder rather than transporting it—since his Calanarian magic worked based on the relative connection between Earth and Calanar, in order for it to function on a foreign dimension he'd need to have the data on where it was located. He could get it, but it would take time—and time was something he didn't have in abundance right now. Even now, he wasn't getting access to the level of Calanarian energy he'd be getting if he were fully on Earth.

He focused on Verity, reaching out to touch her essence. Now that he knew what he was doing, he acted with confidence and care. A short time into the process, he began to sense her presence growing more substantial, and realized she was doing her best to help him from her end. "Good, good…" he said. "Keep it up, Verity. We're almost done…"

With a sudden wrenching sensation, Verity's body snapped fully into being. Her aura blazed bright, solid green, and she gasped and took a staggering step forward.

Stone caught her, holding her shoulders until she steadied herself. "Verity!"

"Doc!" She threw herself into his arms, engulfing him in a tight hug and letting out a long, relieved breath. "Am I glad to see you!"

"Bloody hell, Verity, you scared the hell out of me!" When she let loose, he stepped back and drank in the sight of her.

"Yeah, you and me both. I didn't think anybody was coming." Her gaze sharpened. "What are you doing here, anyway?"

"Kyla called me. Apparently you'd walked off to investigate something on your own, and the next thing she knew she was back in Mason and couldn't remember how she got there. Fortunately she remembered you, or we might have been in trouble."

"Oh, my God." She spun, looking around in all directions. "Where *is* she? Is she okay?"

"She's fine—probably angry with me at this point, because I promised not to go anywhere without her."

"Is she here?"

He looked around. "Do you know what's happened here?"

"Not exactly. I remember looking for a rift near the ley line, but didn't see one. What's going on? Where are we?"

"We're in a little town called Cinder, which has been dimensionally shifted. That's what happened to you—you were stuck between our dimension and this one, just like all the other people of Cinder. Go ahead and reinforce your mental shields now, so it doesn't happen again."

"Already did. I'm good. Where's Kyla, then?"

"Hopefully waiting for us outside, back on our own dimension. Either that, or she's come looking for us and is probably wandering about somewhere since she doesn't have the key to my rental Jeep."

Verity snorted. "She's probably hot-wired it and driven it back to Mason if that happened." She studied the dark, scrubby landscape. "So what's the plan now? We have to get back, and get all these other people back, right?"

"Exactly. We've got to find the rift. My theory is that we can go through it, which will get us back to our own dimension."

"But what about the town?"

He took a breath. "I'm not absolutely certain about this, but I think if we close the rift once we're out, since the town is only shifted and not fully moved to the other dimension, that will be enough to disrupt the energies and shift it back home."

"Ah, right—because dimensional energy has an affinity for its home plane."

"Well *done,* apprentice," he said, grinning. "I thought you slept through my lessons on dimensional science."

"I think I did—maybe I picked it up by osmosis through my head on the desk. Anyway, let's go. I don't like the idea of Kyla wandering around in the wilderness. She's not exactly a country girl. Also, she's gonna be pissed at both of us."

"I'm sure she'll forgive you—and I'll survive if she doesn't forgive *me,* assuming we're able to set everything right. Come on."

Cinder, it turned out, was a *very* small town. Past the gas station and the general store, they found only a few more small businesses along with a collection of residences a short distance out. Stone suspected there might be a few more residences—outlying farms and ranches—outside the boundary of the dimensional shift, but didn't concern himself with those. The rift had to be in here somewhere, but since he couldn't see the ley lines as clearly here, finding it might prove more difficult than he'd thought.

"What's it even look like?" Verity asked after they'd trudged along for about ten minutes and had nearly reached the other side of town.

"No way to know. The two I saw didn't look the same. I think they vary by location and power level. Just keep magical sight up and tell me if you see anything odd."

She walked in silence for another minute or two. "Doc?"

"Yes?"

"What are you going to do? Are you planning to figure out where all those spots on your globe are, then go to them and try to close all the rifts?"

"I…don't know," he said slowly. That was what he *wanted* to do without a doubt—these rifts were clearly dangerous, and who knew what would happen if more of them started to pop up? Certainly, this one was causing trouble for the residents of Cinder, and if others were located in more populated areas they could cause even greater disruption.

"But…" She sounded troubled. "It's not your responsibility to go running around dealing with them. Can't you tell other mages about it? Maybe if you do, they can help."

"Yes, that's definitely an option, but it assumes a lot of things."

"Like what?"

"Well…it's going to take fairly powerful magic to seal the rifts, which means sending minor talents won't do. I already told you what happened with Stefan and Madame Huan. I wonder how many *other* powerful mages are in on this little secret. And even if they're not, trying to convince them to do anything might not be easy."

"But surely they wouldn't want dangerous magical stuff happening, would they? Wouldn't they at least be curious about it?"

"Some of them would." He chuckled. "I think I need to introduce you to more mages. Most of them aren't like us. In fact, the vast majority of mages I know personally are more like Eddie, Arthur, and Walter Yarborough—in other words, content to stay in their libraries, do their research, and avoid adventure like the proverbial plague."

She thought about that. "But that's just the older ones, right? The younger ones might be curious. What about Ian?"

"Ian's not ready to deal with this. He's got the power, but his training has been…spotty at best. And you'd be surprised at how many younger mages these days can't handle the training to become fully qualified. Too many distractions in the mundane world, and too many ways technology can do things it used to take magic for, a lot easier."

"Wow. I can't even imagine knowing magic and not wanting to train it to its full potential." She looked around again. "See, now this is a time when it might be worthwhile to have some kind of mage organization. You could call a meeting and give everybody the details all at once. There've got to be at least *some* mages you could interest in this. And maybe the group could…I don't know…have words with Stefan and Madame Huan for keeping this secret."

Stone snorted. "Oh, yes, *that* would go over well. I definitely wouldn't volunteer to be anywhere near *that* committee. I—" He stopped, narrowing his eyes.

"Do you see something?" Verity stopped too, tensing.

"I think so. Come on."

He set off at a fast walk toward an old barn. Just for a second, he thought he'd seen an eerie green glow from behind it, but then it faded again before he could get a fix on it.

Verity caught up with him, having to run to match his stride, and the two of them rounded the corner at the same time.

Both stopped.

"Shit…" Verity murmured. "That's got to be it."

The thing was huge—at least twice the size of the one in Iowa, rising around ten feet up and stretching out between fifteen and twenty feet horizontally. What Stone had seen pulsing had been the edge of it, which had briefly extended past the edge of the barn before receding again. The whole thing glowed a bright, acid green, darker in the center and brighter around its ragged edges. As they drew closer, Stone felt a bone-deep thrumming that seemed to extend not just into his body, but his soul as well.

"Do you…feel that?" Verity whispered. Her voice shook.

"Yes."

"That thing is…I don't even know how to describe it. So *that's* what shifted the whole town over?"

"Almost certainly, yes. This one is a lot more potent than the other two I saw."

"So…what do we do? Do you want to walk *through* it?" She studied it dubiously, and her tone suggested she wasn't sure that was a good idea.

"I think we have to. I can't shift us back from inside, since I've been using Calanarian energy and I can't get to all of it from here without a lot more study." He too examined the rift, focusing his magical sight on the middle. He thought he could make out forms on the other side, but he couldn't be certain. The green was so intense, it was nearly impossible to see anything clearly past it. "I could go first if you like."

"No," she said quickly. "We'll go together. If something goes wrong, I don't want to be stuck here." She took his hand. "I'll feel a lot safer if we're together. If we end up somewhere weird, at least we'll have a shot of figuring out how to get back."

He squeezed her hand. "Right, then. We'll just step through, and if my hypothesis is correct, we'll end up somewhere not too far from where I left the Jeep and Kyla. Then we'll see about getting the rest of Cinder back where it belongs. Ready?"

"Ready." This time, her voice didn't shake.

Together, still holding hands, they walked forward and stepped through the rift.

The feeling was like nothing Stone had ever experienced before. His body felt as if something was pulling it apart—and worse, his brain felt the same way. It wasn't pain, exactly—that made it even stranger, because it made sense that having your limbs pulled slowly from your body should hurt. Inside his brain, his thoughts careened around, bumping into each other and melding together like some kind of extradimensional drug trip. When he could manage to nail one of them down for longer than a second or two, he felt as if he should be analyzing the feeling, so he could make notes about it when they came through on the other side. Had anyone else ever experienced this?

Before he could solidify the thought, the sensation vanished. Bright, flashing acid green changed first to intense white and then to inky black, like the aftereffects of a whole bank of flashbulbs.

Stone staggered forward, still gripping Verity's hand, and caught himself just before he pitched forward. Next to him, she tripped on something and flailed her free arm to right herself. He held her there until she was steady.

"Holy shit!" she panted, blinking rapidly. "That was—"

But Stone didn't answer. In fact, he barely heard her.

He'd been pointing a different direction than he was, and when his vision cleared, the first thing he saw was a pair of figures standing twenty feet away from him.

"Oh, bloody hell…" he whispered, his whole body growing cold.

One of the figures, he didn't recognize. Of medium height and weight, the man wore a dark shirt, pants, and jacket. His hair was light blond, his face smooth and calm. He stood with a confidence suggesting that he knew exactly where he was and what he was doing there.

Next to him, unmoving but with her face set into a grimace of rage, was Kyla.

| CHAPTER THIRTY-FIVE

FOR A MOMENT, the three of them—Stone, the man, and Kyla—regarded each other in silence. Then Verity spun around and spotted them too, and her eyes widened in shock.

"Kyla!" she called, and made as if to run toward her.

"Stay where you are," the man said, just as Stone grabbed her shoulder. "Both of you."

"Who are you?" Stone demanded.

"Kyla!" Verity yelled again, but didn't move forward. "Are you okay?"

"Yeah, I'm fine—except for *this* asshole." She pointed at the man, then shot a baleful glare at Stone. "Where the fuck did you *go*, Stone? You said you wouldn't go without me!"

Stone ignored her and focused on the man. He couldn't get a good look at him from this distance, but nothing about him looked distinctive. His voice had been soft and pleasant, neither too low nor too high. It was almost as if he were making a specific effort to be unmemorable. Even his aura was unremarkable, a medium blue extending only a couple of inches from his body. "Who are you? What do you want?"

"Step away from the rift, Dr. Stone," the man said.

"You know who I am? I'm at a disadvantage, then. Care to introduce yourself?"

"You don't need to know who I am. It's best if you don't. Please step away from the rift, both of you."

"I'm not going anywhere. I'm going to close this thing."

"No," the man said softly. "You're not."

Stone could feel Verity practically vibrating with leashed tension next to him, but so far she remained quiet. "Suppose you tell me why not."

"Because I won't permit it. You don't know what you're dealing with."

"Then *tell* me!" Stone had about hit his limit of people telling him he couldn't do things for…*reasons.* "Either tell me why I shouldn't do it, or get out of my way. Those are your two choices."

The man chuckled. "I think you've missed a few. You wouldn't want this young lady to suffer any distress, would you?" He indicated Kyla with a head movement.

"I'm not a fucking *young lady!*" Kyla shouted.

"Let her go, whoever you are!" Verity yelled.

"So let me get this straight," Stone said as if neither of had spoken. "You're threatening someone who's got nothing to do with this? Very brave. Why don't you threaten me instead? Let Verity and Kyla go. This is between you and me."

"Like *hell* it is," Verity snapped. "That's my girlfriend over there. That means I'm involved now too." To the man, she said again, "Let her go *now*, you coward."

Stone took a step forward and spread his hands wide. "Go on—it's me you want. I'm tired of all this messing about. Let's have this out once and for all. Or even better: let's talk. Tell me why I shouldn't close the rift. I'm a reasonable man.

Give me something I can work with, and perhaps we can reach an understanding."

"I can't do that, Dr. Stone. I'm sorry."

He narrowed his eyes. "Are you connected with that orange thing that showed up in Pennsylvania?"

"Orange...thing?" The man seemed confused.

"Something—a foggy figure with an odd orange aura— showed up there and tried to prevent me from closing that rift. It killed a man, and told me I was tampering with things I didn't understand, and could be causing trouble I had no way to stop. But it wouldn't tell me *why*. It called me 'scion.' Do you know anything about that?"

"I share no direct connection with this entity, but it was correct," the man said, unruffled. "You have no idea what you're meddling with."

"So why can't you tell me? What's the big secret? What is it that you and Kolinsky and Madame Huan and gods know *how* many other people are trying to keep from me? This is bloody ridiculous. What possible good could come of having these dangerous dimensional rifts popping in and out? They've been here before—I know that. Who stopped them then?"

For the first time, the man showed a recognizable emotion—surprise—but it was fleeting. The pleasant mask was back again in less than a second. "How do you know they have appeared before?"

Stone laughed. "Ah, so I've got some secrets *you* don't know, too. That puts us on a bit more level footing, doesn't it? You tell me yours and I'll tell you mine. Let's start with who you are, and what your connection is with the others."

"I'm sorry, Dr. Stone." The man took a step closer to Kyla. "I did not come here to offer bargains, but to deliver a warning. You will cease your efforts to locate and close the dimensional rifts."

"Or what?"

"Or I will begin by killing this young woman here. Protocols prevent me from attacking you directly without provocation, but she and your apprentice enjoy no such protections."

"Protocols?" Stone demanded, astonished. "*What* protocols? Why am I protected when they're not? Verity's a mage too. Why is she different?" He paused. "It's because of this 'scion' rubbish, isn't it? Is it related to my family? Is this whole *business* related to my family?" A chill ran down his spine as a thought struck him: every member of his family on his father's side, from his grandfather back as many generations as he could track, had been the darkest of black mages, connected with a shadowy organization called *Ordo Purpuratus.* He'd thought the organization long-dead, but what if it wasn't? If that were true, did that mean Kolinsky was connected with them? He was a black mage, of course, so it wasn't inconceivable. But Madame Huan, the most benevolent white mage he'd ever known? Was she involved in this too?

"I cannot share that information with you," the man said. "There are things you aren't permitted to know at this point."

"At this point? Does that mean I'll be allowed to know them later? *When?*"

"Step away from the rift, please. Take your apprentice and this woman and leave now. I won't impede you in any way if you do."

Stone took a deep breath. His heart pounded hard, and his whole body hummed with energy. He glanced at Kyla, who was still glaring at them, and then at Verity, who was glaring back at the man. "You don't listen, do you? I don't know what these 'protocols' you mention are, but I don't care. I'm not bound by them. You might not be able to hurt *me,* but I'm damned sure I can take a dent out of *you* if you don't back off and get your arse out of here *now.*"

His heartbeat increased even more—he remembered how quickly the entity with the orange aura had killed Clyde in Pennsylvania, and he was taking a big risk by goading this man without knowing his capabilities. But neither Verity nor Kyla was as defenseless as Clyde had been. "This is your last warning. Tell me what this is about, or get the hell out of here and let me close this rift and get this town back where it belongs."

The man smiled. "Ah, Dr. Stone, you do amuse me. You have bravado, I'll give you that. You're a credit to your line. But there's no way you can—"

Kyla moved faster than Stone could follow, her own physical form of magic turning her into a blur. With a primal roar, she stomped her steel-toed combat boot down on top of the man's foot.

The man yelped in pain and staggered backward.

Verity acted instantly, grabbing hold of Kyla with a tele- kinetic grip and jerking her free of the man, flinging her nearly twenty feet to the side and taking off after her. "Go, Doc!" she yelled. "Do it!"

The man recovered fast, his face wreathed in rage now. He spun toward Verity and Kyla, raising his hands.

Stone moved faster, and he didn't hold back. He had no idea how powerful this guy was, but if he was on par with Kolinsky and Madame Huan, that would make him formidable indeed. He couldn't risk half-measures.

But he did know from past experience that Kolinsky, at least, could be hurt when he wasn't expecting the attack, and he counted on that being true for this man as well. He opened the conduit to Calanar and unleashed a punishing cascade of pure magical energy, letting it thunder through his body like water from a wide-open fire hose. He didn't try for any finesse or control this time, but merely let the energy channel through him until he couldn't do it any longer. His own roar mirrored Kyla's.

The energy hit the man and blew him backward, and this time the look of astonished surprise on his face didn't fade. He screamed as his body rolled over and over, smashing into the ground and rock outcroppings, his arms and legs flailing. After a couple of seconds a bright shield flared around him, but clearly it was too late to block the brunt of Stone's attack.

Stone let the onslaught continue until the energy pounding through his body went from exhilarating to painful, then cut it off, panting, and examined his work. His shield was still at full strength, and he raised glowing hands as he approached the man.

"Do I still amuse you?" he called, hyper-focused and ready to extend another shield if the man seemed inclined to go after Verity and Kyla.

He didn't seem so inclined, at least not at the moment. Battered and bloody from both the magical attack and slamming into rocks as he flew backward, the blond man struggled halfway up and fixed a painful glare on Stone.

"You…will regret that, scion," he growled, a bright vortex of green light forming around his hands.

"Want more?" Stone hit him with another blast. It wasn't as strong this time, but some of it still punched through the man's weakened shield and knocked him back again. The green vortex faded.

Never taking his attention from him, Stone moved cautiously forward, bathing the fallen figure in enough light to see he wasn't faking the injuries. Stone had hurt him, and badly. Another shot like that might be enough to do serious damage not only to his opponent but to himself, but the man didn't need to know that. "I don't want to kill you, but I don't take well to anyone threatening my friends. Now get the hell out of here."

The man's glare was half rage, half astonishment, his eyes burning out of his bloody face. "How…did you…"

Stone grinned. He couldn't help it. "Secrets. Like I said— I've got a few of my own. Now—*go*."

He spat blood into the dirt. "This…isn't over, Stone."

And then he vanished, leaving behind the faint odor of copper and ozone.

Stone stiffened, immediately unleashing another, lower-powered and wide-spectrum blast in front of him. He couldn't afford to allow the man to turn invisible and attack him—or worse, Verity and Kyla—from another angle.

The blast hit nothing, and magical sight showed no sign of the man's aura.

Stone stood in place, still panting, as Verity and Kyla ran up behind him. Verity's magical shield glowed around both of them.

"Are you okay?" Verity demanded. "Who was that? Where'd he go?"

Stone didn't answer right away. He continued scanning the area, looking for any hint of a lurking figure, an aura, or any other indication that the man was still in the area. As injured as he was, he likely couldn't maintain the spell for long.

Nothing showed up.

"Doc?"

He allowed himself to relax, just a bit, though his body still jangled with tension.

"Is it okay now? Is he gone?"

"I…think so," he said between breaths, then nodded toward Kyla. "Nice diversion, by the way."

"Thanks. I fucking *hate* it when guys call me 'young lady' in that condescending tone. He deserved it." Her gaze sharpened. "Why the hell did you run off? You said you'd take me with you!"

"No choice." Stone took a few more breaths to calm his heart rate. "Wasn't on purpose, I promise. But now I want to take care of this rift before our friend sorts himself out and comes back for round two. Verity, please keep an eye out for anything approaching, will you?"

"Got it. You okay?"

"I will be. Just let me do this. And don't come any closer, so you don't accidentally wander into the town before we've got it back."

She eyed him with concern for several seconds, but finally nodded. "C'mon, Kyla, let's let him work. I want to get out of here. Don't you?"

"More than anything," she agreed.

When both of them walked a short distance away and began patrolling, Stone set to work on the rift. It would be a little harder now that he'd just used all that energy to take down the man, but there was no helping it. He had no idea if the man would return—or if 'protocols' would still keep him from attacking if he did—but he wasn't particularly interested in finding out.

He stood a few feet back from the rift, far enough so he could keep the whole thing in sight, and then repeated the same procedure he'd used on the other rifts, pumping Calanarian energy into it and focusing on bringing its crackling edges together.

It was definitely more difficult this time—and not only because of the energy channeling. This rift was bigger than the others, and more potent, and definitely resisted being sealed. Now that it was here, it seemed to want to *stay* here.

Slowly, though, it began to respond to his efforts. As the edges came together from both sides, almost like a pair of zippers joining two pieces of fabric, Stone noticed at the corner of his peripheral vision that the forms of buildings and other structures were becoming more distinct. He couldn't let go of the energy yet, but a thrill surged through him nonetheless. It was working! Just a little more, and…

There!

The two edges of the rift finished joining the middle with a little astral *pop.* The green light flared brighter than ever, then winked out like the picture on an old-style TV set. In front of him, the tiny gas station, the general store, the sheep, and all the other structures of Cinder, Wyoming shimmered into view and settled into place, solid and substantial. After a moment, a light flicked on inside one of the residences, and several of the sheep in the pen began to *baa* softly.

"Yes!" Stone said with a grin, pumping his fist. "Damn, I'm good."

"Humble, too," Kyla said dryly from behind him. "See, V, I told you he was an arrogant ass."

"True," Verity said, taking Stone's arm and squeezing it to show she wasn't serious. "But you gotta admit, he lives up to his billing sometimes."

"All I gotta admit right now is that I want to get the hell out of here before somebody in that town notices us and starts asking questions." She threw a contemptuous glance toward Cinder. "Besides, I hate sheep."

Stone took a final look around, scanning the area with magical sight. He didn't know what he expected to see, but all around him the area seemed serene, untroubled, and completely magic-free. As he watched, the shimmering yellow aura of a shadowy figure emerged from one of the residences, appeared to take a look around, and then went back inside. With a sense of satisfaction, he turned to follow Verity and Kyla back to where they'd left the Jeep.

He knew this wasn't over—whoever that man was, he'd probably be back for another round. There were still other rifts, a lot of them, out there, and he had to decide what he wanted to do about them. There were too many for him and Verity to close them all—even if they could, it would take too long. Who knew what kind of mischief the things could get up to in the meantime, especially if they popped up in the middle of heavily populated areas? He didn't see any way around it: he'd have to share this information with other powerful mages, and hope they weren't in league with Kolinsky and Madame Huan and who knew how many others.

"Doc? Coming?" Verity had stopped and turned back toward him.

"Yes. Yes, I'm coming." He took off at a jog. He could worry about all this in the next day or two. For now, all he wanted to do was go home.

| CHAPTER THIRTY-SIX

"**S**O—DID YOUR FRIENDS GET THEIR STUFF BACK?"

Jason and Amber sat across from each other at a table in a boisterous barbecue joint in Truckee. Despite the clamor of several TVs playing sporting events, a rowdy Saturday-night crowd cheering their teams on, and rock music on the speakers trying to compete for attention, they ignored all of it in favor of the little bubble of privacy they'd created for themselves.

"Yeah," she said. "Everything was in the truck. You should have seen Darryl—he was practically doing a little dance, he was so happy. Oh—that reminds me." She grabbed her bag from where she'd hung it over the chair. "I owe you and Verity some of the fee I got for getting it back."

He waved her off. "You don't owe me anything. I was happy to help. I'll take V's back to her, but I doubt she cares either. She gets off on that kind of stuff. Adrenaline junkie, my sister is."

"Yeah, I kind of got that impression." She pulled some cash from her wallet and pushed it across the table to him. "But give it to her anyway—I owe her big. If she hadn't been along, that might not have gone nearly as well as it did." Her expression sobered. "Is she okay? I know she was pretty freaked out over…what happened."

"She'll be okay. She's tough, and she's seen worse. It wasn't like she killed the guy." Jason shuddered at the thought of what the mage must have gone through in his last couple seconds of life. "I gotta go back tomorrow and help her move."

She gnawed on a rib, not meeting his gaze.

"So…" he ventured. "What happened with Hank? Did you find him before he took off?"

"Yeah." She wiped her hands on a napkin. "Found him at his place when I got back. He was waiting for a call from the mage about the handoff." She sighed, rubbing her face. "It sucks, Jason. You think you know a guy, you know? I mean, Hank was kind of an ass, but he could be fun too, when he wasn't acting like a jealous prick. And all along…I wonder how many other jobs like this he's had his fingers in."

"I'm sorry, Amber." Surprisingly, he genuinely was. It was never easy to find out that somebody you thought was a friend had betrayed you. "So he's in jail now?"

"Yeah, him and those other two guys. They spilled the whole thing when the cops found them—well, all except the magic, of course. The cops are still looking for the mastermind, but…"

"…but they're never gonna find him. Yeah." The blood they'd found seeping from the wall hadn't been enough to notice easily, and even if the police found it and made a DNA match, they'd still never know the truth of what had happened. "Did they say anything about us?"

"Not from what I understand—not enough to worry about, anyway. They probably didn't want the cops thinking they were crazy, talking about magic and stuff."

"Well, that's good anyway." He leaned back, taking a long drink from his beer, and smiled. "I have to admit, I wasn't sure you'd go for the dinner."

"Why not?" She mirrored his smile, though hers was sly. "Actually, I didn't think you'd call."

"Come on—I'd be an idiot not to." He shrugged, then indicated their bone-littered plates. "Besides, how often does a northern California guy find a woman with a proper appreciation for good barbecue?"

"Damn right." She picked up her last rib and bit off a healthy shred. "So...you do this kind of stuff a lot?"

"What, chow down on ribs and cornbread?" He grinned. "Nah—I have to keep my girlish figure, after all. If I ate like this all the time I'd never catch anybody."

She mimed throwing the bone at him. "No, you goof. The magic."

"Not as often as I used to when my sister was my friend's apprentice and she lived with me. But...often enough, I guess."

"Do you like it?"

He thought about it. "That's a hard question to answer. I'd be lying if I said I didn't wish sometimes that my life was just normal, and I'd never even found out about all this supernatural stuff. But..."

"But?" Her eyes glittered a challenge.

"But..." he said with a shrug, "a lot of good things have happened in my life because of it. I got my sister back from some pretty bad stuff. I met my best friend, even if he does drive me batshit sometimes with how his curiosity gets him into trouble. And my life's in a lot better place than it was a few years back. So I guess all in all I gotta say it was good for me." He hesitated, not sure whether saying anything else was a good idea or a really bad one. "And..." he added, meeting her gaze with a clear, steady one of his own, "Maybe it's still good for me. Or at least I hope it might be."

Something in her smile changed. "Yeah, I hope so too. I'd like to see you again, Jason. But I want to take things slow. You're in San Jose, I'm here, and after Hank, I think I need some time to get my head together, you know?"

"Yeah. I get it. That's cool. I've got a lot going on with the agency, so it's not like I'm not staying busy. Maybe we can...do barbecue again. And if you're ever back in the Bay Area, I know a really good steak house."

She grinned. "There's more to me than meat, you know."

"It's got good beer, too."

The grin widened. "Well, hey, that covers the basics, anyway." She paused, wiped her hands again, and shrugged. "You said you have to go back tomorrow?"

"Yeah, helping V haul some stuff up to SF."

She leaned forward. "What about tonight?"

"What...*about* tonight?" he asked carefully. He hoped she didn't notice how his heart just started to hammer, but then remembered what she was and figured she could probably read him like a book. Ah, well—it wasn't as if his reaction was any kind of surprise.

She chuckled. "If we're going to get along, Jason, you need to figure out fast that I'm not one of those types who drops hints. Bears aren't good with hints. So...you want to go back to my place and...see what happens?" She leaned in closer, and her sly grin was back. "That means sex, by the way. I'm talking about sex."

"Uh…" He swiped his napkin across his mouth and tossed it aside. "Does a bear—"

"Do *not* go there," she said firmly, but the smile never left her face, or her eyes.

| CHAPTER THIRTY-SEVEN

Sunday

STONE WAS HALF-SITTING, half-lying on the sofa in his living room, Raider curled on his chest and the stereo playing softly, when a knock on his door jolted him from his doze.

He jerked fully awake, startling the cat, and glanced at his watch. After ten-thirty. Who would be coming to his door that late? He'd locked the gate for the night, and wasn't expecting anyone—Verity was in San Francisco, Jason was off on a case somewhere, and he'd just gotten a text a few days ago that Ian was in Monte Carlo.

As he hauled himself off the sofa, straightened his T-shirt, and ran a hand through his hair, he realized the wards hadn't buzzed. That shouldn't have been possible; anyone approaching the house would have to pass through his wards, which were normally tuned to alert him to any mundane presence and stop anything unfamiliar that wasn't mundane.

They'd done neither, and that wasn't good.

Tensing, he put up his shield and walked to the front door, but didn't open it. "Who's there?" he called.

"It is I," said a familiar voice.

Bloody hell. Stone tensed. Kolinsky? *Here*? In all the time they'd known each other, the black mage had never come to his home. He'd visited Kolinsky's once—or one of them, at least—but otherwise the two had always confined their visits to either the shop in East Palo Alto or some local restaurant.

He still didn't open the door. "What…can I do for you, Stefan? Bit late for dropping by, isn't it?"

"May I come in?" Kolinsky's voice sounded steady and calm.

"That depends." Was Kolinsky in league with the man from Wyoming? Had the man told him what had happened, and now he was here to finish the job?

"Alastair, we must talk. I give you my word, I mean you no harm. To the contrary—I am taking a risk merely by coming here. Please let me in."

Stone frowned. Taking a risk? What kind of risk? Still, Kolinsky had always been a man of his word. "Fine, then." He opened the door.

Kolinsky stood there, dressed in the same old-fashioned, meticulously crisp sort of black suit he always wore, along with a dark gray overcoat. His expression was serious, almost grave. "Thank you."

Stone stepped aside, realizing as he did that he wasn't sure he'd ever given Kolinsky his new address. If that was the weirdest thing about tonight, though, he'd be surprised. "Come on in, and let me take your coat. Would you like something to drink?"

"Thank you, no."

Stone led him into the sitting room, using magic to flip off the stereo and gather the remains of his earlier takeout meal into a neat pile on the coffee table. "Sit down. What can

I do for you, Stefan? You did a bit of a runner the other day—I couldn't help taking it personally. I also can't help wondering if you warned Madame Huan that I might be coming her way, so she could clear out too."

"I did, yes." Kolinsky sounded unapologetic, and met Stone's gaze with a steady one of his own. He leaned back in his chair, steepling his hands in his lap.

Stone hadn't expected him to admit it quite so readily. "You did. So it's not just your fingers in this little pie—it's hers as well?"

"There are…many things you don't understand, Alastair."

"Stefan, I can't *begin* to describe how bloody *sick* I am of hearing that. If that's all you've come here to say, please go. I'm tired and I've had enough game-playing for the night."

"I heard about what occurred in Wyoming."

"Did you? So then, whoever tried to stop me there is a member of your little secret club too?"

"You bested him in magical combat. That…should not have been possible, even if you caught him by surprise."

"Why not?" Stone glared at him. "Like I told him—perhaps he shared this with you as well—you lot aren't the only ones who have secrets. He was a powerful mage, yes. But so am I. Maybe more so than you know, these days."

"Yes. I am beginning to see that. And I am also beginning to see that no matter the warnings you are given, you have no intention of giving up your crusade to locate and close the rifts."

"Damn right. And I don't have to locate them. I already know where they are. I also know they were here before."

Kolinsky tilted his head. "Indeed?"

"And you know it too, so don't play dumb with me. It doesn't suit you, Stefan."

The black mage's eyes flashed briefly, but then he inclined his head. "As I said, I am putting myself at some risk by coming here, but I have come to the conclusion that the risk would be far greater if I did not."

"What's that supposed to mean? Are you planning to stop me somehow? To kill me?" Stone concentrated for a second, and a shield flared around him. "That might be harder than you thought, if you do—especially on my home ground."

He expected Kolinsky's face to contort in anger, or even for him to attack, but neither happened. Instead, the black mage settled back in his chair and made a dismissive gesture. "You do not need a shield, Alastair. I have already given you my word that I have not come here to harm you."

Stone pondered for just a moment, then dropped the shield. "Fine, then. Why *are* you here? I'm tired of puzzles, and I'm tired of being treated like a child who can't handle the truth. Let's get right to it, then: if you want me to give this up, then you'll have to tell me *why*. That's not negotiable. No other bargains, no other transactions. That's it: either you tell me why, you take your best shot at killing me, or you get the hell out of here and let me get on with my plans."

He hadn't sat down yet; he'd been pacing as he spoke, but now he stopped in front of Kolinsky's chair, nearly looming over the black mage. He noticed peripherally that Raider had made himself scarce. *He's smart. I probably should have done that too.*

Kolinsky remained calmly seated, meeting Stone's gaze steadily as the seconds stretched out. "I should not be here," he said at last. "When…certain others discover I visited you, there will be…consequences."

"What kind of consequences? Who are these 'others'? How many of them are there, other than Madame Huan and whoever came to Wyoming and Pennsylvania? Those weren't you, or someone you sent, were they?"

"No. They were not. And as for how many others…that I cannot tell you. It does not concern you, nor does it relate directly to this situation."

"Is this some kind of cabal of powerful mages? Why have I never heard of it? I'm not exactly a slouch these days, and between my family and Desmond, I've had access to some fairly high-powered people."

Kolinsky held up his hand. "Alastair, stop, please. You have asked me to tell you why you should not interfere with the rifts. You also said you offer no other bargain for this information, but I must insist on one nonetheless."

Stone spun away with a snort. "There it is—I knew we'd get back to that again. What do you want, Stefan? At this point, I don't know if I'll give it to you. You had your chance before, and you chose to hide from me." He turned back, tense and ready to act if necessary. "You can tell me what it is, but no promises."

Still, Kolinsky did not react to his agitation. "It is simple: I require an oath."

"An oath?" That hadn't been what he was expecting. "You mean a magical oath?"

Kolinsky inclined his head.

"What kind of oath? What do you want me to swear to? And why? Is my word not good enough for you? You expect me to respect yours, but you won't honor mine?"

"I respect your word. This is more for your own protection than my own. There are those who seek this information and must not be permitted to obtain it."

"Who?"

"Again, I cannot say. It may be that they are not yet aware of the situation. It is even possible that they no longer exist. But if they do, there are those among them who might have the capability of wresting the information from you, should proper precautions not be taken."

"Let them try," Stone snapped. "I'm not the same mage you knew ten years ago, Stefan. Not even one year ago."

"I am aware of that, and I make no secret of the fact that I am curious as to how you have attained this power—although I have a better idea now than perhaps I did before."

"What the hell does that mean?"

Kolinsky waved his question off. "That is my condition, Alastair. If you will swear a magical oath that you will not reveal the information to anyone else, I will help you to satisfy your curiosity."

Stone took a long, slow breath. He held Kolinsky's gaze for a few more seconds, then paced away, staring into the unlit fireplace. His mind whirled with uncharacteristic indecision, warring between desire to finally know why these powerful forces seemed suddenly aligned to thwart what seemed to be a logical course of action, and a deep reluctance to swear such an oath, to Kolinsky or anyone else. Magical oaths, especially one set by someone with the black mage's power, were irrevocably binding. If he agreed, he would be physically unable to reveal anything to anyone else—so if what he found out required action, he'd either have to take it on his own…or not take it at all, and accept the consequences for inaction.

Without turning, he said in a dull tone, "Tell me the specifics of the oath. What would I be agreeing to, and what would happen if I failed to observe the terms?"

"As I said, you would swear never to reveal anything I tell you about the nature of the rifts and why you should not interfere with them. This also covers any inferences you might reach as a result of information I provide you. I suspect that, once you have divined the truth, you will not wish to share it. But this will prevent you from doing so."

"And if I do?"

"There is no 'if.' The oath will prevent you from speaking of it, or from having it forcibly removed from your mind by any magical means."

Stone shuddered, just a bit. The thought of anyone mucking around in his mind, hunting for bits of data, terrified him. "Do you expect anyone will do that? Some other member of your little cabal, for instance?"

"There is no 'cabal,' Alastair. That much I can tell you."

"So you don't belong to some organization of powerful mages?"

"No. There are…certain individuals whose goals coincide in this case. In all honesty, that rarely occurs. And aside from them, I do not believe any others are aware of this situation at this time."

"What happens if I don't agree? If I decide to continue as I have, tracking the rifts and closing them? Will you get in my way? Will others?"

"I cannot speak for any others, but I suspect they will continue to impede you."

"The one in Wyoming said he couldn't attack me unprovoked. Something about 'protocols.' What's that about? What protocols?"

"That is something I also cannot speak of. Once again, it is not directly related to the rifts."

"And I suppose that means you won't tell me what this 'scion' rubbish is about, either, will you? Is that why he wasn't allowed to hurt me, but he could kill others? He threatened Verity and her friend. I think he would have killed them if I hadn't stopped him."

"You are quite likely correct. And I can do nothing to protect them. As for the protocols—you have made a powerful enemy, Alastair, I can tell you that much."

Something inside Stone chilled. "Brilliant. Does that mean he'll be coming after me now?"

"He might, if you persist in seeking the rifts. I do not think he will do so otherwise. He does respect strength, and your power surprised him."

"So—what—you two got together for tea and discussed this?"

"No. I have not spoken with him directly, but I have heard from those who have."

Stone sighed and went back to the sofa, where he dropped down. "So that's it, then. I agree to this oath, and you tell me what's going on with the rifts?"

"I will…assist you in deriving your own conclusions. It is the best I am permitted to do, without incurring more consequences than I am willing to accept. I value our association— our friendship—but even that has its limits."

Again, Stone hesitated. "Are you sure you don't want a drink? Because I need one."

"No, thank you."

He levitated a bottle and a glass over to him, poured, and took a healthy swallow. Glancing toward the doorway, he spotted Raider lurking there, peering around the corner with wide eyes.

"Fine," he said at last. "I suppose you've never given me cause not to trust you. As long as this oath concerns *only* the nature of the rifts, and my inability to reveal anything to others won't put the world in danger, I accept. I'll agree to your oath. Let's get on with it." He stood. "Do we need to use my circle?"

Kolinsky rose as well. "There is no need. We can do it here."

"Oh?" That was a surprise. Normally, magical oaths required a circle at minimum—but not for the first time, Stone suspected Kolinsky wasn't entirely bound by the rules of normal magic. "What, then?"

He pointed. "Stand here." When Stone did, he drew a small knife, barely larger than a pocketknife, from the inner pocket of his suit jacket, and removed it from its sheath.

Stone, watching with magical sight, narrowed his eyes. The little thing was practically incandescent with magical energy. "A blood oath?"

"Yes. It requires only a drop from each of us." He held out the hand that wasn't holding the knife, and motioned for Stone to do the same.

Point of no return, he thought, but did not hesitate. "Do it."

Kolinsky made a small nick on Stone's palm, and then another on his own. When the beads of bright red blood welled up, he inclined his head. "Clasp my hand."

Stone did as requested, and immediately felt the hum of powerful energies swirling around them. His aura, purple, gold, and silver, swirled around Kolinsky's purple, red, and eerie ultraviolet, mingling but each retaining their own distinct colors.

Kolinsky studied it for a moment, and then said in a flat, steady voice, "Alastair Stone, by accepting this oath you swear never to reveal anything I share with you regarding the nature of the extradimensional rifts appearing around this world. You will tell no person or entity, living or dead, nor will you set the information into any form, including written, spoken, or recorded. This includes any inferences to which you might arrive based on the information I share. You will keep the information to yourself and yourself only. By accepting this oath you acknowledge that upon its execution, you will be physically and mentally incapable of sharing the information in any form, except with me, whom you know as Stefan Kolinsky, or anyone whom I specifically allow. If you agree, state your name and affirm as such."

As Kolinsky spoke, Stone felt the power growing around their clasped hands. The writhing auras, still separate but joined, swirled outward until they engulfed both of them, creating a glowing, shifting barrier around their bodies. *Whom you know as Stefan Kolinsky,* he thought idly. *I wonder what your other names are...*

He took a deep breath, closed his eyes, and then met Kolinsky's gaze. "I, Alastair Stone, do so affirm."

His curiosity had gotten him into some deep trouble in the past—he hoped he hadn't just made a big mistake.

CHAPTER THIRTY-EIGHT

AS SOON AS HE SPOKE the final word, the humming increased, flashing so bright and clear that for a second, Stone could see nothing but the beautiful, otherworldly colors. Something like a multi-pronged jolt of electricity passed through his body, flowing through his limbs and setting his nerves on edge. And then both the sensation and the colors were gone, as if someone had flipped a light switch.

Stone took a staggering step back, breaking the contact, and stared at Kolinsky. "That's it?"

"It is a simple oath, but powerful. It will suffice."

"Right, then," he said, quickly healing the nick on his palm and then taking another drink. "I kept my end of the bargain. Now you keep yours."

Kolinsky returned to his chair as if nothing had happened, and motioned for Stone to sit as well. "You are correct that the rifts have existed previously. I am not certain how you determined that, but it is true."

"How long ago?"

"Several hundred years, the last time."

"The last time? You mean they've appeared more than once before?"

"Yes. "

"So…it's a cyclical thing? They reappear every few hundred years?"

"No. There is no way to predict their appearance. It could be a few hundred years, or a few thousand."

"How do you know this?"

"That is not relevant to our discussion."

Stone tilted his head, glaring at Kolinsky. "You've either got access to research I've never heard of, or you're actually old enough to remember. Honestly, neither one would surprise me. Go on, then—what are the rifts for? What's their purpose, and why are your lot trying to get me to stop closing them? They're dangerous. People have died, and been driven insane, because of them. How is that a good thing?"

"It is not a good thing, *per se.* But in the greater scheme, it is an unfortunate but unavoidable consequence."

Stone started to protest, but Kolinsky held up a hand. "Consider the earthquake."

"*What*?" When Kolinsky did not reply, he leaned forward. "What the hell are you on about? What have earthquakes got to do with anything?"

"You are, I trust, familiar with the way in which earthquakes occur."

Fine, I'll run with it. For now. "Of course. The Earth is made up of a lot of tectonic plates, and they move around. Earthquakes occur when enough pressure builds between a pair of adjacent plates, causing them to slip, or jerk. The more pressure, the greater the quake's intensity. The earthquake releases the pressure between the plates—sometimes violently, sometimes not."

"A simplistic explanation, but sufficient. Just so."

Stone pondered. "All right...I'm trying to work out why you're telling me this. Are you saying there are some sort of magical tectonic plates? I've done some fairly extensive study of magic and ley lines, and I've never heard of any such thing."

"No. The analogy is more...general than that. But consider your own knowledge—how you were able to locate the rift in Wyoming."

Unable to sit still any longer, Stone got up and paced. "I located it because I have access to information that marked locations of rifts I'd already discovered. I extrapolated, assuming the other similar marks indicated similar rifts."

Kolinsky nodded, like a teacher encouraging a prized student. "Yes."

Stone narrowed his eyes. "Wait a moment...you said the rifts have appeared before—perhaps multiple times—and apparently in the same place each time, since I was able to use my source to locate them now. So what you're implying is that their locations are on some sort of...magical pressure points? That makes sense, given that they're all near ley line confluences—though unless my information is incomplete, they're not near *all* ley line confluences, and the number of converging lines doesn't seem relevant to whether a rift shows up."

Again, Kolinsky inclined his head. "Yes."

"So...the rifts appear periodically. And you and your lot don't want them sealed, despite the fact that they're bleeding magical energy into our world from other dimensions, and potentially causing harm."

"Yes."

He let his breath out, still pacing. "I know you, Stefan—you're not a cruel man, but you don't exactly work yourself into a fit of depression over a few mundanes being lost to collateral damage. So if you're content to allow this to happen, it's got to be because there's some greater purpose served by it."

Kolinsky's eyebrow rose. "You are doing very well, Alastair. You are correct in your assumption. Please continue. And once again: consider my analogy."

Stone took another drink and glanced at Raider, who was still lurking in the doorway. "Earthquakes…tectonic plates slipping…I don't see what that has to do with—"

He stopped. Slowly he turned back to face Kolinsky, the sudden chill running through his body mimicking the electrical surge he felt during the oath. "Bloody hell, Stefan…"

"Do you see?" Kolinsky leaned forward in anticipation.

"Bloody hell…" he whispered again, dropping back to the sofa. When he spoke again, he chose his words with careful precision. "Are you suggesting that these rifts are acting as…pressure valves? Fault lines, to continue your analogy? That the dimensions are bumping against each other like the Earth's tectonic plates, and when they get too close to each other, these rifts appear?"

"Yes. Excellent." He leaned back. "I assume you are aware that it is common for adjacent dimensional spaces to…shift relative to each other over time, unless anchor points are established."

Stone thought about the Obsidian's tower on Calanar. He thought about a band of insane women in England, waiting for the confluences to be right every twenty years so they could attempt to summon a massively powerful entity from another plane.

"Yes," he said numbly. "I'm aware."

"The phenomenon you refer to as a 'rift' occurs when a pair of dimensional spaces come into particularly close contact with each other, in a location where the veil between the two spaces is weak. As you might suspect, not all of them occur at the same time—they tend to move in waves, for the most part, with those in a particular area appearing around the same period."

"So..." Stone said, speaking slowly, "right now, the ones in North America are active. Are you saying that if I tried to hunt down those in Europe, or Africa, I might not find them, even though I know where they should be?"

"Likely not. As you well know, dimensional study is not an exact science, and even the others who are aware of this phenomenon cannot predict its specific activity. As it happens, you discovered it before many who should have noticed it sooner—because the intervals are not precise and can vary by thousands of years, it is not surprising that watching for their appearance is not high on these individuals' list of priorities."

Stone swallowed and took a few breaths. "So...these rifts appear at the confluence of two dimensional spaces. They vent energy, taking the pressure off until the dimensions move out of phase again. Is that correct?"

"Yes."

"And how long does this process take? I assume it's not permanent."

"No. Again, the intervals are imprecise, and there is no way to predict the duration, but based on previous study it can be anywhere from a few weeks to several months. They wax and wane during that period, so they are not always at full strength."

"This is…" Stone ran both hands through his hair, trying to get his mind around everything Kolinsky was telling him—or *not* telling him—and then another chill struck him. "Dear gods…I see it now." He leaped back up. "When I seal the rifts—that's the equivalent of preventing the small earthquakes that occur when two plates run into each other. I'm not stopping the pressure—in fact, it's building up *more* because it has nowhere to vent."

"Yes." Kolinsky inclined his head gravely.

"And—every time I do it, I'm making it worse."

"Precisely."

"So…if I were to continue sealing them, eventually the pressure would build to the point where…something blew."

"Yes." Kolinsky leaned back further and crossed his ankle over his leg. "There is more to it than that—more that I cannot tell you. As I've said, I am taking a risk by coming here at all, but I have discussed it with others—some of the cooler heads among us—"

"Like Madame Huan," Stone said dully.

"Yes, she was included in the discussion. And we have agreed that, given your dangerous combination of intelligence, stubbornness, power, and insatiable curiosity, it might be best to—with proper safeguards in place—share the knowledge with you. Now that I have, do you understand why you cannot be allowed to continue in your efforts?"

Stone looked at his feet. "Because if I do, I might—what—blow up the world?"

"No. I will tell you one other thing—something perhaps I should not tell you, since it is not directly relevant, but I think it will help to ease your mind about whatever decision you reach."

"Yes...?"

"The appearance of the dimensional rifts is a natural thing. It is expected, and it must occur. If you continue to disrupt them, you will cause certain events to occur more quickly and violently than expected—but these events *will* occur, regardless."

"What events?" Stone jerked his head back up.

"I cannot say, precisely. But they relate to an increased amount of magical energy in the world. This is natural, as I said. It has occurred before, and it will occur again. But if you interfere, what would normally be a controlled progression could instead become a violent cataclysm—and the world is not ready for that yet."

Stone stared at him. "Wait a moment. I know magic used to be more powerful, hundreds of years ago. Thousands of years ago. We know this because artifacts still exist that were created during those times, and they have power we couldn't hope to re-create in the current time. Are you saying that level of magic is coming *back*?"

Kolinsky rose. "I can say no more, Alastair. I have already told you more than some think wise. But everything I have said has been true—I give you my word."

He straightened his suit jacket and buttoned it. "So, I ask you—based on the information I have given you, do you see now why you cannot be permitted to continue interfering with the rifts?"

Stone bowed his head. He didn't *want* to see. Allowing rips in the fabric of reality to pump foreign magical energy into the world, bringing down unknown effects on the local mundane population, went against everything he believed in.

But...

He sighed. "Yes. I see it now. This is happening. I could stop it, but..."

"But as you have been told previously, you could cause irreparable harm if you do."

"So I have to let innocent mundanes die, be driven insane, be transported to gods know where..." He barked a bitter little laugh, remembering a film he saw a long time ago, on a date with a young woman who'd been into *Star Trek*—"The needs of the many..."

Kolinsky tilted his head, obviously not getting the reference. That was probably good—finding out Stefan Kolinsky was a *Star Trek* fan would have put the weird little cherry on top of the rest of this profoundly strange evening.

"It is the only reasonable decision," he said. "Do you agree?"

Stone spread his hands. "I hate it...but yes. I agree." He glanced up. "Stefan..."

"Yes?"

He didn't want to ask the question, but he had to. "I've already sealed three of the rifts. Could I have already...contributed to something happening sooner than expected?"

"I...fear that is possible, yes." Kolinsky's tone, as always, was even and unemotional. "Only time will tell at this point. We can only hope that the disruption has not been sufficient."

He rose and retrieved his coat from the rack by the door. "I must go now. I am pleased we have come to this understanding, Alastair, and that my instincts to share this information with you were not in error."

Stone only nodded. As Kolinsky reached for the doorknob, he glanced up again. "May I ask one other question?"

"You may ask. I cannot promise to answer."

"Why did they call me 'scion'? Scion of what? Is this related to my family somehow?"

For the first time, the black mage didn't meet his gaze. "I cannot tell you that. It is something you will no doubt discover in time, but it is not something I can reveal at this point."

"But you know."

"Yes."

He let out another loud sigh. "Bloody hell, Stefan, but you can be irritating sometimes. You know that, right?"

Kolinsky's eyebrow rose. "So I have been told, on many occasions. Good night, Alastair." Before Stone could reply, he slipped out through the door and closed it softly behind him.

Stone stood there a moment, then strode over and flung it open. "Stefan—"

But Kolinsky was gone. There was no sign of either him or a vehicle. Off in the distance, the lights on either side of the front gate revealed it to be closed and locked.

Something soft brushed against Stone's leg, and he glanced down to see Raider looking up at him with his usual curious, wide-eyed stare. He continued to stand for a moment, letting the chilly night air swirl around him as he watched the deserted yard, and then bent to scratch the cat behind the ears.

"Come on, Raider," he said, closing the door. "I think I need a good stiff drink."

When he reached the living room, his phone buzzed in his pocket.

Eyes narrowed, thinking for a moment that Kolinsky was calling until he remembered Kolinsky didn't use phones, he pulled it out. He smiled at the familiar number.

"Hello, Ian. How are you?" He dropped back down on the sofa and retrieved his drink, and Raider immediately settled into his lap.

"Hi, Dad." The connection sounded scratchy, and Ian perhaps sounded as if he'd had more to drink than Stone had. "It's not too late there, is it? I can only talk for a few minutes—need to get some sleep after last night."

"I'll just bet you do. I trust you're still having fun?"

"Oh, yeah. We're heading to Paris tomorrow."

"Any idea when you might be back?"

There was a pause. "Not sure yet. I was thinking I might go to England after this—in a month or so, maybe, depending on how things go. Do you want to meet up there? You can introduce me to Aubrey and show me around the ancestral home."

Stone smiled. "Yes, of course. I'd like that, and I'm sure Aubrey will be pleased to finally meet you. I haven't got much going on this summer at the University, so just let me know when you're planning to go, and I'll make it work. I'm glad you're doing well."

"Doing great. Listen—I've got to go, the guys are about ready to leave, but it's good to talk. Anything interesting happening with you?"

Stone lifted his gaze to the door where Kolinsky had exited only moments before. He thought about everything the black mage had told him: about the rifts, about the harm their existence might cause and the greater potential harm he might have already done with his well-intentioned actions. He wondered who Kolinsky really was, and what his connection was with Madame Huan and the others who'd been trying to stop him from his crusade. He thought about his family, and what Ian would think when he found out what kind of mages he was descended from. He thought about what—if anything—he would do about the effects of the rifts, even if he could no longer affect them directly.

"No...not really," he said at last, and was surprised at how casual he sounded. "Same old thing, I suppose. And I could definitely enjoy a few peaceful days back home."

Alastair Stone will return in

HOUSE OF STONE

Book 18 of the Alastair Stone Chronicles

Coming in Summer 2019

If you enjoyed this book, please consider leaving a review at Amazon, Goodreads, or your favorite book retailer. Reviews mean a lot to independent authors, and help us stay visible so we can keep bringing you more stories. Thanks!

If you'd like to get more information about upcoming Stone Chronicles books, contests, and other goodies, you can join the Inner Circle mailing list at **alastairstonechronicles.com**. You'll get two free e-novellas, *Turn to Stone* and *Shadows and Stone!*

ABOUT THE AUTHOR

R. L. King is an award-winning author and game freelancer for Catalyst Game Labs, publisher of the popular roleplaying game *Shadowrun*. She has contributed fiction and game material to numerous sourcebooks, as well as one full-length adventure, "On the Run," included as part of the 2012 Origins-Award-winning "Runners' Toolkit." Her first novel in the *Shadowrun* universe, *Borrowed Time*, was published in Spring 2015, and her second will be published in 2019.

When not doing her best to make life difficult for her characters, King enjoys hanging out with her very understanding spouse and her small herd of cats, watching way too much *Doctor Who*, and attending conventions when she can. She is an Active member of the Horror Writers' Association and the Science Fiction and Fantasy Writers of America, and a member of the International Association of Media Tie-In Writers. You can find her at *rlkingwriting.com* and *magespacepress.com*, on Facebook at www.facebook.com/AlastairStoneChronicles, and on Twitter at *@Dragonwriter11*.

Made in the USA
Monee, IL
05 August 2023

40489848R00236